SHADES OF DEATH

SHADES OF DEATH

DARK GATE ANGELS™ BOOK TWO

RAMY VANCE

MICHAEL ANDERLE

DISRUPTIVE IMAGINATION®

THE SHADES OF DEATH TEAM

Thanks to our Beta Team:
Larry Omans, Rachel Beckford

Thanks to the JIT Readers

Dave Hicks
Veronica Stephan-Miller
Dorothy Lloyd
Diane L. Smith
Kerry Mortimer
Deb Mader

If we've missed anyone, please let us know!

Editor
The Skyhunter Editing Team

Copyright © 2020 by Ramy Vance & Michael Anderle
Cover Art by Jake @ J Caleb Design
http://jcalebdesign.com / jcalebdesign@gmail.com
Cover copyright © LMBPN Publishing
A Michael Anderle Production

LMBPN Publishing
PMB 196, 2540 South Maryland Pkwy
Las Vegas, NV 89109

First US Edition, June 2020
ISBN (ebook) 978-1-64971-003-1
ISBN (paperback) 978-1-64971-004-8

DEDICATION

For Nora Stewart ... I'm damn lucky to have you as a mother-in-law.

—Ramy Vance

To Family, Friends and
Those Who Love
to Read.
May We All Enjoy Grace
to Live the Life We Are
Called.

— Michael

PART I

CHAPTER ONE

A helicopter flew over the New York skyline. Anyone looking up from the streets would have seen nothing special about it, but the aircraft carried within it one of the last hopes of humanity.

The Dark Gate Angels.

And two were motion-sick.

The helicopter's side hatch was wide open, and Anabelle—the de-facto leader of the DGA—sat on the edge, her feet dangling while she watched the city beneath her.

She'd spent years walking through the streets of New York. Eating, visiting galleries, modeling, entertaining guests. Mostly though, she had been stealing secrets.

A part of Anabelle hated New York. The city was always busy, and it had made her busy. The constant rush had transformed into something more than mere restlessness. Anabelle had been a quiet child, but it was hard to remember where that kid had gone.

There could be worse things, though.

Terra sat across from Anabelle, her face shoved into a paper bag as she tried hard not to vomit. Anabelle, a fair-skinned, rail-thin elf with long, night-black hair, was the polar opposite of Terra, who was stacked like a bodybuilder, her hair buzzed to the scalp, and her ears a little too large for her face.

Anabelle was envious of Terra's ears. She wouldn't have admitted it out loud, but she did believe they suited the human just fine. Anabelle touched the point of her own ear absentmindedly as she glanced at Abby to check on how she was holding up.

Though this was Abby's second helicopter ride, she was as nervous as her first time. But at least she wasn't as bad as Terra.

Abby was leaning her head against the side of the copter. The youngest of the DGA, she looked far more suited to a desk job. Her Coke-bottle glasses gave her the air of a pencil-pusher.

The funny thing was, Abby didn't need glasses; she wore them as a fashion choice. A teenager's idea of fashion, at least. Anabelle could appreciate that despite considering it a little silly. Clothes could be used as a form of armor. And how you chose to present yourself could be a weapon in your arsenal.

Abby appeared to be figuring that out for herself, having donned a pair of denim overalls not unlike the pair Anabelle had seen her wearing in an old family photo.

Anabelle moved to her feet, holding on to the support brace as the wind whipped her hair around. She crossed the cabin to sit between Abby and Terra. "You two going to be able to make it to the drop point, or should I send you home?"

Terra looked up from her bag and sneered. "And let you have all the fun? No, I'll be straight once we get out of the air. I hate flying. It always tears my stomach up. You know, once I threw up on a flight attendant while they were trying to convince me not to get a gin and tonic."

"How many had you drunk before?"

Terra raised a hand as though about to relate the memory, but instead, she swallowed hard. "That's not the point of the story now, is it?"

Anabelle laughed as she turned her attention to Abby. "How about you? Are you going to be okay?"

Abby nodded vigorously. "I'll live. Probably will also feel better once I get both feet on the ground. This thing shakes too much. Why'd Myrddin send us in a beat-up ol' chopper? He usually sends us out in style. Or at least comfort."

Anabelle pulled up her HUD menu, which displayed from a more convenient location on her wrist. She was glad Abby had retrofitted a new design for her and the team. Having to pull a HUD visor down over your head, despite it being holographic, was beyond irritating.

A holomap projected from Anabelle's HUD watch revealing New York and its impressive skyline. Anabelle pointed at the Empire State building. "Myrddin is taking a different approach to this mission. We're usually arriving right when a gate is opening, always trying to catch up with what's happening. This time, we'll be early. And we don't want to give the Dark One's forces any reason to speed things up, you know?"

Abby shook her head, appearing to disagree. But Anabelle figured out quickly that the girl was close to throwing up. She grabbed a bag and handed it to Abby, who snatched it and proceeded to hurl.

After a few minutes, Abby closed the bag, leaned against the hull of the helicopter, and sighed loudly. "Does anyone have a breath mint?"

Terra reached into her pocket, retrieved a packet of gum, and passed it to Abby, who popped one in her mouth and chewed loudly.

"Ugh. I don't know why I didn't think of this before," Abby muttered. She closed her eyes and nanobots poured from her skin, covering her in sleek black metallic armor. "That's better. The nanobots will counter the helicopter's movements. Should get rid of this motion sickness in a jiffy."

Abby sat up straighter. She drew in a deep breath, got to her feet, and walked to the open door to peer over the edge. "Thank God for technology, right?"

Terra glanced up from her bag and groaned. "Maybe for you… This exo-suit just seems to make everything worse." She banged her free hand against the suit's side.

Abby laughed. "It has its drawbacks, but also its good side. After all, it'll boost you right up to the strength you had in the coliseum. I been making adjustments to the old suits, so this should work better."

Anabelle thought back to her first mission with humans who'd been wearing similar exo-suits. It had been a disaster. She hoped Abby's version worked better. Otherwise, Terra would be useless in a fight.

Terra moaned loudly as she lay on her side. It was hard to imagine Terra as the sole human who had survived the Game Master, a lieutenant in the Dark One's coliseum on the orcish world. After her successes, Terra had received the title of orc chieftain.

Coliseum survivor, orc chieftain, now defeated by a tiny bit of motion sickness.

Anabelle went to stand beside Abby and give Terra some space to deal with her sickness. The pair looked out at the skyscrapers and traffic below. "First time in the city?"

Abby shook her head. She'd been here once before, also in a battle scenario. And that was when she had met Persephone, a drow assassin who had tried to kill her. But all was well that ended well. The drow might have tried to kill her once, but now...now they were friends.

More than friends.

Persephone, Abby thought, I really miss that mutated drow.

The pilot turned to Anabelle. "We're landing in a few minutes. Get ready."

Anabelle flashed him a thumbs-up and took a seat. Abby sat beside her. The pair maintained splatter-distance from Terra, who was still green in the face.

The helicopter flew to the top of the Empire State building. Abby helped Terra to her feet as Anabelle leapt out the hatch and landed on the drop spot.

Abby jumped, her nanobots' propulsion system slowing her descent so she could land gracefully. Terra followed, landing with considerably less grace, but at least on her feet.

Terra was still swearing under her breath, struggling to get used to her armor as she jogged over to the other two DGAs a few feet away. "Can I get some of them nanobots? I want to float like a butterfly, too."

Abby smiled over her shoulder at Terra. "They'd never take to you. They got taste."

"I never met anything that didn't take to me." Terra pinched Abby's cheeks. "Including redneck teenagers."

Anabelle chuckled at the back and forth between Abby and Terra. The two hadn't known each other for long, but they already sounded like great friends. Anabelle hoped they felt the same about her.

Goddess, maybe cut the insecurity for one mission?

The three Dark Gate Angels strode over to the building's ledge. Anabelle knelt and pulled out a pair of binoculars. She pointed at a building across from them. "That's where the gate is supposed to open up. We don't know the exact room, but we got the floor number. Soon as it goes off, we swing in and tear it up. Sounds easy enough, right?"

Terra cracked her knuckles nervously. "Yeah, I guess so. Do these kinds of things usually go off without a hitch?"

Anabelle remembered this was Terra's first mission on Earth. Correction—it was Terra's first mission ever. Not that Terra wasn't combat-ready—she'd spent almost a month fighting for her life. But this mission would feel different: working with a team, not being in charge.

"No," Anabelle admitted. "Things can go to shit pretty fast. But as long as we're communicating and working together, things usually turn out all right."

Terra smiled faintly as she leaned backward and supported her weight on her hands behind her.

Abby was staring at the skyscrapers, her eyes wide with wonder. "Last time I was in New York, I was in a fight. Second time, and I'm about to get into another fight." Abby chuckled. "Guess this city lives up to the hype. Still, never thought I'd see New York once, let alone twice. Never seemed like a place people like me would go. Ma is going to freak out when she sees this."

Anabelle gave Abby a curious look. "What do you mean, see?"

Abby tapped the side of her eye. "Taking videos and pictures of the whole thing. Planning on showing her as soon as I see her."

"Cute. She'll probably appreciate that. Is New York everything you thought it would be?"

7

Abby shrugged as she kicked her feet over the side of the building. "Eh. Could take it or leave it. Can't miss a jewel you never kissed."

Terra, who was watching the sun reflected in the glass of the building across from them, chuckled softly. "Okay, I'm gonna just say it. Half the things you say don't make sense, kid. Are you messing with us with all your homespun wisdom?"

Abby laughed as the nanobots on her face receded, revealing her girlish smile. "No, no, it's a force of habit. It was something my dad and I did 'cause he thought it was hilarious. You know country folks. Used to drive my ma crazy. We never got tired of it, though."

A silence fell over the Dark Gate Angels as Abby's eyes went dark. The nanobots rolled back over her face, covering her in an obsidian coating. Anabelle hated seeing Abby like this. Usually the kid was a ball of creative energy and curiosity. But recently, anytime Abby's father was mentioned, Anabelle would see the hatred in Abby's eyes.

Anger was a good emotion in a war. Helped motivate you. Kept you going. But hatred? Hatred was an entirely different emotion. A dangerous one. Hatred had unpredictable consequences. Anabelle had seen entire worlds consumed by one person's hatred. She hoped Abby would never become that kind of person.

Terra must have picked up on the vibe from Abby as well. She slung her arm around Abby, pulled the kid close, and knocked on Abby's metallic forehead. "Hey, where you gone to?"

Abby tried to avoid Terra's eyes. "Nowhere. Still in New York."

"You gonna tell me how this armor is supposed to work, or am I gonna have to figure it out myself?"

The nanobots rolled away enough to reveal Abby's bright eyes and her wide grin. "Oh! It's a special version of what Myrddin's marines use. Blackwell's squad. The difference between your model and theirs is energy output. Theirs is set at a standard output, whereas yours is customized to fluctuate with your pineal and adrenal glands through a heart-monitoring system."

Terra raised an eyebrow at Abby. "You know, not all of us speak scientist."

Abby laughed and apologized. "Your suit's performance will

improve the more you are stressed. Or angry. Kinda like back in the coliseum."

"*That* was determination, not anger."

"Whatever you want to call it, if it gets your blood pumping, your muscles'll be next."

Anabelle cleared her throat and pointed at a window in the building across from them. She was glad to have a distraction. "There it is! That glint. The gate is opening up over there."

Terra was on her feet, squinting at the window. "I don't see anything."

Anabelle handed Terra the binoculars. "There."

The nanobots covered Abby's face. "Yeah, I can see it too."

As Terra returned the binoculars, Anabelle caught something else out of the corner of her eye. There was a glint in another room. Then another. And another. "Shit. There's going to be more than one gate."

Anabelle scanned the building to her right. A handful of the tell-tall glints of the impending Dark Gates appeared within. "Ugh. Why isn't intel ever right? Myrddin should start sending us out with a whole army every time we leave HQ."

Abby's back thrusters fired, and she floated a little away from the team to get a better look. "There's gonna be a lot of them, huh? Are we getting any backup?"

Anabelle nodded. "Blackwell's unit is already on their way. I had a feeling that three of us wouldn't be enough. Still could have used an army, though. Would be nice to have my own army."

There was a buzz and a glow as the first gate opened right behind Abby, Anabelle, and Terra. The trio whirled as they heard the sizzling of the gate cracking into their dimension.

A single orc exited the Dark Gate. She wore thin, tattered leather that appeared to fall off her as she moved. Intricate tattoos covered her skin, though none were even slightly indicative of orcish life or culture. Her body was all lean, knotty muscle.

Grok, the Unspoken, watched the Dark Gate Angels silently as she crossed her arms. Her eyes burned with rage as if they were capable of killing.

The last time Anabelle had seen Grok, the orc had almost killed her while leading an attack on Washington, DC. Grok didn't look like a leader, though. The orc was more than that; she was a weapon.

For the first time, Anabelle understood. *This orc isn't chipped. They want this.*

Grok stepped forward and Anabelle flinched, a tiny movement she hoped Grok hadn't noticed.

The orc snickered and waggled her hands at her sides. "You aren't ready for me. None of you are."

"Grok," Anabelle spat, her neck prickling with anger. "Last time, you could barely handle *me.*"

Grok waved her hands around and snorted. "You mean all of your little elf magic tricks?"

Anabelle knew it was a ploy, but she couldn't help wanting to smash open Grok's face for speaking so disrespectfully of the Way. Or was it of Anabelle? "What are you planning to do here? You'd think an orc would understand that attacking civilians is cowardly. Your boss is a bottom feeder. From the number of gates you're opening, it looks like you're sneaking around, trying to pick off unarmed people down on the streets. That's not something a real warrior would do."

Grok laughed, a harsh sound more akin to a cough. "I'm surprised you even know the word 'warrior.' Making your hands hot doesn't make you a warrior. But you are right—the Dark One is no warrior. Neither am I."

"Oh? Then what are you?"

Grok smiled, her sharp teeth shimmering through her orcish snarl. "A force."

It was almost impossible to see. But Grok moved forward, as elegantly as if she were an unburdened river. And Anabelle couldn't help but think, *How beautiful.*

Grok's fist connected with Anabelle's stomach, knocking the wind out of her.

Before either Abby or Terra could move, Grok flipped Anabelle over, and kicked the other girls in the backs of the heads, sending them flying.

Abby went careening off the side of the building, as did Terra, who grabbed hold of the ledge to keep from falling over.

Grok slammed Anabelle's head into the concrete floor. A second later, she pulled Anabelle up by her hair. "I am going to kill you, Wanderer. Wipe the last of you from the face of the Earth. You hear me, elf? I will grind your bones into dust. The Road will be no more, the Way will be shut."

Anabelle leaned forward, preparing to attack. Before she could move, Grok delivered a chop to her throat. The elf's vision blurred for a second and, by the time it cleared, Grok was gone.

CHAPTER TWO

A bby had been caught off guard by Grok's attack; she'd never seen anyone move that fast before. As though she hadn't taken the time to even plan the move. Fortunately, Abby hadn't received the bulk of the attack.

That had been saved for Anabelle.

As Abby flew back to help Anabelle, Grok was already walking through the portal.

Anabelle was still on her knees, staring blankly ahead as though unable to believe what had happened.

Before landing, Abby scanned the area for Terra, who had pulled herself up over the corner of the rooftop ledge and was sprinting toward the elf. "You okay?" Abby asked when she landed beside Anabelle.

Anabelle looked like she'd seen a ghost. Her face was paler than normal and her bottom lip trembled. When she spoke, her question came out as a squeak. "Did you see that?"

Terra was rubbing her jaw as she opened and closed her mouth. "I sure as hell felt it."

"I didn't even have a chance to defend myself. She slipped in and took me down without breaking a sweat." Anabelle surged to her feet, muttering to herself as she stalked toward the edge of the building.

Abby had once seen the same look in her mother's eye after losing a season's worth of grain to a freak cold snap. Nothing any of the Crookins could have done would have made a difference. The cold had come in during the night and frozen the ground solid.

Without warning or mercy.

Anabelle's eyes carried that same look of confusion and anger.

Martin, the AI in Abby's brain, appeared in her peripheral vision as a GIF of a mustachioed latte lazily smoking a cigarette. "Blackwell and the rest of his squad finally decided to show up. 'Bout ten minutes or so."

Abby nodded and strode over to Anabelle.

Terra was meandering back and forth, occasionally staring at the Dark Gate left behind on their building. Unlike those they'd encountered previously, this one hung open, though it lacked the pulsating glow of an active gate.

Either this portal didn't open and close like the ones they'd seen...or someone was keeping it open in... "Sleep mode. The gate is kind of dormant but awake at the same time, like when you put your computer on sleep mode to save energy, but also ready for a quick boot-up. So, what now?"

Anabelle didn't answer, and Abby noticed the elf was still staring off in the distance. "Hey, Belle?" Abby called.

Anabelle snapped back to attention. The confusion had left her face and been replaced by an expression that said she was all business now. "Guess we're going to have to dismantle each and every one of these—" Her words were cut off by the sound of the Dark Gate gearing back to life.

Terra came up from behind the gate, waiting for the portal to open so she could bash in whatever creature walked through. But only a small blue flame appeared in the middle of the Dark Gate's frame. "Hm. This looks different from the last one, right?"

Anabelle groaned. "Of course, it's different. Which means the Dark One is throwing us another annoying-ass curveball."

A bright blue light shot from the flame in the Dark Gate. It flew past the three women, heading toward one of the glints Anabelle assumed were more gates.

Another light fired.

And another.

Abby watched as little blue lights began to glow in a number of buildings across the city block. A second later, a blue line of energy connected all the shining dots in an intricate web. "What's going on? There's nothing in the files 'bout this."

The clouds shifted from white to a deep crimson as black lightning cracked.

The three women looked up as the air around them thickened with energy.

Anabelle shook her head. "No fucking clue."

A giant beam of black energy shot into the streets, cracking the surface of the ground. Cars were thrown through the air as people scurried about, screaming in a panic. "Figures they would go straight for the civvies," Anabelle muttered as she watched the chaos. "How long do we have until Blackwood's squad gets here?"

Abby, who was also focused on the pandemonium below, answered, "About ten minutes."

Anabelle hit her comm. "Blackwell, you need to double time. I want you to take care of the civilians. There's already too much collateral damage."

Blackwell's voice came through to Anabelle. "We're on it."

Anabelle turned to Abby. "You're with Blackwell. I want those humans safe."

Abby was ready to fly off. "You don't have to tell me twice."

Terra grabbed Abby's shoulder. "Hold on. Check that out."

The spot where the energy had landed had caved in. A massive hole was opening in the middle of the street as the asphalt fell in on itself. From beneath came a glowing red light. "That's not going to be good," Anabelle groaned.

A lightning bolt of energy shot up from the earth, connecting with the clouds above.

It pained Abby to know there were people suffering in the streets, but Terra was right. She couldn't go rushing into a situation without having an understanding of what was happening. That would get her killed, and no one would be saved.

The women watched as the ground continued to crumble into the gaping hole, during which, the blue flames in the Dark Gates vanished and the normal portals opened.

A hand the size of a school bus, covered in thick brown fur filled with moss, reached from the hole in the ground, followed by an unholy roar that echoed around the chasm.

The hand was just the beginning.

A creature heaved itself from the flaming maw. Two stories tall with long spindly arms, its lower body was that of a cloven-hooved animal, its torso that of a giant. Resting upon its muscular neck was what appeared to be the head of a deer.

Abby's eyes zoomed in on the monster below her. The creature's head was splitting down the middle. A small man's rotting body, veins bright and clear, forced its way out of the deer's head, screeching as he paused half-birthed, gelatinous fluid flung about as he writhed in pain.

Anabelle shook her head. "They brought a fucking Jotun? Are they insane?"

Abby and Terra both looked at Anabelle with confusion. "Uh, what's that?" Terra asked.

"The ancestors of giants. They thrive in pure chaos and only live to destroy. Shit! Shit, okay, Abby, you're still working with Blackwell when they get here. Not to overtask you, but can you send drones to destroy the gates?"

"I can, but I will need some visual help."

Anabelle nodded. "Terra, I need you to handle the gates. Abby can give your suit control of the drones."

Abby chimed in. "On it. They'll follow you and help, kind of like blockers for a quarterback."

Anabelle smiled. They were one hell of a team. "Good. And Terra? Anything that comes through, you tear the shit out of. I'll handle the

Jotun."

Terra shrugged as she peered over the side of the building at the Jotun. "Sure you don't want me to take that thing out? Looks like it's having a hard enough time living. We could just put it out of its misery."

"Which is why I'll handle it. You can probably clear the buildings faster than I can."

"Well, come on. You don't want to live forever, do you?"

Abby chuckled despite the enormity of their mission. "*Starship Troopers*, huh? Good reference."

Anabelle gave a puzzled look. "What's *Starship Troopers*? Does Myrddin have space squads too?"

Abby and Terra chuckled before Terra stretched and her sternum cracked loudly. The gladiator leapt off the side of the building, rocketing toward the skyscraper across from the Angels. *Man, this suit is cool.* If she had had one during the games, she could have taken down a whole squadron of balrogs without breaking a sweat.

Terra crashed through a window, sliding across the ground as a pair of orcs rushed through the Dark Gate. She grabbed them both and slammed their heads together before picking up one of their axes and tearing into the gate.

Two more orcs came after her, but Abby's drones shot them down, as she had promised.

Anabelle smiled. "Yeah, I think she'll be able to handle this. Get to the ground floor, Abby." Anabelle turned as an orc stepped through the portal behind her. She kicked the creature in the throat, grabbed one of the grenades hanging from its belt, pulled the pin, and threw it into the portal before pushing the orc after it. That was when the elf's hands caught fire and she smashed them into the Dark Gate, splitting it down the middle.

Abby drew a deep breath and sped off toward the ground, scanning for what lay behind the smoke flowing from the chasm in the streets. "Martin, can you do something about that? I can't see anything."

"Adjusting your peepers. So, they got you on boring detail today?"

Abby tried to ignore Martin's tone. "There are people down there who need help, and I'm still killing orcs."

"True. Guess someone has to make sure all the humans don't die."

Abby flew to ground level as Blackwell and his troops were arriving. Turned out there were more than Anabelle had implied, at least fifty. The only person Abby recognized other than Blackwell was Naota.

The two were an interesting pair to be working together. Naota always looked like he had strolled out of an anime convention, not quite cosplaying but pretty damn close.

Blackwell, on the other hand, appeared to have been in the service for some time. He and Naota were about the same age, though Blackwell had an air of sobriety that was constantly aggravated by Naota's inability to take anything seriously.

Abby landed close to Blackwell, who was commanding his squad to assess the situation and move civilians out of the way.

Both Blackwell and Naota wore the exo-suit redesigns Abby had made. They weren't as intense as Terra's, mostly because Abby wasn't certain anyone else could handle it. It was a risk she preferred not to take.

Blackwell jogged over to Abby. "What's the situation?"

She pointed in the direction of the chasm. "Anabelle said there's a Jotun in there. Kinda like a giant or something."

Blackwell nodded as he squinted in the direction Abby indicated. "Okay. We got ground forces of orcs coming in too. There must be gates down here as well. We'll take care of the civilians if you want to handle the gates and orcs we don't pin down."

"On it!"

Blackwell and Naota headed toward the streets, their squad following them, splitting up and searching for any humans who might have been hurt, while still managing to take shots at the orcs who were beginning to come out of the woodwork.

Abby noticed a heavy stream of orcs coming from one of the buildings on her left. She zoomed over to them, weaving between them to fire three quick plasma shots from her hands before soaring away.

The orcs might have the advantage of numbers, but Abby had speed, artillery, and range. She backed up, taking aim at the orcs who were attempting to regroup after the attack.

The nanobots quickly constructed another plasma cannon on Abby's shoulder and she fired.

When the smoke settled, all the orcs were dead. "Hey, Martin," Abby said. "Have Gertrude and the rest start a sweep of the buildings. I want a clear idea of how many of these portals there are."

Martin's sleepy answer of, "You got it, Chief," was slightly annoying. The AI had an amazing ability to appear uncaring no matter what happened during a mission.

High above Abby, Terra flew into the same building, crashing her way inside—not a practical means of entry, but she was having fun.

Martin interrupted Abby's train of thought. "All gates locked on. Thinking about finally doing something?"

"You heard Anabelle. That's Terra's job."

"A job *we* would be more efficient at."

"I don't know," Abby said with a smile. "Terra seems pretty efficient to me. Still, we're a team, so I suppose I could help a bit."

Activating the thrusters on her back, she soared into the air and headed to the other gate in the building where Terra was battling a band of five orcs. "Figures you would try to save all the fun for yourself," Abby commed Terra before bursting through the windows. She fired off two small plasma detonators which attached themselves to one of the orcs. "That one is live!"

Terra surged through the group and grabbed the orc with the detonator. As she flung it through the open portal, Abby landed beside her and focused a thin beam of concentrated energy at the remaining orcs, slicing them in two at the waist.

An explosion shot forth from the portal a second before Terra threw the gate on its side and stomped it to pieces. "There's another one a few doors down," Abby said, pointing to the right. "You want me to take care of it?"

Terra shook her head and raced off.

Abby uploaded the locations of all of the gates to the team's HUDs and sped to the next gate.

Below Abby, Anabelle had finally reached the streets and was preparing to take on the Jotun. Hopefully the elf would be okay. She had seemed pretty shaken up after Grok had made her appearance.

Abby flew to the top of a building, in search of the other Dark Gate. As she scanned the area, a rocket slammed into her back, the explosion sending her careening into the side of the building.

A handful of orcs shimmered into existence. "They must have cloaking devices," Abby muttered.

The orcs circled Abby. Each held an electric rod that they shoved into the ground at intervals. Seconds later, a containment field opened over Abby.

This wasn't good.

The orcs were gloating with each other at having trapped Abby, who was already running through different escape options. Despite the possibility, blasting out was obviously not the way to go. The orcs would be expecting it.

No, she had a better idea.

Abby dumped all of her nanobots from her skin, leaving her vulnerable as her armor disappeared. She was not defenseless, though. Since injecting herself with nanobots, Abby could control them with the slightest thought as though all her white blood cells had been mobilized. Commanding the nanobots was as subconscious an act as walking.

The nanobots zoomed to the electric rods, easily squeezing out from the containment field. They reprogramed the rods, short circuiting them briefly before reversing the energy dispersal.

One of the orcs pressed his face to the containment field and sneered at Abby. "To think, all this is just for a little girl."

Abby smiled as sweetly as she could before the nanobots rejoined her, coating her in her sleek armor. When she was ready, she clenched her fist, disrupting the containment field, and sent it outward to melt the skin off the orcs surrounding her.

"Martin? How's Blackwell and Naota doing?"

There was a buzz and a whir before a GIF of a toddler in a hockey jersey screaming in victorious glory appeared in her vision.

"That good, huh?"

"Their team is—how do you humans put it?—kicking ass and taking names."

"Good." Abby went to the Dark Gate, and with a blast from her suit, shut it down. "Great, actually. Time for me to shut some gates down."

CHAPTER THREE

Anabelle approached the Jotun. The confused creature was struggling and in pain, and likely attempting to make sense of the fact that it was alive. A part of Anabelle felt sorry for the thing. But it had been called by the Dark One's forces, so it could be no friend to hers.

But maybe… Just maybe…

She tried to maintain a neutral stance without leaving herself vulnerable, though she couldn't see or sense any orcs nearby.

Only herself and the Jotun.

Anabelle tried to remember if there was a required manner in which to speak to the Jotun. Though the being appeared monstrous, it was still a demi-god and might possess the superior attitude of what mortal creatures foolishly assume are deities.

There were no real gods. None Anabelle knew of, at least. The gods were either legends or extremely powerful historical figures worshipped by mortals. In Anabelle's experience, anything can be killed. You just had to figure out how.

The Jotun didn't need to die, though, not until it proved otherwise.

Ugh…how the hell do dwarves talk to these things? I know it's formal…ugh, fuck it. Anabelle cleared her throat and performed an elaborate gesture with her hand, feeling extremely stupid for the motion. "Greetings, wise Jotun. What is your business on Earth?"

The Jotun turned to look at Anabelle, its eyes moist and empty. Its hands flailed as though trying to reach for her. Instead, it fell on its face, baying loudly like a dying calf, its hands curving as though gently cradling something.

Anabelle was both disgusted and in awe as she watched the Jotun's body swelling and growing larger—as if it weren't giant enough. Even in its dying pains, it was still showing so much power. But Anabelle didn't know what to do about this. She had expected to walk into a straight-up fight. But whatever was going on with the demigod wasn't so simple.

The Jotun was sprawled in the street like a massive piece of road-kill. It had stopped growing and was now the size of three school buses. And it wasn't breathing anymore.

Anabelle commed Blackwell as she hurried to the peer over the side of the chasm. "How you guys holding up?"

Blackwell replied immediately. "We've got all the civvies a safe distance away from the fighting. Taken down a couple of small squads of orcs too. You'd think they'd be more organized with how many gates they had open. It's like they were just throwing bodies at a meat grinder."

"I was thinking the same thing."

"Any idea about what's going on?"

A rotten scent was coming up from the chasm. "Whatever it is, I'm betting it has to do with this hole in the ground. And with the Jotun. But I got nothing. Let's just clean this up and get going."

"Roger. We'll get the civvies moving to a safe zone and then double back." There was an explosion over the comm. "Goddamn it. Naota, didn't I tell you to stay away from there? Sorry, gotta go. We'll be there ASAP."

Anabelle hurried away from the chasm, trying to piece together all of the seemingly unrelated pieces of the cluster-fuck of a mission. "Abby? Terra? How are you guys doing with the Dark Gates?"

Terra answered first. "There are way too many of these things.

And these orcs can't fight worth shit."

Anabelle didn't hear anything else. Something was moving behind her. When she turned, she saw that a woman had emerged from the chasm. But this was not quite a woman. She was nearly all bones, her breasts hanging like heavy sacks against dead, gray skin. Clumps of her hair were missing, as were patches of her skin. She could barely remain upright. Instead, she stumbled across the ground like a deranged child, groaning loudly and painfully.

Anabelle was caught off guard. All she could do was watch as the husk of a person toppled over and struggled to get back on her feet. "Uh… Ma'am? Do you need a hand?"

The woman looked at Anabelle, her eyes empty of all life. She did not have whites, and her irises were the darkest, deepest green Anabelle had ever seen. The woman answered in a wheezing, hacking growl.

Anabelle wasn't taking any chances. She drew her mana into her hands, setting them aflame, and raced toward the wraith of a woman.

As Anabelle ran, a rocket fired somewhere behind her. She whirled around at the last moment, and tossed up a barrier, catching the rocket before it hit her. The missile exploded, the impact pushing her back a few feet.

She couldn't tell where the rocket had come from. But with only one fired, they hadn't intended to kill her. They had only meant to stop her from interfering. "Team, I want you on my location now."

Whatever this thing was, the Dark One was behind it. That meant *enemy*.

Terra fell from the sky and landed beside Anabelle, breaking up the ground beneath her feet. A few seconds later, Abby landed gracefully a few feet away.

"You need help with an old woman?" Terra asked.

Anabelle pointed to the skyline. "Abby, there are snipers up there. Could you take care of them? I think they're cloaked."

Abby nodded and turned to scan the area. "I came across cloaked orcs earlier, too. I'll take care of these ones now. Martin should be able to find them."

Anabelle gestured toward the old hag, who was still moving to the Jotun's corpse. "If you're feeling up to it, Terra, maybe you want to handle the old lady?"

Terra cracked her knuckles and smiled. "Yeah, okay. I guess I can help her cross the street." She strode to the hag as Abby launched into the air to deal with the snipers. "Hey!" Terra called. "What—"

The woman looked up, her expression feral. She released a low, threatening growl. Terra remained undeterred and strode closer.

Suddenly the woman rushed at her, faster than the frail condition of her body suggested she was capable of. She hit Terra in the jaw, sending her flying back to land beside Anabelle.

After a few seconds, Terra rolled to her feet and touched her jaw gingerly. "Did not see that coming. Double-team?"

"Double-team," Anabelle replied.

The pair raced toward the hag, who had almost reached the Jotun. Terra swung a fist at the woman. She tried to swerve away, but Anabelle landed a fiery punch to the crone's gut.

The woman skidded backward as Terra and Anabelle initiated a second round of attacks.

Anabelle shifted her mana, cooling the flames and covering her hands in shards of ice. She aimed, and fired, a blast of ice, hoping to freeze the hag in place.

But the old woman raised one hand, and a glowing green sphere appeared in her palm and shattered the ice missile.

Anabelle frowned. She hadn't seen this kind of magical energy before; the power wasn't elemental. "This isn't good. We need to put her down."

Two Dark Gate portals opened beside the hag. Dozens of armed orcs came rushing from the gate, taking aim at Anabelle and Terra as the old woman closed in on the Jotun.

The pair attacked the orcs, and Abby landed to join the fray.

As the three women tried to fight their way through the dozens of orcs, more orc forces poured into the streets from the nearby buildings.

At last, the old woman reached the Jotun and knelt beside it. "Flesh of a god…ah…flesh." She sank her teeth into the creature's flesh, tore off a strip, and gobbled it down fast.

As she swallowed, an explosion rocked the streets, spewing green debris, and covering the entire block in a jade miasma. "What the hell was that?" Anabelle shouted.

Energy crackled, and suddenly the smoke was caught in a whirlwind, and the air cleared.

Anabelle turned to the hag who was hunched over beside the Jotun, barbaric and primitive, glaring at the Angels through the horde of orcs.

"Sacrifices…" the hag muttered. "Delightful." She raised her hands, which were glowing green, the same shade as the light now bursting from the holes in her skin.

The orcs went rigid, emerald light shining in their eyes, and soon they were screaming in pain, their bodies convulsing as they rose into the air.

"Uh, you guys might wanna look at this." Abby was looking up at the buildings.

They followed her gaze to find green light shining from the windows closest to the Dark Gates, where many of the orcs would have gathered.

"She's attacking the Dark One's forces?" Anabelle asked.

The orcs in front of Anabelle burst into green flames and were instantly incinerated, leaving only a pile of green ash on the ground.

Green souls rose from the ash and from the buildings, and the old woman breathed them in, standing straighter as she released a sigh of relief. She wiggled her jaw back and forth before snapping it back into place. "Ah, that feels much better." The old woman turned away from the Dark Gate Angels and strode down the street.

The trio exchanged confused glances, and after a few seconds, Anabelle shouted at the old woman, "Excuse me? Are you going to—"

Without looking back, the woman raised one hand, went to the Jotun's head, opened its mouth, and yanked out one of its teeth. She ran her finger over the tooth, transforming it into a long, jagged knife.

When she was done, she closed her eyes, and jade smoke encased her body. When the cloud cleared, she was wearing loose-fitting hide armor made of the Jotun's fur, and a portion of her face was smeared with blood.

She approached the Dark Gate Angels. "Uh…who are you?"

Anabelle scoffed, still trying to process what she was seeing. "That's what we're asking you!"

The hag was now only a few feet away from the three women. "Me? Oh, nobody important." She pointed her knife at Abby. "This one. She's a child, isn't she?"

None of the Angels answered—they were too taken aback.

The hag sniffed loudly. She ran her tongue over her top lip and nodded. "Yep, that's a kid. I'm going to eat your soul first. You cannot believe how good you will taste."

Before anyone could react, the hag tackled Abby, cackling madly as she raised her knife and plunged it into the girl's chest, breaking through the armor. Her laughter was unending, a hair-raising sound like demons cackling as she pulled out the blade and plunged it into Abby's stomach over and over again.

Anabelle and Terra leapt onto the hag, ripping her from Abby. The hag kicked her feet, giggling like a child. "Wait, wait, I haven't even gotten—"

Terra punched the old woman in the face, sent her to her knees, and stomped her head into the ground. Anabelle ran to Abby and helped the girl sit up.

She held Abby in her arms. "Abby, *Abby*, are you okay?"

Abby pulled all of her nanobot armor off. "I need to heal…fast…" She coughed blood and winced when she touched her stomach. "Gimme a minute."

As Abby spoke, the marines finally showed up, driving into the block in military SUVs. Anabelle scooped the injured girl up and raced to Blackwell, who was getting out of one of the vans. She placed Abby in his arms. "She's been hurt. Badly."

Abby groaned softly. "I'll be okay. The nanobots can stitch me up. It'll just be a minute."

"Watch her," Anabelle said as she went to Terra, who still had her boot on the hag's head. "Get her up," Anabelle said, her fists beginning to burn with fire.

Terra grabbed the hag by her hair and yanked her up.

The old woman waved her hands in front of her face. "I'm sorry. I'm so sorry. I'm just…" She screamed loud, her eyes burning bright green. "I'm just so hungry! You know, I haven't had one that young in…oh, ages! I just wanted a taste!"

Anabelle raised a palm at the hag, a fireball growing between her fingers. "Who the hell are you? And how are you helping the Dark One?"

The hag looked confused for a second and started coughing. "The Dark One? That's who woke me up and got that giant asshole off me? Guess that's why he sent so many souls. But orcs? Ugh. Old ones, too. Could've at least sent a couple of newborns. He's getting cheap these days. But payment is payment."

Anabelle punched the hag in the face, burning away some of the woman's skin. "Who are you?" Anabelle yelled. But she merely received a blank stare in response.

The hag's lips twitched. That's the case with all of Myrddin's little cronies, isn't it? You all want to have control. You and the Dark One. Answers and answers."

Anabelle looked at Terra. "We're taking her back with us. She's—"

Terra was still gripping the hag's hair in her hand, but the old woman grabbed the lank strands and pulled them out of her own scalp. She fell to the ground and rolled away. "Fine, fine. Name? Rasputina. Let's go with that. And why am I here? The Dark One must be getting desperate. Even *I* wouldn't summon a lich to help me."

Anabelle's eyes went wide. There was no way she'd heard correctly. *A lich?*

Rasputina could see the fear in Anabelle's eyes. "Now, I'd kindly like that girl's soul now. Or I'll carve you both up first and take it anyways."

"You stay away from her," Anabelle hissed.

Rasputina cackled as she grabbed the side of her face. "Fine, fine. I'm tired of this already, anyway. Maybe the Dark One will have something more interesting for me to do than whatever the hell this was."

Without warning, Rasputina vanished in a cloud of green smoke. Terra pointed at the Jotun; the old woman had reappeared at its side.

Rasputina knelt beside it and plunged her hand into its torso. The Jotun shivered as its fur melted, leaving exposed flesh that pulsated and swelled.

Rasputina rose and grinned madly at Terra and Anabelle. "I think it might be time you two had a certain quality of evil in your lives." And with that, Rasputina erupted in green flames and was gone.

The pair raced to the Jotun. "Is Abby going to be all right?" Terra asked.

Anabelle, who was scanning the throbbing remains of the Jotun, replied, "Yeah, she's healing herself. She'll be fine."

"What the hell is a lich? And what did it do to this thing?"

"A lich is—"

Anabelle was cut off by the sound of flesh tearing. The Jotun was decaying rapidly. Its skin burst open, and the air was filled with the smell of rotted flesh.

Both Anabelle and Terra backpedaled, Anabelle only briefly glimpsing what lay hidden within the Jotun. The gut of the Jotun was lined with hundreds of cocoons, which were all beginning to split open.

Anabelle retreated, grabbing Terra's hand and pulling her away.

All at once, the cocoons popped.

A host of bat-like creatures with the heads of deer, sharp horns, and the bodies of orcs emerged from the corpse of the Jotun.

Anabelle watched as the sky filled with the creatures. "This is not going to be good."

Before she could utter another word, the corpse of the Jotun began to move. It scrambled to its feet, skin hanging like tattered cloth from its body. It screeched loudly as it turned to face the two Angels.

Anabelle swallowed hard. "Goddess, Myrddin really should send us with an army next time."

CHAPTER FOUR

Terra watched the strange creatures spreading their wings, dominating the sky.

Whatever a lich was, it had the ability to assert some control over the dead. The sight of all those mangled orc bodies elicited an emotion within Terra that she couldn't quite understand.

Terra grabbed Anabelle and shouted, "What the hell is going on?"

Anabelle barely registered the question, expression blank as though still trying to wrap her head around it herself.

Terra gave Anabelle two hard shakes. "Hey, we need you in this right now. What's going on?"

Anabelle shook off her funk. "Okay, we need to mobilize our ground forces. Shoot these things out of the sky. Then we need Abby airborne as soon as she can manage it. And...you...do you think you can take that thing?"

Terra didn't need Anabelle to specify which "thing." The Jotun was the biggest creature out there. Terra knew she was the brawn. And that meant the baddest, scariest creature would be hers to eliminate.

She watched the Jotun screeching and lumbering down the street, ejecting a blast of pure fire, scorching everything in its wake.

"Yeah, I guess I can take that." Terra nodded firmly.

"Good. Let's get this taken care of. The faster we can get back to HQ, the better."

Terra could tell Anabelle was still freaked out by what had happened with the lich. Anabelle might have been physically present enough to give orders, but that didn't mean she was mentally available. "You okay?" Terra asked.

Anabelle nodded as a magical aura pulsed around her body. "Okay enough for a fight. You ready?"

"Where are you going?"

Anabelle looked skyward. "Up." She surged into the air, grabbed one of the bat-orcs, and wrangled it to fly toward the mass of wings above.

Terra watched the Jotun amble down the street. "Guess it's game time." She ran after the creature, trying to figure out how to defeat something that large. It made the dragons she'd fought not so long ago look like garden-variety lizards.

The Jotun slowed and turned its head to watch Terra as she closed in. Two seconds later, it released a blast of fire from its broken, necrotic mouth.

Terra leapt aside, managing to avoid being singed. *Guess this fucker means business.* She ran around behind the Jotun and grabbed its tail, pulling with all her strength. The momentum toppled the ancient demi-god onto its side.

The Jotun screeched with rage, kicked its hind legs, and flung Terra away.

Abby lay in the back of a military SUV. Soldiers were moving around her, and she recognized a few. But her attention was focused on Martin, who was explaining what the nanobots were doing. Her internal organs had already been stitched up. Now the nanobots were repairing the damage to her soft tissue.

"How long is this going to take?"

"Maybe you could take a breather?" Martin's voice was annoyed.

"You did just get shivved in the guts."

"If my guts are okay, I don't have to waste any more time, do I?"

Martin sighed. "Guess not. The soft-tissue repair can be completed while you're fighting. Just try not to get stabbed again."

Abby sat up, covering herself in a nanoarmor. "Perfect."

The soldiers closest to Abby opened their mouths as if they intended to say something, but the sound of her thrusters cut them off as she rose into the air.

She flew toward Anabelle's HUD signal. Something huge had happened while Abby had been laid out in the back of the van. She had never seen creatures like this before, not even in the dossiers she'd been studying in her spare time.

Abby caught up with the elf, who was riding one of the bat-orcs. "Need a hand?"

Anabelle smiled at Abby. "Would have taken me a month to recover from that!"

"Modern technology does wonders."

The two Angels headed toward the mass of wings.

Abby peeled away and flew into the thicket of bodies. She stopped on a dime, concentrated her plasma energy, and spun, slicing through anything dumb enough not to get out of the way.

Anabelle leapt off her ride, her hands glowing with white and blue ice-energy. She grabbed one of the bat-orcs, freezing it instantly, spun it to gain momentum, and launched it toward the massive group.

As the creature soared past Abby, she took aim, lining up her shot perfectly. She fired a plasma blast and exploded the bat-orc with a blast of ice magic, which also froze the creatures closest to it.

Abby turned her thrusters up, weaving between the winged fiends, closing in on the creatures she had frozen. She slammed her elbow into one, cracking it down the middle, before whirling and firing her plasma cannons again, cleaning up the rest of the iced-over monsters.

Anabelle came up behind Abby, riding one of the creatures. She snapped its neck, leapt to another, and drove her fiery hands through its body. "We need to make a wave!"

Abby didn't have to be told twice. She flew to Anabelle, grabbed her around the waist, and sped forward as the elf tossed off multiple fire-attacks. The pair burned through dozens of the creatures in front of them.

"We're not making any headway!" Abby shouted.

Anabelle leapt from Abby's arms, snatching one of the bat-orcs closest to her. "The Jotun is what's responsible for this. Kill it, and we get rid of those bat-orc shitheads! Come on, Terra, get it done!"

The Jotun had escaped Terra's grasp. It was moving farther downtown, God only knew where.

Didn't need to know what it was doing to kill it.

Behind Terra, Blackwell's squad was picking off any of the bat-orc creatures that were too close to the ground. "Where do you want us?" Blackwell shouted.

Terra couldn't deal with having to command a squad while trying to figure out how to make the Jotun give her its full attention. "Why don't you ask Anabelle?"

"She's busy! What do you have for us?"

Naota, who was right behind Blackwell, jumped up onto a wrecked car. "We need to have heart, that's what we need!"

Blackwell sighed and rubbed his brow. "Please stop talking for as long as possible."

Naota saluted Blackwell before drawing his dual pistols. "Affirmative, sir."

Terra tried to think of the best course of action. "You guys take care of the back. I'll try to get ahead of this asshole and stop him from moving forward. Anything that gets in the way of that, take care of."

Blackwell, Naota, and the squad tore off, heading toward the Jotun's back legs. Terra sprinted, trying to catch the demi-god, which had stopped paying attention to her and was busy blasting fire at the buildings around it.

She slid in front of the Jotun and waved her hands above her head. "Hey! I'm not finished with this."

The Jotun moved faster than Terra expected. He leaned forward and headbutted her, sending her soaring through the air and crashing into a car.

Terra scrambled to her feet, trying to shake away the spinning in her head. "Okay, so that's not going to cut it." She sprinted toward the Jotun, leapt into the air, and brought her fist down on the creature's head. Its knees buckled and it crashed beside Terra seconds after she landed smoothly on the ground. "If we're going to fight, then we're going to fucking fight."

Abby had dropped Anabelle off on the roof of one of the buildings, leaving the elf to eliminate the few orcs who had survived the mass sacrifice. While Terra took care of the Jotun and the bat-orcs, Abby's main priority was to figure out what to do about the Dark Gates. They couldn't risk leaving them open any longer.

"Hey, Martin, you got anything to help me with this?"

The AI's bored voice rang in Abby's head. "We could commandeer the gates…kind of like what you did back there with that containment field. Reverse the signal. Blow 'em up from inside."

"That's a great idea. Let's—"

"Of course, it is. *I* came up with it."

Abby ignored Martin and glided above the city to locate a suitable spot to access the gates around her—all while dodging and weaving between dive-bombing bat-monsters and plasma-shots fired by orc snipers.

"You think you can hurry this up, Martin?"

"Do you think people rushed Mozart or Michelangelo? Art takes time, Abby."

A plasma shot sailed past her. She spun and fired her own, the blast tearing through the side of a building and eliminating a group of orcs. "Were any of them under threat of death?" she snapped.

Martin hummed loudly. "You know, Michelangelo might have been. Read he didn't get along with the Pope too well."

Blackwell and his squad were attacking the back of the Jotun with all the firepower they possessed, but the demi-god didn't appear to notice; its focus remained on Terra.

She cracked her knuckles and rolled her shoulders. "All right. You ready to do this?"

The Jotun released a roar.

Terra screamed back at the creature before sprinting toward it. She leapt into the air as she had before. This time the Jotun caught her in mid-flight, holding her up for a second before slamming her into the ground.

Every inch of Terra's body revolted in pain as the concrete broke around her. But it was a familiar feeling. She knew it would hurt, but pain wasn't going to stop her.

The Jotun looked surprised, the beady eyes in its bizarre human body narrowing when Terra boosted to her feet. A moment later, the creature lunged for her, leaving behind the soldiers accosting its rear end. It tackled Terra, who grabbed its antlers and held tight.

The demi-god raced through the streets of downtown New York as Terra pummeled its head. She wrestled with the spindly arms of its human half and managed to bite down on its neck as hard as she could.

Above the city, Abby was still flying in circles, attempting to pick up a sufficiently strong signal from all the Dark Gates, evading the echo-blasts of the bat-orcs determined to put an end to her life.

Higher still, Anabelle was holding her own against a group of orcs who had emerged from a Dark Gate. She skimmed easily between the creatures, avoiding their blasts. She drew her mana into her hands, surged forward, and struck them with lightning palms. She used the speed of her electricity to zoom between the orcs, and eliminate every last one.

The Jotun was still raging in the streets, Terra holding onto it with all her strength, trying to wrench its bizarre human form away from the rest of its body.

As Terra finally got a firm hold, the humanoid jaw opened and a wall of fire came spewing out, knocking her off the Jotun. She somersaulted across the concrete and rolled around to put out the fire.

"Hey, guys. This thing is kinda...hard to kill. Anyone think they can give me a hand?"

Anabelle's voice shrieked over the comm, "Terra! You're supposed to be the muscle. Didn't you kill a dragon?"

"Yeah, a dragon isn't a demi-god!"

"Technically, they aren't that far off."

Abby flew overhead, stopping suddenly before boosting upward. "I finally got a signal. Once I'm done..."

All across the city, the Dark Gates detonated, shards of glass exploding from the buildings.

"Kay-kay, I'll be there in a second," Abby yelled.

Terra was backing away from the Jotun when Abby landed at her side. "Anabelle?"

Abby primed her hand plasma-cannons as they continued to move away from the Jotun. The creature was blowing smoke from its nostrils, stomping its back legs, as though ready to stampede down the streets.

Both Terra and Abby jumped at the high-pitched scream as Anabelle fell from the top of one of the buildings. The elf flipped in the air, regained her composure, and landed gracefully beside the two other Angels. "That was planned. So, we're taking down this asshole?"

Terra nodded. "I don't have any spiffy weapons like you guys. Can't get through his hard-ass skin."

"How about you wrangle him and me and Abby will figure something out?"

Terra smiled as she stretched her arms. "Sounds good to me." Terra sprinted toward the Jotun, dodging to the side to avoid another blast of fire. She jumped, pulled back her arm, and punched the demi-god with all her strength.

The Jotun stumbled, struggling to keep from falling. Terra didn't let up. She landed an uppercut to its jaw and the Jotun backpedaled, shaking its head from the blow. She jumped up and grabbed the demi-god by the throat, wrestling its head to the ground.

Anabelle looked at Abby. "Give this fucker everything you got."

Abby clapped her wrists together, her hands combining into an unwieldy plasma cannon. Power pooled in her palms. "Ready?"

Anabelle's fingertips crackled with lightning as energy shot from her eyes. "Let's end this."

Abby fired as the elf ran forward, keeping pace with the plasma blast, only backing up for a second to allow it to hit the Jotun as Terra leapt out of the way.

The plasma blast plunged into the creature's chest, tearing upward through its head. Anabelle's attack followed, and she sent lightning crashing through the demi-god.

When the smoke cleared, the Jotun lay on the ground, dead.

Anabelle rushed to help Terra to her feet. "Sorry about that. Didn't even cross my mind you couldn't kill a demi-god."

Terra motioned to her exo-suit. "Not in this. I know this is supposed to make me as strong as I was in the games, but I feel half as strong. Either Abby severely underestimated my strength, or I'm still working out the kinks." She looked over her shoulder at the Jotun. "That was some pretty good teamwork, though."

Abby joined the two beside the smoking remains. "Never thought I'd say I killed a demi-god."

Anabelle shoved Abby lightly as Blackwell and his squad came over. "Don't think you should brag too much about that. Might give off the wrong impression."

The body of a bat-orc fell from the sky. It was accompanied by more of the winged monsters, falling to the streets like raindrops.

Anabelle looked at Blackwell. "You guys think you can take care of this?"

Blackwell sighed, turning to Naota. "Can you handle this?"

Naota beamed as he addressed the squad. "Guess who's on clean-up detail, guys!"

The Angels exchanged confused glances. "I'm never going to get that guy," Anabelle muttered.

CHAPTER FIVE

When the Dark Gate Angels returned to base, they parted
ways. Anabelle insisted Abby be taken to the medbay, where
she could be observed. Abby tried to argue that she'd already healed
herself, but the elf could not be swayed.

Terra didn't bother explaining where she was heading. Anabelle
was a little jealous that Terra could, in essence, do whatever she
wanted.

Terra reported to only one person, and that was Anabelle.

Anabelle would need to debrief Myrddin and Roy. The briefing
would have to wait for a little bit, though. Abby was supposed to be
present for the discussion, and Anabelle wasn't risking the young girl
sitting through a meeting while still bleeding.

That left Anabelle with some time to kill. She would prefer not to
sit through a debriefing right now, but she also didn't want to be left
alone with her thoughts.

A lich returning to an active life was a troubling occurrence.
Anabelle didn't know much about liches, other than they were
extremely destructive. Also, it was clear the lich knew things, as
though she were communicating with the Dark One or one of his
minions.

Anabelle assumed Myrddin would fill her in on the details.

But, her mind shifted focus to Grok. She couldn't shake her feelings about the orc. Recalling how Grok had defeated her so effortlessly made Anabelle's blood boil.

The elf could mope about how inferior she felt at the moment, but that wouldn't make any difference to her next fight with Grok.

Anabelle went down to the intelligence department of HQ, where most of the spies and recon teams spent their time. It was the least flashy of the departments, constantly darker than necessary, as though the spies could only work in the literal shadows.

The department was almost empty. There were a handful of people around, but they didn't appear to be doing any work. No one was sitting at a computer. They were simply lounging about.

Anabelle hurried through the department until she reached the firing range, where she found Sarah, an unofficial member of the Angels. They had worked on the last mission together, but other than the last time they'd hung out a few months ago, she hadn't seen much of her.

Sarah looked up as Anabelle approached. "Yo."

Unlike Anabelle, Sarah wore standard spy armor—a thin black outfit with a vest. To the elf, she looked like one of those ninjas on human TV.

Maybe she was.

Anabelle stood beside Sarah, who was busy tossing throwing-knives at various targets. "Where've you been? I haven't been able to get in touch with you."

Sarah's knife hit a bullseye. One after another. "Been off-world since our last mission, trying to put together another resistance cell on the gnomish homeworld. Since the last one was crushed, we been hurting to put on another offensive. Mostly guerilla stuff. Just got back today."

"You've been on the gnomish world for three whole months?"

Sarah finally met Anabelle's eyes and smirked. "Yep. It's been good. There's been a lot of time for training."

Anabelle had never had a chance to talk to any of the humans who worked in intel. The department was mostly dominated by elves and dwarves.

Elves provided most of the assassins, and dwarves took care of intelligence gathering.

Technically, Anabelle should have been in this department before her transfer to SWARRT—or rather, the Dark Gate Angels—but in the past, Myrddin had kept her presence at HQ to a minimum.

Anabelle's main interest in Sarah's training was because of her lack of magic. It was wild to think Sarah could handle herself without any of the advantages available to the regular exo-suit-wearing forces of HQ.

"What kind of training?" Anabelle asked.

Sarah smirked as she threw another knife. "Wondering how a human does an elf's job?"

"My team is made up of mostly humans. I've seen what your kind is capable of and can admit, my earlier opinions were…a little harsh."

"That's putting it lightly, but it's a step in the right direction. And I'm not trying to give you a hard time."

Anabelle pulled her mana into her hand, creating an ice spike. She shot it at the target, hitting one of the outer rings. "Thanks for that. And no, I'm just curious. I don't know anything about you. Figured it's some common ground. And I am curious about your abilities. If you have any."

Sarah raised an eyebrow at Anabelle.

Anabelle turned red. "No, I didn't mean it like that. I just…oh, I mean, I train too. It's been a little rough lately since all of my training is mental. You know, meditation, accessing old memories. My physical training was hundreds of years ago. Training is mostly remembering."

Sarah appeared more interested now. "Yeah, you're one of those Travelers, right? I always had a soft spot for your form of training. If I could use magic, that's probably the route I would take."

"So is it mostly stuff like this? Target practice?"

Sarah threw another knife, not bothering to look at the target, and still managing to hit the bullseye. "Humans are born with our own non-magical energy. It's just a little hard to access. My training is mostly about opening up my body's potential through my chakras. I won't bore you with the details, but it allows me to push myself to the limits. Helps with stuff like this."

Sarah turned toward the door and threw a knife over her shoulder. Bullseye. "I don't need to train at this. I'm just bored."

The two chatted for a little while longer, Anabelle was deeply invested in learning more about Sarah. She hadn't expected the human to have such a wry, morbid sense of humor. Calling it black humor wasn't nearly dark enough.

At last, Anabelle remembered her reason for coming to the intel department. "Hey, could you help me with something?"

Sarah retrieved her knives from the target. "Yeah, what's up?"

"I'm trying to get some information on a little problem of mine. An orc named Grok. The first time I saw her, she said she was going to kill me."

"You were in the middle of a battle. That's what I would have said."

"And if you said that to someone, they'd probably be terrified like I was. You're not a regular soldier. How often have you bothered to take the time to tell someone you were going to kill them?"

Sarah's eyebrows scrunched up. "Most killing in my field is incidental, so I'll give you that. It might rattle me a little bit. Come on, I'll check the files."

Sarah led Anabelle to a dwarf seated at a nearby desk. He wore thick glasses and looked like he'd rolled in the dust before coming to work. "This is Vord," Sarah said. "He's this decade's librarian."

Anabelle gave Sarah a confused look. "What do you mean, decade?"

Sarah didn't reply. Instead, she asked Vord, "You got any information on an orc named Grok?"

Vord bit his bottom lip before answering, "Got a couple of files." The dwarf scrawled a series of numbers and letters on a scrap of paper and handed it to her.

Sarah inspected the notes, thanked him, strode away. "Come on," she said to the elf.

The pair headed toward a series of filing cabinets that stretched far back into the department, fading into the darkness. "Yeah, he's on shift for a decade. Myrddin enchants the librarian so that they don't need to sleep, or eat, or anything. He sits at that desk for ten years and never moves."

"Goddess, that sounds horrible."

"Not for him. He loves it. Most of the librarians do. Myrddin's got him psychically linked to every member of the department. Soon as they come on, he gets hit with everything they got in their head. He's also the only person in all nine of the realms who has access to Myrddin's mind. Okay, here we go."

Sarah stopped in front of a file cabinet. She opened it and thumbed through hundreds of manila folders.

Anabelle stared at the files. "Are you serious? You guys use hard copies?"

"Only one copy of anything. Can't hack a piece of paper. Safest option. There you are." Sarah plucked out a couple of folders and handed them to Anabelle. "That's everything we got."

Anabelle eyed the fat folder, almost bursting with notes. "Looks like some good, light reading." Anabelle's HUD watch went off, distracting her with a message from Myrddin that Abby was out of the medbay and it was time for the debriefing. "I gotta go. Thanks again! And don't be a stranger. Just because Myrddin has you in a different department, doesn't mean you're not an Angel, all right?"

Sarah smiled for the first time during their conversation. "Thanks. I'll keep that in mind."

When Anabelle arrived at the War Room, she was surprised to see Terra sitting beside Abby. "Didn't expect to see you here. We're good to debrief without you if you need the rest."

RAMY VANCE & MICHAEL ANDERLE

Terra, who had been talking to Abby, looked up. "I got called in. Totally fucked up my nap."

Abby giggled. "You still take naps?"

Terra put her hands behind her back and stretched. "When you work as hard as me, rest is your best friend. Also, I love sleeping."

"More than fighting?"

Terra nodded. "More than fighting. More than chocolate. And more than sex."

Abby blushed.

Anabelle sat beside Abby as Myrddin and Roy entered the room. Roy took a seat across from Anabelle, his gaze drifting over her for a second. Anabelle counted the microseconds.

Myrddin didn't sit. Instead, he approached the holoprojector in the room. "I'm glad you *all* are here and, well, still standing. How did the mission go?"

Anabelle didn't like the edge in Myrddin's voice. You would have thought Anabelle had been the one who excluded Terra from the meeting earlier. She didn't have any say over who came to these or not.

"Less than stellar," Anabelle said after a few moments. "There were...complications."

Myrddin was still watching the screen. "I assumed so when I heard Abby was being taken to the medbay."

Abby raised her hand, looking awkward as hell. "Uh...I was actually okay. Not even bruised."

"It's still good to see your commanding officer prioritizing your safety. Anabelle, please tell me what happened."

Anabelle mentally ran through the important bits of things to bring up in her head. "Grok showed up. And—"

"I trust you started searching for information concerning her."

Anabelle bit her tongue, trying not to snap at Myrddin. Their relationship had been getting better over the last few months but, sometimes, that tone in his voice made her want to punch the old wizard in the face. "Yes. I did. Can I continue, or do you want to interrupt me again? Because I can—"

"No, please continue."

Myrddin looked over his shoulder, smiling slightly.

One of these days, old man, one of these days.

Anabelle cleared her throat, trying to remain professional. "Grok didn't stick around. She just knocked the shit out of me and bounced. And there were over twenty gates that opened."

At this, Myrddin turned to give Anabelle his full attention. "Only one was projected. Did you shut them all down?"

"Thanks to Terra and Abby, yeah. But even then, they weren't being used for an invasion. It was some kind of ritual sacrifice to release—you'll never believe it—a lich."

The color drained from Myrddin's face. It was the first time Anabelle had ever seen anything resembling fear in the old man. The look was disconcerting enough to make Anabelle think she hadn't taken the lich issue seriously.

When Myrddin spoke, he confirmed Anabelle's worries. "Did you say a lich?"

"Yeah. She said her name was Rasputina. Mean anything to you?"

Myrddin twisted the end of his beard, a nervous habit Anabelle rarely saw him indulge in. "This is not good. This is *not* good."

Terra and Abby stared at the old man. "What's the big deal about a lich?" Abby asked.

Myrddin waved his hand, and the projector switched to an image of Rasputina. Apparently, Myrddin knew exactly who she was. "If the Dark One is willing to reach out to a lich, and this lich specifically, then he is growing desperate. Or too eager."

"Yeah, but what is a lich?"

"Wizards and sorcerers live extremely long lives. I, myself, have lived over 2,800 years, give or take a century or two."

Abby's and Terra's jaws dropped. Anabelle managed to refrain from betraying her surprise, but his revelation came as a shock to her as well.

Myrddin didn't wait for questions. "Generally, we care about knowledge. Many people use magic, such as Anabelle, but there are those of us whose entire lives are dedicated to the pursuit of arcane arts. Some of that knowledge is forbidden, for good reason. Anything that deals with the Old Gods or the Elder Ones, gods as old as the Dark One. A lich has touched that forbidden knowledge.

"A lich is a nearly invincible magic-user. They've gone beyond the veil of what a mortal should know. They do not die. Ever. There are only five in all of the realms. Three are sleeping, one has removed itself from our plane of reality, and the other is Rasputina, the worst of them all."

Anabelle leaned forward. "Is she stronger than the Dark One?"

Myrddin squeezed the bridge of his nose as he shook his head. "It is not a question of strength. It is a question of purpose. The Dark One wants control. Rasputina was not like the other liches. Before she learned how to tap into magic, she was a killer. She was feared throughout the nine realms. There was no reason for her senseless murders. She became a lich, sacrificed her soul and body for one thing: to live long enough to personally kill every living being in the nine realms."

Terra laughed, clearly not taking any of this seriously. "Are you telling me that we're afraid of a zombie Joker rip-off?"

"Worse. She is the only lich who has ever allowed herself to be beaten. I was one of the wizards who sealed her with the Jotun meant to guard her until the end of time. The battle nearly destroyed the dwarfish realm. Not the dwarfish planet, the entire realm."

Myrddin sat, hanging his head. "Entire worlds were wiped out. So many people died. And we knew she let us win. I had to know, so I asked. She told me she simply got bored. And then she did this."

Myrddin unbuttoned his shirt. A scar, surrounded by dozens of other wounds, stretched from the bottom of his neck to his navel. "She froze time and tortured me for hundreds of years, healing my wounds only to disembowel me again. Then she returned everything to normal, and sat there like nothing happened."

From Terra's stricken expression, she didn't appear to find the situation funny anymore. "What the hell was she doing under Earth?"

Myrddin stood silent for a long time before answering. "I needed her close to keep an eye on her." The old wizard inhaled deeply.

"You're dismissed for now. I have to think." He stood, leaving everyone in the room with their questions unspoken.

Roy and each of the Angels exchanged glances. Finally, he broke the silence with a sigh. "I think we all need a drink. Meet you guys in the cafeteria."

CHAPTER SIX

The Angels met Roy in the cafeteria, and they sat in silence while drinking their beers. Terra didn't know what to say. Myrddin had dropped a lot of information on the team. She might not have fully grasped the enormity of what had happened, but she did know it was bad.

Abby, who was sitting beside Terra, slowly sipped a beer that Terra wouldn't have ordered on her worst day. "Are you even twenty-one?"

Abby gulped down another mouthful. "If I can die for the nine realms, I can probably have a beer here and there too."

None of the adults said anything, and they all kept drinking silently. "Well, not that this hasn't been riveting, but I'm heading back to my room," Terra said at last, preferring to avoid more of the awkward silence.

Everyone nodded or waved their goodbyes, still caught up in their own thoughts.

Terra didn't head back to her room. Instead, she went to the orcish barracks. After their last mission, a handful of orcs who had been rescued from the fighting arena had decided to stay on at the base.

Originally, Myrddin had situated the orcs away from the staff barracks. He'd been worried that the orcs might not be well-received by the rest of the base. Orcs made up the bulk of the Dark One's ground forces. Things could get ugly without much reason.

The orcs hadn't minded. As long as they'd been given a place to stay, they were happy. Many of them were lobbying to join the Middang3ard defensive and offensive teams. Myrddin hadn't passed down an order yet, but the orcs were ready.

Terra thought it was a great idea. Most of the time she'd spent around orcs had been in the arena, fighting at their side. It was the first time Terra had ever felt like she belonged anywhere.

She was still surprised it was with orcs.

Terra wanted to speak to one orc in particular by the name of Cire. He was a shaman of a lost orc tribe, one of the last of his kind, and still held to the old ways. He had bestowed the title of chieftain on Terra, making her much more than an honorary orc.

But it was not merely a title. Technically, the small band of orcs that had come back to the base was part of Terra's troop. Orcs were generally informal, but they did speak to Terra with a certain level of respect they didn't give to each other. She wasn't sure if that was because she was their chieftain, or if it was because she had saved their asses so many times. Maybe there wasn't a difference.

Another part of Terra's chieftain status required her to learn orcish history. Cire was relating the orcish oral history. Terra had assumed it would be a drag but found herself more interested in their history than she'd ever been with her own. It was a little difficult to follow, though, with the history being delivered in the orcish tongue through song.

Back in the arena, Cire had performed a rite on Terra that allowed her to understand orcish. Unfortunately, her knowledge was still at the level of a five-year-old. But she was getting better, and that was important.

As Cire had said, hearing their own language in commands would rally orcs in a way that few people ever saw.

Terra found Cire in his room, sitting with Nib-Nib, another refugee from the arena.

Nib-Nib was a mantiboid, a squat, mantis-like alien. Nib-Nib didn't speak much, but Terra could understand a little of what the creature said due to the rite Cire had performed.

Cire and Nib-Nib were conversing furiously, Cire using Nib-Nib's language, a combination of clicks and high-pitched, quiet screeches. When Terra arrived, he rose from his seat and bowed slightly.

Terra crossed the room and punched Cire in the shoulder. "I told you to stop doing that."

Cire rubbed his shoulder as Terra sat on his bed. "The other orcs might not be required to show you reverence, but as your shaman, it comes with the job."

Terra watched Cire closely. As she'd been getting to know the orc, she was learning how to tell when something was upsetting him. Like most of the other orcs, the only emotions that were ever front and center were indifference, anger, or a combination of both.

But there were strong emotions underneath all the bluster. Cire was full of them and Terra was learning it was okay to ask questions. "Everything okay?"

Cire pulled a dagger from his pocket and started sharpening it. "No. It is not. We are still waiting to hear from Myrddin on what will be done about freeing the orcish people from the Dark One's influence."

"Myrddin hasn't said anything more than he did before. It doesn't seem like it's a high priority. At least for humans."

Cire nodded sadly. "What more could I expect? The gnomish world under siege, your own constantly being attacked. If I was in the same position, I would be making the same decision. That doesn't make it sting any less."

Terra rested her hand on Cire's knee. "I know it must be hard. But it's going to happen."

"Yes, and wars take time. And they are constantly in need of bodies. Have you heard anything about our chances to join the war efforts?"

"No. Nothing on that end, either."

Anger flashed across Cire's face, a rarity. The orc was easily one of the most composed people Terra had ever met. "I should have assumed so," he muttered.

"Hey, am I still going to get to listen to a war song tonight?"

Cire's face softened. "Yes, we shouldn't allow Myrddin's delay to get in our way. Are you staying for this one, Nib-Nib?"

The mantiboid's bug eyes were impossible to read.

Nib-Nib stood, chirping and whistling shrilly. All that Terra could grasp was that Nib-Nib thought singing was boring and she was going to go drink with orcs who knew how to have a good time.

Terra laughed heartily as Nib-Nib left the room, leaving Cire with a confused, wounded look on his face. Then he chuckled. "Little gal has quite the mouth on her," Terra joked.

Cire stood and removed his shaman's coat. "You should have heard her before you got back. Shit-talks better than the biggest orc I've seen."

"Can probably back it up too."

Cire prepared for the dance. They were simple preparations: a small wooden bowl and some ash. He placed the bowl on the floor and blew into the ash, sending it flying into his face. The ash stuck to Cire's skin, painting him white as a ghost.

The song came out slowly and was guttural. Though Terra didn't understand all the words, she became lost in Cire's voice. What she couldn't understand could be inferred from Cire's eyes, or the way his hands moved.

When Cire was done, Terra sat quietly, trying to piece together the tale. Many of the orc battle songs did not have beginnings, middles, or ends. They had no lessons. Yet there was a point. One Terra had to decipher.

After giving her some time to think, Cire asked what the song was about.

Terra didn't answer immediately. "A fight can happen at any moment. That was what the singer in the story was trying to get across."

"Deeper. The true point."

"And…because of that, a battle is often lost from lack of prepared-ness…no, it's lost through surprise. Unawareness."

"Perfect."

Cire wiped the ash from his face as Terra's HUD watch beeped. Terra looked at her message. Myrddin was requesting to see her in the war room. "Guess I have another briefing. I'll see you in a bit."

Terra placed her fist over her heart and Cire mirrored the gesture. She left the orc alone in his room, wishing she'd had more time to spend with him.

Myrddin was waiting in the War Room for Terra. She was surprised no one else was there. "Is this another debriefing?"

"No. Please take a seat."

Terra sat and Myrddin took a spot across from her. "Visiting with Cire?"

"Yeah. We've been reviewing orcish history every couple of days."

Myrddin folded his hands as he leaned forward. "You have an affinity for these orcs, don't you?"

"Well, yeah. We fought together. I saw the kind of people they are."

"I mean beyond that."

Terra didn't know what Myrddin was getting at, but she preferred to not beat around the bush. "The way everyone talks about them like they aren't real people, it's disgusting. No one should be thought of like that."

Myrddin snapped his fingers and sat up. "Agreed. But that is not why I wanted to speak to you. I believe I have a new role for you."

"And what would that be?"

Myrddin smiled faintly. "I want you to be our spokesperson."

Terra laughed as she raised an eyebrow. "Me? A spokesperson? You must be out of your mind."

"Precisely the opposite. You're a hero to the humans. And one of the only public faces of the war against the Dark One so far. We need more recruits. Who better to speak to the masses than the person who they watched fight their way out of the arena on television?"

Terra shook her head. Whatever this entailed, it was a bad idea. "I think you have the wrong person."

Myrddin stood, appearing ready to leave the room. "No, I do not. You have limitless potential, Terra. This should be nothing compared to being dragged across the galaxy and forced to fight for your life."

When put like that, Terra didn't feel too bad about the prospects. "Okay, fine. I'll do it. What's next?"

"Next is the Steve Campbell Show."

Anabelle walked down the hall toward the armory and the firing range. She was planning on taking a tip from Sarah to blow off some steam by shooting things, then do some light reading about Grok before bed.

When Anabelle turned the corner, she heard footsteps behind her. She hugged the wall, waiting. The footfalls were too quiet to merely be someone walking down the hall. Whoever it was had been attempting to silence their presence. Which meant she was being followed.

Her stalker turned the corner and Anabelle grabbed the man by his shirt, turned him around, and slammed his back against the wall.

Roy smiled at Anabelle, looking extremely boyish and mischievous. "Oh, shit. Looks like you caught me."

"You're going to have to do much better than that to surprise me."

Roy leaned in and kissed Anabelle lightly. She could smell the aftershave on his neck.

Anabelle glanced over her shoulder, down the hall. "You're getting better at that, too. Come on, follow me." She yanked Roy after her, opening the door to one of the maintenance closets and shoving him inside.

The closet was cramped and barely lit.

Anabelle pressed up against Roy, inhaling the scent of him as his hands caressed her waist. She hadn't allowed herself to think about him since coming back to the base. It was too distracting. If they were caught, they would both be in huge trouble. Officers weren't allowed to fraternize.

Roy had reminded her multiple times of the policy since their last mission, but the long stares from across the room were becoming too much for either of them to handle.

Anabelle grabbed the back of Roy's neck and pulled him closer, pressing her lips against his as he cupped her ass, both trying to keep from stumbling over the cleaning supplies lying across the floor. They failed miserably and ended up tumbling over each other, landing in a heaping mess of brooms and limbs.

Anabelle had lost herself with Roy there for a while. She pulled herself off him only because his HUD watch kept beeping incessantly. "Are you going to get that?" she asked.

Roy sat up and looked at his watch. "Oh, shit. Something about prepping Terra for an interview."

"Wait. What for?"

Roy was already on his feet. "Gotta get her TV ready. She's doing some PR run for recruitment. She's going to be on the Steve Campbell Show."

Anabelle felt her stomach twist, and she was hit with a feeling she hadn't experienced in a while: jealousy. "Are you kidding me? She's going on Campbell? I was an international phenomenon, and I could never get on it!"

Roy gave Anabelle a puzzled look. "Uh...okay. You sound a little upset."

Anabelle quickly regained her composure. "No, not at all. Just surprised."

"All right. If something's on your mind, just give me a call in a bit, okay?"

Anabelle stood and kissed Roy on the cheek. "All right."

Roy walked out of the closet, leaving Anabelle alone with her thoughts. Why hadn't Myrddin asked *her* to be the spokesperson? Anabelle had been famous for nearly a decade.

Whatever. You wouldn't have wanted to do it anyways. It was your idea to leave all of that behind. You didn't get put in charge of the DGA to sit in front of a camera and look pretty. It is not important.

Anabelle left the closet, repeating that last part to herself over and over as she headed to her bedroom. But she didn't quite believe it.

CHAPTER SEVEN

A bby woke up before the sun rose, a habit she'd been unable to lose after leaving the farm. It didn't bother her since it meant she had extra time in the morning to herself to think things over or to simply enjoy the silence.

And there was a lot to think about. Abby had gathered the seriousness of the briefing from the day before. But, if she was being honest with herself, it didn't sound any worse than what they'd been dealing with the last few months.

When fighting a never-ending war with a being hellbent on enslaving all organic life, everything else began to feel like a monster-of-the-week type of situation. And the monsters were growing more powerful, which was unnerving. And frightening.

Abby could still smell Rasputina's rotting breath, and she tried not to focus too much on how easily the lich's knife had penetrated her armor. And there was no way she was spending a second thinking about the lich cackling wildly as she had cut her stomach open.

A chill ran down Abby's spine. She decided she needed to focus on something, and she always had work she could do.

A few weeks ago, Abby had taken a sample of draconic fluid from a human named Alex Bound, one of the Dragon Riders. Or former

Dragon Rider, from what Abby had been hearing. Apparently, Alex had mutinied and had attacked one of the only hopes of destroying the Dark One.

Abby had attempted to talk to Roy about the situation since he was the only person ever around HQ who had worked with her previously. Anytime she questioned Roy about Alex, his expression would become distant, as though he was trying to remember something from a long time ago. Then he would rattle off some official-sounding jargon about capturing Alex, and that would be it.

Something was up, and Abby didn't buy any of it. She'd met Alex. They had been talking regularly—often enough that Abby had felt comfortable designing a tracking device using the draconic fluid and human blood samples she'd taken from Alex. And this design was off-book. She hadn't bothered to write anything down.

Abby worked for a few hours, occasionally checking her messages to see if it was time to go yet. At around eight, she received the request to meet in the hangar. It was time to go home.

The Crookins' farm hadn't changed much, and Abby had returned at her favorite time of year. The crops were just beginning to come in, and Ma's garden was blooming with vibrant life and color.

Abby didn't go to the front door immediately. Her family didn't know what time she was arriving, and she wanted to take this chance to look at the farm by herself. She wanted to see if she still recognized it.

After a while, Abby understood that this place would always be her home, no matter how *she* changed.

She walked around the big house to her old workshop, opened the door, and peeked into the musty old barn. The smell—she'd forgotten the smell of old wood and scorched steel. Everything at HQ smelled sterile. Not like this. *This* was the smell of hard work you couldn't wash off the walls.

I can look at this junk anytime. Maybe after a couple of hours of hellos.

As Abby strode back to the big house, she spotted one of her drones flying over the wheat field, showering the crops with water. She couldn't tell, but it was probably Gertrude, or at least her family's version of Gertrude.

When Abby had left to join the war, she and Creon had sent a team to retrofit the older drone models she had left at the barn. They'd included an AI version of Martin, which they had also named Gertrude.

She was substantially less rude, but still had a little bit of snark.

The other two drones weren't far behind Gertrude in terms of technology and snark. Abby was glad she had left the drones behind for the family. Things would have been difficult without Pa around. Ma and Margie might have been capable on their own, but two extra hands were better than none.

Now, Abby knocked on the door of the big house. A sudden commotion sounded from inside, followed by a startled scream.

Abby's heart tensed. Had the Dark Forces been tipped off that she would be home, away from the team? What if something had happened to her family?

Nanobots poured over Abby, encasing her in her armor as the front door was flung open.

Ma wrapped her arms around her daughter and lifted her into the air before suddenly shrieking and dropping her.

"Who the hell are you?" Ma shouted as she reached for the shotgun resting beside the door.

Abby's nanobots retreated instantly, and she stood unarmored in front of her mom. "Whoa! You can go ahead and put that down. It's just me, Ma."

Ma laughed nervously as she leaned the gun against the wall. "Jesus Christ. You scared the living daylights out of me. What was all that?" she asked, waving a hand at Abby's face.

"I'll explain it later." Abby threw her arms around her mom and hugged her tight. "The farm's looking good. Real good."

The pair went into the living room, where Margie was sitting on the couch, her right leg propped up on a pillow and encased in a cast.

She was reading and looked downright miserable until she saw her sister.

"Abby! You're back!" Margie tried to stand, no doubt out of habit, before glaring at her cast and flopping back on the sofa.

Abby rushed to give her a hug. She kissed her sister on the forehead and said, "I'm glad the farm is in such good condition because you look terrible."

Margie stuck her tongue out at Abby while pretending to focus on her book. "Did you get fired or something?"

Abby laughed as she ruffled Margie's hair. "Yeah, I missed you too. Where are the twins?"

Ma looked at the grandfather clock. "Right now? Probably running around with the gnomes."

Abby's eyes narrowed at her mom. "Wait, did you say 'gnomes?'"

"Oh, yeah, I said gnomes. Come on, give your sister a hand. Would have thought you knew about them."

Abby grabbed Margie's crutches and helped her to her feet. They followed Ma out the back door toward the garden their father used to tend to. Abby didn't allow herself to spend too much time looking at the dried-out plants. Didn't seem like anyone had touched it for a while.

Abby could see the twins in the distance, weaving in and out of the edges of the cornfields. They were giggling loudly, three gnomes chasing them.

For some reason, Abby had assumed the gnomes would be redcaps or garden gnomes, but they were like Creon—small, limber, almost childlike creatures. And younger than Creon, who appeared to be around her father's age.

"Hey, get your sorry butts over here!"

The twins froze and toppled over each other when they heard Abby's voice. The gnomes ran into them, and briefly, they were all nothing but a swirling ball of arms, legs, and shrill giggles. Once they managed to untangle themselves, the two little girls and the gnomes came running up to Abby.

The twins tackled Abby to the ground, covering her in hugs and kisses. When the girls finally calmed down, the three gnomes introduced themselves. Turned out they were siblings of Creon's.

After Abby had left, Myrddin had looked for a way to help the farm out. Creon had mentioned a couple of siblings who were interested in human agriculture and animal husbandry. It had seemed like a good fit, and the gnomes had been on the farm ever since.

Abby was surprised Myrddin had made such an effort to ensure her family was taken care of in her absence.

When Ma asked the gnomes if they were staying for dinner, they declined the invitation. They said it was good to meet Abby, and they let Ma know what time they would start the next day. The twins were upset they were leaving, but the gnomes promised to play with them after work the next day.

After the gnomes left, the family went inside, Abby marveling the whole time at how their lives had turned fantastical so fast.

Everyone helped out with dinner that night, except for Margie, who sat at the table and grumbled. Once the preparations for the meal were finished, Ma asked Margie and the twins to set the table.

When the girls left the kitchen, Ma decreased the oven temperature and sat at the nook. Abby pulled up a stool to sit beside her. "How did Margie break her leg?"

Ma sighed and shook her head. "Acting like a damn fool was how she did it. She got in her head that the shingles on the barn needed to be replaced and decided to do it herself, knowing full well she's terrified of heights. Got up there, got the spins, and practically broke her damn neck."

Abby wasn't surprised. Margie would never admit she was afraid of anything. One day that would probably get her in trouble. "She's getting to be quite the handful, huh?"

"No worse than you were."

Abby scoffed loudly. "Me? A handful? I'm the model of a perfect kid."

Ma kissed Abby on the forehead. "First the out-of-control science-fair projects, then the explosions in your lab. *Then* the robots. You sealed the deal by marching off to war."

Abby heard the sadness in Ma's voice. "You know, if you need my help around here, I can come home."

"No, no. What you're doing is important, more important than this farm. And, to be honest, we're doing better than we ever have. All the help Myrddin's provided has turned this farm around. We were doing good before, but now we're thriving. Now, are you going to tell me how you managed to get so shiny and futuristic earlier?"

Abby didn't want to get into it, but she knew Ma would not allow her to avoid explaining herself. "Okay, but you have to promise not to get mad. Okay?"

"I hate when you start a story like that."

After dinner, Abby and the family stayed up watching TV. She hadn't realized how badly she had missed not having anything to worry about. Sitting in her living room, surrounded by people she loved and having a reason to laugh was the best vacation she could ask for.

But it also was a little bit too much excitement.

Abby decided to go to bed before anyone else, prompting complaints from the twins, and teasing from Margie about Abby growing too old to hang. Abby promised she'd be up working earlier than they all would, so it evened out.

She went up to her bedroom and stood in the doorway for a few moments. Nothing had been moved or changed, kind of like her father's garden.

The thought was caustic, and Abby pushed it away. She changed for bed, pulled the covers over her head, and was asleep within minutes.

It was not peaceful sleep, though. Her dreams were hazy and nonsensical. Images chased her in a panicked frenzy. She watched herself running from orcs, her father's face flashing in front of her from time to time, blood pooling around his head.

Panicked, her need to scream woke her, and she sat up, cold sweat dripping from her forehead. She had calmed a little when something moved in the shadowy corner of the room. She froze, her heart stuck in her throat.

Rasputina emerged from the shadows. She was holding a knife and smiling. "I'm gonna eat you," Rasputina sang. "Gonna rip you up, gut you up, and suck you down..."

The lich leapt on the bed before Abby could move, raising and plunging her knife over and over into Abby's chest as she battled with the sheets, desperate to get out of the bed.

Abby woke up again, frantic and hyperventilating, her blankets and sheets twisted around her. She scanned the room.

Must have still been dreaming.

She went to the bathroom and splashed her face with water. It was a little after midnight, and now she was unable to sleep, with all the adrenaline pumping through her veins. She did what she always used to do when she couldn't sleep: grabbed a thick coat and went out to the barn.

Though darker than her bedroom, the barn was much more comforting. She flicked the lights on just to be safe, though, and strolled around, admiring the half-finished projects covering the workbenches.

Abby wasn't an arrogant person, but she was proud of what she'd created. Her ma had always said that was the finest example of humility: knowing who you were without taking or adding anything for pretense.

All of a sudden, an old, black-and-white television sitting on one of the tables flicked on. "Shit, don't tell me I'm still dreaming?"

Abby had rigged the TV up as a monitor for coding the drones. And now, though covered in a thick layer of dust, an image wavered on the screen.

The picture was distorted, static obscuring what appeared to be a face. A soft voice came through the speaker, but it was too garbled to decipher the words. Abby leaned in to get a closer look.

"Persephone?"

CHAPTER EIGHT

Sarah used the Hadron Collider to teleport to the desert dunes of the gnomish world, which were quiet at night. Few creatures could deal with the heat. Nearly every living thing died out there, leaving it a vast expanse of nothing.

For this reason, the Dark One's forces used it for the majority of their vital transportations. There were no roadblocks, no threats.

Sarah believed it to be the perfect spot for an ambush.

She and Kravis were camped out under the stars. A small fire burned while Kravis lay back and watched the night sky. Sarah was too busy with her map to pay attention to the stars and planets twinkling elegantly above her. She wanted to confirm the Dark One's convoy would be arriving on schedule.

More importantly, she wanted to ensure her reinforcements would depart on time.

Kravis yawned loudly, a gigantic sound for a gnome to be able to make. "You know, we never get to do anything like this anymore. All of our missions are rushed. Get in and get out. Not nearly enough time to enjoy anything."

Sarah agreed with Kravis. There was barely any time to—how did the gnomes put it—polish your gears? "Not like we have much choice.

The whole planet is a goddamned warzone. Figures the only place we could relax would be this hellscape."

Kravis sat up and gazed into the fire, his face barely illuminated by the flames. His eyes were shadowed by an oppressive brow, giving him the look of one who had never known joy. It had always struck Sarah as funny because when they had first met, he had made her laugh all the time. Now, neither of them laughed much. At least, not at what made normal people laugh.

Confident that her reinforcements would arrive on time, Sarah put away her holomap and went to sit beside Kravis at the fire. He rested his head on her arm, as he couldn't reach any higher, which was something Sarah found endearing.

He was small enough to pick up and throw. She'd done it a couple of times, usually during sparring rounds and playful, uh, tussles.

Kravis opened a flask of gnomish liquor. The closest thing Sarah had ever tasted was vodka, and that couldn't compare. This shit burned all the way out of your urethra. But, goddamn, did it make you feel alive, your insides all aflame, ready for whatever came your way.

Sarah took the flask and sipped the liquor. "What's the first thing you're doing when this is over?"

Kravis drank from the flask. "Probably fucking you."

"Which you already do. Anything new?"

"That'll be new. In a room. One of ours. So, I guess, get a place. Or build one. Not sure what'll be standing when all of this is over."

"Here, right?"

Kravis hung his head, staring deeper into the fire as though he'd find answers there. "Don't know. Would be nice to rebuild with everyone else. But I don't know if I'll be able to stomach being here through all that. Seeing what's been done."

"You would hate Earth. Everything is crowded. Humans are loud. Constant bickering. You'd go crazy. Crazier than you already are."

Kravis reached for the bag of food and pulled out a hunk of dried meat. He took a bite and offered it to Sarah. "Me? Crazy? Hardly."

"Maybe not crazy. Sadistic."

"That makes two of us."

Sarah chuckled, but it was a harsh sound. There was too much truth in their jokes, but truth was all they had. Of all the people Sarah had met during the war, Kravis was the one most changed. He held the same opinion about Sarah as she did of him.

All soldiers saw horrible things; there was no way around it. War consisted of atrocities and terror. The difference Kravis and Sarah shared was they didn't merely see these things, they were often the ones undertaking them.

Espionage. Intel. When necessary, torture. A blind eye was turned to the methods the couple used to get results, and Sarah had done things she'd never expected she was capable of, let alone taking delight in. No matter how Sarah looked at it, she knew she was becoming a monster. Both herself and Kravis. Someone had to do it. Unfortunately, that lot had fallen on them.

Kravis looked up from the flames. "What you thinking about?"

For a second, Sarah thought about keeping it all to herself. But she and Kravis had promised to be honest with each other. "About all the shit we have to do in the name of defeating evil." She sucked air in between her teeth. "You know, the Dark Gate Angels wanted me to be a part of their team. Meant a lot to me to be asked."

"How could they *not* want you to be? You're amazing, and you get the job done better than anyone else I know."

"I don't know. It's just...it's been a long time since I've had any friends. Other than you, everything is business. And they don't even know me. I doubt any of them pulled my files. Not that it would have said anything. All the shitty stuff is redacted."

Kravis wrapped his hand around Sarah's. "Which means they like you for you. Not some bullshit they read on a sheet of paper. And besides that, you're more than all of this," Kravis said, gesturing at the weapons spread out on a blanket next to them. "We both are. Might not feel like it all the time, but we aren't only tools used to kill. You know that, right?"

"I do. Still feels good to hear it. Sometimes it just seems like there's no going back. After all this fighting is done, what am *I* going to do?

This is all I've ever done. I don't have a life outside of this fucking war."

Kravis grabbed Sarah's favorite pulse rifle. He handed it to her and selected one of his daggers. He sharpened the blade as he peered back into the flame. "We'll get to have a normal life. And we'll be capable of it. Trust me."

Sarah focused on cleaning her rifle, relaxing with the old automatic movements of taking care of the tools of her trade. Kravis was right. They were both going to live through this. And once it was done, they were going to have real lives.

After some time of working in silence, Kravis said, "I got you a present." He handed Sarah a headband with a spiral emblazoned on it.

She took the headband, which was heavy in her hand. "What is it?"

"I know you've been having a hard time unlocking that last chakra. Got a couple of the boys to whip together something for you. This little guy will help you bypass all of them. Turns all of those unconscious limitations of your brain off."

Sarah grabbed Kravis and pulled him on top of her, smothering his face in kisses. "I can't believe you got someone to make this!"

Kravis still looked at her, his face serious. "You have to be careful, though. You know—"

Sarah kissed him deep and longingly. She didn't want to hear what he had to say. She already knew what she had to be worried about. "Please. Stop talking. Just kiss me."

Kravis smiled. Sarah never grew tired of seeing that smile, the same one he had flashed when they first met. "All right, all right. We got a couple of hours to kill."

CHAPTER NINE

S arah woke up with the sun. They had slept without a tent or sleeping bags. The morning was unbearably hot. They were already burning up wrapped in each other's arms.

Moving silently, Sarah extricated herself from Kravis' arms and started a fire. She brewed a cup of coffee and fried up a couple of eggs to be served alongside the dried meat Kravis had brought.

By the time Kravis woke up, breakfast was ready. The couple ate in silence, which had been their routine for most overnight missions. Talking was distracting. Only one thing required their attention at the moment: the mission.

Once they'd finished breakfast, the pair broke down their camp and checked in with the different teams they commanded.

Myrddin was deeply invested in the liberation of the gnomish world. That being said, he still relied on the gnomish resistance to lay the groundwork. There was only so much the wizard could do all the way from another realm.

Which was where Sarah and Kravis had come in. Both were instrumental in raising up the resistance and keeping it going whenever the Dark One almost crushed it beneath his boot.

Sarah confirmed her reinforcements were making good time. "How about your team?"

Kravis closed his HUD and grunted. "They'll be here in time. We should get to work."

They slid down the sand dunes and headed to the main transportation road. "Road" was a generous description for the worn-in tire tracks Sarah had mapped out over the course of the last two months. She knew these dunes as well as she knew her childhood home.

Once they reached the bottom of the dunes, they split up. They placed mines along the roadside, zigzagging between each other, ensuring the route was covered. Then they added additional mines along the length of the road to slow down the convoy. Once they were satisfied, they returned to the top of the dunes.

Sarah retrieved her pulse rifle, fitted it with a scope, and posted up in a position that gave her a good vantage point to see the convoy coming through the looming dunes.

Kravis went down to the base of the dune below Sarah and pulled a sand-colored camouflage sheet off his dune buggy. Of gnomish creation, the buggy didn't run off gasoline, instead using a clockwork system along with piped steam for power.

In most hands, this would have been an inferior form of transportation, but under the control of the gnomes, the most rudimentary tools had been elevated to deadly usage.

Gnomes possessed the gift of tech. Anything you put in front of them would be transformed into a new creation. At this moment in time, most of what the gnomes were creating were weapons.

Karvis' voice came through on the comm. "I'm in position."

Sarah was looking through her scope, scanning for the incoming convoy and trying to locate her squad. "Okay. Looks like we're just waiting now."

For the following two hours, Sarah and Kravis chatted while waiting for the convoy. These were moments that Sarah most appreciated. Quiet instances before everything grew into chaos. And she was glad to share these moments with Kravis.

Her HUD pinged, and she checked the notification. The convoy was coming through. She peered through her scope.

The orcish convoy totaled twenty heavily armored vans traveling in pairs. Manned heavy-artillery turrets sat on the roofs of every van. That was more firepower than Sarah had been led to believe she would have to deal with. "That's going to make things interesting..."

Kravis' voice came over her comm. "Yeah, but we should be good. Just like we planned, remember. The squads know what's going on. We just gotta make sure to stick with the plan."

"Yeah, I know. I know."

Sarah lined up her shots. Her squad was most likely already in position. All they were waiting for was her signal.

She fired, a hyper-charged beam of plasma that struck the orc manning the turret at the head of the convoy.

All along the road, the ground began to tremble.

The orcs on the roofs of the vans stared at each other, clearly trying to figure out what was happening.

Sarah took another shot, hitting one of the turret riders in the head, sending his brains out into the harsh, dusty wind.

The ground continued to shake as giant drill-bits forced their way out of the ground. The bits were attached to buggies, which were also approaching the surface.

Sarah fired again. And again. Shot after shot, she didn't let up until she had eliminated all the orcs at the turrets. She collapsed her rifle and jumped, sliding down the dunes toward Kravis. Sarah climbed atop the buggy and grabbed the machine gun waiting for her.

All along the road, gnomish buggies were popping up. The orcish convoy bunched together, their vans eliminating extra space on the road.

Sarah slapped the top of Kravis' buggy, shouting, "Go! Go!"

Kravis took off, following the convoy as the gnomish buggies converged on the orcish troops.

The convoy van doors opened, orcs leaning out, some of them brandishing plasma rifles, others flamethrowers.

The gnomish buggies sped up, as though attempting to cut the orcs off. Gnomes hung from the side of the buggies, covered in war paint, hollering as they fired steam-powered buzz-saw shotguns.

Saws tore through the orcs, who screamed in their native tongue as though in that moment, they had forgotten they were under the Dark One's control, firing blazing hot plasma at the gnomes.

Sarah stomped on the hood of Kravis' buggy. "Faster! We gotta drive them!"

He sped ahead, finally catching up with the convoy as Sarah opened fire, spraying bullets at the orcs at the back of the pack.

The orcs at the head of the convoy continued to speed up, attempting to evade the gnomes on one side and Sarah at their rear. Without warning, the gnomes peeled off back toward the dunes and away from the main road.

And the convoy passed over the first set of mines.

Explosions tore the road apart, sending orcs, debris, and shrapnel everywhere as the ground caught fire.

Sarah leaned over the top of the buggy, pointing frantically to her left. Kravis obeyed and veered off the road, attempting to overtake the exploded vans and put some heat on the vehicles still running. "Everyone! Back to it! Pin them in!"

The gnomes drove alongside the convoy, blanketing the orcish vehicles with plasma-blasts and bullets, forcing them to remain on the road.

The convoy hit the second set of mines, explosions tearing through the vans, sending more orcs flying.

"All right, pull 'em in!" Sarah shouted.

The gnomes tightened their chokehold on the orcs and started closing in.

The frontrunner of the orc convoy hadn't slowed down. Its main hatch opened and an orc crawled out on top of the turrets. "For the Dark One!"

The sides of the van split open. Four motorcycles came flying from the left and right panels. Each of the vehicles in the convoy also opened, sending more riders out onto the road.

The orc atop the frontrunner turned to face Sarah. He held a rocket launcher and fired.

Kravis swerved to the side, narrowly avoiding the rocket.

The orc smiled wickedly. "Let her out."

At the back of the convoy, a van opened. A screech tore through the air as two red eyes peered out at Sarah.

Sarah unloaded everything she had at the van but the eyes did not waver. She threw the machine gun away and drew her knives. "Nothing is ever just fucking easy."

CHAPTER TEN

The orcs sped up as the four motorcyclists wove through the gnome's dune buggies, firing as the gnomes performed evasive maneuvers.

Sarah was still preparing herself for whatever would exit the back of the van. She didn't have to wait long.

A wyrm stuck its head out and sent a blast of fire at Sarah and Kravis, who swerved to the left, narrowly avoiding being barbecued. "Who the hell keeps a wyrm in the back of a van?" Sarah shouted.

Kravis' dune buggy began to spin out, and he fought with the wheel to keep from flipping over. Sarah was holding on as tightly as possible as a motorcycle came up on their side. She jumped from the top of the car, kicking the orc rider in the throat and knocking him off. Then she grabbed the handlebars and righted the bike so that she didn't eat sand.

Sarah turned the bike, heading toward Kravis. The best plan would be to regroup, but it was apparent that wasn't happening. Everything was too frantic. All Sarah could hope for was that the gnomes would be able to handle themselves. She would have to take care of the wyrm.

First, she commed Kravis. "What's your move?"

The gnome headed to Sarah. "Cut up to the front. Try to slow down the convoy."

"Sounds good. Be safe."

"Always."

Kravis took off toward the front of the caravan of vans as Sarah headed toward the back. The wind whipped up sand everywhere, and it was becoming harder to see. Looked like a sandstorm was about to arrive.

Just great, if anything else goes wrong, I'm going to call it a day and shoot myself.

The motorcyclists were barely visible in the sand. Sarah was glad because it meant no one could see her. The gnomes would be all right. Their dune buggies were all built with telescopes equipped with heat readers. These were their deserts, and they knew how to fight in them.

Sarah, on the other hand, was trying to figure that out for herself. Getting behind the convoy would not be a problem. Dealing with the wyrm would be. She checked the bike for weapons. All she found was a plasma rifle and a couple of grenades.

Ideally, delivering a few shots to the wyrm's soft underbelly would have worked perfectly. Problem was that the wyrm was lying in the back of the van. Good decision by the orcs. This way, they could have an almost invulnerable flamethrower.

What are they hiding back there? Sarah thought. This is way too much protection for a simple resource drop-off.

She commed the team, "Everyone still alive?"

Someone answered, "No casualties yet. The bikes have backed off for now, but we know we didn't get all of them."

"Okay, slow this thing down until the bikers come back around. Let's take advantage of this storm."

The gnomes moved in unison as if they'd practiced this formation before. Kravis was leading them, trying to get to the front of the van as the other gnomes fought to catch up with the vehicle's wheels.

Kravis reached the front wheels, and opened his side door, holding a harpoon gun. He fired and hit the wheel's axle. Then he slammed a lever that pulled the harpoon's rope tight. "Got one anchored!"

An orc leaned from a window, firing at Kravis, who swerved to avoid the plasma. He pulled another gun and shot the orc in the head.

The driver of the convoy pushed the dead orc from the van and kept driving.

One of the motorcycles came out of nowhere, hitting Kravis' car hard with a plasma bolt. "Could use some backup here!"

Sarah wished she could catch up with Kravis, but she was too far behind. Hopefully, the squad was good enough to keep each other alive. The wyrm had Sarah's focus.

She fell back a little and pulled to the left so that she was directly in front of the wyrm. The giant serpent met her eyes and roared in anticipation. It opened its mouth, preparing to send a jet of flame at her.

Sarah pulled the plasma rifle from the side of the bike and fired. The plasma hit the wyrm in the face, only enraging the creature. It leaned out of the back of the van and swiped at Sarah, forcing her to slow down and put more distance between herself and the wyrm.

Up ahead, one of the gnomish buggies had caught up to Kravis, but he didn't stop there. He kept driving until he plowed into the orc biker.

When Kravis was free, he returned to work. He sped up and cut in front of the van, distracting the driver as another gnome swung around to the other wheel, and fired his harpoon. Once the gnome was certain the spear had stuck, he flashed Kravis a thumbs up.

Kravis disengaged, moving to the right as the orc driver fired from his window. "Now!" Kravis shouted.

He tossed the harpoon gun out of the window. A spike shot from the bottom of the weapon and hit the ground. The spike whirled and spun, driving the gun deep into the earth.

The van bucked forward as the tension from the harpoon guns did their job. The back of the van flipped up, and Sarah watched as the wyrm's eyes went wide with surprise.

Sarah hadn't believed the gnomes were capable of pulling this off so fast. Kravis was probably still alive.

A biker emerged from Sarah's side, firing at her. She turned and headed into the dust, firing over her shoulder, hoping to hit something. Being stuck on this bike wasn't working for Sarah. It wasn't the type of mobility she needed.

She rode over to the side of the van, which was still moving despite the harpoons. *Front wheels are probably shredded to shit*, she thought. *Must be one hell of an engine.*

Sarah leapt onto the side of the van, shooting a grappling hook. She scurried up to the roof, reached over her shoulder, and detached her collapsible sniper rifle. This was going to be a hassle, but she was fairly confident it was doable. Maybe not for everyone.

Ignoring the dust clouds swarming around her, Sarah focused on one thing. Listening. The roar of the motorcycles was louder than the truck's engine. She could pick them out easily. Locating them would be the hard part.

Sarah lined up her first shot, closing her eyes, straining her ears to listen. She opened her eyes after locating her mark.

Bang.

Sarah watched one of the bikers skid out of the sand-clouds, barely able to keep his bike straight, before racing into the truck and exploding.

Beneath her, the dune buggies fell back to attack the rear wheels. Sarah saw that Kravis was still with them.

An orc biker emerged from the left, heading toward one of the gnome buggies. A rocket launcher was attached to his shoulder blade. He fired and the missile connected with one of the buggies, blowing it to smithereens. The orc screamed defiantly as he loaded another rocket.

Sarah aimed at the orc but couldn't line up the shot. He knew Sarah's position and was doing everything in his power to keep from being an easy target. *Goddamn it*, Sarah muttered. She collapsed her rifle and ran to the side of the truck, jumped off, and landed on the bike's handle.

She pulled the orc's sidearm off, fired, and kicked the corpse from the bike as she ripped his rocket-launcher away. Then she aimed at the side of the truck and fired.

The rocket tore through the truck's freight cargo. Sarah hoped that she'd managed to at least ding the wyrm.

With the remaining buggy on her left side, Kravis moved toward the back wheels again as he commed, "Last wheels. Ready?"

The other driver responded and they both fired their harpoons, ripping up the back wheels. As Kravis prepared to drop his harpoon, the wyrm burst out of the side of the cargo hold.

The wyrm hit Kravis' buggy hard, sending it spinning off as the truck began to lose its momentum.

Sarah watched as Kravis spun out. She reloaded the rocket launcher and aimed at the truck-cab and fired.

The rocket hit the driver's side and exploded. She turned to the wyrm. "Your turn."

Sarah aimed the rocket launcher, preparing to fire when the wyrm jumped from the freight cargo, flapping its diminutive wings enough to gain momentum. It slammed into Sarah, knocking her from the bike.

The two tumbled into the sand, Sarah struggling to get away from the wyrm. There was no way she could handle a wyrm at close distance. The serpent could easily rip her to shreds.

Sarah managed to roll out from under one of the wyrm's massive legs. She reached for her gun. It was gone, knocked off during the fall.

She scrambled away as the wyrm came lumbering after her, its jaws open, acidic drool dripping from its fangs. The wyrm towered over Sarah, slamming one foot down, pinning her to the ground.

Kravis' dune buggy hit the wyrm's side, knocking it off Sarah, exposing its soft stomach.

Sarah ran over to her totaled motorcycle as Kravis continued to ram his buggy into the wyrm. She picked up the rocket-launcher which had been flung from her and aimed at the wyrm's stomach.

"You got about ten seconds to get away," she commed Kravis.

The gnome kicked open his door and leapt out of the buggy as

Sarah fired. The rocket hit the wyrm square in the stomach and exploded, sending wyrm guts everywhere.

Sarah went to help Kravis to his feet. "Let's go check on that truck."

The pair returned to the truck, which had stalled. If any other orcs survived, they had already fled. The remaining gnomish driver was waiting for Kravis and Sarah at the freight cargo. "Didn't want to start unwrapping our presents until you two got back."

Kravis groaned as Sarah stalked past the gnome. "You could have come over and given us a hand."

"Saw the explosion. Figured you two were the cause of it."

Sarah climbed onto the back of the freighter and pulled the door open. The hold was nearly empty. She found a couple of boxes, but nothing to justify the size of the freighter. "Were they just transporting a fucking wyrm? That doesn't make any sense," she muttered.

Kravis and the other gnome were also looking through the cargo hold, trying to locate the supplies their informant had told them about.

Sarah finally approached a small black box, the only one in the hold made from steel instead of wood. She opened it and pulled out a vial about the size of her hand. Inside was a black liquid. Sarah held it up to her eye to get a better look.

The liquid in the vial surged forward, trying to attack Sarah from behind the glass.

Kravis came to her side and pointed at the vial. "What the hell is that?"

Sarah was still watching the vial as the liquid in it swirled about. It looked angry. "I don't know, some kind of black goo. I think it might be alive or something."

"Goo isn't alive."

"Myrddin needs to see this, and I want to talk to the guy who did intel. He's got a lot of explaining to do."

CHAPTER ELEVEN

Terra had never been a fan of talk shows. Her mother had watched them often while Terra was a kid. She had distinct memories of people droning on about stories that weren't interesting. If it wasn't that, the crowds were loud enough to be cheering at a sports game. The whole situation had left an odd taste in Terra's mouth, one she could never understand.

Now Terra was backstage at the *Steve Campbell Show*, the second-highest-ranked political talk show in the United States. For the first time, Terra wished she hadn't been ripping the heads off her Barbies while her mom watched television.

Three makeup artists flittered in and out of the room, each time coming back with different palettes and brushes for Terra's face. She had no idea what they were doing. She knew how to use makeup, but these three artists were on a whole other level.

The makeup artists talked as they worked, only speaking to each other, never to Terra, who was happy to be ignored. Having people fuss over her face without asking how she felt about it was beyond irritating to Terra. She probably would have snapped at an artist if they had spoken to her. And then Terra would be the stereotypical image of reality television.

Why the hell is Myrddin having me do this? Like, do people even take this kind of stuff seriously?

Terra knew why, though, even if she didn't like the sound of it. She was a hero to the humans. All of Earth had watched her fights in the arena, thanks to Abby and Anabelle. Terra was the reason humans still talked about the war with the Dark One. It only made sense that Terra be the face of the human cause.

That and Anabelle would leave everyone feeling a little bit shitty.

Terra had no problem with Anabelle.

As a commander, she was good.

As a friend—though using the word might be premature—the elf was surprisingly delightful.

Terra had never had many friends, instead opting for a small group of individuals who she would have died for. She'd been caught off guard at how quickly she'd clicked with Anabelle after the DGA had rescued her.

After spending more time with Anabelle, it wasn't hard to see why. The elf was captivating. She cast a spell on anyone she spoke to, even when she was being a complete dick. Which was why Anabelle probably wasn't doing the show.

Terra had picked up on Anabelle's generally dismissive nature toward humans. It didn't bother her. Generally, Anabelle's opinion about humans not being capable were the same ones Terra had held for years. The difference being that Terra had been one of those humans. Myrddin's decision to not have Anabelle addressing a good chunk of humanity made complete sense.

Still, Terra wished there had been another human readily available. If Abby had been old enough, Terra would have pushed the job toward her. The kid was bright and personable. She would have been great for the small screen.

Roy would have been another good choice. But Terra could already see the problem with him. Blind in one eye, covered in scars, practically needing a cane after his last fight. Roy probably wouldn't make people want to jump up and take up arms.

One of the makeup artists hit Terra in the face with a powder brush, and she flinched. Terra's instinct was to grab the woman and throttle her, but she held her irritation in check. She had to laugh at herself. Six months ago, she never would have imagined being angry enough to speak up about a problem. Now she was ready to fight anything that inconvenienced her. The arena had had a lasting impact on her.

Anabelle entered the room, and the artists momentarily stopped their work. This gave Terra time to glance over her shoulder and wave at the elf. "How you liking the royal treatment?" Anabelle asked.

Terra shrugged as the makeup artists fell silent and returned to their work. "Can't say much. You used to have to sit through this shit all the time, right?"

A shadow danced over Anabelle's eyes but disappeared almost as fast as it had arrived. "Nearly every waking moment of the last thirty years. The worst part of modeling was always having someone on my face. Honestly, I only learned how to do my own makeup so I could grab a couple of minutes to myself. The whole world, it's pretty suffocating."

Anabelle sat on the couch. She crossed her legs, and her eyes zeroed in on Terra. "Any idea what you two are supposed to be talking about?"

Terra squirmed under Anabelle's gaze. She'd seen that look before. It was the same way Anabelle watched her enemies, lining up to take her shots, before eliminating them in the most efficient way possible. So, why was Anabelle looking at *Terra* like that?

"No, not really," Terra replied. "Myrddin only told me I'm supposed to talk with Campbell about the war."

"Well, what are you going to say?"

"Oh...I hadn't really...I mean, I didn't prepare a speech or anything. He's going to ask me questions, and I guess I was gonna try to answer them the best I can. That's how interviews work, right?"

Anabelle leaned back on the couch, stretching her arms out behind her. "Yes, *dear*, that's exactly how it works."

Terra felt the sting in Anabelle's words. She wasn't sure if the bite was intentional or not. Either way, it prickled Terra's skin. "Shouldn't be too hard. Anyone with half a brain can answer a question. My mom used to watch trash like this all the time. Seemed like a bunch of regular people to me."

"This is the *Steve Campbell Show*, one of the most-watched cultural commentaries in the world. 'Normal people' don't go on this show. I never managed to get so much as an invite. I can't begin to imagine who Myrddin had to talk to to make this happen. He must have called in some pretty big favors."

"The way you say 'normal,' you sound disgusted."

Anabelle's gaze softened. "No, I didn't mean it like that. Normal isn't bad. It's just that Campbell doesn't have plumbers or nannies on his show. He has—"

"World-renowned models." Terra heard the acid in her voice. She hoped Anabelle had as well.

Anabelle sat up straight as she cracked her index knuckle. "Anyways, I should get going. Just wanted to stop by and wish you luck. Break a leg out there. Not literally." The elf stood and headed toward the door.

Terra instantly regretted feeding into Anabelle's pettiness. Maybe there was a way to recover this. "Hey, wait. You got any tips for a newbie?"

Anabelle stopped at the door, tossing her hair back with such flair that it was impossible to see her as anything other than a model. "You don't need my advice. Remember, you stared down a balrog while millions watched. What's a couple hundred thousand on live television."

"Seriously, Belle, I'm not trying to be a dick. I'm asking you if you have any advice."

Anabelle turned all the way around and her modelesque mystique vanished. It was as if she'd pulled off a cloak. This was the Anabelle Terra thought of as her friend. "If you freeze, don't panic or rush an answer. Let 'em pile up. While the interviewer keeps asking you questions, getting in his own head, you imagine everyone in their underwear. Block everything else out until you can see them. Always helped me."

"Thanks, I'll keep that in mind."

"I should get going. Good luck."

Anabelle left the room and took all of the coldness with her. The makeup artists breathed a collective sigh of relief.

Now, Terra understood why Anabelle was so intimidating.

Everything was a battle for the elf.

Terra was the third guest on the Steve Campbell Show. She'd hidden behind a giant curtain, waiting through the first two interviews.

In Wardrobe, the makeup artists had tried to talk Terra into either an elegant dress or a more lowkey but still flattering two-piece suit, but Terra didn't feel comfortable in either. Instead, she'd chosen to wear her uniform, complimented by an orcish necklace made of dragons' teeth—a gift from Cire.

After seeing the guests who had preceded her, Terra wished she had chosen the suit.

Finally, she was given her cue, and she emerged from behind the heavy curtains, temporarily blinded by the lights and the applause from the crowd. Once her eyes adjusted, Terra went to the comfortable red seat designated to her.

Steve Campbell was the definition of a posh intellectual. His suit was tailored for a perfect fit, outlining his broad shoulders and chest. His jawline was sculpted for day and nighttime TV, and he managed to straddle the line between allowing his hair to go gray and dying it for the sake of maintaining his youthful appearance.

That smile though… It was like being caught in a tractor beam.

Terra took Steve's hand awkwardly. She sat as Steve did, instantly regretting her decision to be the public face of the DGA and the rest of Myrddin's plots.

Steve was still beaming and clapping, rousing the crowd. "It's great to have you on the show, Terra. We weren't sure if we were gonna be able to pull you away from the dragons and orcs. How are you doing tonight?"

Terra looked out at the crowd, momentarily losing herself in all of the eyes and lights. She knew Steve had said something, but she wasn't sure what it was. "Uh, I'm sorry what?"

"Looks like we got us a live one today, guys."

The crowd laughed. These weren't the same kind of spectators as in the arena. These people were looking for something different, and it made Terra uncomfortable. She forced a laugh, not knowing what else to do.

Steve cleared his throat, and his smile disappeared. "So, thanks to you, we've recently been introduced to the massive threat to humanity. Although your battles were exhilarating, we wanted to hear from you. What do you think this means for humans? I mean, it was horrible that you were dragged to a whole other world to compete in vicious blood sports, but is it realistic to think that all of humanity is in danger because of a single abduction?"

This time Terra heard Steve.

Which didn't change that she had no answer. Her mind had gone blank. She kept looking at the audience, their dark eyes watching her, and glancing at each other in the confusion at Terra's silence. "Uh…" was all Terra managed.

Steve glanced at the producer, who was shrugging behind the scenes. "Well, a lot of our viewers were wondering what your experience on an alien world was like. Perhaps you could shed some light on the details of this conflict with the alleged *Dark One*."

Terra was still quiet. Then she remembered something and chuckled to herself.

Steve, sensing this was the most he would get out of Terra, leaned forward and asked, "Oh, do you have a joke for us? What's got you laughing so much?"

"Just a bit of advice I got from a friend. For remaining calm, apparently, you're supposed to imagine everyone in their underwear."

Steve laughed, relaxing a little more in his chair. "Universally acclaimed advice. How's it working out so far?"

Terra smiled and made a show of checking Steve out. "With you? Perfectly. I feel much more comfortable."

There were chuckles and laughter throughout the crowd. Terra felt a little more at ease and decided to roll with it. "Sorry about your earlier questions. The whole arena was such a…complex experience. I'm still trying to process a lot of it."

Steve shook his head as he waved his hands. "My apologies. It was probably an insensitive question. Let's change gears. Can you tell us exactly what this war with the Dark One entails? We've all heard rumors online and so forth, but it's hard to make sense of it all. It's not like we've had a State of the Union concerning this. Why are the communication channels so bad?"

Terra went on to explain everything she understood about the war with the Dark One. She wasn't privy to all of the behind-the-scenes information, but she knew enough to stress the severity of the situation.

Steve seemed satisfied with her answer. He switched gears again. "We've received some questions from fans of yours that we would like to ask you if that's okay."

Terra firmly planted her elbows on her kneecaps and spread her legs out. "Go for it."

"This is from Jaime, nineteen, living in San Diego."

Terra waved at the camera. "Hey, Jaime! Hope you're listening."

Steve chuckled, noticeably pleased by Terra playing to the audience at home. "Jaime asks, 'Hey, so I've been reading fantasy all my life. What's it like to fight tons of evil orcs?'"

Terra instinctively winced at the question. "Evil? Orcs aren't evil."

Steve reacted about the same way to Terra's answer. "Wait, excuse me if I'm wrong, but don't orcs make up the majority of the Dark One's forces? I mean, other than that, we all saw your fights in the arena. Those orcs were out to kill you."

"Yes, *those* orcs were. But they weren't *all* trying to kill me. Or humanity. For the most part, the orcs serving the Dark One are under mind-control. And, if you'd been watching the fights closely, you would have seen that I was fighting alongside a lot of orcs who valued *my* life as much as their own. The whole idea of orcs being evil as a race is ridiculous. It's an idea we all need to drop."

"How are we supposed to be able to drop that? We've seen orcs invading multiple places on Earth. Yet we've never seen one—"

A sharp cackle echoed from off stage, the sound fluctuating between high-pitched and a low groan—a parody of amusement.

Rasputina stuck her head out from behind the red curtain. Her face was as pale as snow, smeared with bright red blood, and she wore a black designer suit, the fabric sleek animal fur that puffed at the lapels and collar.

Terra jumped to her feet as soon as she saw Rasputina, but the lich waved her hand at Terra, who sat back down violently. Skeletal hands ripped from the ground, grasping Terra's legs and arms.

Throughout the audience, hands emerged from the tiers, pinning the people to their chairs.

Steve turned, motioning for Security. Two armed guards ran onstage, guns raised. "Whoever the hell you are, put your hands in the air."

Rasputina pouted and raised her hands. "Wait, wait, wait. Before we make any rash decisions—"

"We said, hands in the air!"

Rasputina turned to the camera and smiled wickedly. "Don't say I didn't warn them."

One of the guards approached Rasputina, gun raised. When he was close enough to press the gun to her forehead, the lich leaned forward, her jaw stretching wide, jagged teeth shining. She clamped her teeth onto the guard's throat and tore out his jugular.

The guard fell to the ground, grasping at his neck as he bled out.

The other guard turned to run. Rasputina sprinted after him, jumped onto his back, and tackled him to the ground. She rolled him over and pressed her finger to his mouth as he screamed. "Shush, shush. It's gonna be over. It'll hurt, but then it's gonna be over."

Rasputina leaned over the guard until they were nose to nose as she drove her knife into his side repeatedly until his screams eventually faded to gurgles. Then she stood and pointed at Steve. "Sit, please."

Steve did as he was told.

Rasputina approached Terra and pushed her chair to the side. A throne of bones cobbled itself from the crowd, and Rasputina took her seat. She sat there, picking at the loose skin under her nose as she dramatically brushed her hair back from her face. "Uh, this is the part where you ask questions, right? That's what you're supposed to be doing."

Steve's eyes were wide, and his bottom lip trembled. "Wait, I'm sorry?"

Rasputina drove her knife into Steve's hand as skeletal arms appeared and pinned the host to his table. She waited for him to stop screaming. "Come on, I'm on a tight schedule. It took a lot to make time to come see you two today. I don't want to waste it. What you got for me, Steve? Hit me with the hard ones."

CHAPTER TWELVE

The cameras were still rolling. Over a million viewers had watched two security guards bleed out on national television and Steve Campbell swear loudly as he tried to pull the knife from his hand.

Terra was frozen to her seat but not from fear. The skeleton hands wrapped around her wrists and ankles held her fast. No matter how much she struggled, it made no difference. She regretted not having worn her exo-suit under her uniform.

Rasputina didn't seem to mind how distressed the audience, or Campbell, was. She was still preening for the camera, pretending to be slightly uncomfortable but still flattered. "Are talk shows usually this quiet? Or is this something you edit out later?"

Campbell, who was sweating profusely, ran his hand over his forehead and through his hair. "No, no, this is live. We don't edit anything. Don't even take commercial breaks."

"Well, you better start asking questions. I'm getting bored."

Rasputina unbuttoned her suit jacket and pulled out a knife. "But I could easily liven things up." She threw the knife into the audience, hitting a young woman in the chest.

The audience burst into screams.

Rasputina snapped her hand at the cameraman as she stood and walked to him. "Are you getting that?" She grabbed him by the throat and forced the camera on the woman who stared quizzically at the knife in her chest, blood seeping from the wound. "Honestly, Steve, I think you might need to talk to your crew. They're very, very lax."

She returned to her seat and plopped down. "Whoever was filming for the arena did a much better job than your team. Would've thought it had been professionally filmed. Been catching up on that the last few days. Great TV. Just great." Rasputina looked at Terra. "Hey, you'd know who filmed that, wouldn't you? How'd they do it?"

Terra glared at Rasputina, weighing whether or not it was safer to answer the lich or ignore her questions. Although, baiting her might be the best decision. "Don't you already know that?"

Rasputina cackled as she pulled out another knife and pressed it to the side of Terra's face. The lich drew it down slowly, splitting the skin, letting the blood flow free. "See, you could probably run this program better than... Hey, what's your name?" She flung the knife at Steve, and it grazed his cheek.

The host trembled and mumbled, "Steve. Steve Campbell."

Rasputina crossed her legs and picked at the decaying flesh on her face. "We should call this the Terra Show. She's the one with all the *charisma*."

Terra tried again to pull free from the skeletons' grip but to no avail. Where the hell was Anabelle? She couldn't have left the studio already. There was no way she would watch this and not do anything.

Rasputina was still picking her face. "Hm. Okay, so, I don't want to tell anyone how to do their job, but I'm imagining our ratings are plummeting right now. And we have such good shit on at the moment. What do you think we should do to get the people's blood pumping?"

"What are you doing here?" Terra blurted.

Rasputina looked taken aback by the question until she finally smiled, her mandibles visible beneath her pale flesh. "The host speaks! I'm here, oh, why am I here? To check up on you, maybe? Or just to get a whole scoop on your situation. I'm very, *very* interested in you,

Terra. You and all your gal pals. You know, I would have killed for a group like that in my day." She laughed and clapped her hand across her knee. "You get it? Killed?"

When no one laughed, Rasputina pulled out another knife and casually threw it into the crowd. Then she pointed at the cameraman and said, "Make sure to get that!"

Terra tried to block out the screaming of the person who had been struck. Rasputina wanted someone to play with her, and Campbell would never have been ready for this. It was up to her to figure out the rules of whatever game Rasputina wanted to play. "Okay, okay. Just...hold on...I haven't held an interview before."

"You're doing better than this jackass," Rasputina said, jerking her thumb at Steve. Then she snapped her fingers and the audience started laughing. The laughter continued until people were struggling to breathe and the room was filled with the sound of wheezing and choking.

"What brought you out of retirement?"

Rasputina's eyes lit up and the audience stopped laughing. "Retirement? Sweetheart, I was never retired. Sometimes, you gotta know when to take a break, though. Especially as an artist. Things get so—"

"You consider yourself an artist?"

A smile crept across Rasputina's face. "Only in the most basic sense of the word. I create, thus I'm an artist. But I'm not trying to say anything, you know. No big message. I just...create!"

"What exactly do you create? All I've seen you do is destroy."

"I'm so glad you asked."

Rasputina jumped up and climbed onto Steve's desk. She pulled the knife from his hand, dragged him onto the floor in front of Terra, and straddled him. "You see, you look at this guy, and what do you see? A bunch of skin and eyes and hair, and all this boring shit. All of you look the same. Elves, humans, orcs, birds, dragons. Limbs and eyes and skin, and a silly little brain inside all of it. But if you go on and get a little creative..."

She grabbed Steve's ear and pressed her knife to it. "You take one little snip." She sliced off his ear and held it in front of his face as he screamed. Blood poured onto the stage floor. "Now…now you add a little life into the scene." Rasputina dipped her finger into the pooling blood, licked it clean, and shuddered. "Delicious life."

Terra wanted to look away, but she knew that wasn't an option. Anabelle was working on something. The elf had to be. Until then, Terra had to hold it together. "So, you're helping the Dark One to get people to pay attention to your art? No one looking before?"

Rasputina scratched at the side of her face, tearing away a bit of skin with her nail. "What do you mean, no one was looking?"

"I was curious. Myrddin told me that you're supposed to be some unholy, unstoppable creature of death. But right now, it looks to me like you're a pathetic failure, trying to grab everyone's attention by being as sensational as possible. Killing people on live TV is a bad comic-book plot. I've even seen you eat flesh, but you're a lich. I looked your kind up. Liches don't eat flesh, which means you're doing it for dramatic flair. Pretty, uh, what's the word, yeah, needy, if you ask me."

Rasputina stood, her smile now gone. She snapped her fingers at the camera crew and they came running, pushing their cameras with them as she sauntered up to Terra, sat on her lap, and stared into her face.

The smell was unbearable. Terra tried to move her face away from the stench of decay, but Rasputina grabbed her and held her fast. "You know, you're a beautiful woman. You know that, don't you?"

The cameras were getting in closer as Rasputina pressed her nose against Terra's. "I see things, Terra. Things that no one else wanted to see. And no one understood. None of them."

Rasputina reached down and pulled a knife from her jacket. She grabbed Terra's face and held it still when she tried to move away. "I don't care about what the Dark One is doing, but at least he has vision. He can see things. You? All of you are little pawns to that insufferable sack of shit, Myrddin? You will never see anything. *Know* anything. Not even if you try."

She grabbed one of the cameras and held it close to Terra's face. "You know what all those people at home see? A human who defied all odds. Fought for her freedom against orcs and dragons and balrogs. But do you know what I see, Terra? When I look in your eyes?"

Terra could hardly breathe with the smell of rotting flesh filling her lungs. She was doing everything she could to ignore Rasputina's words.

Rasputina's tongue surged out of her mouth, long and thick as a python, and slathered Terra's face as the lich moaned. "I see a little girl...scared...looking out at the world. So beautiful. But so afraid." She pressed her knife to Terra's face. "And blood. Screaming. I see your last breath as you choke on your blood. I can see your soul begging for me. Because you want me. You always have."

Her mouth opened, jaw cracking and stretching as her tongue flopped out of her mouth, onto Terra's lap, wriggling like a possessed worm. A pool of rancid drool formed around it as the lich's eyes burned the purest green.

Terra stared into those eyes and heard wailing in the distance. It sounded like her own voice.

Rasputina's voice was a low growl, something ancient and yearning. "You've been waiting for me to cut. You. Up. Aching for me to eat you."

Terra couldn't deny it.

"Get your fucking hands off her!"

Rasputina turned to look off-stage. Anabelle was radiating pure mana. She reached out and grabbed nothing, twisting it until its existence became obvious: a magical forcefield. Then she drove her other hand through it, tearing it apart.

Anabelle ran through the forcefield as the DGA marines followed her, headed by Blackwell and Naota. She leapt through the air, tackling Rasputina and pulling her off Terra.

The skeleton hands around Terra's arms vanished, along with those holding the audience captive.

Marines moved to secure the civilians, helping them to their feet and out of the studio.

Rasputina appeared behind Steve. She kicked the host out of his chair and sat as Terra got to her feet and joined Anabelle. "Ugh, you!

You're the least fun. Soul's all old and pruny, and you're what elves consider to be young. Took you long enough. Well, guess it's time to get down to business."

The lich snapped her fingers, and the air in the room went hot.

Two Dark Gates opened in the middle of the audience seating area.

Rasputina stood and strode to the gate. "Have a good time. I'll see you when the little girl's around. Thanks for the interview, Terra."

The lich disappeared in a flash of green light.

Anabelle handed Terra her small black compact as orcs poured from the Dark Gate. "You ready for this?"

Grok walked through the Dark Gate and drew a deep breath, releasing it slowly when she saw Anabelle.

Terra glanced at the elf, who was breathing rapidly. "Are you?"

CHAPTER THIRTEEN

Orcs continued to exit the portal as the marines moved the stragglers from the audience out of the studio. Blackwell and Naota managed to clear all the humans before the orcs had recovered from the transportation process.

Grok watched Terra and Anabelle as her forces rallied. "Elf. What a pleasant surprise. I thought I was just exterminating humans today. You will be a pleasant addition."

Anabelle put her hands on her hips and shrugged. "Oh, so you feel like you're ready to kill me today? Did I suddenly jump up on your list of priorities?"

Grok spat as she stretched her right arm. "Hardly. But you don't seem to have gotten any stronger. So much potential wasted—on all of you elves. You look down on us orcs as if we are beneath you, yet you allowed the power in your veins to go unused until it fades away. Worse than humans. At least, the one next to you is still getting stronger."

Anabelle looked at Terra, who frowned, indicating she had no idea what Grok was talking about. "Looks like we got us an old-school standoff."

At Anabelle's side, Terra squeezed the black compact, which

opened, sending the framework of Terra's exo-suit across her arms, spine, and legs. "That's the thing where we both just look at each other for half an hour until someone moves, right?"

Naota and Blackwell moved to the frontline with Anabelle and Terra. Naota pulled his glasses down slightly. "Yep. I've seen this in anime. We gotta psyche them out. Lots of eye-contact. Maybe some whooshing noises."

Blackwell pinched the bridge of his nose as he shook his head. "This isn't a fucking anime—" He was cut off by the sound effects Naota was emitting loudly.

Grok laughed, her bright teeth flashing. "At least you'll die in good company."

Anabelle stepped out from the frontline. "I read your file. Everything I could find on you. What happened to your tribe back home? How could you go on to work for the Dark One? We know you aren't chipped."

Grok's face betrayed no emotion. "Power begets power. What the Dark One did wasn't personal. He was strong. My tribe was weak. What I do isn't personal. I'm powerful. The humans you just herded away aren't. But you...you are personal to me. The last Traveler. Master of the Roads. I've been waiting my whole life to put you in the ground." She closed her eyes, and the earth shook as her mana created an aura around her. "There are many roads to power, elf. Let me show you mine."

Grok dashed at Anabelle. It took less than a second, her hand drawn back, ready to strike.

Anabelle was ready. She already knew how fast Grok was. Grok might be stronger than her, but what had happened last time had been a fluke. She'd just been caught off-guard. Anabelle threw up a magical barrier, deflecting the attack, then fluxed her mana. She sent the shield outward, pushing Grok back.

Grok wouldn't let up. Which Anabelle had expected. That was the orc's style, so Anabelle had to play it smart. She waved her hands, her fingers moving like streams as she flash-froze the air in front of her, firing dozens of razor-sharp icicles at Grok.

The orc swiped the ice attack away.

By that time, Anabelle had already slipped into the shadows. Grok's shadow to be precise, following the Path of Silence.

Grok whipped around, searching for the elf.

Anabelle thrust her hand out of Grok's shadow, grabbed her foot, and stabbed it with a long icicle. As the orc stumbled, Anabelle pulled her other foot from under her. Grok hit the ground, but Anabelle wasn't done yet. She clenched her fist, and the icicle in Grok's foot sent ice running through Grok's veins.

"Guess you didn't see that coming, did you?"

Grok scrambled to her feet and pulled the shard of ice from her foot. "Simple, weak elf-tricks. That is all." She crushed the shard, letting the dust fall to the floor.

The battle broke out around them, the marines shattering the spell of their personal fight. Blackwell fired first from his double pistols. The marines all wore exo-suits—Abby's redesign. Sleek and functional. More than enough to keep up with the orcs.

The orcs had taken cover behind the chairs and platforms where the audience had been seated. They laid down suppressing fire, forcing the marines to look for cover. Blackwell, Terra, and Naota tried to find somewhere to hide.

Grok and Anabelle had ignored the plasma blasts flying past them and were focused on their own battle. They danced between the plasma fire that heated the air as they swung fists and kicked at each other.

Terra, Blackwell, and Naota took cover behind Campbell's desk. "Looks like they kinda have the advantage," Blackwell said. "We're gonna need to force them from cover. Any ideas?"

Naota drew his dual tasers. They were attached to his exo-suit by retractable cables. "How about a little crazy-fun time?"

"Goddamn it, English please!"

Naota took off his glasses and looked into Blackwell's eyes. "Senpai, please never forget me." He flipped the desk over and ran out from cover, drawing the fire of the orcs.

"Naota, you fucking idiot!"

Naota threw one of his tasers, hitting an orc in the chest and electrocuting it before it could return to cover. Then he retracted his taser, pulling the orc with him, before throwing another taser at a nearby orc.

Terra watched Naota moving. "He might be stupid, but he's got guts." She ran out from under the desk, dropped and rolled, and grabbed a plasma rifle from the ground. "Ugh, did no one bring an axe?" She fired at the orcs, who were distracted as they focused on Naota. Unlike Naota, though, she wasn't moving laterally. Terra was heading for the wide, squat pillar where the orcs were hiding.

She hit the column hard before anyone could process exactly how insane she was. Her fists plunged into the pillar, tearing into it with ease as adrenaline pumped through her system, sending her exo-suit into hyperdrive.

Terra came out the other side of the pillar, grabbed an orc, and slammed him into the ground. She grappled another and shouted, "Got anything other than a gun on you?"

The orc mumbled under his breath, "Uh…uh…uh."

Orcs nearby were quickly lining up their shots.

Terra groaned in irritation, lifted the orc up, and threw him into the three closest shooters. Before they hit the ground, she was already on them. She grabbed the orc she had thrown moments ago and ripped away the small hatchet hanging from his side. Terra drove the blade into his back and turned her attention to the other three orcs.

When she looked up, she was covered in blood. She flipped the hatchet and caught it. "Hm…light. I like that."

A shot of plasma hit Terra in the back, knocking her forward. As Terra fell, she twisted, throwing the axe and nailing an orc in the chest.

The television studio was pure chaos. The enclosed space was overrun with orcs and marines fighting for their lives.

Blackwell had joined Naota, and they fought back to back. Naota whipped his tasers around, shocking anything dumb enough to get close, while Blackwell carefully put orcs down with clean, precise headshots.

Terra had glanced at them just as a troll exited the Dark Gate, falling onto Blackwell and Naota. She knew the troll was hers to handle. Still, as long as these two gates were open, this fight was a lost cause. "Hey, Anabelle!"

Anabelle flew right in front of Terra, skidding across the ground before screaming with rage, her arms catching fire as Grok tackled her. "Guess you're busy," Terra muttered.

Terra ran toward Blackwell and Naota, who were both caught up in the troll's huge fists. The creature wasn't affected by their defensive attacks, its hide too thick to penetrate.

Perfect. That means it can probably take a decent enough beating, Terra thought.

She tackled the troll, and it dropped the two commanders. Both Terra and the troll hit the ground.

Naota and Blackwell scrambled away as Terra turned and shouted, "We need to get that gate closed! We are *not* ready for anymore of this shit!"

"On it!" Blackwell shouted. "Naota, bring in the guns."

Naota stared blankly at Blackwell. "From your tone of voice, I'm assuming you're speaking about something big, right?"

"Naota, I told you to bring the railgun. Three times. I told you three times!"

Suddenly, Naota pushed him to the ground, then he helped Blackwell to his feet. "Sorry, I thought you were in danger. So, how are we closing the gates?"

Blackwell groaned in irritation as he shot an orc who was running at them. He pulled its plasma rifle off as it fell. "Come on, we gotta go figure this out."

Terra was still struggling with the troll. It was stronger than any of the trolls she'd fought in the arena. And she was still getting used to the power difference between her suit and her former strength.

Those were the thoughts on Terra's mind as she was flung through the air. She hit the wall and the troll bounced on her, bringing its fists down on her chest, knocking the wind out of her.

Anabelle and Grok were still locked in their fight only a few feet away. The elf's hair was disheveled, the first time Terra had seen it in such a condition. She was practically drenched in sweat, breathing heavily, and covered in small wounds.

Grok was not nearly close to Anabelle's state. She still seemed in control. A little winded but, other than that, fine.

Terra cracked the troll across the face, wondering where her axe had gone. As the creature slumped away, gathering its bearings, she called to Anabelle, "You want to trade dance partners?"

Anabelle blocked a jab from Grok and backflipped away, landing beside Terra. "You think you can keep up with her?"

"Can't promise but might make things a little more interesting. Plus, I always like an orc who can get down."

Anabelle helped Terra to her feet. "I could use the breather. She's fast. Really fucking fast."

"He hits hard. And smells like old scrotum. So, there's that."

Terra and Anabelle stood back to back as they squared off against their new targets.

Grok chuckled when she saw Terra raise her fists. "Really, human?"

Terra spat and pounded her fist to her chest. "Speak to me with the respect I deserve. I am Terra, Hewn from Orc Bone, Chieftain to the Ul-Kurah tribe, Stewarded by Cire the Black, Slayer of the Four Champions, and Bane of Traitors to our Traditions."

Grok scoffed loudly. "To *our* traditions?"

Terra kicked the plasma rifle in front of her out of the way and approached Grok. "Sorry. I meant *my* traditions."

"Do you think you're more orc than me?"

"Guess we're going to find out."

CHAPTER FOURTEEN

Grok came at Terra. Faster than Terra could have imagined. Watching Grok attack someone else was not the same as Grok coming for you.

The orc's fist slammed into Terra's stomach.

She felt her insides churn and twist as her knees buckled. Her eyes crossed and her vision went blurry.

Grok leaned close to Terra and whispered in her ear, "Still feel like an orc?"

Ignoring Grok's words, Terra focused on herself. She wasn't going down. It was that simple, just like in the arena. It didn't matter what was thrown at her. She didn't know anything about magic, orcish and elvish rivalries, or any of that shit. And it didn't matter.

Grok reached for Terra's throat.

She grasped the orc's wrist, twisted it to the side as she threw her weight, and rolled them both onto the ground.

Grok went down fast, and Terra was on top of the orc before she knew what was happening. Terra cupped both of her hands together into a fist and screamed as she brought it down on Grok's head. Terra's exo-suit whirred loudly as it attempted to divert more power to her.

The orc took the hit and lay there, dazed, staring up at Terra. Then Grok chuckled. "Shit and mother's piss…you are an orc, aren't you?"

Terra smiled despite herself. "Yeah, kinda surprised myself too."

Grok stretched and slugged Terra in the face, throwing the human backward. As Grok leapt to her feet, *she* was smiling too. Not the disconcerting, murderous smile Terra had seen before. No. Grok wore the same grin sitting on Terra's face.

"I…hm…there isn't a chip. You know that, don't you?"

Terra stood and popped her neck. "Yeah, it's been established."

"All I've ever wanted was a fight—one that would matter to me and only me. One that is going to feel right."

Terra couldn't say she fully understood what Grok was talking about, but she did understand it on some level. It was the same conflicting feeling she'd experienced in the arena. The constant desire to escape, yet waking up every morning, excited about the next fight and what she might have the chance to take down. "You think I might be enough?"

Grok laughed and shook her head. "No. But you might be the closest I'll ever get. Try to enjoy this as much as I'm going to."

The orc surged forward. Terra tried to keep an eye on her movements, but it was impossible. Grok was already in front of her. She threw a jab at Terra, who blocked it instinctively.

Grok smiled, her toothy grin reminding Terra of Cire's wry, argumentative grin. "I'm not holding back. You understand that, right? I am going to kill you."

Terra threw right, which Grok easily blocked. But Terra wasn't right-handed. Her left was coming fast, and it connected with the orc's trachea.

Grok stumbled backward, clutching her throat and gasping for breath as Terra lunged for her. She grabbed the Grok's head, clutched it tightly, and drove her knee into it, breaking the orc's nose.

Terra rolled her shoulders and released a primal scream. "Fuck me, right? If you're gonna kill me, fucking do it already."

Grok wiped the blood away from her nose. "Hm…Terra, correct?"

"Yeah. But say it with some respect next time."

"Your name is too long. Probably given by a shaman. Let me give you a new name. The Unbreakable Bone. Live through this, and I'll gladly pay you your proper dues."

Before Terra could blink, Grok was in front of her. The orc delivered a quick punch to the side of Terra's head. Dozens of blows to her face followed, so many that she didn't bother to count.

Terra hit the ground.

Anabelle had watched the fight out of the corner of her eye, reluctant to interfere. She couldn't figure out how Terra had kept up with Grok.

Jealousy was a new feeling for Anabelle, and she wasn't dealing with it well.

But she wasn't stupid. Anabelle might not be able to take Grok, but Terra had begun to prove she was capable. And it had been important to allow Terra to do her best.

But Anabelle had seen that was not the case. She had witnessed the devastating attack Grok had delivered. Terra was seconds away from being killed.

Anabelle looked at the troll she'd been wrestling. "Sorry, dear, but playtime is over." The elf's hands caught fire and she shot out as much mana as she could spare, engulfing the troll in flames. Even if she didn't kill the damn thing, her fire would ensure it wouldn't recover for a while.

She hoofed it over to Terra and Grok, throwing a handful of lightning at the orc, forcing her to step away and open a path to Terra.

Terra looked up when she saw the elf above her. "Switching was a really shitty idea."

Anabelle knelt and cradled Terra in her arms. "Yeah. You should have thought that one through better. You're gonna get through this, though."

Terra groaned and flexed her chest. She struggled to her feet without Anabelle's help. "You're fucking right, I'm going to get through this. I'm gonna rip her fucking head off."

Grok was watching the two. "Huh. Gods and goddesses fuck me, I admire you, Unbreakable, but I could also kill you. But together... together you two are something interesting."

Terra and Anabelle looked at each other. "Uh, are we doing doubles now?" Terra asked.

Anabelle shook her head. "Fighting together isn't like it is in the movies. We don't—"

In the next instant, Grok was before them, swinging a wide haymaker at Terra. Anabelle slid in front of her and blocked the punch. Terra reacted instinctively. She grabbed Grok's arm, straightened it slightly, and snapped the orc's elbow.

Grok screamed but didn't back off. She headbutted Anabelle, who was closer. As the elf stumbled backward, Grok tried to grapple her.

Terra grabbed Grok's limp hand, gripped her shoulder, and pulled her arm out of its socket. Then she dropped low and punched Grok's kneecap in.

Grok limped away, laughing under her breath. "Oh, you two. You're just what I've been waiting for." She quickly reset her arm and leg. "I've been waiting so long for you."

Blackwell and Naota were plowing through as many orcs as they could. They watched each other's back, working together seamlessly, their hours of training together paying off. Blackwell had come up with a plan. Overload the Dark Gates with the charge from Naota's tasers. But the tasers weren't strong enough. They needed more juice.

To boost the tasers' power, the pair had collected cores from the plasma rifles they had lifted from the dead orcs. Blackwell wasn't a genius like Abby, but he knew enough about electric wiring to make it work. Still would have been better if Abby had been on the mission.

The other marines were doing their part to help with the growing mass of invading orcs but wouldn't be able to keep going much longer. More orcish forces kept pouring through the Dark Gate, replacing those the squad took down.

If the gate wasn't closed soon, the whole studio would be overrun.

Naota snapped his tasers back and grabbed another core from a plasma rifle. "Think this is going to be enough?"

Blackwell checked the mound of cores at his feet. "Should be. Watch my back." He knelt and got to work while Naota sheathed his tasers, picked up a rifle, and started firing.

Anabelle and Terra looked at each other. "Uh, you wanna go first?" Terra asked.

The elf's right hand crackled with lightning. "Sure." She ran at Grok and swiped at her face. But the orc easily sidestepped the attack.

Terra came up behind Anabelle, aiming a right hook at Grok. As the orc raised her hand to block the punch, Anabelle dropped and swiped her leg at Grok's ankles. The orc lost her balance, but she landed with her hand supporting her weight. She flipped herself upright and knocked both Angels backward.

Grok went on the offensive, first swinging at Terra—who managed to block the attack—then aiming a punch to Anabelle's gut. The orc alternated between the two Angels using an obscene amount of speed; it was all Terra could do to keep Grok's blows from landing.

Anabelle pulsed mana and an aura formed around her, pushing Grok back. The orc didn't waste any time in unleashing her own mana aura.

You kidding me? Terra thought. These superpowered assholes should be able to take care of themselves.

Grok sped up her attacks, pushing Anabelle and Terra back. "Slow her down!" Terra shouted.

Anabelle grabbed Grok's wrist and froze it to her palm. The orc tried to pull away, but she was bound to Anabelle.

Terra took advantage of the moment. As Grok tried to wrench herself away from the elf, Terra slid close to Grok, grabbed her neck, turned, and tossed her through the air. Anabelle dissolved the ice handcuff and blasted the orc with water.

Grok was wiping her face when Terra grabbed Anabelle's wrist and flung her at the orc. The elf's hand charged with lightning, and she drove it into Grok's chest.

The orc backpedaled before regaining her footing within seconds, a burn mark smoking on her chest. She shook her head and rushed Terra, delivering three quick blows to her stomach.

Terra coughed blood and fell to her knees.

Grok stretched her fingers and a sharp bone shot from her palm. When they had first encountered Grok, she had revealed no necromancy talents. Now...now was different.

Grok might have been hiding her powers, or she'd since received an upgrade courtesy of the Dark One. Either way, she was more dangerous than ever.

Grok grabbed hold of the bone and swiped at Anabelle. The sharp tip grazed the elf's cheek. As Anabelle backed away, Grok kicked Terra in the face and raised her hand. She aimed her palm at Anabelle and fired three ten-inch razor-sharp bone shards.

Anabelle flipped out the way. As she landed, Grok appeared in front of her, shooting out another bone-dagger. The elf kicked up a stray rifle and used it to deflect the oncoming bone.

Terra raced to them, crept up behind Grok, and put the orc in a chokehold.

Grok smiled, and flame surged from her mouth, as though she were a dragon.

Terra held on, but Grok pushed a wave of energy at Terra and forced her to release her hold. In shock, Terra and Anabelle backed away. But they moved too slowly; when the flame exploded, it sent both DGA's soaring through the air.

The moment Anabelle hit the ground, Grok fell on top of her. "Wondering what else I got up my sleeve?" the orc teased.

An explosion went off, and Grok looked over her shoulder. Above her, one of the Dark Gates was on fire, its portal shutting down. "How the hell..." she muttered as she moved off Anabelle. She scanned the room for the source of the commotion, and her gaze fell on Blackwell.

Blackwell held a shoddily made plasma grenade constructed from the left-over plasma cores. He saw Grok's eyes fall on him. "Oh, fuck."

The orc sprinted toward Blackwell, but before she could strike, Naota stepped in front of Blackwell, shouting, "Senpai, do it!"

The orc's fist connected with Naota's face, shattering his jaw. He dropped to the ground as Blackwell lobbed the last grenade at the gate.

Grok attempted to grab the grenade but missed. She watched it explode on contact.

The explosion threw them to the floor. Blackwell crawled to Naota to check if he was still alive.

Grok pushed to her feet and stood watching the flaming Dark Gate. She approached Anabelle and crouched low until they were face to face. "You took care of my army, but guess who you're locked in a room with?"

As she spoke, the side of the studio exploded, sending concrete and debris everywhere. Grok glanced over her shoulder as dozens of marines stormed into the room. "Count yourself lucky. If you and your friend ever get your shit together, hopefully we'll have a real fight. Maybe then you'll be worth killing."

Without warning, Grok pressed her hand to Anabelle's arm and fired a bone shard into the elf's shoulder. "Something to remember me by." She stood as Anabelle's agonizing screams melded with the increasing roar of firepower. "Lich, I need an out." After a second, Grok's body glowed bright green and she vanished.

Terra crawled over to Anabelle as the marines mopped up the last of the orcish invasion. She pulled the bone out of the elf's shoulder. "Fuck. That does not look good."

Anabelle tried to sit up as Terra collapsed beside her. "You look like you got the shit knocked out of you."

"Funny, I was thinking the same about you."

"Good first interview?"

"Oh, yeah. It was fucking great."

CHAPTER FIFTEEN

Persephone's face was starting to clear up on Abby's old television monitor. Her voice was still shaky, and it was difficult for Abby to understand her. "You're breaking up, I can't hear you," Abby complained.

The image of the drow shook as though Persephone was tapping whatever object she was transmitting her video through. "Is that better?"

This time, Abby could hear Persephone as clearly as if the drow were in the barn with her. "Perfectly. What's going on? I been trying to get in touch with you for weeks."

Persephone smiled, fading into the darkness for a moment. "Same here. Connection underground is terrible. I had to surface for this one."

"Underground?"

Persephone laughed heartily. "Yeah, I thought I told you. Drow spend most of their lives underground. It's not normal for us to live above ground, out there with all the sunnies. That's what we call surface dwellers. Or some people do. I never really cared for the term. But the dwarves love it. Ever want to get a rise out of one, call them that. They'll lose their shit. But that's not why I called—"

"*How* exactly are you calling?"

Persephone shifted uncomfortably. Abby still didn't know the drow well, and she wondered why Persephone seemed awkward. "I ain't upset or anything," Abby offered quickly. "Just curious, that's all."

The drow relaxed and leaned in closer to look at Abby. "I have a gnome friend down here, kinda like a surrogate dad. He's really good with tech and tracking. He pinged a signal you sent out to your base and figured it out from there. Honestly, I don't quite know what he did, but I didn't really care. As long as I got a chance to talk to you."

Abby blushed and looked away from the TV for a second to collect herself. "I'm glad you did. How you been doing?"

Persephone sighed loudly as she scratched her scalp. "Ugh, it's been such a hassle since I got back. Reintegration is mind-numbing. I can't wait until all of it's over."

"Wait. What's reintegration?"

"Oh, I've been away for a long time. I mean, it's probably been three or four years. And drow communities are very insular. Think of it as a debriefing. But one that you have to do with your family and close friends. Maybe an elder, if you're unlucky enough. Thank the goddess that I didn't have to do that."

"So, you could serve the Dark One for three years and not have to talk to someone in charge?"

Persephone's eyes narrowed. "I wasn't serving the Dark One. I was under mind control."

Abby instantly regretted her phrasing. Persephone recoiled from the monitor, her movement noticeable despite such a small screen. "That's not what I meant... I just didn't know what else to call it. Sorry."

Persephone cast a glance over her shoulder. "No, no, I know what you're trying to say. I'm just on edge from the interviews. Every day, six hours or so. It starts to wear you down. But, yeah, it wasn't that big of a deal. Drow society is much more forgiving than most. Actually forgiving. Forgive and forget. But that's because we need a lot of it. Plus, I think everyone sees how hard I'm trying to fix everything, and they might be cutting me more slack than usual."

"What do you mean?"

Persephone raised her hand. Her fingers exploded outward, tentacles flowing from her arm. "This whole thing."

"Is there something wrong?"

Persephone cracked up, deep guffaws that made Abby giggle. "You know having tentacles isn't a normal thing, right?"

Abby shook her head, feeling stupid for not knowing anything about drow physiology. "Can't say I do."

"Well, this is definitely not a normal thing. That's mostly what everyone has been concerned about. No one cares about the Dark One. The drow are protected against whatever he wants to throw their way. But the tentacles have everyone a little bit worried."

"How'd you get them?"

Persephone squirmed in her seat. "Uh, it's kinda a long story."

"I haven't talked to you in almost a month. It can be as long as you want."

Persephone sighed, hanging her head a little bit. "Okay, but it's not a *fun* long story."

"When I was a kid, my birth parents sold me off. I never met them. But that's what my guardians told me. Still don't know how true it is. And I call them my *guardians* because that's what they were. Not parents. I was sold into…I guess you could call it a cult.

"When I was fourteen or so, I was offered up as a sacrifice. I didn't really know what it all entailed at the time, obviously. No one told me it was a sacrifice, just a birthday party. I was taken to a shaman, one of the oldest in my realm. Which is saying a lot because a healthy drow can live to be a couple thousand years old. No one knew how old this guy was. Other than ancient."

Abby had no idea that anyone could live that long other than Myrddin. But now that she'd thought about it, she'd heard Anabelle and Roy both reference the elf's age. Abby had always thought it was a joke between the two of them, but now it was starting to make sense.

"You're kinda like elves, right?" Abby asked.

"We *are* elves. Dark elves. Not dark like evil. We're just darker. But we're still elves. But, anyways, the shaman was…he wasn't like a regular drow shaman. He did something to me, brought something from the Netherverse and put it inside me. I don't think they understood what it was that they were doing. They couldn't have. A lot of people died, and that was when the Dark One found me."

Persephone was quiet for a while, looking down at her hand.

Abby wished she could hold Persephone, whisper to her that everything was going to be okay. But they were realms away from each other. All she could do was watch Persephone hurting. "What did they put in you?"

"Something ancient. The elders have been trying to figure out exactly what, but there's nothing concrete. They think it's older than the Dark One. An Old One. I'm praying that's not true, though. I can't imagine what it would take to get rid of that if it's even possible."

Abby had heard of the Old Ones. A few weeks ago, she'd received a message from Alex, the leader of Boundless, a Dragon Rider team. It had been a hectic, confusing message. Something about aliens and telepathy. The most succinct part of the message had been concerning the Old Ones. Apparently, Alex had discovered a weapon infused with the power of these things.

"What are the Old Ones?"

Persephone shook her head slowly as she tried to put her fears into words. "It's hard to explain, mostly because we don't know what they are. I guess you could say that they're kinda like gods. But not really. They were the first beings. Immensely powerful monsters that defy our understanding. They don't care about us. We're like ants to them. But some crazy people pray to them, offer them sacrifices...all for the sake of power."

"Sounds like the Dark One to me."

"There are a lot of drow who think the Dark One is an Old One. They believe that's where he draws all his power. No one knows for sure, but there are rumors that he's trying to tap into the Netherverse and bring back whatever is there to serve him."

Abby wanted to change the subject. She could see that Persephone was obviously upset. "When are you going to come visit me? Shouldn't be too hard if you know where I am all the time."

Persephone laughed, a pleasant break from the tone of the conversation so far. "I don't! But hopefully soon. My reintegration should be over in a few days. And then I can come and go as I please. I'm not sure whether or not I'll be allowed back onto your realm, though."

"Why would they keep you from coming here?"

"Oh, it's not them. Myrddin seems to have final say over who can come and go between the military bases of the realms. But if he has a problem with me visiting you at the base, I can get to Earth or Middang3ard. You might just have to do some sneaking."

Abby didn't have a problem with sneaking, though she found it hard to believe Myrddin would keep Persephone from seeing her. The drow had helped out with the battle in the arena to save Terra, so what other proof of her loyalty would the old man need?

"I miss you," Persephone said softly.

Her words caught Abby off-guard, and she jumped in surprise. "I miss you too."

"That's good to know. I've been thinking about you a lot. Probably too much."

Abby's heart swam up to her throat. She'd been thinking about Persephone a lot as well. They hadn't spoken since their short "field trip" in Japan. Since then, Abby had been wondering why Persephone hadn't been returning her comms. Now she knew the reason, and she wished she could have been there for Persephone during all of this.

"I been thinking about you too," was all Abby could manage.

"I don't know when I'll be able to talk to you next, but it'll be soon. Take care."

The television cut out unceremoniously.

Abby sat in the dark of the barn, watching the screen, hoping Persephone would come back. She didn't.

CHAPTER SIXTEEN

Anabelle stormed into Myrddin's study. There was probably a better way to handle this, but she didn't care. The old man had to know what was on her mind.

Myrddin didn't appear disturbed by the disruption. "Can I help you with something?"

Anabelle was almost vibrating out of her skin with anger. "You better fucking be able to. What the hell was that at the show? Two gates opening up without even a little bit of warning from you? Do you know how many lives were put in danger from that?"

Myrddin sighed, looking tired and defeated. "Do you believe I would not have informed you had I been aware of incoming Dark Gates?"

Anabelle thought it over for a second.

It didn't make a whole lot of sense for Myrddin to keep that information from her.

The whole point of her squad was to eliminate the gates. If they weren't given the intel, they were pretty much useless. "Okay. Then what happened?"

Myrddin appeared beyond tired.

For the first time, Anabelle could see the sag of his skin, as though hundreds of years were threatening to catch up with the wizard. Even the way he moved seemed slower. "This is a different game now. Rasputina and Grok are something beyond what I've been planning for. They…they are anomalies."

Anabelle sat across from Myrddin, trying to hold her anger in check. "How so? They're just more generals. Nothing we haven't seen before."

Myrddin shook his head and waved his hand over his desk, conjuring a glass of wine. Another glass appeared in front of Anabelle. "No. They are different. I'm assuming you retrieved the file on Grok."

Anabelle sipped the wine as she nodded. "Glanced at it. There wasn't anything particularly useful. An orc who studied the Old Ways of combat. Has a vendetta against elves. But, honestly, who doesn't? Didn't see anything that I thought would make you lose your cool."

"I was not being dramatic when I spoke to the DGA about Rasputina. She is a game-changer. And Rasputina, coupled with Grok, is a disconcerting turn of events."

"Are you going to tell me what the deal with the orc is or keep tap-dancing around it?"

Myrddin looked wounded but recovered quickly. "She's first-generation from the schism between your two people. That's not in the file. No one knows how long she's managed to stay alive. But years ago, she dedicated herself to the extinction of the Travelers. Grok is the reason that you are the last of them."

Anabelle wouldn't have thought such information would hit her hard. But it did. Even if she wasn't certain of how she felt about relearning the ways of the Path, she was still floored by the idea that one orc had destroyed over five thousand years of knowledge. "Okay, are you saying she and a couple of other—"

"No, I am saying that *she* did it. Only her."

Anabelle was beginning to understand the hatred that burned in Grok's eyes every time the orc looked at her. This was beyond Anabelle, she was merely an extremity in the situation. "What's she been doing in the meantime? Her file is obviously lacking some pertinent information."

"We don't know. She showed up with the Dark One about five years ago. Everything before that is a mystery. I've done everything I can to dig into her past, but haven't found anything."

"And the lich?"

Myrddin recoiled at the word as though he'd been slapped. "I've told you all everything that I know about Rasputina."

"Then why do you seem so uncomfortable?"

Myrddin's face reddened, and the room pulsed around him as if he were pushing it outward with his mind. "What more do you want to know? Specific details of the time she spent torturing me before we were able to lock her up?"

Anabelle remembered the tale of torture that Myrddin had laid on them last time. Even with the revelation, Myrddin's response was uncharacteristic. The wizard never became angry about anything. What else had happened?

"I want information that will keep me from ending up dead. And it feels like you're hiding something from me. What aren't you telling me?"

Myrddin shook his head. "I'm not keeping anything from you—"

"Why did Terra have so many soldiers with her for the interview? It was almost like you were expecting an attack."

The room grew hotter as small sparks of electricity snapped across Myrddin's face. "What exactly are you suggesting?"

"That you knew about this, and you let it happen."

"I am constantly expecting attacks. I assumed that the Dark One would take the chance to strike out at my two toughest lieutenants. That does not mean I allowed anything to happen, merely that I'm not stupid. There is no time for slip-ups. Not at all. Grok is proving to be a bigger threat than I imagined. And the introduction of the lich...I don't have time for petty arguments like this."

Anabelle wasn't ready to pull back from Myrddin. "You could have warned us what to expect. Or at least given Terra a heads up. Do you know how upset she is? She thinks people's lives were put in danger because of her."

"Do you seriously walk around at any point in the day and not assume the Dark One is coming to kill us all? The only person who should need this kind of babying is Abby. Frankly, I'm disappointed that this is so upsetting to you."

"You need to start letting us know everything, Myrddin. It's beginning to feel like you don't trust us."

Myrddin stood, electricity still coming off his body. "I expect you to do your job, and I will continue doing mine. There are gates still opening. You will have to take care of these ones by yourself. Terra has another interview."

"Give her some time to recover from the last one."

The holoscreen on Myrddin's desk beeped with an incoming comm. "Time is something we do not have much of. Dismissed."

The conversation was over. Myrddin looked like he could have killed Anabelle, but the elf felt the same way.

She stormed out of Myrddin's office.

Back in her room, Anabelle mulled over her conversation with Myrddin. She wasn't certain Myrddin had been unaware of the attack, despite his assurances.

Roy would give her the information, but she didn't want to drag him into the situation.

Since they'd started dating, Anabelle had discovered that Roy had been kept in the dark as much as she was. It appeared Myrddin was not straightforward with anyone anymore.

A few of his recent decisions had made Anabelle question whether or not Myrddin was the best person to lead this war. She wished she could talk to someone about her concerns, but there was no one. Her team didn't need the burden of this worry either.

I need to get out of my head, Anabelle thought. She sat with her folder on Grok, reading through as much as she could about the orc. Still, nothing struck her as overly important.

Anabelle thought back to her last encounter with Grok. Fighting alongside Terra had slightly increased their chances of defeating the orc. What unsettled her more was Grok's enjoyment of it.

The Dark One's two new lieutenants were a frightening combination. Anabelle had never come up against an agent of the Dark One who relished causing pain so much. To willingly side with the Dark One seemed like such an insane thing to do: he was trying to enslave all of existence!

Maybe some people don't need to care.

Anabelle sat on her rug and crossed her legs. She closed her eyes and entered into a deep meditation. She was trying to access more of her lost memories, lessons from her training. She might not find an answer to her problems there, but it would at least occupy her time.

She sank further into the blackness of her mind, experiencing emotions about events she'd long forgotten. There was a lot of anger there today. As Anabelle meditated, she understood she was angry at everything.

The war.

Myrddin.

She was also pissed at Terra, and she didn't know why.

An image flashed into Anabelle's mind. She was an elfling at the Traveler's temple. There was another elf the same age as her. They were fighting each other as their teacher observed. Anabelle watched herself getting her ass kicked.

She surged to her feet, breaking her concentration. "Ugh, I'm not getting anywhere tonight." She flopped onto her bed and turned on the news.

CHAPTER SEVENTEEN

Sarah and Kravis returned to base camp during the night. The encampment was one of the newer gatherings of the resistance. For months now, the gnomish homeworld had been under siege by the Dark One. The gnomes were fighting a losing battle. The most they could do was strike back in these small guerilla cells.

Myrddin had ordered Sarah to help the gnomish world with her espionage skills, but since there was no government or real organization, she and Kravis had spent the majority of their time organizing attacks across the cells. The two had become the unspoken heroes of the resistance.

Some gnomes didn't see it that way, though. They believed Myrddin had less than scrupulous reasons for helping, pointing out that the wizard hadn't been invested in the gnomish cause until the war had toppled the world.

Sarah and Kravis had done everything they could to reverse that opinion. They were all fighting against the Dark One. If one world fell, all the realms would suffer.

The human and gnome took care of their first duty upon returning: debriefing the gnomish squad, explaining what had happened on the mission. Then they found the friends of the two gnomes who had fallen in battle. They provided them with their friend's personal effects and anything that was recovered from the dunes. Once that was taken care of, Sarah returned to her tent while Kravis went to attend to his own business.

The last thing Sarah had to do was personal. She took out a notebook and recorded the names of the two gnomes who had died. The notebook was full of other names. Everyone Sarah had served with, she detailed as much as she could.

The nature of Sarah's position didn't allow her to create close friendships. She was always moving, going wherever she was assigned. Her last few months on the gnomish world had been the longest she could remember having remained in one place. The notebook was the closest thing she had to a friend.

Her records were her way to remain grounded. Of all Myrddin's operatives, Sarah's job was perhaps the hardest. She and Kravis were given assignments that were murky, to say the least—one of the reasons some gnomes didn't trust Sarah.

As an assassin, Sarah rarely had the luxury of feeling like one of the good guys. She got the job done by whatever means necessary— even if those methods consisted of actions she would rather forget. And there were many of them. Most nights, Sarah was kept awake by memories of past missions. She often felt like a monster; there was more blood on her hands than anyone she knew.

At least the notebook helped to ease some of that.

Once Sarah was finished honoring the dead, she pulled out her HUD communicator and scanned for any urgent messages. There was only one—a message from Anabelle, thanking her for providing information on Grok.

Sarah wrote a quick message in reply. She wanted to keep in touch with the elf. Though Sarah might not spend any time with the DGA's, the honorable induction into their squad meant a lot to her. But she thought it best to continue to maintain some distance from the DGA. She was glad Myrddin had reassigned her to the gnomish world.

The closer people became, the more likely they were to discover what kind of person Sarah was: a killer. That was different from Anabelle or Terra. Those two were warriors. They were cut from a different cloth.

Desperate to get out of her head, Sarah left her tent and wandered through the camp. It was a fairly large establishment containing at least two hundred heads. The gnomes had managed to make it as homey as possible with barely any supplies. They had all been annoyed that the truck had been emptied of anything useful.

Raiding orc convoys was the only way the gnomes' camp sustained itself. There wasn't nearly enough game around to hunt, and their own supply lines were non-existent. Sarah would have to find something else soon, or it would soon be time to fold this camp and start moving again.

There were some families of gnomes at the camp as well. Most of the resistance groups had had no choice but to accept refugees. The gnomes displaced by the war didn't have anywhere else to go. There had been rumors about trying to go back underground, to abandon the surface world as the dark gnomes had done years ago.

But that was a foolish hope; the dark gnomes had also been run out of their homes. If anyone was honest with themselves, they would assume the Dark One was already busy converting the ancient underground gnome cities into another machination of his war.

Sarah took a seat at one of the many fires throughout the camp. A pair of orphans sat across from her, sharing a meal. They smiled at her, and she forced a believable grin for the kids. The sight of these children tore her up more than anything else. Children weren't supposed to ever experience life like this. They should have been running and playing, not squatting in squalor and starving.

Kravis came to sit beside Sarah. "We're in the process of hunting down another convoy. And the spy who gave us the bad intel should be joining us soon."

Sarah watched the flames and sighed. "Do you think we can talk about something else for a little bit?"

Kravis handed Sarah a piece of salty dried meat. "Does it have to be child-appropriate?"

Sarah glanced at the kids, who had finished eating and were now playing with a stick, drawing figures in the dirt. "Preferably not something that we have to shoo them away from."

Kravis leaned back and looked up at the stars. "What did we ever used to talk about? Feels like this has been life for so long. How about this…tell me about the first time you ever went to the beach."

"The beach? God, it's been forever since I was at a beach." Sarah couldn't help but laugh. Anytime Kravis had to think of something to talk about, he ended up getting sentimental. A very noticeable change for the gnome who, for the most part, projected an image of an insufferable grouch. "The first time…I think I might have been ten or eleven. We didn't really have beaches where I grew up."

"I thought humans went to the beach all the time."

"Only if you live near one. My home was pretty landlocked. I actually learned how to swim at the beach. It was terrifying. My dad and mom took me out to the water, and I looked out at all that ocean. I started crying and wanted to go home. My parents had to sit down in the water with me for an hour or something like that."

Kravis took a bit of meat and chuckled. "You being afraid is very hard for me to wrap my head around. Granted, you were only a kid. Still, you being afraid of anything sounds downright false."

Sarah nodded as she began to lose herself in thought. "Yeah, I used to be scared of everything, especially of dying. That's what I was thinking at the ocean. Everyone thinks the ocean is beautiful but for me, for a long time, all I could see when I looked out at the waves was something that could drag me to death. But I love the ocean now. First place I want to go once we get some time off. What about you?"

"First place *I* want to go?"

"No, first time you went to the ocean."

Kravis screwed up his face while he thought. "I think I was twenty or so. There's a lot of lakes all over the place where I grew up, and the ocean wasn't too far off. But I couldn't believe it when I saw it. There was so much water. We took a boat out and spent the day sailing and fishing. It was a really good day. I wouldn't mind taking a trip out again once we can take a break from—" Kravis stopped talking abruptly. He was staring at the children, who were watching him and Sarah with wide eyes. "From what we do," he finally finished.

Behind them, a gnomish spy walked to the fire, the same spy responsible for the faulty intel. He sat beside Sarah.

One thing Sarah loved about gnomish culture was the lack of formality on all occasions. Gnomes spoke to you as though they knew you, and rank meant nothing. If this gnome was in trouble, there wouldn't be some huge meeting. They would simply sit and talk. The most formal Sarah had seen any gnomes was during briefings, and even that was usually done over a beer.

The spy handed Sarah a jug of wine. "You wanted to see me. There were problems with the intel I provided?"

Sarah nodded as she took the wine. "Yeah, there were problems. The truck we found was empty. No supplies. Only some weird black goo."

The spy raised his eyebrow. "Black goo? I didn't find out anything about that."

"I don't know if you got duped or not, but you're gonna have to keep that from happening again. Good intel is all that's keeping any of us alive right now. That falls through, we're dead."

The spy sipped the wine and nodded. "Understood. On that note, I have some more information. This time it's not good news."

Sarah sighed and shook her head. "When is it ever *just* good news? What do you have for me?"

"There are reports of the Dark One making moves on the Northern Front. We've been anticipating that for a while, but it looks like it's actually happening. But that's not the real news. We've been getting reports from different camps. They're being wiped out. The Dark One is pushing to break the resistance. There've been over ten attacks over the last twenty-four hours."

"Any idea how he's finding the camps? They're pretty secluded, and we have security measures in place."

"We think he's hacking our communications. There's also always the chance there's a spy. Not likely that each of these camps was infil-trated, though. Most likely, it's someone who works with communica-tion between camps."

Sarah took a deep swig of the wine and passed it to Kravis. "Any word on how that's going to be handled yet?"

"We've put in a request with Myrddin to help us improve our communication encryption. And the remaining camps are looking into all of their soldiers. We haven't found anything on our side yet."

Sarah stood, still staring into the flames. "Okay. I'll touch base with Myrddin and make sure you get what you need soon. Send me a copy of the details for the next truck you're planning to hit."

The spy agreed and Sarah left, heading back to her tent. She closed the tarp behind her and sat on her bed as she sent in a comm request to Myrddin.

The wizard picked up quickly. He appeared stressed out. "Looks like you're in a great mood for some shit news," Sarah joked.

Myrddin put on his glasses and cleared his throat. From the looks of it, he had probably only recently woken up. "I'm always ready for bad news. What do you have?"

"We hit a truck for supplies today. The whole thing was empty. We either have a mole in our communication squad, or someone's hacking us. Either way, we put in a request for someone to strengthen our lines. I wanted to emphasize the need for this."

"I'll have someone on it immediately."

"Second thing, we also found something really weird on the truck. It was a vial of some kind of black goo. The stuff reacted when it saw me. Tried to break out of the glass and attack me. I have it stored now, but it reminded me of something I read in one of the recent briefings. About the shard that alien Vardis on Middang3ard left behind when he died. There was a reactive liquid in that too, right?"

Myrddin stroked his beard. "Yes, there was. And the shard is a weapon. The substance might be more important to the weapon than we previously thought. We're still running tests on it. Before Vardis died, he said the weapon would have had the potential to destroy the

Dark One. If this is tech that the Dark One has as well, we're in a lot of trouble. I believe the endgame is finally upon us."

"Are we ready?"

Myrddin reset his glasses, his eyes distant. "I believe we will find out soon enough."

CHAPTER EIGHTEEN

Terra and Roy were on an elevator heading to the thirteenth floor of the Ciacom television studios. The company was a media beast, owning nearly seventeen cable channels and a handful of newspaper outlets. They were known for their hard-hitting, confrontational style. Terra had been bummed to hear that the show she was appearing on was their most openly conflictual.

The last talk show was still fresh in Terra's mind. It had been such a clusterfuck. And there had been no downtime between both interviews. This wasn't Terra's strong suit. She didn't think she could handle another bout of questions, especially knowing she would have to answer ones that dealt with what had happened on the Steve Campbell show.

This was beyond stage fright. Terra's stomach had been bundled up in knots since Myrddin had informed her of the second interview. She tried not to let anyone know, though. To be fair, this wasn't any more dangerous than her time in the arena. She knew how to handle herself in a fight. The civilians made her feel uncomfortable. Hopefully the producers had the common sense not to be filming in front of a live audience.

The elevator stopped, and Terra and Roy walked out. It seemed like something was on Roy's mind as well. Terra wondered what it was. She had been told at the last minute that Roy would be accompanying her on the show, so maybe he was also nervous. "You ever do the tv thing?" Terra asked.

Roy, who was looking around the corner as if he was watching for shooters, distractedly looked back at Terra. "Huh? Television? No, never done this talk show crap. Don't know why Myrddin would send me on something like this. There are a lot more important things that I could be doing."

"Yeah, he's putting a lot of effort into getting a media presence. Never would have thought this was the place for our resources."

The two walked down the hallway, looking for someone to direct them, but the studio was bare. "Necessary evil. Honestly, if you don't have a viral twitter, no one is going to be listening to you. You wouldn't know it, but we have an entire social media department. Myrddin's only being this hands-on because of you."

"What do you mean, because of me?"

"You're green. That's probably why I'm here. You and Abby are two of our newest recruits. I mean for special-agent situations. Myrddin probably knows this is going to be stressful. But he's right. We do need you front and center. Anabelle hasn't really polled well with humans because...you know, she can be kind of a dick. But you, people been watching you for a minute. If humans were going to pay attention to anyone, it would probably be you."

Two young women dressed in suits were waiting at the end of the hall. One of them waved Terra and Roy over. "Hi! Sorry about the lack of a welcoming party, but we're running a skeleton crew today. Everyone was pretty spooked about working today in case there was an attack."

The two women looked at each other hesitantly. "Do you think there's going to be one?" the other one asked.

Roy looked sincerely at the two women. "We've doubled our security already. In all likelihood, there probably will be. If you guys wanted a day to call in sick, I'd suggest this one."

One of the women laughed. "Yeah, sick days? In this industry? Come on, let's get you to makeup."

The two women led Terra and Roy down the hall to the makeup department. Terra prepared herself for the irritation of having someone playing with her face for the next hour. She had no idea why makeup had to take so long.

Terra was not disappointed about the length of time it took to do wardrobe and makeup. What was a welcome surprise was how much Roy enjoyed all of this. His gruff demeanor vanished once he got in front of the mirror and had two artists grooming his beard.

Roy was all jokes as he was worked over. It was the most Terra had ever seen Roy talk, let alone to strangers. He seemed to be in a great mood. "So, this is kinda your thing?" Terra asked.

"Not the television part, but I love being pampered. Do you know when the last time was that I was able to just lie back and let someone pamper me?"

One of the assistants lathered Roy's beard and started shaving it. "I've been wanting to get a shave forever now, but I hate doing it myself. Years ago, I used to go to this barber a couple blocks away from my house. Friend of my dad. He only used a straight razor, and every time you came in, he made you feel like a goddamn god. You guys are doing a pretty great job too, just so you know."

The other assistant leaned over Roy and said, "You know, we could use a straight razor."

Roy beamed, the biggest smile Terra had ever seen across his face. "Hook that shit up, friend."

While Roy had his face shaved, Terra tried to relax and enjoy the experience. She'd never gotten pampered much either. Maybe she could enjoy someone taking care of her for a bit.

That feeling vanished once one of her makeup artists asked if she wanted her eyebrows plucked. "Stick to the makeup, please. I happen to like my bushy brows."

The artist smiled at Terra. "Glad you do. They are pretty fierce."

Terra and Roy continued to be prepped. As the makeup artists took care of their work, Roy prepped Terra on a couple of talking points. He encouraged her to defer questions about policy to him. Anything relating to human efforts would be her job. "Also, I want you to know that the bit you said about orcs went over really well back at the base," Roy said. "Not a thing that gets talked about nearly enough. Glad you spearheaded that one. Which brings me to my next point. Wanted to know if you were interested in a little surprise? Some shit-stirring."

Terra's interest was piqued. "What did you have in mind?"

"I hate the idea of orcs not being able to speak for themselves, you know? Who are we to talk for them? So, Cire's here. We talked about this a little bit. If you don't mind sharing the spotlight, we could bring Cire on too."

"Wouldn't Myrddin be pissed?"

Roy laughed as he stood to inspect the suits being brought to him. "Of course he's going to be pissed. But he still enjoys the initiative. And if you're going to be the face of the human resistance, you should have a bigger role than just reading off a script. These are calls you can make."

Terra hadn't spent much time with Roy since she'd come to HQ. She was glad to see that he was such an individual. Her first impression of him was someone who followed Myrddin's rules blindly. Maybe Roy was someone she could talk to about what was on her mind. "Hey, you know Anabelle pretty well, right?"

Roy slipped on a bright pink suit jacket, casting a glance over his shoulder at Terra. "Uh, you could say that. Why are you asking?"

"She seems pretty angry with me. Or, maybe not angry. She...she just doesn't seem like when I first met her. I don't know what I did wrong, and it's kinda irritating me. But I don't know if it's just in my head. Figured you may be able to give me a little perspective."

Roy turned and took his pants off to try another fit. "Yeah, she can be a little tough to read. But she's got a good heart. When did she start acting weird?"

"A day or two before the Campbell show."

Roy laughed before checking to see if Terra was looking away before changing again. "Oh, that. I can't believe she's still being weird about that. You know she used to be a model, right?"

"Yeah, if you could even call it that. She's a fucking icon. I used to watch everything she ever made."

"Does she know that?"

The makeup artists had ducked away.

"Why would I have told her that? You think I want her to know I'm fangirling over her?" Terra asked.

"She'd be flattered. But anyway, she never got a slot on the Campbell show. And to say she's having a hard time reconciling all of her time being in the public eye versus now would be an understatement. She's having a weird-ass time. That's all."

Terra checked herself out in the mirror, content with how she looked. "Okay. I wanted to talk to her about it but didn't know where to start. Glad to hear it's not only me she's pissed with."

"No, this is about Anabelle, not you. But let me give you a little bit of advice. If you wanna get this out in the open, you're gonna have to talk to her. She's not gonna say anything."

A production assistant entered the room. "Hey, we're ready for you guys."

Roy held up two suit jackets, one pink and the other bright green. "Okay, which one do you think?"

"Are you serious?"

"What do you mean?"

"The pink would look great on you."

Roy looked at the pink suit jacket. "Yeah, that's what I was thinking."

The tone of the show was evident from the moment Terra and Roy entered the studio stage. Larry Omans and John Ashmore were waiting for them, already seated. There was no music to play either of the agents out.

The audience was absent as well, replaced by HQ soldiers. Naota and Blackwell were sitting front row, the former eating popcorn. Where he had managed to find the popcorn eluded Terra.

Terra took a seat across from Larry and John, and Roy sat beside her.

Larry and John extended their hands to Terra and Roy. "I'm glad you were able to make it here with such little warning," Larry said. "We've been dying to have you on the show since we began to see what was happening on the...what was it, orcish world? We actually have a couple of questions to ask you about just that."

Terra leaned forward, grinning into the camera. "You know, I have someone who would be great for answering any orc related questions. Cire, do you think you could come out here?"

Cire emerged from the audience, the only orc amidst them all. He went to the desk, one of the production assistants running from offscreen to provide the orc with a chair.

Larry and John looked at each other uncertainly. "Oh, we didn't realize you were bringing a guest. Uh..."

The hosts softly spoke to each other before turning to Terra and the others. "Excuse me if I'm blunt," John said, "but how are we humans supposed to trust you, given what orcs have been doing? Launching attacks. Abducting people such as Terra. I know we've been told that orcs are not all following the Dark One but there has been little to any evidence of that. Honestly, I believe you are the first orc that myself and our viewers have seen who isn't actively trying to kill every human in sight."

Cire drew in a deep breath, his face looking stern yet approachable. "The orcs were the first race to be conquered by the Dark One. We've had the most physical and mental casualties. The Dark One used us as a foundation for his army, destroying my world and culture. The few of us who remain have sworn to fight him as long as possible."

"Yes, but that doesn't—"

"The reason that you do not see more orcs is that the majority of us are dead, hollow husks used by a psychopath. There are most likely fewer than a thousand free orcs. I understand your misgivings, even if

I think they are deeply rooted in racism. But the truth of the matter is that you have not seen many orcs because there are so few of us with the most rudimentary control of our bodies and minds."

The two hosts seemed extremely caught off guard by that answer. "Okay, well, let's take this another route. We're both curious about the details of who is running everything. If Earth really is in danger, why is it that Myrddin, a private CEO of a video game company, is running the show? Shouldn't the governments of Earth be responsible for making the kind of calls that he is? What do you have to say about that, Terra?"

Terra choked on her answer. She had no idea why Myrddin was in charge of anything. "Uh, I'd like to defer that question to Roy. He's one of our heads of operations. He'd be more suited to answer this."

Roy crossed his legs as he said. "Myrddin isn't only the CEO of a video game company. He has been working tirelessly with various governments to get this threat noticed and addressed. It would be more appropriate to ask why more global leaders haven't listened to Myrddin by now. They've been given the information yet few have taken action. The war efforts would be greatly strengthened if the global community was giving this the proper attention it deserves."

Larry checked the notes in front of him. "You say it's a threat that should be taken seriously globally. Talking about elves and other fantasy races and the dangers that they are experiencing. So far, all that we've seen has been human casualties and a rogue agency making claims that none of us can substantiate. How are we to know what's true or not?"

Terra scoffed loudly. "There's an orc sitting in your studio. Are you going to tell me that this is fake?"

"No, not that it is fake. Merely that we aren't being given the whole truth."

Terra decided not to mince words. "Okay, so I'll be real with you. I don't know all the ins and outs of what is going on. But I do know that I was taken from Earth. And there was one group of people who found me and worked their asses off to get me back—the Dark Gate Angels. A human, elf, and a host of other people and races came together to save me and everyone else. You all saw the battles. There was no way I could have kept surviving there."

"Yes but that doesn't necessarily mean—"

"I was given a fighting chance. And that's all that we're here to ask for. Until people start taking this seriously, we're all just pissing in the dark, looking for a toilet. So, couch the condescending prick attitude when you're asking these questions."

"And Myrddin, this savior is the same who allowed for the lives of innocent audience members to be put in danger?"

Roy took this one. "We didn't allow anyone to be put in danger. We are fighting a war with a conniving, vicious pyscho with resources that we can't even understand. What happened was unfortunate, but we're trying for transparency."

One of the cameramen began laughing maniacally, a laugh that Terra recognized.

The cameraman leaned his head out from behind the camera and Rasputina grinned menacingly. "Please tell me you have room for one more."

Before anyone could answer, the lich disappeared in a fog of green light, appearing right beside Larry and John. "If we're going to discuss the state of the war and all of the realms, we should at least have a balanced conversation, am I right? And here you go, not letting each side of the argument be voiced. Well, come on, let's get this going? We have *so* much to discuss."

CHAPTER NINETEEN

Neither Terra nor Roy moved. They had both been expecting Rasputina to make another appearance. It would have been too easy an opportunity for her to skip up. But Terra was still uncertain as to why Rasputina was making a game out of this. The lich seemed to be doing this for shits and giggles.

Like now, for instance, Rasputina hadn't bothered restricting either Terra's or Roy's movements as she had before. Instead, she was sitting in between the two hosts, acting chummy as if she were a guest host or something. This was all a game for her, but Terra didn't quite understand why or what it was that Rasputina was playing.

Roy looked equally confused but more cautious as he watched the lich, no doubt trying to figure out his next course of action. The armed soldiers in the audience continued sitting, watching the show. Naota was still chomping on popcorn.

As Terra studied the soldiers, she realized one of the reasons everyone seemed so calm was that, even if this wasn't the plan, this is what had been expected.

Rasputina seemed to have noticed as well. She eyed the soldiers with a greedy smile before turning her attention back to the two hosts. "So, how do you want to do this? I don't want to overshadow your journalistic integrity. Should I be over here or over there."

Larry, who was keeping his cool much better than John, said, "Well, I have a few questions for you. We've been waiting to have a chance to talk with one of the Dark One's lieutenants."

Rasputina clapped her hands manically and leaned back in her chair. "Oh, this is my first interview. Hit me with them!"

"What exactly does the Dark One want from us? Why is he bringing humans into this mess that he has with elves and gnomes? Humans did nothing to him, so why make us a part of a problem that we aren't?"

Rasputina flipped over the desk and landed on Terra's lap. Terra did everything she could not to recoil from the lich and behave as though this was normal. It seemed Rasputina was less murderous when she was being indulged. "Do you know how war works, Larry?"

Larry and John exchanged glances. "Of course, we're news analysts."

"Then you know some people have things they want. That's all it ever is. Someone in charge wants something bad enough and goes about getting it whatever way they want, no matter how terrible it is for anyone else. The Dark One has a desire. It doesn't have to do with you being human or not."

"And what is that desire?"

"To remake every living being in his image. Sounds kinda interesting, right? Unlike so many gods before him, the Dark One didn't make anyone in his image. No one did, really. But he wants to fix that. He thinks you could all be…better."

Terra had heard some of this before but, though she was terrified and uncomfortable, she was still interested.

Rasputina flirtatiously ran her finger over Terra's cheek. "Do you have any questions? It seems like such a waste to only have these two asking."

"What are you doing here?" Terra growled. "Is this all a joke to you?"

Rasputina shook her head as she picked at the hole in her face. "A joke? Not at all. I deeply value the human lives I endanger. Not unlike your boss Myrddin. Did you see what he allowed to happen last time? Obviously, he must have seen how badly it polled. Couldn't waste any time getting you back on the tiny screen."

"This isn't about tv ratings."

"Oh, it isn't? You're an image, Terra. One to be wielded as inefficiently as the old man can. Did you know that I knew the guy way back when? I know the kind of person he was."

Roy sneered. "You tortured him. I'd hardly say that counts as *knowing* anyone."

Rasputina pulled out a knife and held it to Terra's face. "You've obviously never tortured anyone before." She pressed the blade against the side of Terra's eye. "There's a lot you can find out in these little moments. What they love. What's important to them. What they're willing to sacrifice to make the pain go away."

Roy moved to stand, and Rasputina clicked her tongue at him. "Don't bother. You know I could suck the life out of this entire room. We're having such a civil conversation. Why would you want to bring an air of violence into all of this? Just because we're on two different sides of the coin doesn't mean we can't try to see eye to eye."

John had finally snapped out of his frightened stupor. "What did you mean about Myrddin's ineffectiveness?"

"The Campbell show was a great example of the faults in his leadership. Even if he didn't know we were planning an attack, he could have at least prepared. He knows that I'm back and still dead as ever. Yet he didn't bother warning the studio. Or the audience. Allowing so many souls to be put in danger."

Roy interrupted Rasputina. "That's bullshit. We had enough soldiers with us to make sure that no civilians were hurt."

Rasputina waved her knife at Roy. "That's the script. You really think I didn't manage to steal one of those precious little souls. But even then, that's beside the point. Waiting for me to appear shows Myrddin's weakest point. He's a watcher. A reactionary. People start making moves, and he starts making his plans. It's going to be what gets all of you humans killed."

Terra was only half-listening to the conversation. She'd been struck by something Rasputina had said. It was a sentiment that she'd felt in the arena more than once.

Larry and John looked to be back on their game. They exchanged notes quickly. "Uh, what is your name?" Larry asked.

The lich beamed as brightly as a movie star on the red carpet. "Did I not tell you? Rasputina, my dear."

"Can we ask why you've decided to help the Dark One? Do you believe in his vision of remaking humans in his image? And if so, why?"

Rasputina laughed wildly. "Believe in his vision? No, no, I don't give a shit about that. That's the Dark One's business. Not for me. All that making-order-out-of-chaos stuff isn't really me, it's not Rasputina. Never has been."

"Wait, I'm afraid I don't understand. If you don't support the Dark One, why are you working with him? You are working with him, aren't you?"

"First off, why would you even call this work? I'm doing what I love! Secondly, maybe a better term would be working tangentially."

John shook his head, confused. "Wait, I'm sorry, but could you explain this to me?"

"Do you know what a lich is?"

John and Larry exchanged wary looks. "No, I'm afraid I don't," Larry replied.

"Years ago, I searched out the knowledge of immortality. I sacrificed everything I had to become this... Do you know why people choose this unholy half-life, this hell between humanity and monstrosity? For understanding. They think knowledge will help them understand the universe that they live in."

Rasputina stretched out on Terra, cradling the human's head in her arms like a lover's. "But the longer the other liches lived, the more exhausted they became from their search. They faded away and died their last death. But I didn't fade away. Because I found the answer. There is no understanding because there is nothing to understand. There's no meaning to any of this. None. If the Dark One wipes away humanity, in the grand scheme of all reality, it doesn't matter. He'll die one day, and the universe will keep on going. One day it'll be like he never existed."

Rasputina got up and crawled onto Larry and John's desk. She grabbed John's face. "The elves will all die off. It doesn't matter how. So will the orcs. All of existence will fade and be reborn as something unrecognizable. These small instances only matter to us."

John struggled against the lich's grasp. The skin around his face was glowing green, and his eyes were sinking into his skin. He began to scream.

Rasputina didn't release him. Terra jumped to her feet and tried to pull the lich away from John. She stared into his eyes. "We have to make them count, John, these small, precious moments. But you can't appreciate what you take for granted. If Larry lives through this, he's going to appreciate it after watching you die."

Rasputina leaned forward, her jaw stretching and clamped her fangs down on the side of John's face. She threw her head back, bright green energy flashing from her body, tossing Terra away as a shrill laugh came from her crouched body like a demon from old.

A Dark Gate opened behind Rasputina as she continued to eat and cackle.

CHAPTER TWENTY

R asputina kicked the corpse of the news anchor out of the chair. She sat in the empty seat, casually grabbed the anchor's body, and tore off one of his arms. She peeled back the coat and shirt sleeves and gnawed the skin off the forearm.

Larry, who was covered in John's blood, stared in horror at Rasputina aghast, incapable of processing what had just happened.

Both Terra and Roy were also watching Rasputina in horror as she happily devoured John's arm.

Terra wanted to get up, to pound Rasputina's face to mush, but every time she tried to move, her body refused. Rasputina wanted everyone in the crowd watching her.

The lich, face smeared with blood, pointed the bloody stump at Terra. "So, what do you think we should do now? You're the big star, right? What do you think the American people want to see?"

Terra could hardly meet Rasputina's eyes. She wanted to kill the lich with every fiber of her being. "You're kidding me? How about you let me get up, and I'll show you some ideas I have."

Rasputina laughed, which sounded like broken glass jangling against steel, the sound of emptiness and evil. "Is that how you think that would end? Are you just that tough and strong?"

Terra didn't care what Rasputina was saying. It didn't matter how powerful the lich thought she was. Terra would kill her and make her pay for all the harm she had done this day.

Larry was crying softly, his hands in his head as the lich took another bite of John's arm. "Why are you doing this?" he whimpered.

Rasputina hit Larry with John's blood stump. "Didn't you listen to anything I said before? There's a lesson in all of this. Look at Terra. All you humans lined up at your televisions every day like you were watching divine moments with god. Why? Why? Why! Because she's strong. You see her strength and forget that you all are actually tiny, weak, insignificant creatures. A strong wind could kill most humans. But you forget that. And when you forget how weak you are, you start to think you might be powerful. Or that you matter. I'm just here to remind you all. Wouldn't want you lying to yourself."

The lich tossed the piece of John at Terra, who flinched, trying to move. "But you look at Terra now, and she doesn't seem that strong to me. Couldn't even save your friend. Everyone in the room just sat here and watched. Not that you didn't want to. There was just nothing for you to do."

Roy struggled, trying to get to his feet. "We aren't weak! You're just a psychotic bitch who thinks she knows how the world works."

Rasputina jumped to her feet, motioning for the cameraman to follow her. The cameraman zoomed in as Rasputina kicked Roy out of his seat and stomped on his face. She grabbed the camera, focused it on her face, and laughed. "Hello, folks out there in TV-land. Did you see what happened to the big, strong man? And these are the people who are supposed to save you?"

The lich took Roy's seat, smacking her lips and licking the blood from them, her eyes a bright, lively green against her pale, dead skin. "Come on, tell me what you think everyone wants to see. Obviously you! They didn't tune in for me. But what do you want to give them?"

Rasputina ran her knife along Terra's stomach. "Do you want to show them your guts? Maybe that way they'll really believe in you."

"Terra's a hero. Nothing you say is going to make us stop believing that, you freak," Naota shouted.

Rasputina stared out into the crowd. "Freak? You say freak? Come on, you. Come on." She walked over to the crowd and grabbed Naota, dragging him onto the stage. She tossed him next to Roy. "You all think you're so...good, don't you? That's where you think you have meaning. You see someone like me and think, oh, look at that monster. How could she have done that to herself? But you're all just waiting. You only need a little incentive. Get up. Come on, get up."

Naota, now released from the lich's control, stood. He looked around for a moment, trying to figure out if this was a trick.

Terra believed wholeheartedly it was. The lich could have freed her instead. It might have been a fairer fight, but the lich had picked someone she knew could easily be dominated, just like she had done with John. "Don't play with her, Naota. This isn't a fight—"

Naota didn't listen. He ran at the lich, fists raised. He threw two jabs to her face. Both of them connecting. The lich didn't even register she'd been hit. "You're all violent people, cutting down waves of orcs. And I'm the monster? How many people have you killed, my dear boy?"

Naota hit the lich again. "We're nothing alike. This is a war. We're—"

"And what is a war? People killing people. You're all little pawns for big things happening in the universe. But you don't think of the lives you take. You tell yourself that they're under mind control like they don't still have families or friends. You make them... Actually, let me show you."

Rasputina struck Naota across the face, bringing him to his knees. She grabbed his head between her hands and looked him in the eye. "You ever feel someone's soul leaving their body?"

Naota tried to look away and Rasputina redirected his head, shouting, "Look at me! Have you?"

Naota shook his head.

"Then I'll show you."

Rasputina's eyes glowed bright green, and the light shot into Naota's eyes. The young man tried to flinch, but Rasputina straightened his head. He screamed, and tears rolled down his cheeks.

The light went out, and Naota fell limp. "That's what you do when you kill," Rasputina hissed. "All of you soldiers."

Naota shook his head, tears still streaming. "If we don't defend ourselves, all of us will die."

"You don't get it! It doesn't matter! Take you and...that one!"

Rasputina pointed at Blackwell. "He obviously cares about you. You. Get over here."

Blackwell flew over to the lich. "You don't have to be under mind control to get a little crazy."

The lich grabbed Terra as well. "Why don't you join our little social experiment?" She tossed Terra on the ground and straddled her. "Encouragement is all you need."

Green light poured from the lich's eyes and skin into Terra's, bathing Blackwell and Naota in the dim, unearthly eeriness.

The studio melted away, and all Terra could see was the green. She felt it crawling up inside her, digging into her skin, worming its way into her brain.

Naota was standing over her dead body, his hands wet with her blood. The image disappeared. Terra was walking down a crowded street.

Blackwell entered the street, holding a machine gun. People were running around and screaming as Blackwell gunned everyone down.

Image after image, Terra watched Naota, Roy, and Blackwell commit atrocities upon her and innocent people. She felt her stomach turning as the lich cackled on top of her, but Terra didn't hear the lich's laughter. All she could hear was the screaming of innocents at the hands of her friends.

Abby woke up and rolled out of bed, landing on the floor and staring at her shoes for a bit.

Martin's voice caught her off-guard. "Do you want me to help you with that?"

Abby stared at the ceiling, thinking about how much she had missed seeing it. "Help with what?"

"The waking up thing. I could jump-start your endocrine system and get your adrenal glands pumping. Should wake you right up."

"Sure, go for it."

The fog of sleepiness hanging over Abby vanished. She felt like she'd just had a cup of coffee minus all the jitters. "Yeesh, your human bodies are so touchy," Martin muttered. "Never seen a computer take so long to boot up."

"Hey, how did you do that?"

"Wake you up?"

Abby went to the sink in her bathroom and rinsed her face. "No, access my glands. Never said you could do that before."

"Ooooooh, well, your body's changing with all these nanobots. First it was just your blood, and then they started multiplying. Then I tried to keep them from multiplying. There was kind of a revolt, and they gained sentience and merged with your nervous system. Oh! And I merged my consciousness with them, and that caused them to kinda commit suicide, and I guess I died for a bit, but it all worked out, and now I'm integrated into your nervous system."

Abby expelled a deep breath as she tried to process what Martin had just said. "Okay, that was a lot. You're saying you have control over my body?"

"Not hardly, but I do have the ability to regulate your unconscious bodily functions. Heart rate, eyes drying out...you know, that kinda crap."

"Martin, I told you that if there were any changes going on that I wanted to know about it as soon as it happened!"

Martin sounded embarrassed when he said, "I did tell you as soon as it happened. That was twenty minutes ago. For one, I think I handled the possibilities of all your bodily functions shutting down quite well, especially for it being my first time."

Jeez, the little guy sounds like he's learning how to be sensitive.

Abby had been about to start brushing her teeth, but she paused to say, "Sorry, sorry. Didn't mean to hurt your feelings. Thanks for making sure I didn't die. Don't want to take you for granted or anything."

"It's nice to be appreciated once in a while. I'm only constantly improving your quality of life. Oh, and you have a bunch of messages from Anabelle and Myrddin. You might want to take a look at them. They're pretty urgent."

Abby spat and wiped toothpaste off her mouth. "I'll check them in a little bit. I'm on vacation, remember?"

Next, Abby imagined what outfit she wanted to wear, and her nanobots covered her in a pair of jean shorts and a baggy hoody. Then she went downstairs, where her mom was standing in the kitchen, watching the television.

"Morning!" Abby said.

Abby's mom jumped. "Sorry. I didn't know you were up," she replied, though her attention remained on the screen.

"Anything for breakfast?"

Ma still hadn't turned to look at Abby. Whatever she was watching on television must have been very interesting. "Don't worry about it. I'll make a couple of eggs. You like them scrambled, right?"

Abby's mom nodded as she leaned over the television.

Abby grabbed a couple of eggs from the fridge, cracked them in a bowl, threw some pre-cut garlic in, and got to stirring. "Whatcha watching?"

"This talk show your pa and I used to watch. It's...very disturbing today."

Abby hadn't heard her mother talk about her pa since he passed. Anytime the two of them spoke, Abby tried her best to steer the conversation away from that. Her heart still jumped at any mention of him, but she was tickled to hear her mom and dad used to watch talk shows together. For years, he'd sworn he hated them.

The smell of cooking eggs filled the room. Abby wasn't much of a cook, but she knew how to make eggs. "What's so messed up about it?"

"There's this...zombie woman. She just killed and ate someone."

Abby only half-heard her mom. The idea of a zombie on a talk show was ridiculous. It could be a little funny, but it sounded like that anti-comedy crap her sister liked. *Really? A zombie eating a host?*

"Is it funny?"

Ma answered as if she were in a daze. "No, it's really fucked up."

Abby dumped the eggs onto a plate and brought them over to her mother. "Language, Ma." She placed the plate beside her mom's hand and glanced at the television.

Rasputina was looking into the camera while Terra, Blackwell, and Naota writhed in pain in the background. "Been waiting to see you all morning, sweetheart," the lich growled. "You're looking unbelievable scrumptious."

Abby screamed as she backed away from the television.

Ma turned the television off and said something, but Abby didn't hear her. She was looking at her HUD, reading through her emails. Anabelle was already on her way to collect her.

The image of Rasputina had scared the living shit out of her. She knew the lich had been talking to her. There was no mistaking it.

Abby hit her comm and called the elf. "Belle?"

Anabelle answered instantly. "You see that what that fucking psycho is doing?"

"How long until you get here?"

"About twenty minutes. Myrddin gave me a teleportation spell. One-time use, but it'll get us into that television studio, and we can put a stop to that fast."

Ma murmured under her breath, "Oh, my God."

Abby turned to see her ma backing away from the television.

Rasputina dragged Naota and Blackwell to a window overlooking the city, the camera crew following her.

Terra watched what was happening. She'd been released from Rasputina's mental spell. She still didn't know where she was, but when she looked at Blackwell and Naota, she was filled with an overwhelming desire to bash their heads in.

Rasputina kicked the window, shattering it out into the open air. She knelt and looked at Naota and Blackwell. "You see, all you two need is a little push." She clicked her hand, and the green fog in both of the human's eyes lifted.

Blackwell and Naota stared at each other for a moment. The hatred in their eyes was the same as what Terra felt deep in her bones for the two of them.

Naota moved first, lunging at Blackwell. Blackwell was too fast, though, and he scrambled around Naota, getting him in a headlock. He tried to choke him, but Naota head-butted him.

As the two former friends tried to murder each other, Terra could only watch. She felt like they both could die, but something in her told her that was wrong.

They shouldn't be fighting. Not like this.

Rasputina approached the Dark Gate that appeared earlier. She snapped her fingers, and the portal opened. "You see, you're all just waiting to kill each other. I'm only speeding up the process."

As the Dark Gate opened, there was a bright flash across the room. Abby and Anabelle walked through the portal.

Nanobots covered Abby's body as her armor encased her, and she blasted Rasputina with a plasma shot.

Rasputina went flying as Anabelle rushed to Roy's side and helped him up.

Blackwell and Naota were still fighting.

Naota had gotten the upper hand, and Blackwell was backing up against the open window. Suddenly, Naota kicked Blackwell in the chest, sending him flying out of the building.

Terra saw Blackwell heading toward the window in slow motion as the orcs were beginning to pour from the Dark Gate. Her body reacted before she knew it.

Whatever feeling she had about Blackwell dying, it wasn't hers.

She was already on her feet, running toward the window. She grabbed the compact exo-suit, slamming it to her chest, and it stretched out and connected to her spine.

Terra jumped out of the window and held her arms close to her sides to make herself more aerodynamic. It didn't take her long to catch up with Blackwell. She wrapped her arms around him and held him close.

Tucking her body into a ball, she held Blackwell close to her as they hit the ground.

Terra lay there for a moment, Blackwell beside her. The suit had saved them.

Blackwell peered at her, his eyes confused. "What...what's going on?"

"Why would Naota kick you out a window?"

Blackwell shook his head. "What the fuck is going on?"

Terra stared up at the building as a fireball shot out of it. "I don't know, but we're going to fucking find out."

PART II

CHAPTER TWENTY-ONE

The news show studio was filled with pure chaos. Orcs poured out of the Dark Gate as Anabelle helped Roy off the ground and tried to move him out of the room.

Abby was at her side, firing at the orc attackers, and at last, the marines seated in the audience finally broke free from their spell.

As the marines gathered, drawing their weapons to join the fray, Rasputina, the Lich, stood from behind the desk where she'd been knocked onto the floor. Half her face was missing, though the bones were re-stitching themselves fast, while her worn and rotting skin grew over her wounds.

Rasputina ran at Abby, who boosted her thrusters and soared back. She fired shot after shot at the lich, who dodged them with ease, her eyes emerald and hungry.

As Rasputina closed in on her, Abby constructed a small thermal grenade using her nanobots. Martin's voice rang in her ear, informing her that she was using less than two percent of her nanobots.

Abby hovered in place, drawing the lich in. And when Rasputina lunged, jaws wide open to take a bite out of her, Abby plunged her grenade into the lich's throat. She fired another plasma blast, tossing the lich away as Anabelle shouted for the marines to retreat.

Abby followed them, the agents and the marines ignoring the Dark Gate. When she was certain the last marine had left, she detonated the grenade, and the studio went up in flames.

Anabelle was herding the marines, one of whom held Larry, the host of the show, whose face was still pale with shock. The elf also supported Roy, who appeared ready to pass out, his eyes dancing wildly.

"We need to get out of here and on the ground," Anabelle instructed.

The elf led the marines down the hall, toward the windows through which Terra had jumped.

Anabelle blasted the windows open with a flash of lightning from her hands. "Everyone out!"

The marines leapt from the window, tossing grappling hooks out to make their descent easier. They all wore exo-suits and were moving at above-average speed.

Abby flew past them, searching the streets for Terra.

She spotted her lying near Blackwell, curled into a ball on the wreckage of a car. As Abby approached, Dark Gates started opening inside the buildings all along the city block, the way they had when the lich had risen from the ground.

Terra sat up slowly when she spotted Abby flying toward her. "Aren't you supposed to be on vacation?"

Abby landed beside Terra and helped her and Blackwell to their feet. "Not looking like a good time for a vacation. What happened?"

"Rasputina decided to stop by for another interview. She gets worse and worse every time I see her. She's a fucking nightmare."

Abby looked around at the Dark Gates shining in the windows of the nearby buildings. "What do you think is going on?"

Anabelle ran up to the trio. "We need to get to the control room ASAP. Whatever is happening, we need to have a plan."

Abby and Terra stared at the elf, both confused. "What control room?" Terra asked.

Anabelle pointed at the sky. Above them, a massive floating aircraft carrier shimmered into existence.

Abby whistled as she stared at the carrier. "Whoa, this is going to be big, huh?"

Anabelle nodded as she scanned the area. Marines were already heading to the carrier, which had launched tractor-beams to lift the troops to safety. "Full-scale invasion," Anabelle said. "Come on. Let's get you inside and get you up to speed."

While the DGAs hurried to the carrier, Roy and Blackwell were glaring at each other, their eyes filled with hate. Unlike Terra, dispelling the mind control would take some time with the two men. Whatever Rasputina had done to their minds had been more powerful than what Terra had experienced.

Or maybe Terra was more resilient. Anabelle wasn't sure.

The carrier beamed them up. Abby wondered what Anabelle meant by "full-scale invasion." No way things had escalated that quickly.

Guess I'm going to find out.

The control room was a smaller, modified version of the war room at HQ. A holoprojector sat in the middle of the room, surrounded by chairs for agents or VIPs. Creon was already there, waiting for the DGAs and the other special agents to arrive.

Abby's face armor peeled away when she saw Creon. The goblin smiled and waved. "Good to see you," he called.

Anabelle strode past the goblin and took a seat, the one Myrddin would have taken had he been present.

Blackwell, Roy, and Naota were still staring at each other like rabid dogs as they took their seats.

Abby watched them, confused by their strange behavior. "What's up with the dudes?"

Terra, who had taken a seat beside Anabelle, explained how the lich had invaded their minds, forcing them to watch their friends committing horrible acts. Terra admitted she wasn't sure why she'd been able to shake off the psychic attack when the other three hadn't.

Anabelle chimed in. "It's because of your will. We all saw it back in the arena. I don't know many other humans who could have willed themselves to be as strong as you. Definitely not these three. You're on a whole other level. Might even have a stronger will than the lich."

The elf pointed at the three men. "You all need to handle your shit. I don't have time to babysit you, and I will not have you attacking each other until this gets figured out. You understand?"

Roy rubbed the side of his temples as he cleared his throat. "Yeah, got it. I'll hold it together."

Blackwell and Naota muttered a similar response.

Anabelle turned her attention to the holomap, which displayed a grid of the buildings around their immediate location. "Long story short, we're in a fucked situation. At best, we thought this would be a repeat of the last time Terra made a public appearance. We were prepped to put heat on the lich, or on Grok if either showed up. We weren't expecting this."

Abby raised her hand. "What exactly is *this*?"

The holomap changed, revealing the interior of the studio. Glowing spots dotted the Dark Gate where the machine had begun to heal itself.

"You were right when you said this was too similar to what happened before. I commed Creon, and he pulled up a scan showing how many Dark Gates are opening up. Almost four times more than before. We can only assume this is another kind of ritual."

Terra leaned into her chair as she released a deep sigh. "Ritual for what? The Dark One already summoned an undead, immortal, pretty all-powerful, lich. What the fuck else could he bring out here?"

Anabelle swiped through a couple of options on the holoscreen. They were all terrifying. "You don't read a whole lot of fantasy, do you? Realistically, I have no idea what they're summoning. It's not a type of magic people often use anymore because of how unpredictable whatever is summoned can be. Look at the lich. The Dark One obviously summoned her to help him with his army, but she seems much more content doing her own thing."

"So, you're saying they might be trying to summon something else the Dark One can't control?" Abby asked.

Anabelle sat in her chair as the holoscreen returned to a map of the city. "I'm saying we have no idea what the fuck will come through whatever portal that lich opens up."

Abby groaned. "So, the Dark One and this lich are going to open up a...what? A super Dark Gate?"

Anabelle shrugged. "Your guess is as good as mine."

"Also, I've played DnD. A lot of it. The only way to kill a lich is by destroying its phylactery, right?"

Another shrug. "In theory. But this lich is older and more powerful than anything I've ever heard of. I'm guessing that means all bets are off. All I do know is the Dark One's forces will arrive through those Dark Gates. Hundreds of them. Grok is probably coming too. So, we need a plan."

The control room was silent as everyone mulled over possible options. Finally, Roy spoke. "We look at what we know. The Dark One never just throws enemies at us. He's strategic. I'd bet he will release a heavy ground- and air-force. You say this looks like a summoning? Let's look at what we know you need for a summoning."

The humans in the control room stared at each other, dumbfounded. "I'm going to assume from your silence that none of you know anything about this," Roy said. "So, let me break it down. To summon anything from another plane of reality, you need to perform a ritual. A ritual had to be performed just to break the lich out. Seeing as the lich seems to be the magical arm of the Dark One at the moment, it'd be safe to assume *she* will be the one performing the ritual.

"If I was going to have one of my most powerful agents performing a ritual, I'd be doing everything I could to keep us away from them. That means the Dark One's forces will probably be more interested in pushing us back than attacking us. Which puts us at an advantage."

Abby considered Roy's theory. "Wait. If the lich is as powerful as Myrddin said, why would the Dark One need to protect her?"

Anabelle raised three fingers. "One, maybe she's not as powerful as we think. Two, the ritual might need to remain undisturbed until completed. Three, she's more vulnerable than usual during the summoning. Any of those reasons are good enough for me."

The door to the control room opened and Cire entered. "Those are all reasonable assumptions."

Anabelle stood and crossed her arms. "I'm sorry, but did you receive clearance to be here?"

Cire sat beside Terra. "The human world is under attack. If you really want to take this chance to play bullshit politics, be my guest. But I came here to fight the Dark One, if that's all right with you."

Anabelle smiled and relaxed. "You're a shaman. What can you tell us?"

"The lich is a creature of immense magical power. She won't waste her time summoning something small. And she's already mentioned multiple times that she has no care for life. Whatever she summons, will be similar. An elder one, perhaps. Regardless, it will be a labor-intensive ritual. Which means you will have time for an attack."

Abby watched Anabelle consider their next move. She was happy the elf was the one heading up this mission and not her. It would have been impossible for Abby to tell where to start. But Anabelle seemed more ready for this than anyone else in the room.

The elf checked the holoscreen, which showed more Dark Gates opening. "There's too many for us to close. This is going to be full-scale. Thank God, Myrddin had most of the city's businesses shut down for the day. Scrambling to make sure humans don't get caught in the fallout would have made this so much worse. Here's what we're going to do."

Anabelle outlined the plan for the squads. Abby would head an airborne team of marines on hoverbikes. Their main mission was to keep the skies clear and destroy any Dark Gates on the nearby rooftops. Secondary focus was providing backup to the ground troops when possible.

Terra and Cire were given their own squad of ground troops to command—much to the orc's surprise. They would lead the first advancement, breaking through any blockades erected around the location of the ritual.

Roy's mech was on its way, and he would be leading another advancement of the bulk of the marines from the other end of the block.

Blackwell and Naota were sitting this one out. Anabelle still didn't trust their heads to be in the right place.

Creon would be monitoring the overall state of the battle, providing support with the carrier's artillery when possible.

"Any questions?" Anabelle asked.

"Yeah. When do we move out?" Terra asked.

"When we see the lich. None of the Dark Gates are active yet. If we make the first move, we lose our advantage. So, we wait for them. Then we go on the offensive. Martin has Abby's drones scanning the area for visual confirmation."

They all watched in silence as the feed from Abby's drones played over the holoscreen. Abby wasn't sure how long they'd been watching, but the tension was real. She gasped when the lich finally showed up on one of the screens, limping down the street, clutching a book to her chest.

Anabelle snapped her fingers. "There we go. Now we wait for her to set up shop. Then we roll."

CHAPTER TWENTY-TWO

Rasputina did not take long to select a location for her ritual. The team watched her wander cheerfully through the financial district of New York, as though she were a tourist. Her tattered face twisted into a grizzly grin as she gave herself a tour of the desolate streets.

The new Dark Gates hadn't opened yet. Anabelle and Roy discussed the best places for deployment while everyone else watched the screens, waiting to see how the battle would start.

Abby studied Rasputina's image on the holoscreen. There was something almost child-like about the way Rasputina went about her business. Abby had seen that purity before a few times in her life. Watching the twins play, and once when she had observed a litter of wolf cubs playing with the carcass of their prey.

It was unsettling, to say the least. Abby had been briefed on what Rasputina had done on the talk show, and she had watched some of it herself. She couldn't understand the reasoning behind most of what Rasputina had said. The lich had made no sense.

Even if everything was meaningless, how did it mean you had the right to wipe away whatever you wanted?

"Something on your mind, kid?"

Abby looked toward the source of the voice. Terra was waving her over to take a seat beside her and Cire. Abby was glad Cire had joined the mission. Since the orc had returned to the base with Terra, Abby had accepted that her blind hatred for the orc race had been misplaced. Orcs hadn't taken her father away from her, the Dark One had.

Abby and Cire had shared many long conversations late into the night when she found herself wandering the hallways of HQ, unable to sleep. Cire was almost always awake and willing to sit and talk for a while. Sometimes Abby would only listen. The orc enjoyed talking about big ideas, concepts she didn't often find herself pondering. Terra would sometimes join them if she were awake.

Abby sat between Terra and Cire. "You okay after everything that happened?" she asked Terra. "That all looked...pretty horrible."

Terra's laugh was harsh. "I feel like shit, to say the least. Whatever Rasputina did...it felt like she was cracking my head open. I saw things I didn't want to see. And it's still hard to unsee them. But I'll be okay. That shit just did not feel normal."

"What do you think about all that crap Rasputina was going on about?"

Terra flinched as she prepared to speak. She fidgeted in her seat. "Doesn't mean anything. They're just words."

Cire was watching Terra closely as she spoke. He put his hand on her knee and squeezed tight.

Terra's eyes watered, and she pitched forward, pressing her head into her hands. "I can't get that shit out of my head. Fuck!"

Everyone in the room turned at the sound of Terra's outburst. She stood awkwardly and cleared her throat. "Just need some space for a bit."

Anabelle shook her head. "I'm sorry, but we don't have the luxury of that right now."

"Fuck you, man. You didn't see what I saw. Look at how messed up everyone else is!" Terra pointed at Blackwell, who was sitting across the room from Naota. Both were covered in a layer of sweat and looked like they were ready to pass out.

Anabelle cleared her throat and moved closer to Terra. Her gaze was stony. "Step out with me."

Terra returned the stare but followed as Anabelle walked out of the control room. She leaned against the wall and folded her arms as the elf stared at her silently.

After a long moment, Anabelle coughed and studied her feet. "Okay, this isn't easy for me to say, but I've been kinda shitty to you."

"Wait. Are you serious?"

Anabelle finally peeled her gaze away from her feet. "Yeah, so, I'm trying to say I'm sorry. For that."

Terra shifted her weight from one foot to the other. "It's okay. Things have been stressful."

"Yeah, they have. And I don't want to do that catty shit. I'm not good with all this relationship stuff. But you're my friend. And we have a potentially devastating battle conveniently looming in the immediate future. So, I want to be an adult about this. We're DGAs. And I need you with me on this. Abby, Cire, and you are the only people I can rely on to get the job done. Roy is out of it. So are Blackwell and Naota. We need to take care of this, and I can't do it by myself."

Terra grabbed Anabelle and embraced her, squeezing hard enough that the elf gasped for breath. "Shit, man, I didn't think you were going to drag me out here for a Hallmark moment."

"I can't breathe, Terra."

"Is it because you're filled with so much love?"

A voice squeaked from inside the control room. "Uh, could I have a hug too?" Abby poked her head out.

Terra beckoned her to join them. Anabelle scooped Abby between her and Terra and squeezed as tight as she could. When she dropped Anabelle and Abby, the girl was crying. "Yo, kid, what's wrong?"

Anabelle began to put her hair back into a bun. "Goddess. I didn't bring you out here so we could start having a therapy session. Someone needs to be watching the screens." She headed back to the control room, ruffling Abby's hair as she walked by. "You're strong, Abby. Remember that."

Abby was fighting back tears as she nodded in agreement with Anabelle. Then she looked at Terra, searching for the right words. "Can I talk to you about, I don't know, all that stuff Rasputina said? About everything not mattering. What if she's right? What if everything we're fighting for is meaningless. Like, people just die, and that's all. And there's nothing you can do about that."

Terra didn't answer for a while. "You're talking about your dad, aren't you?"

Abby wiped away her tears as she chewed on her lip, struggling to speak. Terra grabbed the child and held her close. "He mattered to you, which means he mattered. Maybe life is meaningless, and there's not a point to any of this. You really going to trust the opinion of a half-dead demon monster who eats people alive, on the matter? Fuck that. What we're fighting for matters. I'd rather be alive and fighting for my freedom than dead. This matters to me."

Terra released Abby and stared into the girl's eyes. "You're a smart, kind, and strong young woman. You matter to me. That orcish hunk in there with those baby eyes? He matters to me. Even that rude-ass but surprisingly sweet elf is important to me. That's the whole reason we're fighting. And we all need to remember that. Rasputina is just some Joker knockoff. Anyone can spew that shit."

Abby laughed as Terra shoved her toward the control room. "Yeah, yeah, she *is* kinda derivative."

"She probably watched *The Dark Knight* like a thousand times before she made her TV appearance, practicing in the mirror and shit."

The pair returned to the control room, where Creon, Cire, and Anabelle, were watching the holoscreen. "It's starting," Anabelle said. "Get over here."

Rasputina had found a suitable place for her ritual. She was at the base of the Empire State Building, drawing a pentagram that stretched from one street corner to the next. Candles appeared around the pentagram, while a Dark Gate emerged at each point. The lich stood in the middle of the magic circle and opened her book.

All at once, the Dark Gates around the pentagram began to open.

Anabelle assigned the gates to the different squads to focus on. Then she split Naota and Blackwell up, sending them to separate holding cells on the carrier. Five marines escorted them both out of the control room.

"If everybody is finally tired of sitting on their asses, let's get going," Anabelle said.

Abby and Terra followed the elf as they headed toward the exterior level of the carrier, where the aerial team was waiting for Abby.

Anabelle ran through their orders one more time. Abby would lead the team of hoverbikes, eliminate any threats in the sky, and shut down as many gates as possible.

Terra would drop with Abby's squad, using a set of jet-packs Creon had developed. She would push through any defenses protecting Rasputina's location.

Anabelle would take another squad and flank Rasputina. From what they had seen through Abby's drones, their approach would encounter a strong resistance on both sides of the lich's position, but it would be possible for their team to shut the summoning down.

At least two hundred marines were waiting outside for their squad leaders. Abby hadn't seen this large a force for any of their previous missions. This was going to be a big battle. She was glad Myrddin had had the forethought to prepare them for this.

Abby's armor flowed over her body as she approached her squad. They were all equipped with exo-suits and jetpacks. They sat atop one of Creon's new creations: hoverbikes he had reverse-engineered from the Dark One's tech.

Martin said, "I'm having the drones continue with their recon. They haven't been spotted yet. That should give you a little bit of an edge. I can tap you directly into their feed, or let you know when something important is happening. It's up to you."

Abby thought it over. "You can handle the drones. If they get into trouble, get them out."

Then Abby turned to her squad. She was still uncomfortable commanding her own team, but she'd realized that if she didn't display some kind of confidence, her squad would feel worse, which could lead them to make mistakes. And any screw-ups could result in the deaths of members of her team. "Squad C. You know our mission. Don't bother trying to stick with me. Stay together, and if you're in any trouble, let me know. Keep comms open on all channels."

Abby leapt off the carrier, her thrusters activating as she soared toward the closest building their intelligence team had pinged as containing a gate.

Terra glanced at Anabelle, her face smug with pride. "She's turning into quite the commander."

Anabelle smiled as she watched Abby speeding away. "Yeah. She really is."

Suddenly, a voice tore through the minds of all the DGA agents and marines. Abby stopped midflight and scanned the city block for the source. But it only took one word to identify the speaker.

Rasputina.

"In your darkest home, your silent insanity, I call to you, I call to you. Child of eyes, giver of knowledge, you who lay dreaming, I call to you. Let us see, let us see your dreams of wild fantasy. Wake, my father, wake my mother, wake my love to our fading dream. Fill us with your eyes. Fill my mind with sight. Sleeping Child of Beyond, I ache to be seen."

The lich chanted the words incessantly, and they rumbled within Abby's mind making it hard for her to think. "Martin? Is there something you can do about this?" Abby asked.

"Already talking with Creon about it. He's working on using your HUDs as a way to block it. I can handle this for you, though."

Rasputina's voice cut out, and Abby's mind was silent again. Abby wasn't waiting for anyone else. She flew toward the Dark Gate that showed up on her HUD. Within moments, she spotted the gate on the top floor of the building ahead.

Abby burst through the window, hovering in place as she fired at the Dark Gate, blowing it to pieces.

A plasma blast hit her in the back, sending her tumbling through the air. Her feet touched the floor and she skidded a few yards back, cursing herself for not scanning the room for enemies before she entered.

Rasputina's chanting had thrown Abby off. There was something unsettling about her words. They had crawled into Abby's head and, though she couldn't hear the lich anymore, she could still feel the chant.

Abby boosted to her feet, zeroing in on one of the orcs hiding in the darkness. Before she could say anything to Martin, her eyesight adjusted, allowing her to see the heat signatures around her. A pair of orcs were holding a massive cannon, and Abby could see the energy fluctuation as it charged up.

She soared forward and tackled one of the orcs. When he dropped the cannon, she spun around and fired at the second orc who had leapt toward her with a plasma ax. Abby raised her arm, the nanobots quickly constructing a shield to block the blow.

Looks like the Dark One finally decided to upgrade his basic-ass tech, Abby thought.

She fired at the orc as she fell backward. She rolled to her feet and slammed her hands together, forming a small cannon. She fired a thin ray of plasma that surged out the side of the building and spun about, slicing through the room.

"How are my power reserves looking, Martin?" Abby asked as the orcs in the room sank to the ground.

"Solid so far, but you might not want to keep performing stunts like that. You'll drain yourself too fast, and you'll have to take a while to recharge. Not too long, but it won't be a good idea in the middle of a firefight. Since the nanobots multiplied, you have more energy, but it's not infinite. Try to play it safe."

"Sounds good," Abby said as she blasted off, looking for the next gate.

CHAPTER TWENTY-THREE

Terra's troops were on the ground floor with Cire and roughly forty marines. These guys weren't the same caliber of soldier Terra had seen at HQ. They also wore slightly different uniforms from the marines Terra was familiar with. Their faces were hardened, and they looked like they had seen some shit.

The plan was to push through the defenses surrounding Rasputina. Terra hoped they had moved fast enough to ensure they reached the lich before the orcs fortified her location.

When the orcish forces had begun to exit the Dark Gate, Terra had hit the ground running. She had a vague idea of where the orc troops might position themselves, but real-time spatial strategy on a large scale was something Terra was a little new at.

That didn't make Terra any less excited.

The rush of the fight was getting her blood pumping. Which was good because it meant her exo-suit would be able to push her strength further. Creon had made some improvements to it in Abby's absence. Hopefully, it could boost Terra to her strength-levels from the arena.

A plasma shot came from above, and Terra dove forward as the marines split up, taking cover. "We got contact!" Terra shouted.

At the moment, the orcs up ahead had the high ground. Anabelle had assumed the orcs would attempt to take the fight to the streets, but it appeared the elf had been wrong.

The marines returned fire as Terra tried to pinpoint the location of the shooters. She could see the glint of a Dark Gate in the building to her left. A cluster of orc snipers was positioned there, laying down suppressive fire.

Though Terra preferred melee weapons, she'd been given a plasma rifle. It was a practicality. For now, she grabbed one of the grenades attached to her belt. She felt her heart thumping as her exo-suit beefed her muscles up. Then she pitched the grenade as hard as she could at the fourteenth-floor window hiding the Dark Gate.

The grenade broke through the glass and rolled inside the room. Back on the street, Terra hit the remote detonator.

Balls of fire shot from the window as two orcs were blown out of the building. "Just two," Terra whined. "I was hoping for more."

One of the marines turned to Terra. "Most of them probably hit the ground. Left those two up there to pick us off."

"Makes sense. We keep going forward. Keep your eyes on the windows."

The squad resumed their approach, the marines on the far edges of the formation watching for movement in the buildings around them. They progressed down the street until Terra raised her hand, signaling for them to stop.

Four mountain trolls stood in the middle of the street, surrounded by dozens of orcs, some on hoverbikes. All were strapped with plasma rifles, upgraded plasma-swords, and shields. Terra also spotted goblins, many armed with dual plasma-daggers.

Terra slung her rifle off her shoulder. "Guess this is the first wave, huh? I call the trolls."

One of the marines looked at Terra aghast. "*All* of them?"

"Yeah. Four trolls seems reasonable."

The marine shook his head. "Damn, lady. We heard you were crazy, but I didn't think you were *this* crazy."

Abby soared above Terra's location, giving chase to a band of orcs riding hoverbikes ahead of her. As she flew over them, she fired, blowing one away with a massive, arcing plasma-blast.

Terra snapped her fingers. "Fuck. Guess I'll just have to settle for three. Let's go." She slammed her hand to her chest, and Cire, who was by her side, did the same. They rushed at the platoon up ahead.

Terra leapt through the air, soaring toward one of the trolls. She slammed into the troll, tackling it to the ground as the other two stumbled away.

Cire raced for the goblins. He kicked one in the head, snatched its dagger, and threw it into an orc nearby. As a plasma blast came at him, he grabbed a goblin as a shield, which was obliterated by the explosion.

The marines were firing at the orcs, forcing them off the street, toward cover. Hot plasma filled the air as Terra wrestled with the troll.

Another troll picked Terra off its compatriot. Terra wrapped her hands around its elbows and forced them upward, snapping the bones in its arms.

Terra dropped to the ground, turned and slugged another troll before a third grabbed her by the throat and slammed her into the concrete.

The wind went out of Terra. Her heart was leaping for joy, though. This was a real fight. She rolled over and grabbed a plasma ax abandoned by one of the fleeing orcs.

A plasma blast whipped past Terra. Another sped toward her, and she sliced through it with the ax. "Oooooh, this is a toy I can get behind."

Terra ran at the troll who had attacked her last. She sprang into the air and slammed the ax down on the orc's arm, slicing clear through the limb.

"How have I not had one of these ever before?" She glanced over her shoulder at Cire, who was fighting six goblins simultaneously. "Have you tried the plasma ax? This thing cuts through bone like butter."

"No. Trade you!"

Terra tossed her ax to Cire, who threw two daggers at her. She glared at the daggers, disappointed. A troll distracted her by punching her in the face, and she soared into the air and landed a few feet away.

The two remaining trolls lumbered over to Terra. Once they were close enough, Terra leapt to her feet and jumped onto one troll's shoulders, driving the daggers into its chest. She kept hacking and hacking at the troll's chest until it fell to its knees. "Hm...not too bad."

Terra pushed to her feet, covered in blood as she stared down the remaining troll. "I could get used to these."

Anabelle proceeded along the streets of New York, her squad flanking her. She hadn't brought any weapons with her, though she had changed into her HQ suit, thick black tactical armor with DGA emblazoned on the chest.

While she walked, she focused her mana, drawing in as much as possible from the world around her, a technique she had only recently rediscovered through her rigorous, often fruitless, meditation. Mana was everywhere. All she had to do was tap into it and pull it within her body.

Anabelle hoped it would be enough. It would be stupid to assume Grok wasn't going to show up. She was probably leading one of the many platoons.

Where the hell is everyone? It wasn't as though the Dark One's forces bothered to create elaborate plans. All the Dark One's efforts so far had simply been shows of brute strength. Grok was capable of more, though. And the Dark One was leaning into using Rasputina.

Anabelle wasn't too worried about what the lich would summon. The DGAs had already fought off a Jotun, and that was a demi-god. They'd survived the lich as well, and what could have been worse than either of those?

Up ahead, a group of orcs raced across the street. One of the orcs cast a glance toward Anabelle and her squad.

Anabelle commed Roy. "Hey. How you doing on getting that mech ready?"

Roy's voice came through loud and clear. "Should be dropping down in a bit. Any good spots for me to get some action? Not that kind of action, just so you know."

Now was not the time to be flirting.

"There's hardly anyone in the streets. I was expecting a full-on army keeping us from Rasputina, but it looks like they left us a wide-open path."

"Obviously, a trap."

"That's what I was thinking. We're going to take it slow. Check the tact-map before you get out here, but that's all you."

Next, Anabelle patched into Abby. "Hey. You got any reads on the orcs down here?"

Abby answered quickly enough. "Terra's engaged on the other side of the city. Didn't see anything 'round you, though. Why?"

"Think you could do a quick sweep?"

"Kinda busy right now, but I'll see if I can make my way over."

A sonic boom pulsed somewhere in the sky. Anabelle looked up to see Abby speeding toward her, an orcish hovertank in close pursuit of her.

The elf clicked her tongue. "Huh. Probably should have looked up to see how busy you were."

Abby descended, spinning to fire at the tank.

As the girl zoomed closer, Anabelle drew her mana to her lower body and leapt upward, soaring over Abby and the tank. She pulled the mana to her arms and slammed her fist into the tank.

The sheer force of Anabelle's mana stopped the tank in mid-flight, its steel casing reverberating from the kinetic force.

Abby zoomed to the side of the tank and opened fire, peppering it with small plasma shots that tore through the metal. As Anabelle dropped to the ground, Abby said, "Looks like there's a battalion to your front. There's a blockade. Grok is there."

"Where else would she be than right where I want to go?"

"Hey, at least you have a super rival or something."

Anabelle raised her eyebrow at Abby. "A rival who wants to kill me. How does that sound like something anyone would want?"

Abby shrugged. "I don't know. Sounds like it would make things interesting, at least. All I got to fight is grunts."

A ferocious roar silenced both DGAs. Above them, the marines on hoverbikes were being pursued by an elegant yet terrifying silver dragon. Abby whistled as she stared at the beast. "Well, looks like I at least get a dragon. Can't be worse than wrangling a bull, right?"

"You've wrangled a bull?"

Abby shrugged. "Wrangling a bull can't be much harder than a pig, I figure."

"Get out of here and kill that dragon."

Abby hovered a few feet above the ground and saluted Anabelle. "You got it, Big Boss Belle."

"Don't call me that."

Abby blasted away, heading for the dragon. Anabelle motioned for the marines to follow her as she went ahead to meet the battalion. And Grok.

Anabelle realized she'd seen the orcs running in the opposite direction from where Abby had said Grok was waiting. She was glad she'd asked Abby. That little piece of information had helped her squad to avoid being flanked by Grok and her orcs. Granted, they would be moving in the opposite direction to Rasputina, but that was better than being jumped from behind.

As Anabelle turned the corner, a rocket came flying at her. She threw up a shield and deflected the attack.

Grok was sitting on the roof of a tank, smiling widely. Orcs, trolls, and goblins surrounded her. There were at least five tanks, the tech more advanced than anything Anabelle had seen at HQ.

The orc leader reloaded and fired again. Anabelle deflected the rocket with ease, and Grok laughed. "Didn't think you were ever going to show up, knife ears," Grok shouted.

Anabelle instinctively touched her pointed ears. "What the fuck are you talking about? You have sharp ears, too."

Grok jumped off the tank and sauntered toward Anabelle, who

was walking briskly to meet her. "The difference is, I don't care. *I* wasn't the one pretending to be a human for a hundred years."

Anabelle felt her mana spiking, and she continued to pull it from everywhere around her. For the first time since she'd met Grok, she wasn't afraid. She was excited. "Goddess. You talk so much shit. I'm going to enjoy breaking that jaw."

Grok tossed her rocket launcher away as she pulled out a plasma sword. "Where's the scared rabbit I saw last time? The timid little elf afraid to do anything other than rely on her little Pathway tenets?"

Anabelle let herself go. The final Path, that of the Lost.

Her skin broke apart, her whole body becoming nothing more than mist. The haze rushed ahead, catching Grok off guard, and reforming behind the orc. Anabelle slammed her hand at the orc, energy crackling in her palm.

Grok turned, raised her sword, and caught the energy ball. Anabelle tried to force it down Grok's throat, the elf's eyes bright and flaming.

The spheres of energy exploded, sending Grok skidding across the ground.

As the smoke swirled, it combined with the thick, blue mist, reforming Anabelle's body. She solidified and exhaled smoke.

Grok smiled widely. "Ah, little rabbit. You are a worthy kill now."

The elf and the orc ran toward each other as the marines and orc troops opened fire around them.

Between the two battling factions, Rasputina sang and swayed in rhythm to her own song. But the music was not merely coming from her lips. The sound of a million voices rose from a place within and outside of time and space. A blackness that was nothing more than a cage for that which could not be spoken of, but always was.

A pair of orcs sprinted to Rasputina to report the situation, but they could only stare as the lich floated into the air, her skin healing, her body aging in reverse, her patchy, hairless scalp blooming with deep auburn hair.

She hovered above the pentagram, her dress flowing around her as if it were nothing more than the breeze, and the orcs had been invited to see the wind for the first time.

As the orcs watched, their eyes bled, but neither noticed. All they could pay attention to was Rasputina floating through the sky as her dress fell to the ground, her body contorting in bizarre formations, twisting in ways a body should not be capable of.

The sky darkened as clouds gathered.

Rasputina's maddening cackles could be heard everywhere, as the lich lay suspended in the air. Her eyes beamed green lights into the darkened sky as though they were a pair of maddening beacons.

Beneath her, the orcs fought each other, their hands wrapped around each other's necks. And in the next moment, they fell to jabbering and speaking in tongues, prostrating before Rasputina and her wild dance.

A few blocks away, Terra stopped dead in her tracks, as did everyone else. A collective shiver ran down their spines, and they turned to stare at each other, confused as to why they were fighting in the first place. Not because they didn't see the point in the violence, but because, for a brief moment, something else filled their minds, a bigger thought, if one could call it that.

The feeling passed quickly, as though it had never happened.

Across from Terra, Cire impaled an orc with a plasma ax. He cut his way over to Terra, who was staring up at the sky, watching Abby weaving in and out of orc forces as she was chased by the silver dragon. "You see, it's like everyone else gets all the fun shit sometimes. Those trolls were nothing."

Cire fired his plasma pistol, killing a goblin who had been sneaking up on Terra. "Did you feel that?"

Terra glanced over her shoulder at Cire. "Feel what?"

"The lich is nearly done with her ritual. We need to get to her and stop this."

Terra nodded and commed Anabelle. "Hey. Cire says that this shit is about to go off. Any idea how far away you are from the lich?"

When Anabelle answered, she was out of breath. "Don't know if I can make it. I'm kinda tied up right now. You and Abby will have to make the push."

Terra could hear Grok screaming in the background. She was glad Anabelle sounded like she was handling the orc better than she had the last time.

Now Terra turned her attention to the lich, shouting to the marines, "Let's clean this shit up and get going."

As the marines began to make their final push against the orc platoon, Terra patched into Abby. "Hey, kid. We gotta get to the lich. You think you can hurry it up and meet me there?"

"How about I meet you where you're at, and you give me a hand?"

"Like a dragon hand?"

"Exactly the hand I'm looking for."

Terra scanned the street until she spotted two plasma axes. "Bring it to me!" Terra shouted.

Abby was coming around one of the buildings, trailed by the silver dragon. She flew between an explosion as two fighters slammed into each other. Abby cleared the smoke and flames, speeding toward Terra while the silver dragon shot blasts of lightning at her.

Abby whirled, flying backward as she fired at the dragon.

Terra bounced from foot to foot, excited at what was about to happen. She didn't notice the four orcs in the windows of the buildings around her, nor did she see them line up their rocket launchers on Abby as the girl glided between the buildings.

The orcs fired in unison.

Abby was struck by four rockets simultaneously while a second group of orcs fired a net that stretched between the two buildings.

Abby slammed into the net, still on fire from the rockets. The silver dragon collided with Abby, and they tore through the net and crash-landed together.

Terra watched as Abby skidded across the ground, her nanoarmor retracting from the shock, blood pouring from a deep cut in her stomach.

Terra rushed to Abby as the dragon struggled to pull itself free from the net. "Holy shit, Abby. Are you okay?"

Abby sat up with Terra's help and pressed her hand to her stomach. "Just a minute," she mumbled. "A minute to heal. Can't armor…"

Abby passed out.

Terra lifted the girl's shirt to inspect the wound. She could see the nanobots working to stitch Abby up.

Cire came up on Terra's side. "Is the child okay?"

"She's hurt, but she'll be back up soon enough. Guess I get the dragon I wanted. Let's go show that thing why it doesn't fuck with my friends."

CHAPTER TWENTY-FOUR

Anabelle and Grok were fighting up and down the street while the marines and orcs attempted to stay out of their way. The elf was doing a better job of keeping up with Grok this time around. She could feel her mana flowing freely, and she was able to pull as much as she needed from the orcs around her, sapping some of the orcs' strength to keep from tiring out.

And beyond that, the fear was gone. Each attack Grok threw at Anabelle failed to fill her with dread. She took her time with the fight, thinking through every move, rather than remaining on the defensive of Grok's onslaught of attacks.

The orc was still sticking to her original fighting tactics. Hard, fast, and relentless. Anabelle could see why. It was difficult for Anabelle to land any strikes. Or at least it had been.

Now, it was Anabelle's turn to put Grok on the defensive. Whenever the elf needed a breather, she would dodge, turn into mist, and recombine a few feet away, or behind the orc.

The fight took on the nature of a dance. Anabelle felt it as her movements flowed and she played off Grok. She could tell the orc sensed it as well. The pair engaged in a violent waltz, fighting to see who would lead, competing to see who the better partner was.

Grok's fists charged with mana, and she swiped at Anabelle, who threw up a shield and slipped in close to Grok. The elf swung her fist upward, only for Grok to grab her by the wrist and fling her aside. Anabelle's heels slid across the ground, and she couldn't help but wonder if they were trying to hurt each other at this point.

The fight felt more like her early sparring matches. Testing technique against technique to see which would break an opponent's guard. And Anabelle was most definitely trying every move and skill she'd learned. And, rather than merely relying on her elemental magic, she was using a combination of all three Paths. Slipping into the shadows when available, disintegrating and reforming her body, managing her mana with short bursts of violence.

In many ways, the elf was the true opposite of Grok. Anabelle moved in a calm and measured way, reacting to what was in front of her, and attempting to come up with a solution.

But, as the elf had already admitted to herself, Grok's fighting style didn't need any improvement. The orc possessed the stamina and the mana-control to deliver bone-crushing blows—something Anabelle was well aware of. She had seen Terra take an uppercut from Grok in their last fight and had wondered how the human had managed to get back to her feet so quickly.

Grok rushed at Anabelle to close the distance, barreling into a marine. She ripped the rifle from the man's hand, surged into the air, and slammed the rifle down on Anabelle, who simply heated her hand with white-hot energy and sliced through the rifle with ease. The orc wielded the two halves of the rifle like clubs, attempting to beat Anabelle over the head with them.

Anabelle stepped away, deflecting both of Grok's attacks before jumping up, her feet bursting with ice energy as she kicked the orc in the chest. The connection was solid, and ice spread across Grok's chest and to her feet as the elf guided the energy. Annabel froze Grok in place as the orc stepped back.

The elf took her shot, pulling as much mana from Grok as possible. She redirected the energy to her fist and slugged Grok in the face with all the power she possessed.

Grok's eyes bulged, but she didn't go anywhere; her feet were frozen to the ground.

Now it was time for *Anabelle* to be relentless. As the orc fought to break free of the ice, the elf pounded her face in repeatedly.

The strain of attacking with mana while also trying to keep her prior attack from unraveling turned out to be too much, and keeping it up any longer would tire her out before the fight was over. She dissolved into mist, reforming beside a rifle as the ice melted from Grok's foot.

Anabelle kicked the rifle up, caught it, and fired at Grok, peppering the orc with plasma blasts. She hoped a few full-on blasts would be enough to eliminate the orc.

The smoke cleared, and Grok was standing, breathing heavily, a thin shield of mana covering her body. "Nice one, knife ears. Didn't think you had it in you. Where's all this coming from? The first time I fought you, I was worried the Travelers had picked a whelp incapable of defending herself."

Anabelle released a deep sigh. She was tired. This amount of mana usage was costly. She was technically able to keep from running out, but her body would punish her for it. Maybe Grok knew that and was drawing the fight out for that reason.

Grok straightened her spine and smiled before cracking her neck and stretching. "Looks like I can really let myself go." The orc closed her eyes.

Anabelle could feel Grok's mana rising dramatically. *By the gods. She has this much power?*

Anabelle felt like she was looking at an infinite pool of magical energy. "Confusing" wasn't the right word. Grok had barely used magic. The most Anabelle had seen had been simple manipulations of her strength and speed. Was Grok going to use all that mana just for physical means? That would kill her.

As Grok's mana continued to rise, Anabelle could see her muscles tensing and flexing.

Grok took a step forward, and the ground shattered under her foot. "I've been waiting a long time for this. To look upon the final

Traveler and know that they have the strength to finally test me, to let me see how strong I truly am."

Anabelle felt a twinge of her old fear. This fear had initially scared her. "You don't hate the Travelers, do you? They never did anything to you. You don't really give a shit about them."

Grok took another step, and the concrete beneath her exploded. "One enemy is as good as another, as long as they're strong enough."

Grok surged forward, and her elbow connected with Anabelle's chest. Anabelle felt her entire body explode with pain as she gasped for air. Grok leapt up, whirled, and slammed her foot onto Anabelle's head.

Anabelle managed to shield her upper body with mana, keeping Grok's attack from breaking her neck. For a moment, she considered running. But she wasn't going to give Grok the satisfaction. Instead, she turned, preparing to attack.

Grok was gone.

Anabelle whirled, and Grok's fist hit her in the head. She felt the mana traveling through the orc's fist and into her skull. The elf soared backward and crashed into a nearby building.

She tried to sit up, but her body refused to move. *At least I have a good view of the battle. Looks like we're winning.*

Grok hadn't bothered to walk over to Anabelle. She was staring off in the distance, unconcerned with the elf, or the battle around them. "I'll be damned. She actually did it," Grok muttered.

Above the city, the sky was turning black. Anabelle felt a distinct sense of dread, but she didn't know why. It was as though the feeling had been inserted into her accidentally, and then it had vanished.

Grok turned her attention back to Anabelle. "If you survive this, we'll finish where we left off."

A Dark Gate opened behind Grok, and she walked through it, leaving her forces behind.

Anabelle released a sigh of relief. "Ugh. Live to fight another day." She struggled to her feet as an orc ran at her. She raised her hand and let loose a stream of fire, scorching the creature. Then she commed Terra. "What the hell is happening?"

Terra sounded shaken when she replied, "Cire says the ritual is nearly complete. I just gotta get through a dragon, and I'll be at Rasputina."

"A dragon?"

"Yeah, we're kinda having a pretty epic stare-down right now. How are things on your end?"

Anabelle scanned the block. Her marines had the upper hand, and they could easily make their way to Rasputina. Even more so now that Grok had been polite enough to leave. "Should only take a couple of minutes. Abby with you?"

"She's a little banged up, but she should be good."

Anabelle was already limping in Rasputina's direction. Above her, the sky had returned to normal. "Hurry up. We gotta stop this quick." She hung up and then punched in an order to the other marines. "Finish off the orcs and make your way toward the lich."

Terra and Cire stared the silver dragon down as it roared and spat sparks of lightning.

"What's the plan?" Cire asked.

Terra shrugged noncommittally. "I was going to punch it until it was dead. That sound good?"

"That is a working plan."

Terra ran at the dragon, Cire following closely behind.

The dragon sprang forward. As Terra and Cire got closer, the creature turned, whipping its tail around and catching Terra with it.

She grabbed the dragon's tail and held on for dear life. The wind had been knocked out of her, and she needed a second to catch her breath.

Cire ducked and managed to avoid the attack. He brought his ax up into the dragon's neck, but the plasma blade wasn't strong enough to cut through.

The dragon dove to snap Cire up in its jaws, and the orc dodged to the left. Lightning crackled around the dragon's body.

173

The sparks traveled along the dragon's spine and electrocuted Terra, but she didn't let go. She gritted her teeth and fought through the pain. Once the lightning had passed, she started crawling up the dragon, who seemed to have forgotten her in its attempt to deal with Cire.

Cire lunged, closing in on the dragon's head. He swung his ax and hit the dragon broadside across the face, stunning the creature. Another pulse of lightning flowed through the dragon, this time catching Cire in its wake.

The orc slumped forward, stunned. He was leaning against his ax as the dragon's maw opened, and a blast of lightning hit him square in the chest.

Cire soared through the air, hitting a car near Abby, who had two marines watching over her as she healed.

Terra, still clutching the dragon's tail, screamed with rage and leapt into the air. She slammed her fists into the dragon's spine.

The dragon screeched and slumped over to the side for a moment before regaining its composure. It rolled over, catching Terra underneath its bulk as it leaned close to her, its mouth open.

Terra grabbed the dragon's jaws to keep it from biting her. She stared into the creature's mouth as it began to charge up its lightning. Terra either had to wait for the dragon to fry her, or she had to release its jaws and risk electrocution.

Cire was picking himself up when Abby stirred. She was speaking under her breath. "What am I at right now, Martin?" she muttered. "Eighty percent? Internal bleeding? Now…okay, stitch me up later. Let's go."

Nanobots rolled over Abby's body, covering her in armor. The thrusters on her back fired and she rocketed toward the dragon, slamming into the side of its head, her hands glowing with charging plasma blasts. She fired again, the bursts tearing through the creature's jaw.

The dragon reeled away, giving Terra the opportunity she needed. She leapt up and grabbed it by the throat, slinging herself over its neck. She pulled down as hard as she could, wrestling the dragon to the ground. "Let 'em have it, kid!"

As the creature opened its mouth, roaring in pain, Abby slammed her hands together to form her massive plasma cannon. The charge whirled loudly, and she fired. The blast plunged into the dragon's mouth, tore through its body, and ripped out its backside.

The dragon slumped over dead.

Terra looked at Abby. "We need to get to the lich. Fast."

Abby scooped Terra up in her arms. "All right, then. We'll get there fast." Her thrusters went off, and she sped down the street.

Terra and Abby zoomed around the corner. Abby stopped suddenly, and Terra toppled out of her arms.

Rasputina was in the middle of the block, floating above the pentagram.

Across the block, Anabelle had just arrived, followed by her marines. There was a platoon of orcs, along with a balrog, between Anabelle and Rasputina.

Terra whistled loudly. "That's probably gonna be a hassle to get through."

Abby didn't answer. When Terra looked at her, Abby was gawking at Rasputina. "Is she...naked?" Abby asked.

Terra shoved Abby. "You're not allowed to get a crush on someone who's trying to kill us and destroy reality as we know it."

"I don't have a crush. Just ain't something you see every day. You think Belle's going to need help?"

As Abby asked this question, a loud whooping echoed over all the comm. Roy's mech fell from the sky, landing on top of the balrog. The marines screamed in response and charged the orcs around the fallen beast. "Finally found a good landing spot. Holy shit. Is that Rasputina?"

Anabelle's voice came over the comm. "Could you pay attention to our mission?"

"Yeah, yeah. Just caught me off guard. Don't think I've ever seen that before. Pretty weird."

Rasputina's cackle cut off the conversation. She laughed as she dove to the concrete. She collided with an intense force, her body lying flat, leaking thick green fluid from parts of her body she had busted open.

Abby's face scrunched. "Fuck, that's nasty."

"Did she just kill herself?" Terra asked.

Anabelle, who was on the other side of the block, fighting through orcs and goblins, shouted, "You could go and check instead of sitting around blabbering about it!"

"You don't have to be a dick about it."

The marines behind Terra and Abby were approaching Rasputina's body. As they drew closer, the lich's laughter started up again. She lurched off the ground, her body moving as though controlled by a puppeteer, bones broken, arms akimbo. "Open all of our eyes! Let us see!"

The ground split open, a chasm gaping wide and terrible. The marines stopped in their tracks, as did everyone else.

Black flames shot up from the broken ground, and a putrid smell billowed out, the stench of millions of bodies rotting for an eternity. A cry came from deep within the souls of all who watched.

What came forth did not come from the shattered earth. Nobody would have seen how it manifested. It was unlike the opening of the portals that had accompanied the lich's arrival.

There was a moment in time when the space was empty. And then a moment in which it was filled.

And that which came forth, the creature the lich had summoned, was a thing of horror, one who had not walked within the realms of mortals since the elves were but children, still forming the basics of their language. For language had been necessary to describe the horror that pulled itself into existence while the lich laughed, and while the sky rained blood.

A womb was the simplest description of such a thing. A placenta that writhed and pulsed in the middle of the city block. A horrid screeching emanated from the womb as it expanded, a heart beating beneath the thin layer of bleeding skin.

All watched. Orc, goblin, and human alike. Many of the marines and orcs screamed, incapable of comprehending what they looked upon.

When the placenta burst, it sent waves of amniotic fluid pouring down the street, catching human and orc alike in a tidal wave of fetid fluid.

A god was being born. That which was dead and sleeping was now awake and living.

Something slithered out of the deflating sac. The thing was growing rapidly, its tentacles spreading out as its liquid skin began to solidify.

"I've seen this before," Abby murmured.

Terra was staring at the grotesque pile of tentacles and eyes, all opening in the same moment, all staring about and rolling, as though peering into a world unseen by those who now beheld this obscene abomination.

"Where?" Terra asked Abby.

"The shard...the liquid in the shard. I think it's the same stuff...I'm getting the same readings."

The mass of tentacles and open eyes began to take shape. A chaotic pile of slithering life, moving incessantly as though incapable of remaining in this realm. It grew larger and larger, a screech bursting forth, a sound none but the lich had ever heard. Such a noise would drive the weakest minds to the brink of insanity, and already, humans and orcs were turning upon each other, slaughtering without reason, without discretion between friend or foe.

Abby grabbed Terra with one arm and Cire with the other, and she surged into the air. Across the street, Roy raced to Anabelle. He slowed only long enough for the elf to jump on top of the mech before he sped to Abby and the others.

The five were perched on a building above the chaos in the streets as the Elder God before them took its final shape: an almost humanoid creature, body covered in eyes, three heads protruding from its neck, each opening its mouth to reveal gums and throats lined with more green eyes.

Leathery wings spread out, showing hands pushing against the skin. Its bottom half was a mass of writhing tentacles.

"It's like Persephone's arm..." Abby murmured.

The Elder God towered over the tallest building, its tentacles tearing up the ground.

Anabelle sighed as she leaned her head back. "How the fuck are we supposed to stop *that?*"

There was a flash of bright light next to Anabelle, blinding everyone.

Myrddin appeared at the elder's side. He sighed softly. "So, it seems she was successful. That is unfortunate."

"What the hell are you doing here?"

Myrddin conjured his wand. "It takes a god to kill a god."

CHAPTER TWENTY-FIVE

The DGA and Myrddin watched as the Old One stumbled through the city, lumbering along as though still getting accustomed to its body.

Abby couldn't believe what she was seeing. Nor did she want to continue looking at the creature. The sight of it made her head swim and felt like she was going to fall off the side of the building. "How are you going to stop something that big?"

Myrddin studied the Old One. "Huzmurrth is one of the youngest of the Old Ones. Weaker than the rest. Rasputina probably didn't have the supplies, or time, to perform a ritual to summon one of the stronger ones. I can manage this one as long as we can strike before it solidifies fully."

Anabelle shook her head in disbelief at the monstrous being tripping over its own tentacles and smashing into the building beside it. "It's like a giant baby."

"For now. A half-hour or more, and it's going to be a rampaging monster hellbent on chaos."

Terra waved a hand. "Uh...I'm just gonna throw it out there. That thing is already rampaging. Pretty effectively, too. It's been like thirty seconds, and it's already destroyed two buildings. New York is going to look fucked up after this thing is done with it. Oh! Is anyone else getting major *Ghostbuster* vibes? You know, like when they accidentally summoned Zuul."

Abby and Anabelle stared at Terra, their faces blank. "Do you really think *now* is the right time to be playing eighties' movie trivia?" Anabelle asked.

"I am of the opinion that a joke here and there helps ease the tension of constantly being in danger of dying. But, hey, that might just be me."

Roy poked his head out from his mech. "I'm with you, Terra. Heavy *Ghostbuster* vibes. So, Myrddin? What's the game plan?"

Myrddin pointed at Rasputina's pentagram. "There's no way she's going to leave without watching the destruction. She's baiting us right now. Waiting for a fight, knowing full well you'll only be able to choose one: her or Huzmurrth. She probably thinks you'll choose her, hoping it'll destroy the Old One."

Anabelle, along with everyone else, was avoiding looking at the creature. "And you're saying that's not going to work?"

"No. The ritual is done. Huzmurrth is awake. Fighting Rasputina will only waste time and allow Huzmurrth to grow stronger. But Rasputina must be exhausted. Summoning something this powerful, no doubt, took a lot out of her. I assume her body reverted to its former liveliness."

Abby nodded, blushing slightly as Terra jabbed her in the side. "Yeah, she did. She got much younger."

"When a lich uses most of their power, they revert to the appearance they'd held moments before losing contact with their soul. She must have been only a few years older than you, Abby. No more than twenty, or twenty-one. And she believed she was already at her peak."

Anabelle was tapping her foot impatiently. "Okay, cool history lesson, but what are we going to do about this? Feels like we're kinda wasting time."

Myrddin pointed his wand at Huzmurrth. "I will handle the Old One if you can make sure Rasputina doesn't interfere. Then I will deal with the lich."

The DGA members stared at Myrddin, shocked.

"You were serious? You think you can take that thing by yourself?" Anabelle asked.

Myrddin unbuttoned his suit jacket and loosened his tie. "If I cannot, you can say I told you so at my funeral." He waved his wand and floated into the air. Then he vanished.

Anabelle crossed her arms as she pouted. "He knows how badly I want to gloat over his casket. And there he goes, sucking the fun out of even that."

The elf peered over the edge of the rooftop. "Who's ready to go beat the shit out of a sleeping old lady?"

Terra pumped her fist as she prepared to jump off the side of the building. "I have been waiting to smash this lich's face in since we got here."

Anabelle went to Abby and gently placed a hand on the girl's shoulder. "How about you? Ready for this?"

Abby nodded. She was still a little frightened of what the lich could do to her. But she wasn't going to let her fear get in the way of doing the right thing, which was supporting her team. "Yeah, let's fuck her up."

Privately, Abby reached out to Martin. "Hey, is everything healed up yet?"

Martin answered quickly enough. "Yep. You're running a hundred percent again. Try not to get stabbed this time. Or at least, if you do, not in the same place."

"Yeah. Because I'm really making it easy to get stabbed in the gut."

"Just saying. It's been twice in two weeks."

"How are my power reserves?"

Martin hummed for a second while he checked. "You're looking like you're overclocking a little bit. You could stand to burn off some nanobots. So, if you want to get creative, or a little crazy, now would be the time. I'll set a bare minimum to hold onto so your suit doesn't go out or anything."

"Good. Maybe we can finally finish this lich off."

Anabelle clapped and turned to the DGA, Cire, and Roy. "Myrddin wants us to distract the lich. I say we try to end her. If she's as weakened as he suggested, let's throw everything we have at her. Let's go."

Anabelle jumped on top of the mech, and Roy leaped toward the lich. Cire climbed onto Terra's back as her muscles bulged, and she leapt to the building across the street, before sliding down the exterior, her hands tearing through steel and glass. Abby's thrusters fired, and she took off after her fellow warriors.

Myrddin appeared in front of Huzmurrth. His suit was glowing white, as was his skin, shining a light on the swirling green bleakness of the Old One. "Huzmurrth, Toppling Mass of Insanity. I hail you, the All-Seeing Madness."

The Old One stopped walking, its many thousands of eyes shifting to look upon Myrddin. The air around the Old One turned rank, the scent of death and decay.

Myrddin didn't back down. He raised his wand, light shining from its tip. "This is not your realm. You do not belong here, and I humbly beseech you to return from whence you came."

A bubbling sound rose from the Old One as its flesh jiggled and contorted. A voice, ancient and loud, sounding as if it were the beginning of life itself, answered in a pagan tongue unspoken in the realm of mortals for nearly a millennium.

Myrddin understood what had been said. He had hoped this would have gone better. "I will ask you one more time! Please, return to your home. This world is not yours yet. You have no servants here. It was only a lich that summoned you. No one here sings your songs, nor do they wish to."

The voice came forth again from the Old One, this time like thousands of blasting horns, almost throwing Myrddin out of the sky. But the wizard held on.

Slowly, the eyes of the Old One turned from the wizard as Huzmurrth the All-Seeing Madness began to lumber onward, its skin reaching out in violent thrusts, attempting to snatch up anything around it.

Myrddin hadn't wanted it to come to this, but he had assumed it would have to. An Old One hadn't been reasoned with since the Mad Prophet had retired. Myrddin hadn't assumed his negotiating powers concerning these eldritch abominations was anything on par with the Prophet. *The least I can do is give him a warning,* Myrddin thought.

The wizard raised his wand high, and a bright flash of light went off, yet it grew brighter until it seemed as though a miniature sun had just been born into existence on the skyline of New York.

Huzmurrth recoiled, its skin reaching out and covering its multitude of eyes as a grating screech sent Myrddin's skin crawling.

"Go home, Huzmurrth."

The Old One wheezed its ancient language once more as hands burst from its skin and darted at Myrddin.

Fingers and bones wrapped around the wizard as the Old One started chanting a spell in his foul, dead language. Myrddin struggled against the force of the being but could do nothing as he was held in place.

The chanting grew louder and louder, and Myrddin stared at his hands, which were disintegrating in front of his eyes. He continued to struggle as his body burst into flames, his skin turning to ash and floating away in the wind.

Huzmurrth dropped Myrddin's bones, and they were caught up in the mass of tentacles slithering over New York's streets.

The wizard's skull rolled onto the street, stopping beside the remains of a car. His wand fell next to the skull. The wand glowed brightly, and white light shot out of the skull's eye sockets.

The eyes on Huzmurrth's back opened, watching the light.

Myrddin's body reformed from ash and dust. The only indication that he had been attacked was the faint layer of dust on his shoulder, which he promptly brushed off.

"If you insist on fighting, fine," Myrddin growled. The wizard raised his wand. "Incinerate."

An explosion the size of a small nuclear bomb went off, engulfing Huzmurrth in flames.

The DGA and their teams were closing in on Terra when they saw the explosion from afar. Buildings were simply gone afterward, and a cloud of smoke rose into the sky, followed by a shockwave that nearly toppled everyone over.

"Was that Myrddin?" Anabelle asked.

Roy watched the smoke. "Guess the old man thinks this is serious. Come on, we need to hurry before Rasputina notices their fight."

They booked it down the street until they reached Rasputina, who was sitting in the middle of her pentagram, her robe hanging loosely from her body. She looked up at Myrddin's agents, her hair hanging over her rapidly decaying face.

"Didn't think any of you were going to make it here. Glad to see you brought the whole family."

Rasputina's eyes flashed bright green when she spotted Abby. "Ah, and *you* came as well. Not one to let the terror get to you, are you?"

Abby ignored the lich, trying to remain focused.

Rasputina moved to her feet slowly, swaying as if she were going to topple over. "Do you like what I've done with the place?" she asked as she gestured to the ruins of the city. "It's amazing what a couple of chants and a bit of paint can do to liven up an area."

Anabelle moved ahead of the other DGA members. "We didn't come here to listen to more of your B-level bad-guy bullshit." Mana flowed to Anabelle's legs, and she darted at the lich.

Abby and Terra glanced at each other, surprised. "Guess we don't need a plan for this one," Abby said.

Terra cracked her knuckles and then took off after Anabelle. "Hit her with everything we got. Looks like the plan to me."

Anabelle fist connected with Rasputina, her knuckles hitting the lich's face, and cracking her jaw.

Rasputina's eyes blazed emerald, and two bolts of green light shot out. Anabelle barely managed to move out of the way.

As the elf stumbled backward, Terra came up behind her, leapt through the air, and sliced her plasma ax downward at the lich. Rasputina raised her hand, shot a shard of bone out, tore it free, and used it to deflect Terra's attack. Terra landed and sliced at the lich, pushing her back.

Abby rocketed behind Rasputina, stopped abruptly, and launched a charged-up plasma blast.

The lich ducked, her green eyes flashing before she loped toward Abby on all fours, her jaw stretching open, her tongue dragging across the concrete. As the lich leapt at Abby, Cire tackled her in mid-air.

Rasputina hit the concrete and rolled smoothly back onto her feet. She straightened before firing four bone shards, which Cire narrowly avoided.

Anabelle and Terra were both on Rasputina, flashes of fire shooting from the elf's hands as Terra swung her ax. The lich backed away, dodging each attack until she jumped into the air, a green orb of energy forming in her mouth. She fired it at Anabelle and Terra.

Before the blast could hit, Roy bounded over to Anabelle and Terra, knocking them out of the blast's path.

Abby fired a concentrated beam of plasma that hit the lich in the side. Then she swung the beam, cutting Rasputina in half.

The top portion of the lich's body floated into the air while her intestines plopped onto the ground. Then her innards suddenly waved about as though they had a mind of their own. They stretched out and wrapped around Anabelle's throat as the lich's torso clawed its way toward Abby, cackling as green slime oozed out of her.

Roy's mech landed in front of Rasputina. He slammed the mech's dragon claw onto the lich's head, over and over, pounding her into the ground.

Rasputina lay there, still for a moment. Then her body dissolved into green sludge, sliding underneath Roy's mech and reforming the lich's entire body on top of the mech. She reached into the hole in her side and broke off a rib that stretched and sharpened into a long dagger. Then she drove the dagger into the mech's cockpit, attempting to cut Roy out.

Terra soared through the air and dropkicked Rasputina. Cire, who was on the other side of the mech, reached up and grabbed the lich by the hair and threw her through the air.

Anabelle leapt up and punched Rasputina in the face with her electric-charged fist. As the lich hit the ground, Anabelle focused her mana and covered her in ice, freezing her in place. "End it, Abby!"

Abby had already combined her hands into a plasma cannon. She'd also constructed four additional cannons on her shoulder. All the tech she could spare was going into this battle.

Roy was also powering up his mech's missiles and cannons. He nodded at Abby, and they fired simultaneously.

Anabelle leapt out the way as Rasputina was hit with Abby's and Roy's attacks.

Off in the distance, there was another explosion and shockwave.

When the smoke cleared over Rasputina, there were only bones. Terra walked over to them and stomped them to dust. Then she helped Anabelle to her feet. "That wasn't so hard," she said, laughing.

Anabelle bent over, breathing heavily. "Pish. Speak for yourself."

There was a flash of green light that blinded everyone. When they could see again, the lich was standing in the crater that had held her bones. She shook her shoulders as she bobbed her head. "Now, that was impressive. Truly."

Terra threw her arms up in the air. "You have to be fucking kidding me!" She pulled out her other ax and ran toward the lich, and Anabelle followed suit.

The elf swung at the lich, who ducked and blocked Terra's attack. Rasputina knocked Anabelle away, grabbed Terra's arm, and bent it backward, snapping her bone in two.

Terra screamed and stumbled away, cradling her broken arm.

Cire roared and charged Rasputina as Anabelle approached from the other side. They both met the lich at the same time. Anabelle shifted into mist, forming again behind Rasputina. She put the lich in a full nelson as Cire prepared to hack off her head.

Rasputina headbutted Anabelle, then leapt to her feet and kicked Cire in the chest.

Roy's mech was heading for Rasputina and was only a couple of feet away. It bounded through the air, opening its mouth to fire another round of missiles.

Rasputina sprang upward and shot a spear-length shard of bone out of her palm. She tore it free, and drove the spear through the mech, narrowly missing Roy's body.

The mech slumped to the ground, and as Rasputina walked lazily past Cire, she tossed a knife into the orc's chest.

Rasputina was towering over Anabelle, who was pushing herself to her feet. The lich grabbed Anabelle by the throat and peered into her eyes. "I am going to tear your soul from your body," she growled as she pressed her lips to Anabelle's ears. "I'm going to feed on you for a thousand years."

Rasputina's eyes glowed, and green mist poured out of her body and wrapped around Anabelle.

Anabelle's skin shriveled, and she started aging rapidly.

A plasma blast hit Rasputina in the back. She glanced over her shoulder at Abby, whose hand was still smoking. Anabelle also looked at her hand, which was covered in liver spots and wrinkles. But the condition reversed as soon as the lich let her go. Whatever magic Rasputina used did not last. One's life energy would return...provided they survived the lich's attack.

Rasputina dropped Anabelle and turned to face Abby. She pulled another knife from the open hole in her chest. "Oh, Abby. My sweet, sweet, Abby. Did you think you were going to kill me?"

Abby shook her head as she fired again. "No. But I ain't gonna to sit here and let you hurt my friends."

The lich laughed sharply. "Let me? Goddamn, you are adorable. None of you have any say in anything! Your lives are pointless. None of this matters! Not any of this!"

The lich suddenly vanished and appeared again in front of Abby. "I'm going to show you," she said as she grabbed Abby by the neck and forced the girl to stare into her undead eyes. "You'll see. I'll make sure of it."

A blast of white light hit the lich broadside, sending her flying away from Abby.

Myrddin, covered in black goo, wand smoking, had arrived.

The lich picked herself up off the ground, her body steaming. "Myrddin! Finally decided to come out of your little hidey-hole and face me? We have so much catching up to do. I wanna see how many organs you have left to play with."

CHAPTER TWENTY-SIX

Rasputina's hands began to glow with a green aura as she circled Myrddin. "I haven't had an excuse to use magic in such a long time. Your playthings are cute, and tough too, don't get me wrong. I can see why the Dark One's been so worried about you. Who would have thought little ol' Myrddin would have grown up to be the hope of all the realms?"

Myrddin removed his suit jacket and tossed it aside. "You are not going to get in my head. I am not the same young wizard you met all those years ago."

"You know, I should thank you for sealing me away. There was so much time to think and to dream down there. You wouldn't believe all the things I've seen, the worlds I've been to, the lives I've lived. The knowledge I've found."

At the word "knowledge," Myrddin began to look uneasy.

Rasputina noticed and smiled widely, her jagged teeth gleaming. "Did you think I stopped learning in that pit like the rest of the liches did just because I didn't have books? That's not where you found knowledge, Myrddin. I tried to teach you that all those years ago. You find it through pain, through suffering. Knowledge comes to you when you're half-mad, soul-starved, forgetting whether or not you even exist. That's where you really begin to learn things."

She looked in the direction of the explosions. "I'm assuming you killed...uh...what's his name, right?"

Myrddin watched Rasputina as she glanced at Abby, who had rushed to Terra and was helping her up. "Yes. I sent him back to the hell he came from."

"You know Old Ones don't come from hell, right? Oh, of course, you do. Myrddin knows everything. You do know where the concept of hell comes from, though. You must. A human religion. Christianity. Or are the religious concerns of these monkeys something that's beyond you?"

"I don't look down on humans like you do."

Rasputina laughed, the sound hoarse. "Like *I* do? We'll pick that up later. I got a little knowledge to give you. You see, the early Christians, they would do this ritual where they ate the blood and body of their God. It saved them. Strengthened their soul. Kinda what I do, you know? Eating for strength. You ever wonder where the soul is, Myrddin?"

"What are you getting at?"

"It's in the blood, you sweet, sweet fool. The blood and the flesh."

Rasputina raised her hands toward where the Old One's corpse no doubt lay. A tidal wave of viscera and gore, the remains of what Myrddin had left in his wake, came flowing through the streets. The blood from Myrddin's coat floated toward Rasputina as well. All of it combined and condensed into a black ball roughly the size of a walnut. "That's an old god's soul right there," she chirped before popping it into her mouth.

Myrddin's eyes widened as he turned to the recouping DGA. "You need to get out of here now! Everyone return to HQ."

Anabelle shook her head as she took a fighting stance. "No way. We're not leaving you here by yourself."

"You must leave. She's too—"

Rasputina let out a primal scream as black goo poured from the wound in her chest, and a green light flashed from her eyes. She hit the ground, wheezing and grunting, her body twitching as though she were trying to fight something.

Myrddin shook his head. "How could I have been so stupid…"

A barking sound came from Rasputina. "They speak to you in the dark, in your dreams," she growled. "They tell you everything you know so you can use them because they're just like everything else in this universe. They think they're powerful gods. They think they're important. They don't realize they're just food."

As Myrddin and Rasputina glared at each other, Terra went to Cire and propped him up. "Shit, shit, shit," she murmured as she pressed her hand to his wound. "We need to get him help."

Abby rushed to them and knelt beside Cire. She pressed her hand to his wound, and nanobots flowed over it. The nanobots began to stitch up the orc's wound. "We still need to get him out of here fast."

"Already on it," Roy said through his comm. "We got an evac already on its way."

A few feet away, Rasputina raised her knife at Myrddin, the blade shape glowing. "What do you say to a duel?" she asked Myrddin.

Myrddin raised his wand as well. A white bolt of energy shot out of it.

A green jet of magic burst from Rasputina's knife. The two blasts collided, sending sparks flying, resulting in enough energy blowback to shake the ground and cause a rush of wind.

A small explosion broke the energy chain between the two wizards.

Myrddin waved his wand, and clouds formed in the sky. A column of lightning crackled and rushed at Rasputina.

The lich pressed her finger to her mouth, and, as the lighting hit her, it turned into thousands of falling snakes. She whipped her knife around, and the snakes rolled together, oozing into each other's bodies until they became one red snake the size of a dragon. Rasputina jumped on the snake's back as it lunged for Myrddin.

Myrddin didn't move. He raised his wand to his mouth and released a ball of fire, easily swallowing the snake in its flames.

Rasputina came flying through the fire, green flames shooting from her mouth. Myrddin whispered, "Incinerate," and exhaled a ball of flame, much larger than the last.

The lich appeared behind Myrddin, slashing at him with her knife. The wizard raised his own, blocking the attack, sparks of energy flying off the wand and dagger as the duel intensified.

Myrddin lunged forward, kicked Rasputina in the chest and shouted, "Eviscerate."

Blades of energy slashed Rasputina across the body, and she screamed as she fell to her knees. She slammed her knife into the ground, sending a shockwave at Myrddin, who rose into the air. The lich grinned as she tossed her knife at the wizard, who easily deflected it, only for it to explode a moment later.

Rasputina surged in front of Myrddin, her hands glowing green. She grabbed the old man by the head and began to drain him of his life.

Myrddin screamed, and a bolt of lightning struck them both.

When the smoke cleared, Myrddin was back on the ground, breathing heavily, and Rasputina was stumbling away. She turned and slashed at Myrddin, sending an energy attack his way.

It hit the wizard in the shoulder, flinging him through the air. He raised his wand, stopping mid-air and whirled, thrusting fireball after fireball at Rasputina. The lich simply pointed her knife, caught the fireballs, and turned them back on Myrddin, who took to the ground as the fireballs exploded around him.

Myrddin touched his wand to the rubble on the ground, the debris coming together to form a rock golem behind Rasputina. The golem grabbed Rasputina and started squeezing.

The lich laughed maniacally as she wriggled, trying to escape. She spat on the ground and chanted in the foul, ancient language of the Old Ones.

Bones burst from the ground and grabbed Myrddin. They pulled him down, wrapping around the wrists and ankles, trying to choke him.

Rasputina opened her mouth, and a slug-like creature poured out. The lich's skin deflated as the slug slithered its way across the ground, growing limbs and a head until Rasputina was standing again. She spun and blasted the golem to bits.

Myrddin's body melted into water and flowed toward Rasputina, reforming a moment before he slashed at her with his wand.

Rasputina deflected, kicked Myrddin in the kneecap, and pressed her dagger to his temple. The wizard disappeared, reappearing behind her as the tip of the dagger exploded.

Myrddin touched the end of his wand to the back of Rasputina's head. Bone grew over Rasputina's back as he fired a magical energy blast. When the smoke cleared, Rasputina's head spun backward, her arms cracking and reforming until she was facing Myrddin. Her jaw hung open, and a bright green light burst from it.

Myrddin stumbled backward as Rasputina jumped on him, knocked him to the ground, and drove her knife into the wizard's chest. As the blood flowed, Rasputina continued her attack, slowing at last to look over her shoulder.

Myrddin was behind her.

The Myrddin beneath Rasputina exploded as she leapt off it, laughing madly. "So many tricks, Myrddin! You could have been a court wizard! Where's the power I've been hearing about ever since I was released?"

Myrddin took a step closer, pausing momentarily. Sweat dripped down his forehead. He straightened, his eyes bright. "Power? Is that what you want?"

He vanished, and appeared in front of Rasputina, his wand pressed against her right shoulder. A blast tore through her arm, hitting the building behind them, and tearing through glass and steel.

Anabelle, who had joined everyone else around Terra, stared in awe at the battle played out before them. Abby was speechless as well. None of them had suspected that Myrddin was this strong.

Rasputina looked shocked as she stared blankly at him. She fell forward as Myrddin backed away. He pointed at Rasputina, muttering an incantation under his breath.

Rasputina stared at the ground in front of her as Myrddin charged up his attack. She looked at what was left of her shoulder. "No...no...

no…" she muttered over and over in time with Myrddin's incantation. Then she started laughing as she grabbed her knife. She plunged it into her stomach, cackling louder and louder as she shouted, "No! No! No!"

The lich grabbed at her intestines and pulled them out as she laughed. Before Myrddin could fire, she teleported behind him. She threw her intestines over the wizard's neck and pulled tightly as her innards transformed into snakes.

The pair stumbled while Rasputina sprouted another arm. She withdrew another knife and drove it into Myrddin's stomach as the wizard struggled to break free.

"I'm going to rip 'em out," Rasputina shouted. "I'm gonna rip them all out!"

Myrddin reached behind him and pressed his wand to Rasputina's head. The wind flashed, and energy pooled. An explosion rocked the street, and Myrddin stumbled out of the smoke, holding his side, trying to heal himself with his wand.

The evac helicopter had just arrived, dispersing the smoke while Anabelle and Terra helped them move Cire into the chopper.

As the smoke cleared, Rasputina stumbled to her feet, headless. She aimed her knife at Myrddin as a new skull built itself out of his exposed spine. "Shall we end this as we were taught? One final chance to see who really is stronger, winner takes all."

Myrddin slumped forward, breathing heavily as blood seeped from his nose. "The Dark One will never win."

Rasputina cackled loudly. "The Dark One? I don't care who wins or loses. I'm just having fun again." She raised her knife to her chest.

Myrddin did the same. "May the best wizard survive."

Rasputina sent a curving green blast at Myrddin, hitting him in the chest. The lich grinned as she lowered her knife.

But Myrddin didn't fall. He held out his wand. It was still glowing, the wand having absorbed the lich's attack.

Rasputina screamed in rage, slashing her knife again.

Bloody gashes opened on Myrddin's face, but he muttered quietly under his breath and did not stop charging his spell.

Rasputina continued to attack, unrelenting, laughing mindlessly, her skull tilting backward as she tore Myrddin's skin apart with her magic.

Myrddin collapsed, barely able to stay on his feet as his body began to glow bright white, Rasputina's attacks still slicing him up. Finally, he opened his eyes. "I banish you."

A white energy blast the size of the entire street shot out from Myrddin. It obliterated everything in its path. When the blast died, nothing remained but rubble.

Myrddin fell to his knees, coughing up blood.

The evac helicopter was already in the air, the DGA leaning out of the open door, watching the fight. Abby leapt out of the helicopter, thrusters blasting as she soared toward Myrddin. She scooped him up in her arms before he fell over. Then she returned to the helicopter and placed him beside Cire.

Terra was still staring out the side of the helicopter. "Do you think he did it? He killed the Elder One. You think he could kill her?"

Anabelle shook her head and pointed at the rubble.

A skeletal hand forced its way out of the dirt, pulling itself up as skin began to wrap around partially decomposed muscle.

Once fully formed, Rasputina sat there, watching the helicopter flying away. When the chopper faded into the distance, she slumped, her eyes lifelessly staring at nothing. Then she chuckled softly.

CHAPTER TWENTY-SEVEN

The ride back to HQ was silent and somber.

Terra, Anabelle, Abby, and Roy, watched over Myrddin and Cire. The orc's wounds were mostly sealed, but he had not woken up yet. Myrddin was another question altogether. Abby had tried to heal his wounds with her nanobots, but they hadn't helped whatsoever.

The helicopter flew to the carrier, which was only a few miles away. They boarded with no problems. The orcs Abby had fought in the skies above the city were gone, no doubt due to the summoning of the Elder One.

Once aboard, Myrddin and Cire were rushed to the medbay, leaving the DGA and Roy alone with their thoughts on the day's horror. Usually there would have been a debriefing, everyone offering up what they had witnessed to Myrddin. Now, there was nothing.

The carrier activated its miniature hadron collider under Creon's supervision, jumping to HQ as quickly as possible.

They arrived within minutes, and Cire and Myrddin were transported to the main medbay. Information on the prognosis of their recoveries still wasn't available.

As Anabelle wandered off the carrier, she tried to think about what the next course of action would be. There were things to be taken care of; a chain of command. But first, a decision had to be made on how involved Myrddin was going to be.

Anabelle felt callous for looking at the situation in this way. Wasn't she supposed to be upset by Myrddin's defeat, and Cire's injuries, and her frustrating stalemate with Grok? Yet, all she felt was a coolness, a sort of detached awareness. There was simply too much to process.

Terra and Abby drifted away without saying much. Anabelle knew that as the team's leader, it was her responsibility to say something to rally her troops. However, she had no idea where to start. She let them handle the impact of today's mission however they thought best.

Anabelle went to her room and lit a few candles. She sat and closed her eyes, trying to center herself.

What she'd seen had been beyond her understanding—the raising of an Elder God of such tremendous power. Rasputina using Myrddin as a pawn for her own schemes of absorbing the Elder One into her own body. And how much strength had that given Rasputina?

That wasn't beginning to touch on Grok, and how Anabelle felt about their fight. There had been something almost magical about it. And that wasn't a feeling Anabelle was used to.

She tried to silence her thoughts, to concentrate and meditate. She failed miserably as her mind jumped between the things she believed needed to be done.

At last, quitting the attempt to silence her mind, she commed Roy. "Hey, we need to talk."

Roy picked up quickly enough. "Yeah, I know. Can I come over."

"Yeah. Hurry up."

Anabelle waited for Roy to show up, pacing back and forth, uncertain of what the future held. Myrddin not being in charge had never crossed her mind before. It seemed like an impossibility. There had never been a threat she had expected him to engage with, let alone one he couldn't defeat. Myrddin's power was an unspoken thing. Now, having seen it on full display and having been in awe of it, the knowledge that it was not enough to defeat the lich was terrifying. Which only begged the question of how powerful the Dark One was.

A knock sounded at Anabelle's door. She opened it, and Roy was standing there, looking tired and worn out. He was holding a bottle of whiskey, and he tossed it to Anabelle before sitting on her bed. "Fucking hell," he muttered.

Anabelle cracked the bottle open and took a gulp. "How's he holding up?"

"Stabilized at the moment. But there's shit they don't understand. Everyone has a lot of questions, and I don't have the answers. There's something keeping Myrddin from being able to heal, even with all the magic and tech. Whatever Rasputina did to him, it's nullifying any of our attempts to get him back in shape."

"Is he going to die?"

Roy hung his head, rubbing his brow. "They don't know. It's hard to tell. Honestly, the med staff is confused as well. People like Myrddin don't just die. Wizards of that caliber? The lich is stronger than any of us could have imagined."

"So, what now?"

Roy looked up at Anabelle, his face uncertain and worried. "There's a chain of command that follows. I'm after Myrddin. If he's incapable of leading, then I have to step up to the plate."

Anabelle sat beside Roy and passed him the bottle. "That's good, right? You're as close to Myrddin as anyone is."

Roy shook his head as he pulled up his HUD. "That's what I thought, too. But I'm not ready for this. I don't know the first thing about leading an army, let alone one that's spread through the realms. Myrddin has contacts with governments that I don't even know about. And the moment he couldn't be resuscitated, all of his credentials passed to me. There's shit in here that I've never even heard about."

Anabelle glanced at the projection of Roy's HUD files. "Was he keeping this stuff from you?"

Roy shrugged as he peered at the files. "Honestly, I don't know. Most of the shit in here doesn't even make sense to me. I wouldn't even know where to start."

"We could take a look through it together."

Roy cast a dubious look at Anabelle that quickly softened. "I'm not supposed to be doing that. Myrddin expected me to step up to the plate and handle this."

Anabelle wrapped her fingers around Roy's. "Drop the macho-tough guy bullshit. This is a lot. None of us were ready for this. If you need help, don't be a fucking idiot. Just admit it, and we'll go from there. If you can handle this on your own, then do it."

Roy took a swig from the bottle of whiskey. "Fuck. You know I need the help. This isn't my thing. I'm not a fucking general. I'm a grunt with a lot of authority. Even more now. So, yeah, give me a hand. Myrddin left a bunch of contingency plans in case all this shit in New York went bad. We can start with that."

Terra sat in the medbay by Cire's side. She held his hand, watching the nurses and doctors bustle about, occasionally being asked to leave the room, and coming back when she was allowed.

Emotions weren't something Terra dealt with often, not that she didn't have any. She was awash with them most of the time, but there was a time and place for each one, which was usually when *she* wanted to deal with them.

This was different. A wellspring of feeling had overcome her as she watched people she didn't know, standing over Cire's body, doing God knows what to him.

On an intellectual level, Terra knew they were helping Cire. But she wanted to be in there with him. She knew—though she also knew it was false—that she could help Cire better than they could.

After two hours of surgery and mage-healing sessions, Terra was finally allowed into Cire's room. She pulled up the only seat there, and sat beside the orc, wrapping her hand around his, hoping he would open his eyes.

After another hour, Cire's lids fluttered open. He smiled at Terra as he tried to sit up. "The only tolerable thing I could imagine waking up to."

Terra scoffed loudly as she disentangled her hands from Cire's. "Tolerable thing? O-fucking-kay."

Cire's face went stony. "No, that's not... I didn't mean it like that. We..." Cire sighed loudly as he fumbled for words. "We don't talk like—"

Terra raised her hand, smiling. "I'm just teasing you, that's all."

Cire relaxed, sinking back onto the bed. "I'm glad you're here. There's no greater honor than waking up from a battle with your chieftain at your side."

"That's the only reason you care?"

Cire looked up at Terra, his eyes softer than she had ever seen before. "There is no greater honor than waking up to *my* chieftain at my side. The only greater honor would be dying in battle."

Terra laughed as she kissed Cire's forehead. "You gotta work on your pillow talk, dude. Because you're fucking horrible at it."

Cire groaned as he touched his wound tentatively. "Orcs aren't used to pillows. It will be something to learn."

For a moment, Terra thought she shouldn't speak. It would be easier to let this go unsaid. Maybe it would shrivel up, and she wouldn't have to ever deal with it. But that's not what she wanted. "I was scared...I thought you were going to...you know, die or something."

Cire smiled sweetly. "That tends to be what warriors do. We die."

"No, that's not what I meant. I mean...fuck it."

Terra leaned over and kissed Cire, holding him as close as she could, letting herself melt into him as he did the same. When she finally pulled away, Cire looked as if he'd been punched in the face.

Cire released a heavy sigh. "This is the best way I've ever woken up after a fight."

"Consider it payback for all of those 'sessions' you gave me."

Myrddin was sitting silently, his breathing heavy and haggard.

Abby was sitting beside him, watching the old man breathe. In the entire time she'd been waiting with him, there had only been a few visitors, mostly nurses and mages. She couldn't understand why Anabelle and Terra hadn't stopped by to see the wizard.

Myrddin looked emaciated as if all of the life had gone out of his body, reducing him to a sheet of paper. Abby suspected that she could have pushed her finger through his forearm and it would have come out through the other side.

He was dying; Abby knew it beyond a shadow of a doubt. Whatever the lich had done to him, it had left a lasting impression. It was not something the mages or nurses could overcome.

She wondered if she could solve a problem they hadn't.

An image of Abby's father flashed in her mind, but she pushed it away. It wasn't helpful. Nothing would be solved by thinking about it, but her hands trembled still as she held them over Myrddin's chest. "Martin, scan for anomalies and cross-reference with everything in the database. Everything."

Martin answered, but he sounded hesitant. "When you say everything, you're just talking about HQ, right?"

"No. Break into every system. I want to know it all. How long do I have to wait?"

"Already done. I got a couple of things you might think are interesting."

Abby pulled up Martin's list. "What are they?"

"There is an anomaly in Myrddin's wound. Some kind of black contagion. It's similar to the material within the shard that was transported from the Wasp's Nest. It also shares a host of similarities to readings taken from Persephone. I don't quite know what to make of it yet."

"Pull it up. I want to see."

Abby stared at the holoscreen projecting from her HUD. There was a pattern, and all of it was connected. She was going to find out what linked them together.

Myrddin wasn't going to die on her watch.

CHAPTER TWENTY-EIGHT

The next few days at HQ were quiet. Anabelle didn't see much of the DGA other than in passing. She visited both Myrddin and Cire in the medbay. That was the only time she saw Terra, who had barely left Cire's side. Abby was watching over Myrddin, but Anabelle still had other duties to take care of, which restricted the amount of time she could check in on the old man.

Anabelle found herself in the medbay with Myrddin more often than she had expected. It was never like she intended to go visit him either. She'd wake up, meditate, grab breakfast, and start walking. Then she'd look up, and realize she was in Myrddin's room.

The wizard was still in critical condition. The nurses and mages hadn't been able to figure out exactly what had been done to him. His wounds had healed, but there appeared to be some kind of residual magic working in his body, keeping him sick.

Creon had been back and forth to Myrddin's room as well. He thought there might have been a technological aspect to the problem, but he hadn't found anything.

Anabelle sat on the opposite side of the room, watching people come and go, watching Myrddin struggle for life. She had never seen him like this before. The wizard's skin looked as if it had aged a hundred years. He looked thin. In his sleep, he muttered in a language Anabelle couldn't identify.

She thought about her first few years under Myrddin's watch. Those had been trying times for the elf, having only finished her training as a Traveler a few months prior. She'd been excited about joining the war effort, but Myrddin's plans for her had not been what she had wanted.

Regardless, as a Traveler, she knew it was her duty to serve the common good in whatever way it presented itself. So Anabelle had done what she'd felt was necessary.

The two had butted heads constantly. Myrddin had not expected her to be as vocal about her issues with him as she had been. But it seemed like Myrddin also treasured that about her. Or at least tolerated it.

Over the last few months, since the creation of the DGA, Anabelle had felt that she and Myrddin had been repairing their relationship. She wouldn't have gone as far as calling it a friendship, but it had been more than just business.

But that hadn't changed any of Anabelle's growing doubts concerning what Myrddin had been planning. She'd assumed Roy and Myrddin's relationship was much more transparent than it had been. Now that Roy was meant to step up to the wizard's position, both he and Anabelle had discovered Myrddin possessed a wealth of secrets that Roy was not privy too.

Even more disconcerting was that, despite having received the wizard's credentials, certain information had not been instantly available to Roy when the change in leadership had occurred.

Information Roy needed right about now.

It was as if Myrddin couldn't fathom a situation where he was not in charge. It was frustrating to think their leader had been so full of hubris.

That being said, Anabelle couldn't help but feel a large measure of respect for the old man. He had risked his life, knowing full well he probably wasn't going to live, just to give her and the other DGAs a way to escape.

Just how powerful was the lich? Anabelle wondered. *Myrddin killed an Elder One…those things are practically gods. But he couldn't kill Rasputina, and she was able to do this to him.*

Anabelle was wondering if this war against the Dark One would have to switch to Rasputina. Then she remembered that the lich didn't appear to have any motivations, no reasons for the chaos she was sowing. It made her erratic but was also a blessing. She wouldn't be raising any armies anytime soon.

Someone cleared their throat, and Anabelle looked over her shoulder. Abby stood on the threshold. "Mind if I visit, too?"

Anabelle motioned for Abby to sit beside her, and the child obeyed. They sat there in silence for a bit, both lost in their thoughts, watching Myrddin from afar. "You think he's gonna die?" Abby asked at last.

Anabelle felt something tugging at her chest, and she choked on her words. "He better not."

"Me and Creon been looking through our credentials and everything. Looks like the only way Roy gets full access is when Myrddin dies. Then it all reverts to Roy."

"Any way to work around that yet?"

"We're trying to figure something out."

They fell back into silence, Anabelle thinking about how close Myrddin and Abby had grown over the last few months. He was becoming a surrogate father, much like Roy. She couldn't imagine how difficult it must be for Abby to lose another parental figure.

Anabelle stood and straightened out the creases in her pants. "I need to go meet Roy. He's supposed to be officially making the announcement about Myrddin and the change of command in a little while." She turned to go but caught herself. She couldn't leave Abby like this, even if this sort of shit wasn't her strong suit. "Uh…I'm not really good at this kind of stuff. You know that. But if you need to talk…about anything, let me know."

Abby, who hadn't looked away from Myrddin, nodded dully, and said, "Thanks. I will."

Anabelle walked out of the room, leaving the child alone with the ailing wizard.

Anabelle stood at Roy's side, Terra at hers, as Roy addressed the marines and the main agents of HQ. He explained Myrddin's injuries and his condition and informed them he would be stepping in to take over the position until the wizard recovered.

The marines cheered when Roy said, "We will not be defeated by the Dark One. He might strike at us, but we will not yield. None of our sacrifices will be in vain. Victory will be ours. Fuck this lich, and fuck the Dark One. The realms will know peace again."

The marines were dismissed, and Terra, Anabelle, and Roy retired to the war room. Roy's armpits and brow were stained with sweat. He collapsed into Myrddin's chair. "How did I do?" he asked.

Terra and Anabelle sat with him. "You did great. Very Helm's Deep, " Anabelle said. "Besides, the men love you. Myrddin might be the brains of this operation, but all of those soldiers know you. You don't have anything to worry about."

Terra nodded her agreement. "So, what are we doing here? Don't tell me you already have missions for us."

Roy nodded as he pulled up the holoscreen. "Yeah, I do. Nothing big, though. Without access to some of Myrddin's main strategies, we're kinda fucked in that department. But we have a lot of collateral damage to take care of, either way. We haven't heard anything from any of the fronts other than the usual, and Creon said there have been no energy spikes from potential gates. The Dark One is probably preparing for another push. Which means we have some time to figure things out."

"What kind of things?"

"Creon and Abby are upgrading all of our equipment, and I have intel coming in on how to deal with this lich. But you two will have your own assignments. Terra, we're keeping you on the news circuit, once Cire is able to get out there with you. It is imperative that we don't let public opinion change about what's happening, and after New York, you know it's going to have swayed straight to shit."

Terra sighed and nodded. "He should be up by tomorrow. He's been getting a lot better. We'll have security, right?"

"As much as we can spare. But after New York, I'm starting to think it won't matter. But that brings me to you, Anabelle."

Anabelle braced herself for whatever shit assignment she was about to get. Roy hadn't given her any inkling of what it could be, and she was already annoyed. Taking orders from Roy was going to be a tough one.

"The battle has left a good chunk of that area of New York in shambles. Over a billion dollars of property damages. We're having our alchemists on that already, and we'll be able to fund the restoration process. But I need a face there—you. You're going on a work/press show tomorrow. On the ground floor, meeting with people, helping out where you can. Pure politics, but it's something we need to do."

Anabelle believed her talents would have been better suited someplace else, but she held her tongue. This was Roy's first mission briefing. She could give him shit about it after he got used to all of this. Or she could just talk to him later when they were alone. "Okay. I can take care of that. Anything else?"

Roy looked surprised that Anabelle had taken her assignment so easily. "Oh, okay. Well, you're dismissed."

Anabelle and Terra got up and left. As they walked away, Terra said, "You went pretty easy on him back there."

Anabelle laughed as she flipped her hair out her face. "He's a sensitive guy. Don't want to ruin his first day. We'll wait until he does something stupid first."

The two women walked off laughing.

Abby was in the lab before most people in HQ were awake. Generally, she rose before dawn, but since returning from the battle with the lich four days ago, she was getting out of bed early even by her standards.

There was a problem that needed to be solved: Myrddin wasn't getting better. Cire had been released from the medbay without complications. Myrddin, on the other hand, was still under twenty-four-hour surveillance.

A couple of theories floated around in Abby's head. One thing she knew was that the attack had something to do with the lich, obviously. The second was that it was specifically the lich's knife.

At the moment, Abby was waiting for Martin to deliver a compiled list of steps the nanobots had taken to heal her when she'd been stabbed by the lich. So far, Martin was only able to confirm that some anomalies were present that he hadn't noticed at first. The wound had been healed, but the nanobots had been trying to hunt down the traces of foreign agents in her blood.

Creon walked into the lab, yawning loudly before using the wall conjurer to get himself a cup of coffee.

Abby briefly looked up from her computer screen. "You know you don't have to get here this early just because of me."

Creon grimaced as he sipped his coffee. "How bad would it look if my partner was showing up a good four hours before me?"

"Might look like she's gone a little crazy."

Creon laughed as he booted up his computer. "Won't find me disagreeing there. I found those research articles you asked about the lich. Emailed them to you last night."

"And what about the Old One's stuff?"

"That was a little harder to come across. Most of the information we have on the Old Ones is in old Elvish or in the celestial tongue. I pulled whatever I could, but I can barely read Elvish, let alone old Elvish. There's no guarantee what I got will be of any use."

"Martin can take care of that for me. Thanks."

Abby pulled up her messages. There were a handful from Creon, as well as two others: one from Persephone and another from Alex, the leader of the Team Boundless of the dragonriders.

Naturally, Abby wanted to open Persephone's message first, but the message from Alex was interesting. They had met during the battle to free Terra from the battle arena and had kept in touch since then, but something had recently happened with Alex and her team.

Apparently, Alex's team had been disbanded due to mutiny. The details weren't included in the basic information portal Abby had access to, so she couldn't tell why. Also, she'd noticed something odd happening every time she tried to remember anything about Alex. It was as if her brain was getting fuzzy, like the vague haziness of trying to bring up a memory from childhood. Then Abby would find herself stuck.

She opened the email and read through it quickly. At first, it appeared to be a followup about a question Alex had asked earlier, about the way her blood had metabolized draconic fluid. But the further Abby looked into the email, the more it seemed like Alex was hinting at something she couldn't talk about.

"Hey, Martin, do you know anything about breaking codes?" Abby asked.

Martin popped up in the corner of sight. "More than your average computer program. Want me to take a look at this?"

"Yeah. And I have some old celestial and Elvish texts I need help with too."

Martin yawned as his avatar disappeared. "I'll tell you when I'm done. Ooooooooh, these are long. Might take me a little bit. Half an hour, maybe."

As Abby prepared to open her email, she received a visit from Creon. "What's this?"

Creon conjured two plates of food: *Elkor*, a goblin breakfast of stewed intestines served over buttered oats. It had quickly become one of Abby's favorite meals.

He placed a plate in front of Abby. "Finally got into Myrddin's encrypted files—without Martin's help. Now, just to let you know, this is grounds for a court-martial."

"I think they might cut us some slack if they know we're doing this to help Myrddin. You should also forward these to Roy. Make sure he gets those credentials. Oh, and thanks for the grub."

Abby ate while she read through the email and documents. Martin had slowly been increasing the speed at which her eyes could move, allowing her to read faster. At the moment, she could finish *War and Peace* within fifteen hours. Getting through these documents took no time.

She couldn't believe what she was reading. It was a compilation of briefings Myrddin had had with Alex and Suzuki, the leader of a very successful MERC group responsible for war efforts in Middang3ard. He had also been a part of the siege on the battle arena, and his crew, the Mundanes, were legends.

Alex's report was the easiest to digest. It detailed a battle she'd had with the Dark One. How a living meteor had almost destroyed Middang3ard, and how Alex had battled it psychically. One thing Abby noticed referenced often was a sickly green color. It was reminiscent of the green aura and the magic Rasputina used.

Next was Suzuki's briefing, in which he detailed a conversation with a river god of some kind who had spoken to him about the Dark One and where he came from. Suzuki referred to it as Netherverse, a place outside our time and understanding and the same place the Old Ones were from. But the Dark One didn't dwell there. Suzuki seemed to think the Dark One *was* the Netherverse.

More pieces of information had been included in the package. A description of a weapon left by a psychic alien at the Wasps Nest, the HQ of the dragonriders. The weapon was a shard of some sort, filled with a black liquid that appeared sentient.

These briefings had been grouped together by Myrddin. He obviously believed they were related.

Martin interrupted Abby's train of thought. "Got two things for you, sweet child of mine. Got Myrddin's toxicology reports back. Turns out, the anomalies we found in your blood are in his as well, but much more. I'm sending the reports on how the nanobots scrubbed you to the technicians. Should have him right as rain in no time."

"What's the second thing?"

"Incoming call from Persephone."

Abby's heart raced. "You mean, right now?"

"As in, right now."

Abby pushed her hair back and sat up straight, checking her reflection in her computer screen to see if she'd rubbed the sleep out of her eyes. Then she patched Persephone through.

The drow smiled at her. Abby thought Persephone was the most beautiful tired person she'd ever seen. She was so enamored she didn't realize she was staring blankly at her screen. "Hey, Abby, is there something wrong with your connection? You're frozen."

Abby laughed nervously. She was embarrassed by how flustered she still got when she spoke to Persephone. "Oh yeah, yeah. Sorry. I didn't notice. How are you doing?"

The two chatted for a bit, playing catchup. Not much had been going on with Persephone since her reintegration. Abby felt it was better not to stress Persephone out with news of the lich and the people she cared about being hurt. But a thought did pop into her mind. "Hey, I was thinking about what you told me about your tentacles coming from having a bit of an Old One implanted into your body. What did the Old One look like?"

"Kinda like this black liquid, but not quite liquid, kind of solid. Like liquid that is alive."

Suddenly, things began to come together. "If I can find a way to get you here today, can you come?"

Persephone smiled. "All I've been able to think about is seeing you. Of course, I can."

CHAPTER TWENTY-NINE

A nabelle arrived in New York around ten in the morning. She was set to do a press conference with the mayor. Roy had put together a press team for Anabelle and Terra. They'd been drilled on questions that would be asked. Rather than create a set list of answers, the two agents had been encouraged to come up with their own.

As Anabelle waited for the helicopter to land, she thought about how much she appreciated Roy's approach to handling the DGA. It was probably because he'd heard and experienced most of the same grievances Anabelle had.

The helicopter touched down, and Anabelle was ushered to a conference room where the mayor waited for her. They exchanged small talk, a practice the elf considered herself an expert at. After they were finished, they went outside for the press conference.

Questions came hard and fast. The reporters were at the top of their game, probing Anabelle on the responsibility Myrddin had to the city. Many of the questions pertained to what the wizard would do to fix the amount of destruction wreaked in the last battle with the lich.

Anabelle held herself with a calm and poise she'd practiced for years. "We've already started our efforts to bring relief to the city. Five million dollars are being given to the city as a stimulus package, and we are funding a three-hundred-billion-dollar restructuring effort which will be dispersed throughout the city."

A reporter raised his hand, and Anabelle chose him for a question. "What about the orc issue? Even further than that, it seems like humanity has been made a target since Myrddin chose to involve us in this. Many humans are wondering if we would be better off ignoring Myrddin's claims and handling this with our own military and diplomatic leaders."

Anabelle waited for the commotion among the other reporters to subside. "That is actually a misperception. The Dark One has been working against Earth for nearly a hundred years. We have documentation to prove it. And most of your political leaders do, as well. You can take up the disclosure of that information with them because ours is all public at the moment.

"To answer your question about what to do going forward, I won't lie to you. Humanity is a target now because the Dark One has been decimating the majority of the nine realms. Even if he backs off now, he will be back soon. This is a question of what humanity wants to do at the moment. We will all continue waging this war for our collective freedom, but we can't defend humanity for itself. There will come a time when you will have to fight alongside those of us who have been laying our lives on the line as well.

"Our forces are a collaborative effort between the different races of the realms. Elves, goblins, dwarves, humans, and gnomes are all working to fight the Dark One. Our fight has even begun to incorporate free orcs. But the extent to which humanity can defend itself is dependent on how much humanity wants to fight."

The press conference continued, and Anabelle grew tired of the questions. They all ended up revolving around the same thing: How can we be saved without saving ourselves? That was the reason Anabelle was annoyed with humanity; they seemed to want everyone to fight for them without being willing to put in the work themselves.

Anabelle tried to answer the questions with as much calm and politeness as she could muster. She knew this was bigger than herself.

They needed as much support as possible, and if she revealed her irritation at such a widely-broadcasted press interview, and in light of the destruction of New York only a few days ago, the results could be catastrophic. Fortunately, the reporters hadn't been prepared for Anabelle to be so frank with them. Probably because this wouldn't have happened if Myrddin had been speaking.

Once the press conference was over, Anabelle was taken to an office to discuss the PR-related stuff she would be engaged in for the day. The first was visiting Times Square, the section of the city that had taken the most damage.

Anabelle was carted off in a nondescript van. When she arrived, the streets were full of police, firefighters, and anyone else willing to give a hand.

She was shocked at the extent of the damage. While in the midst of the battle, Anabelle had been concerned with many other issues. But now that the fighting was over, she saw just how much had been destroyed. The city was in shambles.

A police chief and a fire captain were waiting for her. Neither seemed particularly interested in talking to Anabelle, and the same was true for her, but her mission was to play nice. She said what was expected and tried to assuage the egos of the two men.

Anabelle was led on a tour of the damage throughout the city. She watched as humans worked with each other to clear away the rubble and look for survivors. A group of firefighters was clearing a building and bringing out the bodies of a few humans who had been caught in the crossfire.

Her heart skipped a beat when she saw the lifeless bodies. Anabelle had been under the impression that the entire area had been cleared out, but there had been apartments they hadn't been able to evacuate in time. She wondered how many lives had been lost.

It was a painful realization. Even if she had some disdain for humans not fighting for their own freedom, these were civilians; humans who probably didn't have the strength to fight. And now they were dead.

Anabelle toured the rest of Times Square. She listened to what the police chief and fire captain had to say. Her judgment was reserved. The humans had not been able to defend themselves, but they were capable of taking care of their community. It was something that, as an elf, she could appreciate.

"Is there anything I can do to help?"

The question slipped out of Anabelle's mouth, and even *she* was surprised to hear it.

The fire chief looked at Anabelle curiously. "Uh, we're starting a new excavation a couple of blocks away from here. We could always use extra hands."

"I'd like to come."

Anabelle was led to an apartment complex. The destruction was disturbing. Most of the complex had been burnt to a crisp, and rubble littered the streets. Humans walked back and forth, working to find any survivors.

She fell in with the humans, blending in seamlessly, and taking her orders. Three hours went by before she realized it, digging and digging, hoping to find life.

Finally, Anabelle's team was told to take a break. She walked over to a group of humans sitting and talking amongst each other.

Two stuck out to Anabelle more than the rest. They were older folk, heavily tattooed, and they looked like they had just come from a music festival.

Not knowing what else to do, Anabelle walked up to them and said, "Hello."

The man looked at her and smiled widely, his eyes full of compassion. "Name's Sugar Owl. This right here is my ride or die Star Breeze."

Star Breeze smiled at Anabelle with the same level of radiance. "You're Anabelle, right? The elf with the guy who is in charge of all of this."

Anabelle felt her gut clench. Is that what people thought? That she was part of the group responsible for this? "No, not quite. We're the ones who are responsible for trying to keep this from happening."

Star Breeze nodded as she looked at the rubble. "Yeah, I think we met another one of your guys. Talk, dark, and handsome one. Laid into a couple of orcs with him."

Anabelle was surprised to hear that, then it clicked. She'd heard Roy talking about two old hippies who had joined the cause at Burning Man. These two fit the bill. "What are you doing all the way out here?"

Sugar Owl pulled out a flask, took a sip, and handed it to Anabelle. Whatever was in the flask smelled like rubbing alcohol. "We follow the flow, man. You know, ley lines and the like, guiding us to where we're supposed to be. No questions asked. We just go and let the source guide us."

Star Breeze took the flask next and nodded emphatically. "Yeah, my dude. We can't be plugged up and missing out on all the humanity. If there's a need this big, there's nothing we can do but go and make ourselves useful. What about you? What brings you out this way?"

Anabelle considered lying for a second. But she didn't know these people, and it didn't matter. "I was here…when it happened. My boss thought it would be a good idea to have a friendly face around. Show we're willing to help clean up the mess we were a part of."

Sugar Owl knelt and picked up a handful of dirt and rubble. "Ain't nothing like a little bit of accountability. But some of us know this ain't your fault. We're being attacked, man. Interdimensional aliens coming through to pick us up and scoop out our eggs, to milk us until we can't walk. Old gods come for this earth to remind humanity that we might not be anything but a blip in the whole matrix. Ain't nothing any of us can control, really. Just react to."

Anabelle stared dumbfounded at Sugar Owl. She hadn't expected to hear anything sensible from the hippies, or for the hippie's words to sound sensible.

A crowd of humans was gathering, some having noticed Anabelle. Their faces were angry, and they were walking toward Anabelle and the two hippies.

Someone threw a soda can at Anabelle, and it hit her in the forehead. "You coming here to make this worse for us? Haven't we suffered enough?" the man shouted.

Anabelle's initial reaction was anger, but she swallowed it. These people were hurting, and this was their city. They had a right to be angry. Maybe more of a right than her.

Blood trickled down her forehead, the first blood drawn by anyone other than the Dark One's forces. "You have," Anabelle shouted. "You have suffered enough. And I'll be honest with you, this shit sucks. My homeworld hasn't been hit nearly as hard as most of the nine realms. If I was digging my family out of a ditch, I'd be beside myself. But that doesn't change what we have to deal with right now. The Dark One is making a terror of our lives. Whether I'm here or not, isn't going to make a difference. All I can do is try to fight him. And hope I am making a difference and saving lives."

The crowd was quiet. It wasn't until Sugar Owl stepped up and shouted that the crowd changed their tune. "She's right. Regardless of whether or not we fight, this fight is coming to us. What are we going to do about this now? We can't just ignore the spirits. Can't just ignore where the universe is guiding us. If we hide in our homes, our homes are gonna become this."

The crowd didn't cheer. They didn't agree. But they pulled back. They returned to their work, occasionally casting glances at the elf and the two hippies sitting with her.

After half an hour, Anabelle and the two hippies returned to working in the rubble. A young girl walked up to her and tugged on her sleeve. "Excuse me," the child said. "Are you the elf lady?"

Anabelle wiped the sweat off her brow. "Yeah, I am. What of it?"

The girl smiled brightly, dancing about a little bit. "I just wanted to say thank you. My daddy told me you fought to keep the city safe against monsters. We saw them from our window. He said you killed them all, and that's why we're safe."

Anabelle knelt beside the girl. "Not all of them were monsters. Some of them were orcs who don't have any control. A monster is hurting them, and we're trying to make sure no one is hurt anymore."

The girl screwed up her face like she was trying to understand what Anabelle had said. "They're not all monsters?"

Anabelle stood as she nodded. "We don't always see the monsters. Sometimes we just see what the monsters make."

The child's parents walked over to Anabelle and the hippies. The father said, "We've had a pretty long day of this so far. We were thinking of heading back to our shop. It's a couple of blocks away, a little Middle Eastern spot."

Sugar Owl's eyes widened. "Do you have shawarma? I've always dreamed of trying shawarma."

The father laughed. "We have a lot more than that. Here's the address. We're closed because of, you know, all of this. But give me a knock, and we'll have ourselves a little dinner."

Anabelle said she'd call them once she was done at Times Square. The family went off, walking through the destruction of New York looking more hopeful than Anabelle could have ever imagined.

After another hour or so, she received a call from the child's parents, asking if they could still make it for dinner. She spoke to the fire chief and told him she'd be sending out a squad to reinforce the efforts of the city. "This isn't a one-day thing. We have the resources, and we want to share them," she said.

Anabelle and the two hippies headed to the address the child's parents had provided.

It was in a slightly run-down part of town, but one that had managed to avoid the collateral damage of the battle a week before.

The child greeted Anabelle at the door and led her into the apartment.

Anabelle had been expecting a storefront. Instead, she was greeted by an array of scents she'd never smelled before.

The child guided the elf and the two hippies into the kitchen, where a variety of Middle Eastern foods were laid out on the table.

Anabelle took a seat as the father poured glasses of juice for everyone. He said Grace in a language Anabelle had never heard before and began to pass around the plates of food.

The meal took place mostly in silence, Anabelle trying to savor every bit of flavor she had never known existed. The meat was savory and juicy in a fashion very different from elvish cuisine.

Anabelle didn't speak a word until the meal was finished. "That was amazing," she managed. "Utterly amazing."

The child's father looked up and smiled as he started clearing the table. "It's the least we could do for someone risking their life for all humanity. The least we could do."

CHAPTER THIRTY

Terra, Cire, and Nib-Nib were sitting in the reconnaissance wing of HQ, waiting for a feed to come in from the orcish homeworld.

When Cire had first arrived at HQ, he had spoken with Creon about setting up a network to allow him to check on the orcish homeworld. Creon had thought it was a novel idea.

Access to the orcish world had been nonexistent for some time. Most of the nine realms had lost contact with the orcs before they had known of the threat from the Dark One. The orcs had always been more private than the other races of the nine realms, so no one was surprised.

Cire was currently explaining to Terra, Nib-Nib, and Creon, why that had been the case. Orcs had no problem with the other races of the nine realms. As a society, they had also forgiven elves for the fashion in which the elves had distanced themselves from orcs.

Terra was confused as to why orcs and elves had any sort of relationship with each other, to begin with.

Cire smiled gently as he scratched his brow. "You don't know much about the nine realms, do you?"

Terra watched the video screen and shrugged. "Honestly, up until I was abducted, I would have laughed at anyone who claimed that orcs existed. But, as you can see, I'm pretty open-minded about what's in front of me."

Cire explained how thousands upon thousands of years ago, orcs had been elves. When the Dark Elves broke away from the fairer folk, a few drow decided they didn't want to live underground anymore. Their society had become so different from the elves who lived above them that they felt it was proper for them to carve their own place in the realms.

Through the magic they developed, they found a way to another realm. Here they began to change even further. By the time they came across their elvish brothers again, they were nearly unrecognizable.

This did not sit well with the elves. The elvish folk began to think of orcs as a lesser race, something beneath them because orcs did not follow any of the elvish religions or gods. Orcs had made their own.

That was the beginning of the first Orc War. The war had been heavily documented in most elvish literature. Orcs, on the other hand, maintained their tradition orally. Thus, the story that many people heard of the conflict between orcs and elves was one-sided.

Once the war ended, the orcs continued with their lives, building their culture as they saw fit. One of the aspects of orcs that rose to the forefront was their love of fighting.

"The way orcs think of fighting is quite different from the other races," Cire explained. "Orcs consider fighting to be the way in which we assert ourselves, our existence. Through strength, we continue to grow. There is nothing more satisfying than a challenge that can be overcome."

Terra didn't need much more explanation. From the moment she entered the arena, she'd understood that. Conflict wasn't something to be avoided. It was a tool used to sharpen yourself. When Terra explained this, Cire nodded with understanding. Then he continued.

As orcs perfected their own martial arts and turned away from magic, the nine realms began to view them as barbarians. They were said to have no culture, to be practically machines with only the desire to maim and kill.

Naturally, orcs didn't care what was said about them. Rather than engaging with the other realms, they turned inward and became reclusive.

Cire hung his head after recounting the history of his people. "That was why we were such easy prey for the Dark One. We were completely cut off from the other realms. And we were assumed to be violent and evil from the beginning. What better people to enslave for your armies? Before anyone knew of the Dark One, it was assumed that orcs were just going on a genocidal rampage. It was believed to be in our nature."

Terra watched Cire's eyes, how they grew deep and sad as if he had been there himself. But she knew why. Cire had spoken to her in length about the role of the shamans in his culture. Shamans were responsible for upholding the magic and rituals of orcish history. Though Cire hadn't been there in person, he had absorbed enough of the stories to feel as if it had been his life.

Creon broke the spell Cire had cast over Nib-Nib and Terra. "Looks like we got one. One of the satellites I dispatched a week or two ago has been in position long enough for us to have gathered some reconnaissance. I wouldn't be surprised if it didn't last, but it'll give us a general idea of what's going on."

The holoscreen they were watching began to show the feed from the last couple of days.

Cire gasped when he saw the footage.

Terra didn't understand what was so surprising to Cire. "What is it?"

Creon pointed at the screen. "This is…this is not the orcish world. We would have never done something like this. It goes against everything we stand for, all our principles."

The orcish world had been transformed. Monolithic, technologically advanced buildings formed massive, expanding cities. Orcs walked about as if they were performing everyday business.

Hoverbikes and hover ships floated throughout the city.

Some of the orcs caught on the surveillance had undergone technological improvements, many of which Terra didn't recognize.

Creon confirmed they were far more advanced than anything he'd ever seen.

Terra clicked a section of the video, zooming in on the orcs moving about. "What do you mean? What's wrong with it?"

Cire puffed out his chest. "Orcs have always prided ourselves in our connection to our land, to our planet. We were born within the world, and we have taken our pride with us. Never in all my years would I have imagined that our world would have been carved up like this. I've seen all I need to see."

The holoscreen cut off as Creon awkwardly shifted his weight from side to side. "I'm sorry, Cire. It hurts me to see this done to your people."

Terra could understand Creon's emotional response, something she'd rarely seen from the goblin. In the Nine Realms, orcs and goblins were both considered evil races. Cousins of sorts. In many ways, Creon probably felt like someone had defiled a distant home.

Cire went to the door. "I would like to be alone for a bit."

After Cire left, Terra received a comm from Anabelle. "What's up, my dude?"

Anabelle sounded panicked when she spoke. "You need to turn on the news right now. BCN."

Creon was already tuning the holoscreen to the channel.

Terra was horrified by what she saw. It was a protest in the middle of New York. Humans were carrying signs and shouting in the streets. One of the signs read, Defeat the Orc Menace! Another, Orcs Beneath Our Boots.

"Fuck. I'm glad Cire wasn't here to see this," Terra muttered before hitting her comm. "What's going on, Anabelle?"

"Human public opinion about orcs has grown pretty strong over the last few weeks. Guess the battle with Rasputina and the Dark One's forces tipped it over the edge. People here are livid. I've been on the ground for a while. Nobody is making a secret about this. They're out for blood."

"Are any of the interviews Cire and I are giving making a difference?"

Anabelle took a little while to answer. "They were for a bit, but things have gotten worse. They've had their homes destroyed. They can't grasp what the Dark One represents. To them, it's just orcs killing humans."

Terra looked from Nib-Nib to Creon, not knowing what to say. "What are we supposed to do?"

"You guys have that interview today. Knock it out of the park, and get Cire on the camera, talking."

Terra took the stage to an onslaught of boos. She was accompanied by Cire, who wore his traditional shaman garb, and Nib-Nib, whose eyes fluttered in the bright lights of the soundstage.

The crowd was incensed. They screamed curses and held signs describing the depth of their hatred for orcs.

Terra was still surprised that public opinion had swayed so much. Before the last attack, it had seemed humanity was only slightly worried about orcs. For the most part, humanity had still been ignoring the war with the Dark One.

Once the interview got underway, Terra could see why opinions had changed.

Terra had been briefed on the content of the show she would be on. Anabelle and Roy had described it as a fear-mongering telecast that appealed to the basest fears of the people. Terra knew something about these types of people. Her younger brother bought into these kinds of conspiracy theories.

When Terra visited him, she expected to be greeted by a television show host ranting in the background about globalists, or how solar technology had been developed by aliens as a means of brainwashing Americans into paying social security.

The talk show host, Frank "Don't Tread on Me" McCarthy, was the most well-known peddler of conspiracy theories. Terra had been surprised when Roy had assigned her to appear on the show, but he had explained that McCarthy had recently risen to superstardom with his coverage of Terra's battles.

Anabelle had been a little ashamed to admit it, but Frank was responsible for getting Terra's fight out there when many other television stations had deemed it too risky to show such violent material. Now, Frank was capitalizing on his fame to get the blood of humanity boiling. And what better way than with hate.

Frank motioned for the DGA agent and her guests to take a seat. The soundstage had the look of a professional newsroom with a flair for the theatrical. A flag fluttered behind Frank, and his desk was filled with piles of paper, as well as a typewriter.

Terra could smell the liquor coming off Frank the moment she took her seat.

Frank slammed his fist on the table and stared into the camera. "Welcome back, fellow patriots! Today we managed to wrangle Terra from humanity's so-called savior, Myrddin the White Liar. She's also brought along some of her alien friends. Terra, these 'allies' as you call them, are they the same ones who helped you escape the arena?"

Terra, who had been getting used to these interviews—they were, in fact, battles of a different nature—straightened her spine and folded her hands politely. "Yes, Cire and Nib-Nib here were instrumental in helping me survive as long as I did."

"And how are we to know they aren't spies for this Dark One? If he even exists. This orc looks very similar to all the orcs that have been killing humans by the thousands. And what kind of name is Nib-Nib? How do we know that isn't some kind of code meant to activate a sleeper agent in the crowd? Hell, we could have all been Mk-Ultraed. Our brains are not meant to be tampered with. Would you—"

"First and foremost, Cire doesn't look like 'the orcs who have been attacking.' He just looks like an orc, like we all look like humans. And Nib-Nib is a nickname. We couldn't begin to pronounce her actual name."

For some reason, this answer elicited rage from the crowd, and their booing drowned Frank out until the host slammed his hand on his desk, eating up the attention he was getting.

"Well, hold on," he began once the crowd calmed down. "Let me hit you with this. Does this orc even feel the slightest remorse for the..." Frank shuffled through the different papers on his desk until he held one up triumphantly. "For the three thousand New Yorkers displaced in your last orchestrated battle?"

Terra's eyes scrunched. "What do you mean, 'orchestrated'?"

"Oh, you can't fool me, Terra the Bootlicker. Can't fool ole 'Don't Tread on Me!' We know these attacks are all part of the globalist agenda to destabilize our economy and topple this great state! What do you have to say to that?"

Terra was done listening to Frank. "Okay, I'm going to spell this out for you. There is no agenda behind this. We aren't orchestrating anything. A multi-dimensional force is attacking humanity, along with orcs, elves, and everyone else. You're a big fan of talking about the different dimensions and planes of reality on this shithole of a show. Are you going to tell me you think it's all fairies and giggling gators out there? Are you so dense that you don't think there could be a potential threat? And is all that hippie stuff you've been talking about a lie?"

Frank's mouth hung wide open. He obviously wasn't used to being spoken to like that.

Terra didn't let up. "Secondly, you're a straight-up racist. People do this every time a war happens—you demonize whoever we're fighting until people are in such a blind rage they don't know the difference between anyone. Thirdly, Cire is sitting right here. Any questions you have about orcs, you can ask him. So, let's hear what he has to say about your first one."

Cire cleared his throat as he waited for the booing from the crowd to subside. It took a while, and Terra admired Cire's patience. Finally, the orc said, "The loss of human lives deeply grieves me. I was at that battle. I watched my brain-washed brothers and sisters engage in atrocities none would ever have wanted.

"What is happening *is* horrible for humanity, and my heart aches for you. That is why we are trying our best to fight the Dark One. No one needs to experience what my people have—to exist as something other than yourself, purely for the purpose of another. I speak for all orcs when I say we would never want to do any harm to any of you. We were weak, and the Dark One took advantage of that."

Cire began to cry, and he made no attempt to hide it. "The truth of the matter is, if you are going to hate orcs for anything, it should be for being too weak to have stood up to the Dark One when we had a chance, and now we are paying the price. That is why we must stop the Dark One. He will destroy all of you if he is not stopped, just like he has destroyed my people."

Cire wiped away his tears and sat in silence, looking all the stronger for being able to show such raw emotion in front of so many.

Even Frank seemed caught off-guard by Cire's response.

Someone in the crowd started clapping, then another. Before long, the entire studio was applauding.

The tone of the interview was different after that. Frank was on the defensive, and Terra and Cire were beating him into a corner. Nib-Nib chittered along as best as she could.

By the time Terra, Cire, and Nib-Nib left, Terra knew they had won the fight.

CHAPTER THIRTY-ONE

Sarah and Kravis sat beside a spy who had traveled from almost three hundred miles east of their current position. The spy didn't talk much, and Sarah was okay with that. He presented his information quickly, gave a detailed explanation for his arrival, and set out his plan.

The spy was a hacker. He had infiltrated the Dark One's fortress a year ago and had been siphoning information since then. It was imperative that his findings be sent to Myrddin immediately, and Sarah made sure it happened.

The next issue was a necessary extraction. The Dark One possessed valuable information concerning something that would interest both Sarah and Myrddin's forces.

"What is it?" Sarah asked.

When the spy spoke, his voice was grave. "You came across a shipment of a black liquid a few days ago. There is information concerning that. I'm not quite sure of the contents, but I know it is heavily guarded."

"Why would you need us for this? We don't have any particularly good hackers here. Definitely don't have the tech for it."

The spy shook his head as he raised his hand. "The tech isn't the problem. I have the necessities. I need backup."

Sarah looked dubiously at Kravis. "Neither of us is much into that kind of tech."

The spy knelt and rifled through his knapsack. He extracted two VR-helmets and handed one to Sarah. "It's a fully immersive combat-hacking software. Firewalls appear as enemies that have to be eliminated. The program is closer to a combat simulator than anything else. And from what I've heard, you're one of the most accomplished fighters the resistance has to offer. You were my first choice."

Sarah took the VR-helmet. "Okay, what do we have to do?"

"We need a place to sit or lie down. We slip them on. Once they boot up, it'll be self-explanatory. It'll be a tough fight, though."

Sarah motioned toward her tent and began to walk in its direction. She looked at Kravis, who nodded discreetly. They both knew the rules for situations like this. If something seemed sketchy, Kravis would handle it.

She wasn't too worried, though. The insignia the gnome wore was one Sarah recognized. In addition, the Dark One primarily used gnomes for manual-labor camps. Rarely combat situations. He lacked faith in gnomish combat abilities. A flaw the resistance was hoping to exploit.

Sarah and the spy lay on the bed, and she slipped the VR-helmet on. The world around her faded as she felt herself uploading into a digital world.

She saw nothing but a flat green plane. The spy was next to her. "What now?" she asked.

"I'll access the firewalls. We're going to try to break through all of them at once. Your avatar should be a perfect reflection of yourself in real-life physical abilities. You'll have to deal with all of the enemies. I'll be concentrating on navigating through the system. There should be no more than three firewalls. And it will be difficult."

Sarah had to admit she was a little excited. She'd never tried a VR combat-simulator.

"Also," the spy said. "Be careful. If you die in VR, you will go braindead."

Sarah nodded. She was glad there was a little bit of a challenge. Now might be the chance to see if she could push past the seventh chakra gate. If it was possible in VR, it could be possible in real life.

"Well, what are we waiting for?"

Abby was in the lab, and it was well after midnight. She was still working on processing the material Creon had given to her. There were more than just elvish and celestial texts now. Creon and Martin had managed to hack Myrddin's entire database.

The day before, Martin had prompted Abby with a question that seemed impossible at the time. *What if I could help you think faster?* The way the AI explained it was that since he was already helping Abby's system operate on an unconscious level, he could probably regulate most of her unconscious bodily function. He could, in essence, increase her neural pathways, and regrow all of her brain's grey matter.

Abby didn't waste too much time thinking about it. She gave Martin permission to get to work. She hadn't noticed anything at first. Not until her mood slumped in the mid-afternoon. She took a nap in the middle of the lab, and when she woke up, her mind could not stop racing.

She got straight to work, practically absorbing every bit of information Myrddin had locked up. Hundreds of years of notes. Both she and Martin combed through them together.

When Abby began to tire, Martin reduced the amount of lactic acid in her muscles and put her body to a relaxing, sleeplike state. She retained her higher cognitive abilities and continued to read and think.

Part of Abby wondered if she could still claim to be human. That was less of an interesting thought than what was in front of her, though.

As Abby pieced together Myrddin's disparate ideas and theories, she received a conference call from Roy, Terra, and Anabelle, through Zoom.

Terra waved, smiling widely, and Abby returned the smile. Roy looked noticeably less excited than everyone else. Anabelle looked tired.

"How's everyone holding up?" Roy asked.

Anabelle grinned the way a cat looks at its prey. "Oh, so informal…"

Roy tensed as if he'd just had a jolt of electricity run through him. "Don't see the point in pulling all that rank crap with you three. We've been on the same level for a while. But what do you all have to report?"

Anabelle started first. She explained how she'd been helping with the efforts to clean up New York. Meeting with different families who had lost their homes and helping to organize efforts to rehouse displaced persons. She was also working with a committee to deal with the issues of homelessness in the city.

Abby was surprised to hear Anabelle talking about helping humans. She'd worked with Anabelle long enough to know the elf didn't hate humans. That didn't mean Anabelle didn't hold some fairly problematic ideas about humanity. From the look on Anabelle's face, Abby would have bet the elf was starting to care a little bit about humanity.

When Terra spoke, she hit the nail on the head. "Looks like someone's cold, little elf heart is growing. Are you getting warm fuzzies helping people out."

Anabelle turned away from the camera and raised her nose. "Hardly. I am merely enjoying doing a good job. What about you? Tired of living your life in the limelight?"

Terra shook her head, smiling wide enough to make Anabelle cross her arms and pout slightly. "Nope, me, Cire, and Nib-Nib, are finally starting to get the hang of everything. People are starting to come around. And we haven't been attacked since the last fight we got into. I could probably make a career out of being Myrddin's ambassador.

Speaking of attacks, what's been up with that, Roy? How come the lich and Grok have gone silent. I've practically been begging to be ambushed."

Roy looked up from a stack of papers. "Huh? What?"

"You okay, my dude?"

Roy ran his hands through his hair. His eyes were droopy, and he appeared to have aged a couple of years. "Actually, to be completely honest, no, I am not. This kind of leadership, having *everyone* depending on me—there's so much to sign off on—but long answer made short: nope, not at all. Still trying to make sense of the information Myrddin left behind."

Abby raised her hand to get everyone's attention. She tried to put her words into simple sentences because her mind was racing with theories she and Martin had uncovered. "I've been reading Myrddin's files. I think we're up against a very large impending problem."

Roy hung his head as he sighed loudly. "You know, what else could I expect?"

"Sarah found something that Myrddin was trying to figure out. It was something a few Dragon Riders had found in the form of a weapon as well. And something we've seen the Dark One use on Persephone. It's this black goo. The same crap that came out with the Old One that was summoned."

"What exactly are you trying to say?"

"I think...and I think Myrddin was on this same train of thought... that the Dark One has direct access to the Netherverse. That he's harnessing some kind of—"

Roy interrupted Abby. "That black junk you're talking about came from Vardis, not the Dark One."

"In briefings concerning Vardis, he said he was from a similar plane as the Dark One. It would make sense that Vardis had access to the same stuff."

Roy leaned back, whistling. "How much of Myrddin's files have you read?"

"At the moment, everything written in English."

Anabelle raised her hands, waving them around to communicate her frustration. "Okay, everyone needs to slow down. I have no idea what anyone is talking about. Do you, Terra?"

Terra was picking her nails. She looked up, bored. "Honestly, until I have a clear idea of whether or not we're talking about something I need to kill, I'm mostly not listening. I'm much more of an action kinda girl. Plot can suck it."

Abby took a deep breath as her screen dinged, showing another person was ready to join the chat. "I told Persephone to join us. She's at the base. But I think she'd be able to explain some of this better than me."

Persephone's face popped up in the chat meeting. Her arms were bunched close to her body, and her eyes moved from one box of faces to the next quickly.

Abby continued talking as her mind raced. "The Netherverse is the realm the Old Ones exist in and it's kinda like antispace or antimatter. It's the polar opposite of ours, a place that exists in all the ways that the nine realms don't."

Terra folded her arms and leaned back in her chair. "See, *this* is why I don't care about plot. I practically need a Ph.D. in quantum physics to understand anything. Hey, Terra, punch this. Tackle that. See how that makes more sense?"

"The Netherverse is a place of pure energy. What I'm trying to say is that the Dark One has access to that. I've been running tests, and I think I've figured out how the Dark Gates work. They're teleporting *through* the Netherverse, but there are only certain access points, which is why we're always able to get readings on them when they do open. And I think the gnome homeworld is the largest touching point."

Everyone in the group chat looked at Abby with blank faces. "Abby, when was the last time you slept?" Anabelle asked.

"That's not important. Persephone, tell them what you told me."

Persephone held her cursed arm in her other as she spoke. "The Dark One was the one who introduced the Black Melody to my people and me. That's what we call it, and it is from the Netherverse. The Dark One uses it to bolster his armies. But the Melody, it's…"

The drow started to panic. Her breathing sharpening, her lips trembled, and she started to shiver.

Abby looked up what floor Persephone was. The drow was in the medbay, not too far from Abby's lab. She got up and raced over there.

Persephone was sitting in front of her computer, her back heaving as she sobbed.

Abby walked up behind Persephone and rested her hand on the drow's back. Persephone whirled to see Abby, who sat on the bed beside her. She hugged Persephone tightly as the drow cried.

Terra pulled at her shirt collar as she made mock kissy-faces.

Anabelle's eyes widened and she slashed her hand across her throat, signaling to Terra to stop joking.

Once Persephone's tears dried up, she spoke again, gripping Abby's hand tightly. "The Melody, it gets in your head. It starts to take over. You start to lose yourself as it asserts itself over you. It doesn't talk to you, not the way that we talk, but it's always speaking to you."

Persephone held up her hand, and her fingers slowly peeled apart as tentacles forced their way through her skin. "At first, I couldn't control it. That was why the Dark One had me chipped, so he could control us both. But now...now I can, but the Dark One is starting to infect his army with it, along with the chips. He's getting better at control."

Roy finally picked his head up off his table. "Ugh, this is the single worst week I've ever had."

CHAPTER THIRTY-TWO

Sarah was waiting for the second wave of enemies, and she was already exhausted. She'd had to push herself to the third gate, and the effort was taking a toll. Usually, she had time to work her way up to the gate, but the onslaught of enemies had meant she had to dig deep and quickly.

She wasn't certain how many she'd taken out. The bodies had disappeared almost as fast as they had appeared.

The spy was already queuing up the next batch of firewall enemies for Sarah to dispatch. Sarah wished the gnome had said something about the sheer volume of forces she was expected to fight.

"You ready for the next ones?" the spy asked.

Sarah inhaled, held her breath, felt it in her. She centered herself, rooting her feet to the ground, feeling her energy flowing through her. "Yeah, go ahead."

The gnome typed into his handset, and the green plane shifted and morphed. They were in a replication of an old gnomish city, one built above ground. The buildings didn't extend far into the sky, but they did feature much of the famous gnomish clockwork mechanisms.

The wave of enemies appeared in front of Sarah. Thirty orcs and goblins faced her, all armed with plasma rifles and plasma axes.

Sarah had been wanting to stretch herself for some time, to see what she was truly capable of. Today was going to be the day. Usually she had a multitude of tools at her disposal. Right now, the only thing Sarah had was her fists.

She didn't wait for the orcs to come to her. She concentrated on her breathing, on where her feet were, and she opened her fourth chakra—the heart chakra.

Energy exploded within her body, and her heart raced, blood pumping faster than before.

Sarah surged forward, throwing herself into the midst of the orcs.

They opened fire as she sailed through the air, twisted to avoid the blasts, and landed in the middle of the horde. Her fist connected with the ground and her ki reverberated around them, pushing the orcs back.

Sarah bounced to her feet, swung a fist at the closest orc, and hit him in the jaw. The bone cracked on impact, but another orc was attempting to grab her. She gripped his hand the moment it touched her shoulder, snapped the arm at the wrist. She did a backflip. Sarah landed behind the orc and tore his arm off.

She whirled and clocked an orc who was slashing at her at her face with its ax. She dropped to her feet, swiped at the legs of another orc, and rolled backward. As she got to her feet, the orc swung its ax at her again.

Sarah caught the ax between her palms, the plasma burning her skin. She fought through the pain, twisted the ax away, and flipped it in the air before throwing it at the orc. She was reaching to grab the ax when she heard rifle fire.

A blast of plasma flashed past Sarah, and she ducked to the side.

She sprang into the air, pulling all her ki into her chest, letting it burn. And she unleashed it in a large burst of flame. *Just enough,* she thought as she landed. She dashed forward, picked up an abandoned ax, and eliminated two goblins aiming their weapons at her.

Sarah could feel her body vibrating. If opening the gates didn't numb part of her pain, she'd be able to feel her muscles screaming.

More orcs materialized: a small army. Sarah pulled herself out of her head, nestling her consciousness back within her body. It didn't matter how many there were. She could do this.

Sarah unlocked the next chakra gate. Was she at the sixth now? It didn't matter. She would know once she encountered the eighth gate.

Her body flowed like a river through the mass of orcs and goblins, tearing through flesh with the precision of a butcher's blade. She weaved between plasma blasts as she increased her speed, her eyes now incapable of keeping up with her physical movements. Sarah was trusting that her hands and feet would find their way.

Finally, when Sarah stopped, the dead lay at her feet in droves. She sat beside the spy, slowing her breathing, feeling her ki, and preparing for the next wave.

Abby's meeting had taken a break until everyone could reconvene in the war room. Until then, she and Persephone were sitting together quietly on the drow's bed.

"I didn't think that was going to happen," Persephone said. "We aren't supposed to do that...get that emotional. My parents would be so embarrassed."

"Really? My dad would've been proud of me if I'd been able to do that. He always said you can't judge a man based on what he lets you see. Walls are meant to be unbuilt."

Persephone's eyes were still teary. She looked dreamily at Abby. "I'm glad you came to see me in person. I didn't want the first time we saw each other again to be over a computer screen."

"Sorry, I didn't come straight to see you. There's been a lot—"

"You don't have to apologize. I know you have a lot of responsibilities. I can't imagine how stressful this must be. If I was put in this position in a drow army, I would have quit by now."

Abby blushed and scooted closer nervously. But she shifted away from Persephone again. "Doubtful. You seem to be pretty capable."

"You saw Persephone under the control of the Dark One. Usually, I'm just a nervous wreck."

"Not true. You handled yourself pretty well with that dragon we fought together in the arena. And there wasn't a microchip in you. It was all you."

Persephone smiled from underneath the mass of her hair. "You're really sweet." She was quiet for a little bit, and then blurted, "I missed you a lot. I think about you every day. Is that weird to say?"

More than anything else in the world, Abby wanted to move closer and kiss Persephone. She wanted the war to be over. She wanted to be someplace far away, alone with the drow. "No, I don't think it's weird. Been thinking a lot about you too."

Persephone wrapped her fingers around Abby's. Her skin slowly broke apart, and little tentacles slithered over the girl's fingers. Nanobots poured from Abby's body and rolled over the drow's pale skin.

Abby stared deep into Persephone's eyes, unable to pull herself away. It was as if each moment was slipping away too quickly. She was desperate to grab them and keep this time together from ever ending.

The door to the medbay opened, and both girls jumped, Abby almost falling off the bed as she scrambled to see who had entered.

Terra stood on the threshold, drinking a beer and shaking her head. "Jesus, did I just interrupt you two from *holding hands*? How old are you?"

Abby stuttered as she said, "Sixteen."

Persephone stared at her cursed arm. "One hundred and ten."

Terra downed the last of her beer. "All right, so the first part of being a teenager who is a special agent in a secretive military base is to take advantage of the fact that you have your *own goddamn rooms!* Now get your asses up. We gotta finish this briefing."

The third wave was coming. Sarah could feel them forming in the ether of the digital plane. She hoped whatever the spy was looking for was worth it.

Sarah stood.

An army of a hundred orcs and goblins appeared before her.

She relaxed her body, focused with all her power, and visualized the eighth and final gate opening wide. She opened her eyes as her irises turned white. Her whole body trembled, and she felt like her skin was coming undone. If she didn't move, she might explode.

Her body moved forward almost of its own accord. She felt like a passenger in a car whose driver had greatly overestimated their ability to handle wide curves while speeding.

Sarah hit the first orc with enough force that its head exploded. She was on to the next, gliding through the mass of bodies, each orc moving slower than she'd ever seen a living creature move.

Snails surrounded Sarah, beings barely capable of movement.

And all the while, Sarah could feel her muscles coming undone, the lactic acid having reached a point where it had begun to burn her alive from the inside.

Bodies of orcs soared into the air as she plowed through them, moving at a truly superhuman speed, her body slowly tearing itself apart.

But the adrenaline kept her going. That, and the sound of cracking skulls and crushed bones. She barely registered the ax that hit her shoulders, but the blow wasn't enough to slow her. Sarah continued to decimate the orcs as though she were a tornado.

A plasma blast came flying at her, and before she could think any better, she slashed at it with her hand, cutting through the plasma, and searing her skin almost down the bone.

Yet, the severe injury did not stop her. She barreled through the orcs, circling them, moving faster than any of them could see. She picked off the stragglers on the outside before leaping into the thick of it.

Then it was suddenly over.

Sarah sat up in her bed and started coughing blood, holding her chest tight. It felt like her lungs were caving in. She pitched over the edge of her bed, the last hour of combat catching up with her within an instant as all eight gates closed simultaneously.

Every blast, ax-wound, and attack hit her system, coupled with the internal damage she'd received from the stress on her body.

Sarah couldn't stop screaming. Everything hurt so much. All she could do was lie on the floor, blood seeping from her eyes, nose, and ears as Kravis rushed to her side.

The world faded.

Abby, Terra, Anabelle, Roy, Creon, and Persephone sat in the war room. Roy was pacing back and forth, occasionally looking at Myrddin's chair, but refusing to sit in it. "What are our options? Anybody got a plan?"

Terra laughed loudly as she finished her beer. She pulled a twelve-pack from under her chair and tossed one to each person in the room. "Plans? I thought that was your department."

Roy threw his arms up in the air. "If it isn't obvious by now, I'm a fucking grunt! Plan a mission or extraction what-fucking-ever. Yeah, I can do that. Figuring out how to run a whole goddamn war is a little bit outside of my field of expertise."

Anabelle stood and went to Roy's side. She put her arms around him in an attempt to calm him down.

Terra looked from Abby to Creon and inhaled sharply. "Damn, Roy, I was kidding with you. I didn't mean it like that."

Anabelle gave Roy a kiss on the cheek, and he retired to Myrddin's chair. "No, I know. I'm just not...this isn't what I trained for. Abby knows more of what was going on in Myrddin's head than I do."

"Then maybe we should ask Abby," Anabelle suggested.

Initially, Abby's heart jumped, but Roy was right. She and Martin *did* have the best understanding of Myrddin's thoughts. "The gnome world is the nexus of the Dark One's operation. It's his tie to the Netherverse, so we need to hit that. Sever his center point for the Dark Gates."

Roy pulled up an image on the holoscreen. "The Gnome World is completely overrun by the Dark One. All we have are small resistances here and there. Nothing capable of taking back the planet."

"I'm not saying take back the planet. The majority of the Dark One's forces are in one spot. Sarah's done countless recons on it. We hit it, then we take it further. Dump everything we got into cutting off the gnome world from the Dark One. Surround it with our own defenses. Contain the threat on the planet. Starve it out."

The DGAs and the other exchanged glances. Anabelle spoke first. "That's a very dangerous strategy, Abby. If we put all our resources into that, we'll be defenseless across other theaters."

Abby wasn't going to back down. She knew this was the only real option. "If we cut the Dark One off from the Dark Gates, he can't attack Earth anymore. He's being held off on all other fronts already. It'll buy us a lot of time."

"And the lich?"

"I'm still working on something."

An incoming message blinked across the holoscreen. Roy accepted it, and Kravis appeared on the holoscreen. "Urgent news. You need to hear this now."

Roy motioned for Kravis to continue.

"We recently received intel on the Dark Gate structure. Got a read on their network. There's a gate that doesn't seem to go anywhere. We don't know what it is, but it's heavily guarded. In addition, that black crap we found earlier? All of the shipping routes for it are coming from that gate. Whatever the hell it is, it's pretty fucking important."

Anabelle and Roy looked at Abby as she nodded solemnly. "All right, Kravis. Anything else?" Roy asked.

Kravis looked over his shoulder. Sarah came limping onto the screen. She looked like hell. "This was the Dark One's most heavily guarded secret on the gnome world. Put it to good use."

"Will do."

The holoscreen turned off as Roy leaned forward in his chair. "Okay, Abby, you got it. I'll divert whatever I can to the gnomish world for an offensive, but I'm not sending all of you. I can't risk it.

Abby, you're staying here to help coordinate. I don't care what you have to say. You know too much, and I need you here."

Abby couldn't disagree. Even now, her head was flooding with potential plans.

Roy continued, "Terra, I know you want to get out and fight, but we still need you for recruitments. You and Cire have been turning the tide for us. People are finally beginning to pay attention. We'll get you out busting heads again soon."

"Which leaves you, Anabelle. You're going to handle this mission." Roy activated his comm. "What's the status on Blackwell and Naota? They getting along yet?"

A voice piped up. "Yes, sir. They're buddies now. Took a lot of *Clockwork Orange* reprogramming, but we got there."

"Good." He shut off his comm and turned to Anabelle. "I'll send Blackwell and Naota with you. A small squad to break into this Dark Gate, disable it, and get the resistance defenses up and running. We'll coordinate with Sarah and Kravis. We move out tomorrow."

Silence fell over the war room before Roy stood and said, "This is our big push. If Abby's right, this offensive will make or break the war with the Dark One."

CHAPTER THIRTY-THREE

Anabelle woke up and meditated. She'd never been comfortable with a morning practice, but recently, the early sessions had been growing on her. If she thought about it, she was inspired by Abby, who was early to rise and late to sleep. Anabelle wondered what her life would have been like if she'd had a similar work ethic as the child.

Memories were becoming easier to access for Anabelle. Many still remained hidden, but Anabelle was beginning to feel more complete and at home within herself.

Is it because of Grok?

Anabelle had never been challenged by an opponent like Grok before. The orc's skills were the closest to Anabelle's Traveler training, and even that hadn't been so much a challenge as an obligation.

The elf's time with Myrddin, playing the role of a model while also stealing important national secrets, hadn't been challenging in the proper sense of the word. The hardest part of the job was keeping from punching her marks in the face.

Grok had presented a different problem. One Anabelle hadn't faced before. This was the first time Anabelle had come across a problem she could not solve with the tools she possessed.

The option of a charming Grok was laughable. And no matter how much Anabelle pushed her body, she didn't seem capable of besting the orc.

Still, seeing Grok's face light up during their last battle had taught Anabelle something she'd never known about herself.

When she had first witnessed Terra's delight in battle, she'd been floored. She had been envious of someone who enjoyed pushing themselves to their limits. Anabelle had never needed to *really* try at anything before. It had all come so naturally. Many younger Travelers who had gone before her had failed. Anabelle had only ever been slightly annoyed.

Grok was the first thing to actively push against Anabelle in a way she couldn't easily ignore. And it was exhilarating. Initially, she'd been terrified by the look of murderous lust in Grok's eyes. Now, the elf saw something else entirely; she saw a door to possibilities.

But focusing on Grok during meditation was stupid. Anabelle should be looking at the past, finding lessons there. But she didn't care. She wanted to think about Grok. It felt good to allow herself to finally start obsessing. The orc was doing the same thing. Probably lightyears away, Anabelle knew Grok was thinking about her.

There was nothing else either of them could do; they were connected. Neither would be able to rest until the other one lay dead at their feet.

Anabelle found Blackwell and Naota in the hangar, speaking to Creon and Abby. When Abby and Creon spotted Anabelle coming toward them, they moved away, leaving Blackwell and Naota alone.

Anabelle hadn't seen the two humans together since the battle with the lich where they had almost killed each other. She hadn't given their recovery much thought; there hadn't been time. Everyone had been in crisis-mode since that day.

What surprised her was she hadn't been worried about either of them. Not that she hadn't cared. But rather that she had known they would pull through. They were strong. Naota was a little bit odd, and Blackwell probably a little too rigid, but the two men were tough. Besides, they hadn't been in the medbay. Anabelle would have had to hunt them down. She couldn't imagine having wasted time on that.

Even Anabelle had to admit that her feelings toward humanity had changed. When she had first met Blackwell, she'd believed he was a child, incapable of defending himself and needing to be babysat during the entire mission.

Blackwell had proven her wrong, revealing he was more than capable of leading his squad. And he'd only continued to impress her with his dedication and leadership.

Naota had been another story altogether. Her initial impression of Naota was that he was an idiot who was going to get himself killed. She had been taken aback by his decision to join the fight at an amusement park he'd worked at, knowing nothing about the stakes and being—what she had believed at the time—a lowly human.

Now Naota was leading alongside Blackwell. And his demeanor hadn't changed ; he was still the same confusing oddball.

The words came out of Anabelle's mouth before she realized it. "Of all the people to go on a suicide mission with, I'm glad it's you two."

Blackwell, who was tying his laces, looked up at Anabelle. "Couldn't agree more, ma'am. It's been an honor to serve with you. I'm looking forward to continuing that service."

Naota saluted Anabelle, who was only slightly annoyed the human still hadn't learned the official DGA salute. He said, "Same here. Couldn't think of anyone else I'd love to risk my life with. Other than Blackwell, of course."

"Sorry, I didn't visit you guys when you were... What happened with you afterward?"

Naota removed his shades, his eyes bright with excitement. "Oh, you would not believe it! You know how we were going to kill each other, right? Wild. Me and this guy? We're practically in love. Seriously. *In. Love.* And here we are trying to kill each other."

Anabelle snapped her fingers impatiently. "Less talking soon, please."

"Gotcha, boss-lady. Creon figured our brains had been tampered with by the lich. So, I told them about this story I read about how Deadpool and Wolverine can't be affected by telepathy or mind control because their brain cells are constantly regenerating. He thought it was a pretty interesting idea, and he regrew our brain cells until they weren't affected by the lich's magic anymore."

Anabelle raised an eyebrow at Naota. "Are you telling me you were saved by your god-awful extensive comic book knowledge?"

Naota grabbed Blackwell and pulled him in close for a hug. "The both of us were. Might even be used for a big reveal later. And now we can continue our passionate annihilation of the Dark One."

Blackwell pulled himself away from Naota and returned to suiting up. "I wasn't sure how much weaponry to bring. Abby and Creon supplied us with the means to pack in a lot of heat. Think they got one for you too."

Abby and Creon approached Anabelle as the two soldiers continued prepping. The girl handed her a circular compact. "It's pre-loaded with a buncha weapons and crap," Abby said. "Not quite sure what all is in it. I just made the tech. Here you go."

Anabelle took the compact. "Sorry you have to stay home and miss out on the life-threatening fun."

"Actually, I'm more than happy to sit this one out. Roy needs help with this. And honestly, my head is full of so much right now, I think I'd be pointless out there."

"And what else?"

Abby groaned loudly as she turned and walked away from Anabelle. "And Persephone's here. Are you happy now?"

"Very."

Abby and Creon departed, leaving the marines and Anabelle alone. The trio approached the hadron collider.

Anabelle, Blackwell, and Naota were transported to the sand dunes of the gnomish world, about forty miles off from the coordinates Sarah and Kravis had supplied. With the heat, it would take a few hours to reach the camp. Most of that journey would be completed at night to avoid overheating.

According to Roy's and Abby's calculations, they could only risk sending a small group via the hadron collider. The others would have to go by ship, which would make timing difficult. After all, anything to do with hyperspace was always complicated.

Once Anabelle and the humans got their bearings, they began their trek to the camp's coordinates.

Anabelle had never been to the gnomish world. Now that she thought of it, she'd only seen the elvish, human, and dwarven realms in person, not counting Middang3ard since it was an in-between of all the realms.

She wondered why she'd never been interested in seeing where the gnomes lived. The elf had been alive long enough to have visited the Gnome World before it fell. But she'd been a child back then. More than likely, she'd been too interested in living her own life.

Such a shame that this is what it's taken for me to come here, Anabelle thought. *Not quite what I was expecting...*

After an hour of walking, it became apparent that it was too hot to continue. Naota and Anabelle scouted the area to ensure none of the Dark One's forces were nearby, while Blackwell worked on locating a water source.

When Anabelle and Naota returned, Blackwell had found a collection of cacti that he suspected held water. He sliced them open, and they drank the fresh liquid while sitting on the sand dunes, watching the sun set.

Once the oppressive sun sank beneath the golden sand dunes, the trio resumed their journey. They were silent as they walked, their shadows stretching across the sand as if they were totems of old. Occasionally, they took breaks to forage for water and rest their legs. But it was not long before they were walking again.

Anabelle was happy to find the humans had a good grasp of basic survival techniques. She could have gone for hours without water or food. Over a week without water, if necessary. Her body would have just begun to burn mana. Over time, she would have been depleted, but elvish bodies were more resilient than they appeared to be.

That being said, it was good to have water and rest.

In the fifth hour, Blackwell used his binoculars to glass what he suspected were fires in the distance. He checked his map and confirmed they had found the camp.

Anabelle commed ahead, informing Kravis and Sarah that they would reach the camp within minutes and to relax any defenses present. Kravis assured Anabelle that they were awaiting them.

The trio strolled into the camp—if you could call it a camp. There was a smattering of tents, and a handful of gnomes wandered about as though they had lost their purpose. They had the same look in their eyes as the displaced humans Anabelle had seen in New York.

Kravis came out to meet them at the fire. "It's good to see you." There were introductions around for those who hadn't formally met. "Follow me. Sarah's waiting for you."

The gnome led them through the ramshackle camp to Sarah's tent. He pulled back the tarp, and Anabelle entered.

Sarah lay on a bed, her chest bandaged up to her neck. She sat up and smiled at Anabelle. "You're a sight for sore fucking eyes."

Anabelle sat beside Sarah. "Looks like that isn't the only sore thing you've got. What happened?"

"Just pushed myself a little bit too much, that's all. I'll be up in a few hours. Hopefully."

Anabelle retrieved a bottle of elvish wine from her knapsack, along with a few cups. "Let's keep our fingers crossed that this'll work." She poured a cup for everyone. "I was expecting a bigger camp than this."

Kravis sipped his drink and nodded slowly. "It was. We disbanded it. Sent smaller groups around. Trying to get everyone organized for the big push. Can't do that if all the folk are spread out."

Sarah winced as she swallowed. "Yeah, we're on a skeleton crew. But we're small enough not to be bothered. Once we leave, the gnomes who remain here are going to try their luck underground.

Should be safe. So, fearless leader of the DGA...got any good war stories?"

Anabelle chuckled as she poured herself another cup, her eyes deep and far away, caught within her memory. So much had happened over the last few days. "Saw a lich get resurrected, then watched the same lich summon an Old One, which she baited Myrddin into killing for her so she could eat its soul and gain its power. Needless to say, we got our asses kicked in that one."

Sarah snatched the bottle from Anabelle and laughed. "I take back what I said before. I don't ever want to be officially reassigned to the DGA. You can keep your liches and Old Ones. Just give me a good, old-fashioned planet in need of liberation."

The tent rang with laughter. A little tense, but laughter all the same.

CHAPTER THIRTY-FOUR

The next day, the group rose with the sun as it began to peek over the humps of the sand dunes. By the time Anabelle got out of bed, the camp had already been broken down. All that remained was her own team's tents. Sarah and Kravis were already sitting by a fire, roasting meat rations for the day's trip.

Anabelle sat beside Sarah, who passed her a piece of smoked bear flesh. The elf turned her nose up at it, but she took a piece nonetheless. It was gamey but easy enough to get down. "Should I wake those two up?"

Sarah shook her head. "No, we got up early for preparations. We wanted to make sure the refugees got off in the right direction. They won't have a whole lot of support, and it would be better for them to move before they can be tracked easily. How'd you sleep?"

Anabelle stretched. Her back was a little sore, and her legs were killing her. "Haven't had to rough it like that in a long time."

"Yeah, it's kinda funny for how much you agents risk your lives, for you to still be a little bit on the soft side."

Normally, Anabelle would have been livid at someone calling her soft, but she could see the faintest hint of a smile on Sarah's face. And besides that, Sarah was more than just a coworker. She was a fellow warrior and friend. There was nothing wrong with a little chiding.

"Yeah, those beds at HQ are a little bit soft. And the blankets. Don't even get me started about the blankets."

Kravis snickered as he stoked the flames. "Sarah's been going on about blankets for at least a year now."

Sarah shoved him playfully. "Every time I get called back to base, I demand at least fifteen blankets. Otherwise, I'm not coming back. If I'm going to be home, I want to be as comfortable as humanly possible. Makes coming back out here a lot easier."

Anabelle was surprised by Sarah's attitude. "Really? I would have thought having any shred of comfort would make roughing it out here even harder."

"No, not really. The whole time I'm in those comfy-ass beds, the only thing I can think about are the gnomes out here who are happy to have a chance to sleep on anything other than rocks. The faster I get back out here in the field, the more work I can do to make sure there aren't children sleeping out in the cold."

Anabelle didn't think of her work in the same way as Sarah. But it was admirable to see someone so committed to the cause that they couldn't enjoy their own comfort knowing people out there were suffering.

There was a lot to admire about Sarah. And, much like with Terra, Anabelle was starting to realize that it was okay to see those qualities in people and respect them.

By the time Blackwell and Naota were awake and tearing down their tents, the final preparations for the day had been made. Enough water had been drawn and stored for all of them. Now it was time for the journey.

According to Kravis, it would be a two-day hike. They would have to pass through an orc encampment at the halfway point, but that was the only way to make good enough time for the incoming satellites.

Anabelle informed Kravis that it was still going to take the satellites four days to arrive, and the gnome assured her that he was prepared. If the Dark One was scrambling to figure out what had happened to his base, there was a good chance the forces on the planet would be too distracted to look skyward. It would be a perfect time for the satellites to slip into position without being noticed. "In essence, *we're* going to be the distraction."

Kravis and Sarah led the way, and they marched south as the heat of the day began to make itself apparent, their shadows short, stubby imitations of their bodies.

Anabelle and the two humans were not used to this kind of strenuous "hiking." From their departure, they had kept a pace that was more of a brisk jog. If the trio hadn't been in great physical condition, they would have been wiped out much earlier in the day.

The heat didn't seem to bother Sarah or Kravis; they were obviously used to it.

Not Anabelle, though. She didn't complain, but so much sweat was dripping down her face that she almost couldn't see through it. The thought that Sarah and Kravis made these treks regularly when moving camps seemed obscene. And Sarah was traveling while still injured.

Anabelle was curious about that. She jogged up to Sarah and tried to keep pace with the human. "Hey, I wanted to talk to you about your injuries. You seem to be dealing with them pretty well. How'd you get them?"

Sarah pointed at her forehead, the space in between her eyebrows. "The ninjutsu art of the eight gates. Opening up all of your chakras. Generally, those are there to keep you from burning yourself out. You pull them up, and you can push your body. Push too far, and you can do irreparable damage. Luckily, that didn't happen. The body heals fast enough. But the soul...the mind...that can take some time. I don't think I'll be doing that again anytime soon."

She pointed at the gun hanging from her side. "I'll remember I have other options."

"How do you push yourself further?" Anabelle asked. "Say, someone has a block. Or someone they can't overcome. How—"

Sarah giggled and quickly suppressed it. "You know I know who you're talking about, right? I gave you the files on Grok. I know this isn't a hypothetical."

Despite the heat, Anabelle had somehow managed to blush brightly. "Okay, sorry. Grok is definitely stronger than me. And every time we fight, I feel like I walk away a little bit tougher. But I can't figure out how to take it to another level on my own. Before I come across her again."

"The way of the Traveler isn't that much different from my practice. You have mana or magic. I have ki or life energy. Both of us manipulate that for tangible results. What I've found is that generally, you can only push yourself as far as your will can take you."

"Like Terra."

Sarah snapped her fingers as the group climbed and descended a hill. "Exactly."

Kravis held up his hand, and the group stopped. As he scanned the hills with a pair of binoculars, Sarah said, "When she was off-Earth, Terra was able to tap into the natural process of using her ki. But once back on Earth, the way our planet and realm works, you need a lot of training to get to that level. She could probably do it one day. Ditch the exo-suit and be as strong as she was. But it won't happen overnight."

Anabelle sat beside Blackwell and Naota, who spoke quietly to each other as they shared a sack of water. "So, what am I supposed to do?" Anabelle asked.

Sarah tapped Anabelle's forehead. "All blocks we experience in life are up here. You remove those blocks, you remove the limitations of your growth. Until you stop holding yourself back, you're never going to move forward."

Anabelle felt like she had just been transported to the past. That sounded like something her former masters would have said. "Didn't know you were so enlightened."

"No need to get snarky. Just repeating what I was taught. Feels like it helps sometimes."

Kravis interrupted their philosophical discussion. "That's it. Up ahead. The orc encampment. Last spot of defense from this side until we get to the massive setup they got going on. We move through here to the safe spot, and we'll be good for the night. You guys ready?"

Blackwell chugged more water and nodded.

Naota lifted his sunglasses for a moment to stare defiantly in the wrong direction. "Born ready," he said stoically.

The orcish encampment resembled a small fort, nothing like the Kravis' and Sarah's camp. Its walls were built high, and sentries were posted all along its length. Kravis informed the party that there would be a small army in the encampment as well. "It's going to be a hell of a fight if we don't plan this well."

Anabelle looked at Sarah. "Well, this is more of your guys' thing. What's the plan?"

Sarah used her binoculars to scan the encampment for a few moments. "We have to take out those sentries first. I've seen the general setup of these kinds of forts. The walls are nearly cut off from the rest of the camp. They're on a different level. If we can take out all of the sentries at the same time, we should be able to slip in undetected."

Sarah and Kravis were taking the eastern and southern parts of the wall, while Anabelle and the marines would handle the other sides.

The party split, each going their separate ways. Anabelle's worked their way around, using the dunes to provide cover. Once they got to their position, they opened their compacts, looking for the most appropriate weapon.

Blackwell, who had been in charge of outfitting, had packed a sniper rifle for each with a powerful scope.

Anabelle clicked the rifle, and it downloaded into her hand from her HUD. She believed the weapon was inelegant, but she would rather have followed Sarah's lead than mess up. Stealth wasn't exactly her field of expertise.

On the opposite side of the fort, Kravis and Sarah were getting into position as well. Instead of picking a good vantage point, they had snuck up to the wall and were preparing to scale it. Sarah sent Anabelle a confirmation that they were about to move and to wait for her signal to fire.

Anabelle lined up her shot, as did the two commanders. Then her HUD dinged. She fired, taking out one of the orcs as Blackwell and Naota followed suit.

Sarah and Kravis quickly scaled the wall, the pair flipping up onto the top and rushing the four orcs standing guard. Kravis took two and Sarah the others.

Kravis fired his crossbow twice, hitting both orcs in the head as Sarah tossed a kunai at both of the orcs. Without breaking her stride, she ducked under cover of the wall, scanning for the other orcs that weren't easily visible. "We have a cluster of three over on our side, and there's two more on yours. They should be visible in about ten seconds."

Sarah scooted around the corner of the wall, leaning over for a better view. She motioned for Kravis to go forward, and he fired twice, dropping two orcs while Sarah took care of the last one. As the orc fell, Sarah could hear the familiar sound of silenced sniper-rifles firing. "Everyone's down up here," Sarah confirmed. "Get on up."

She and Kravis went to the most likely spot on the wall for Anabelle and the marines to scale. She'd guessed correctly. Within minutes, the trio was scrambling up the side of the wall.

Once they were all atop the wall, Anabelle waved at the other side. "Down there?"

Sarah nodded. "Yeah, there's usually a set of barracks. Three, generally. We roll in. Take them down, sweep the area, and make camp for the night."

Anabelle peered over the ledge of the wall, looking for the barracks. "Sounds good."

CHAPTER THIRTY-FIVE

Anabelle prepared her grappling hook and waited for the signal from Sarah. She wasn't used to following direct orders from anyone other than Myrddin. This was something she could get down with. Being along for the ride was much more tolerable than she had expected.

Blackwell and Naota were bickering quietly, and both Sarah and Kravis were waiting for them to shut up and get their grappling hooks ready.

When Naota realized everyone was waiting on him, he looked away bashfully as he quickly prepared his hook. Blackwell said nothing and betrayed no emotion, but he worked fast as well.

Once everyone was prepared, Sarah took the first leap. Everyone else followed her.

As they slid down their wires, Anabelle noticed the distance from the top of the wall and the ground was greater than she'd expected. Either tech or magic had augmented the space between the wall and the ground. It made sense. The added distance would give the orcs at the bottom enough time to prepare. That is, if they had been properly warned.

"The ground should be coming up soon," Sarah whispered.

Sarah was right. It felt like the bottom came out of nowhere. Anabelle and the marines hit the ground with a heavy thud, while Sarah and Kravis landed gracefully on their feet, barely making a sound.

The barracks were in plain sight, but the space beneath the walls was expansive. Anabelle had been expecting the buildings to be clustered together, but they were spread wide over the length of about a football field.

Sarah pointed at the barracks closest to them and crept toward it, keeping to the shadows. Everyone followed suit until she raised her hand. The party halted, and Sarah sprinted ahead. She climbed up the side of the barracks, to the roof, and disappeared for a few moments. She returned to the edge and raised six fingers.

Anabelle looked from Kravis to Sarah, confused as to what to do next with this information. They were obviously trying to be as quiet as possible, and Anabelle was not used to sneaking around. So, she shrugged at Sarah, who smiled back and winked at Kravis.

The gnome grabbed Anabelle's hand, tugged her toward the barracks, and pointed at the window.

Anabelle peered through the window and ducked quickly. A group of orcs were seated inside. She gathered it was her job to do a headcount. Slowly, she peeked up again. She counted four that she could see and raised four fingers for Sarah.

Kravis was moving, preparing to take point, but Anabelle waved him down. She didn't want these two to have all the fun. She pointed at herself, and Kravis took a step back. Up above, Sarah smiled widely.

Anabelle pushed open the barracks windows. She concentrated her mana, her body dissolving into the shadows cast by the windowsill. The darkness slithered into the barracks as the window shut quietly.

Still dark and intangible, Anabelle crawled up the side of the wall and slipped into the shadow cast by a nearby orc. Her hand emerged from nothing and pulled the orc into his shadow.

The other orcs reacted, but by then, Anabelle had jumped out of the shadow. She drew her mana to her arms and legs, increasing her speed, delivering blow after blow in a whirlwind. She spun and knocked each of the orcs out.

Anabelle felt the exertion from the successive attacks, but she pulled mana from the orc's last breath to replenish herself. Then she slipped out the window.

Sarah was waiting for Anabelle and nodded her approval. "That was impressive. Didn't see you as someone who could be that stealthy."

Anabelle tried not to look too proud of herself. "We don't get to be stealthy very much. Myrddin's always throwing us into the boiling shit pot."

Sarah pointed in the direction of the next barracks, this one still caught in the shadows. The party moved silently as a unit, despite never working together in this capacity before. Anabelle could see the natural leadership Sarah possessed, even if she'd heard through HQ gossip that Sarah didn't consider herself a leader.

Once they closed in on the barracks, Blackwell and Naota took point, lining up their shots to eliminate the three orcs chatting out front. Kravis, Sarah, and Anabelle snuck around to the back of the barracks.

Sarah boosted Kravis up to peek through the window while Anabelle held the window up.

Anabelle gave the signal to Blackwell and Naota, who fired as Kravis took care of the two orcs in the barracks.

They were about to rejoin when a whirring alarm went off.

Blackwell and Naota looked at each other as one of the orcs they had shot stumbled to his feet. Naota took aim again and fired quickly, dropping the orc, but it was too late. The alarm had already been rung.

At least twenty orcs came running out of the last barracks. When they saw the small party of resistance fighters, two of the orcs ran back into the barracks, returning within a few seconds with two vials of black liquid.

Anabelle recognized it instantly. It was the same stuff that Abby and Persephone had briefed her on.

One of the orcs took the vial and slammed it against his skin. When the glass cracked, the black liquid forced itself inside his mouth. The other orc did the same.

Black tendrils ripped out of the orc's bodies as they fell forward, the other orcs forming a circle around them.

When the resistance party rejoined each other, Naota was already sputtering an apology for missing his shot. "I thought I had it lined up. I'm so sorry, I thought—"

Sarah clapped Naota on the back. "Don't worry about it, everyone misses shots. Honestly, things usually go ass-backward way before this. You guys did good for your first time."

Naota's face brightened as he smiled and flipped up his glasses. "Really?" He turned to Blackwell. "Permission to WYL out, sir."

Blackwell stroked his brow as he sighed. "I've told you before to stop asking me for that."

"Is that a yes, sir?"

"Goddamn, yes. And stop calling me 'sir.'"

Naota whipped out his chain tasers and flipped them over his shoulders as he turned to face the orcs. "Let's show them how we do this at HQ."

A blast of tendrils hit Naota in the chest, sending him flying, his screams echoing through the cavern.

The two orcs who had ingested the fluid were back on their feet. Tendrils were shooting chaotically out of their bodies, like some kind of foreign agent. Their eyes rolled into the back of their heads, and they were foaming at the mouth.

Anabelle whistled loudly. "Guess that's what the black goop is for. That's not too impressive. Naota? Are you okay?"

Naota sat up, scratching his head, looking around as if he were lost. "Uh...yeah...I'm still alive. Not exactly kicking, but still alive."

"Let's take care of these sons of bitches."

Anabelle sprang into action, sprinting to the orcs with the tendrils with Sarah hot on her heels.

Naota joined up with Blackwell and Kravis, who were drawing the other orc's attention with suppressing fire.

As Anabelle leaned in close to take a swipe at the tendrilled orc, the orc reached out with a speed Anabelle hadn't been expecting and landed a punch to her face. As the elf flew off, her comm rang. She hit the ground and accidentally picked up.

Terra was on the line. "Hey, Anabelle, do you know anything about dinner etiquette?"

Anabelle climbed to her feet as the tendrilled orc leapt over its brethren and landed in front of her. It slammed its hands down to crush the elf, who managed to roll to the side. "I'm kind of busy right now, Terra!"

"Yeah, I know, but I don't know who else to ask. I'm kinda at this fancy dinner and there's a thousand forks to choose from, and honestly, they all look the same, but I remember seeing in a movie that picking the wrong fork is a huge deal or something."

Anabelle flipped up to her feet and caught the orc in a flaming uppercut, sending the creature stumbling backward. "Uh…how many forks are there actually? A specific number. And what are you eating?"

Anabelle was hit in the chest by the tendrils, which sent her flying over Sarah, who was grappling with the other tendrilled orc while Naota leapt into the large mass. He spun, electrocuting any orc dumb enough not to move out of the way.

The elf slid across the ground, rolling to her feet and charging her arms with lightning.

Terra answered, "We're eating salads right now."

Anabelle connected with the orc, sending it stumbling backward. "It's the really thin one with all the prongs bunched together."

"All of the forks are tiny and have prongs close together."

"Goddamn it, Terra. Just Google it!"

Terra sighed loudly as Anabelle dodged another tendril attack. "I did. They all look the same."

Blackwell crashed into the tendrilled orc's side, but not from tackling it. He was thrown and he crumpled to the ground, then realized where he was and opened fire on the orc.

Anabelle flipped over the orc, shooting electricity from her hands. "Do you even like salad?" she shouted.

"No," Terra answered. "But I don't want to be rude."

"Ugh, why don't you ask Abby?"

A timid voice spoke up. It was Abby. "Uh, I told Terra to call you."

The tendrilled orc picked Blackwell up and tossed him at Kravis, who nimbly dodged out the way as he fired his crossbow. Kravis hit two orcs in the head as Sarah ran up behind him, scooped him up in her arms, and tossed him into the thick of battle.

The gnome sheathed his crossbow and drew two daggers, slashing at anything that moved as he sailed through the orcs. He landed beside Anabelle, who was deflecting the tendrilled orcs' attacks. "Why don't you just send her a picture, Abby?" Anabelle shouted.

"I did. She said they all look the same."

Terra groaned in irritation. "Forks all look the fucking same! Oh, shit. Sorry, sorry, sorry."

"You don't have to apologize to me," Abby said. "I've heard people curse before."

"No, I was talking to the Prime Minister."

Anabelle grabbed the tendrils from the orc, trying to drain as much mana as she could from the creature. "Wait, you're eating with the Prime Minister?"

"Uh, I think a couple of them," Terra answered. "Prime Ministers plural, at least."

Across the battlefield, Sarah unleashed a massive blast of ki as she jumped on top of the tendrilled orc, and started beating the shit out of it.

Anabelle felt something welling up in her. "Wait, you're with how many prime ministers right now?"

"Wait, Anabelle, I got to go. I think I did something very wrong."

The line clicked, and Anabelle screamed with rage, her body filling up with mana. Her hands caught fire, and she drove them deep into the tendrilled orc's body, burning the creature alive from the inside. When she stood up and looked around, the other orcs were dead.

Sarah was also pushing herself off a tendrilled orc. "Now that was a fight," she said as she walked over to Sarah. "What brought that out in you?"

Anabelle laughed as she looked at the orc. "You know, I was upset that Terra was having dinner with a bunch of prime ministers. And then I realized I was upset at myself for being upset about such a stupid thing. I don't even want to be doing that. I want to be out here. And I was being pissy about something I don't even care about."

Sarah punched Anabelle in the shoulder. "That's what I was talking about. The only block is you. Come on. Let's get this place in order. We're camping here for the night."

CHAPTER THIRTY-SIX

They woke early, before the dawn, and walked through the shadows of the cavern by the light of their HUDs like silent wraiths hellbent on the impending destruction. By the time they finally came to the surface, the sun was beginning to rise.

In the distance, Anabelle could see the orc defense-tower looming. It was not that different than the towers she'd seen the Dark One using across Middang3ard in briefings provided by Abby. The construction was not orcish. Even from this distance, Anabelle could see the bright blue lights given off by the Dark One's advanced technology.

The party stopped on a hill as Sarah peered through binoculars, gauging the situation. "So, what's the plan?" Anabelle asked.

Sarah handed the binoculars to Kravis, who looked through them for a moment before passing them to Blackwell. "Similar to before. We're breaking into two groups, and we work our way through the base. Set detonators across the foundation, a couple of other hot spots. Call in reinforcements from the resistance to deal with the hell that's going to come afterward. Try to get out alive."

Kravis was hunched over a collection of grass and twigs, striking a piece of flint to start a fire as Blackwell and Naota watched. "You know, we have fire starters," Naota offered.

The gnome shrugged as his fire caught flame. "And what do you do when you don't have your fire-starter?"

Naota frowned as he removed his sunglasses and looked out at the defense tower. "Guess you got a point there."

Kravis took out a pot and steel framework, placing the pot on the frame before pouring water into it. "You can't be too reliant on tools: fire-starters, vehicles, guns, swords, whatever. You depend too much on them, you forget what to do when they're gone. Say you don't have any of your flashy weapons, and an orc comes at you? Is the only reason you know how to kill an orc because you got a gun?"

"What would you do?"

Kravis looked up from the fire. "Kick it in the nuts, or tear through its ankle with my teeth. Something that big. Only chance I got. Then get on top as fast as I can, and get my hands around its throat."

Naota hunched beside Kravis. "That's deep. Pretty morbid, but pretty deep."

Kravis reached into his pouch and pulled out some raw meat. He held it over the flame and watched it cook. "That's just the way I am. Ain't changing anytime soon, I suppose."

Naota clapped the gnome on the back. "It's sick. Don't think I've ever met anyone with your outlook. You're a cool little dude."

Kravis stared at Naota, appearing confused by the compliment. "Uh...thank you."

As they continued to talk, Blackwell walked over to Anabelle and Sarah, who were still surveying the defense tower.

Sarah looked over her shoulder at Blackwell as he approached. "Looks like those two are getting along fairly well. Don't see that very often. I can't remember the last time I remember Kravis making a friend."

Blackwell sat beside Anabelle. "He's an all right guy. Can't see why he'd have any problems."

Sarah's face softened—something Anabelle hadn't seen often. "He's been out here for a long time. All he's known for a bit has been me and war. Not exactly the most stimulating environment for conversation skills to flourish."

Blackwell shrugged as he motioned for the binoculars. "Nah, I don't think either of you is doing too bad. Maybe the extra company is what you guys needed."

Sarah winced at Blackwell's words as if she'd been slapped. Then she smiled and handed Blackwell the binoculars. "I'm not going to lie...it has been good to have you three around. Practical. You're a good fighter, and you follow instructions well. What more could I ask for?"

Anabelle felt the words bubbling up in her again, as it had in New York. "You know, it's okay to enjoy being around people sometimes. Even better to be around friends."

Sarah met Anabelle's eyes. The elf felt like she could see something working behind Sarah's gaze, her mind churning to understand what had slipped out of Anabelle's mouth. Then she smiled. A real smile, her eyes bunching up tight as if she were about to cry. "I haven't heard someone call me that in a long time. But don't think I'm going to start getting all gushy on you guys just because you start saying nice things. It's appreciated, though."

Anabelle stared out at the defense tower looming in the distance because there was nothing else to look at. "They're not nice things. It's the truth. We're your friends, and I for one am happy to be out here with you."

Blackwell nodded as he stood up. "Same here." He glanced over his shoulder and asked, "Food time yet?"

Kravis grunted, annoyed. "If you want it any faster, you can get your ass over here and take care of it."

Blackwell walked over to Kravis and Naota as he said, "I'm gonna go show Kravis how to barbeque with some style."

Anabelle and Sarah sat quietly alone for a few moments before Sarah cleared her throat and coughed. "One of the first things I was taught was to work alone. The second thing was that you should never get close to the people you're working with. In my line of work, your friends die pretty quickly. Slows you down over the course of years. If you cut them out, nothing slows you."

"Yeah, okay, Ms. Assassin. You know the emotionally distant sole warrior trope is a little old. Been there, done that. Seen enough of it as well. The way I see it now is, fighting beside your friends reminds you why you're fighting. And no one is watching your back like someone who cares about you. That's the whole thing with you and Kravis, right? You guys are always there for each other because of that love. You'd probably give anything for him and vice versa. That's how I feel about my team too. The DGA, Blackwell, and that idiot Naota. And I know they feel the same way."

Anabelle took Sarah's hand and squeezed it tight. "And you're DGA, whether or not you want to admit it."

Sarah stared at both their hands before pulling hers away suddenly. She rubbed her eyes and stood. "Thanks. I'll keep that in mind. We should go get something to eat."

Sarah strode off before stopping abruptly. Her eyes were wet, and she wiped them repeatedly. "I don't know how to do these things. But I don't want to ruin it...I don't know what to say...I just...you know, it's lonely...very lonely..."

Anabelle came over to Sarah and wrapped her arms around the human, holding her while she cried.

Over by the fire, Blackwell and Kravis looked at Sarah and Anabelle. Blackwell scoffed softly. "Looks like they're having a moment."

Kravis turned his attention to the coffee brewing. "Just having a good cry. Ain't nothing wrong with having a good cry. You should try it sometime. You might loosen up enough to actually be able to take a shit, and stop looking like you've been constipated for a decade."

Naota burst out laughing, but he caught himself when he saw how red Blackwell had turned. Then he scooted over as Anabelle and Sarah found places to sit around the fire. Without warning, he burst into tears, loud, booming sobs as he threw his arms around Anabelle, who quickly tried to crawl away. "What the hell are you blubbering for?" she shouted.

"Your friendship! It's so beautiful!"

Anabelle and Sarah exchanged glances before the fae gave up and held Naota as he wept loudly. Once his tears dried, the party ate and drank coffee.

Sarah outlined the plan in greater detail. There were four power generators in the tower. That was their first priority. Cutting the power would give them a bigger window to work within. From there, one team would take care of knocking out the hangar, and the other would make their way for the main general of the tower. If they took care of that, then the orcish forces would be in disarray. After that, blow the charges around the foundation, and hope the whole thing toppled.

Kravis stomped out the fire and packed their belongings. "All right, how are we splitting up?"

Sarah pointed at Anabelle. "I'm taking the elf. After that last fight, I want to see what Anabelle can do. You mind babysitting Naota and Blackwell?"

Blackwell snorted derisively. "I don't need a babysitter."

Naota, on the other hand, brightened up instantly. "Oh! Bro time! Sweet!"

Kravis sighed and shook his head slowly. "Yeah, that's good by me. We should get going, though. Now that we got a little food in us, let's get this over with."

As they approached, the party split in two, one heading toward the western side of the defense, and the other taking the eastern route. There were few orcs along the way. Sarah told Anabelle it was because the orcs were lacking in resources around the defense tower. It took a lot to hold the entire gnomish world, and the Dark One's forces were spread throughout the planet. That, and the orcs didn't believe the gnomes had the slightest chance of rising up.

"We'll show them, though," Sarah said. "They've made the worst decision you can in a fight. Two of the worst: underestimating your enemy, and the sheer power of desperation."

A small camp of orcs was situated outside the defense ring, barely large enough to be called a camp. It only took Anabelle and Sarah a few minutes to sneak in and deal with them. They hid the dead to avoid drawing any attention to themselves if someone were to pass through the camp.

From there, they scaled the defense tower's first floor. An air duct was built into the side of the tower, a construction flaw that Sarah meant to exploit.

As they climbed, Anabelle couldn't help but be impressed with Sarah. The way she'd gone about planning this mission was impressive, and its execution was razor-sharp. Anabelle could learn from Sarah, and she felt no shame in admitting that.

They came upon the air duct, and Sarah popped the grating off. She grabbed it so it didn't fall and tied it to the side of the tower before pulling herself into the vent, Anabelle following closely. The vent was tight but high enough that the two women could crouch and make their way through.

After almost fifteen minutes of silent crab-walking, Anabelle's legs were beginning to ache. She wondered how much further they had to go.

Sarah held her hand up, signaling for Anabelle to stop. She pointed at the vent's grate.

Anabelle could see a few orcs walking back and forth beneath her. "First generator," Sarah whispered. "The guards will probably just be technicians, and they won't be expecting us. Assess the situation and hit hard. I'll get the door."

Anabelle nodded confirmation, and Sarah pried open the grate. She dropped to the floor silently, and Anabelle came after her, pooling her mana as she clung to the wall, melding into the shadow cast by a chair.

Six technicians were in the room, many working with the generator ahead of them, a hulking mechanical creation sending out temporary blips of energy. All the technicians were armed.

Sarah was already creeping up behind the technicians.

Anabelle picked a shadow of one of the orcs, and leapt across the room, landing in it as though it were a black pool of still water.

Sarah struck first, driving her blade into one of the orcs as Anabelle seized another's foot and dragged him down into his own shadow. Once the orc's shadow disappeared, Anabelle materialized behind the other orc. She gripped it by the shoulder and pulled back, throwing the orc off its feet as she drew her mana into her fist and punched it in the throat.

Another orc grabbed Anabelle, pulling her away. She spun, grasped his hand, and pulled it back. Anabelle jumped into the air and kicked the orc across the room.

Sarah was still moving as well, sliding past Anabelle, drawing another kunai, and tossing it into an orc's chest.

Anabelle retrieved her kunai from the orc, filled it with mana, and threw it at another orc. When the blade struck, a small blast tore through the room, killing another orc.

When the smoke settled, Anabelle and Sarah were the only ones still alive in the room. "Not bad," Sarah said as she searched the corpses of the orcs. She smiled when she found a key card. "This'll make things a lot easier. Come on, let's set those charges."

The two went to the generator and inspected its perimeter. They planted two charges on the corner of the generator.

Sarah commed Kravis. "You guys ready yet?"

"Just cleared out the room and set the charges. How about you?"

"About to blow the generator. Should kill about half the power in the area."

"Wait, hold on…Naota is doing something." After a few seconds of waiting, Kravis said, "Hold onto those explosives. Naota found an orc to get into the system for us. We'll disable all four generators remotely. Just make sure you fuck the thing up some, so we don't have them turning it back on."

"Sounds good to me."

Sarah hung up and pulled off the generator's electrical panel. "This is going a lot smoother than I thought it would."

The lights in the room flickered. "Guess the generators are going offline. Would you do the honors?" Sarah asked.

Anabelle charged her hand with mana, and struck the electrical panel, frying it and sending sparks flying.

The lights in the room cut off. "Okay, now we just need to get to the general. Kravis will take care of the foundation explosives and the hangar. We can help after we take out our target. Let's go. We're taking a direct route. Can you stay out of sight?"

Anabelle scanned the darkened room. If the rest of the base was this dark, staying hidden would not be a problem. "Yeah, I'll be good."

Sarah smiled as she phased in and out of sight, turning invisible. "Good."

A beeping green light, hardly noticeable, floated through the air. "Follow me."

The light headed toward the door. Anabelle slipped into the shadows, her body losing its consistency and becoming one with the darkness. She followed Sarah through the door and out into the halls.

Orcs ran along the hall, barking orders to each other. A couple went into the generator room as Sarah and Anabelle slipped right past them. The two continued to make their way down the hall, passing orcs who didn't notice the waist-level green light bopping faintly in the darkness like a drunken firefly.

Anabelle did her best to keep up with Sarah, who was moving extremely fast, turning corners into new hallways. *The human must have memorized the entire floor plan,* Anabelle thought.

Finally, the two came to a massive double-door bejeweled in a fashion quite different than the rest of the tower, which had been built to showcase its technology.

Sarah pushed the door open, and the two women crept into the room.

The throne room was ornately gaudy. Trophies of animals hung along the wall, alongside the heads of decapitated gnomes. The room was vast and empty, giving the feeling of an elusive power. A huge orc, covered in scars and warpaint, sat on the throne. He was talking to someone who appeared to be human.

Rasputina, the lich.

Anabelle's heart went cold once she saw the lich's pale, rotting skin.

The lich turned from the orc captain and looked in the direction of Anabelle and Sarah. "Hm. Dethrok, I believe someone came in here to kill you." She waved her hand and mimed a yanking motion.

Anabelle was torn from the shadows and Sarah shimmered into sight.

Rasputina motioned for them to approach.

As Sarah and Anabelle walked toward the lich, Sarah spoke into her comm, telling the reinforcements to start rolling out.

The lich conjured two seats in front of the throne. "Sit, sit. There's no need for us to behave barbarically. Let's have us a chat. For one, what are you doing here?"

Anabelle took a seat. She knew better than to not play along with Rasputina. Besides, she wasn't sure what the lich wanted. And she knew that neither she nor Sarah would win in a flat-out fight.

Sarah crossed her arms as she sat. "What do you think we're here for?"

Rasputina jerked her thumb at Dethrok. "This big 'ol guy? You came all the way here for him?"

A loud explosion shook the room. "Oh. I see it's more complicated than just Dethrok. You came for what he has, didn't you? The gnomes."

"What are you doing here?" Anabelle shot back.

Rasputina shrugged and sat on the arm of Dethrok's throne as the orc glared menacingly at Anabelle and Sarah. "Bored, really. That's all. The Dark One is moving rather slowly. I'm starting to think the poor boy doesn't know what to do with himself. He might work better under pressure. Or maybe he's spread himself too thin. It's kinda hard to be everywhere at once."

"You seem to be doing a pretty good job at it."

Rasputina laughed as Dethrok squirmed in his throne. "This? Oh, this was just luck. I'm just as tickled as you are. Tell me, how is Myrddin doing? Has he gotten better yet?"

"What do you fucking care?"

Rasputina raised her hands in mock offense. "Hey, hey, why the tone? Me and Myrddin are closer than any of you ever could be. I've had my hands inside him. We're practically lovers."

Anabelle and Sarah stared silently at the lich, the elf's lips tight with hatred.

Rasputina sighed. "Okay, okay. How about we have a little truce, okay. You want something here. I want something from you. A bit of information. Let's just play nice, and I'll let you go so you can keep playing war or whatever the hell you mortals want to call it."

Neither woman spoke.

The lich pulled out her knife. "Okay, I'll go first." She leaned over and drove her knife into Dethrok's throat, sawing at it like a maniac before tossing the weapon onto the floor. She straddled the orc, caressing his chest while she tore at his throat with her teeth. He screamed as he tried to bat the lich away, but she merely pushed his head with her hand and kept eating.

Dethrok eventually stopped screaming and moving. Rasputina stood, and Dethrok slumped over before the lich tossed his corpse onto the floor, taking the orc's seat at the throne. "See. I'm not all that bad. Now all you have to do is answer my teeny little question, and you can go."

Anabelle swallowed hard. "What is it?"

The lich pulled a bone out of her side and picked at her teeth with its sharp edge. "The girl. The one with the tentacles. Did Myrddin do that?"

Anabelle was confused by the question. Why was that something Rasputina would care about? "No. She was like that when we first met her."

Rasputina brow furrowed. "Hm...interesting. Well, thanks."

Anabelle's seat popped out of existence, and she fell flat on her ass, along with Sarah.

Rasputina stood and walked off. "And Myrddin will be okay in another week or two. His body's probably sensitive to ancient magic, like a bad cold. Oh, and you can take credit for…all of that," she said, waving at Dethrok's body. "Have fun with your battle."

The lich's body began to decay rapidly until she crumpled into a pile of green dust that was swept into the air before vanishing.

Sarah raised an eyebrow at Anabelle. "What the ever-loving fuck was that?"

Anabelle shook her head as she walked over to the orc general's body. "I don't have the slightest clue."

Another explosion rocked the defense tower. Kravis' voice came through the comm. "Last one, and the reinforcements are outside. We got a comm saying most orc forces are already outside, ready to engage. You two take care of that general?"

Anabelle kicked the orc's corpse. "Yeah, he got taken care of. We'll meet up with you as soon as we can."

CHAPTER THIRTY-SEVEN

It didn't take long for Anabelle and Sarah to join Blackwell, Naota, and Kravis. The three men were down in the recently exploded hangar. They had managed to nick five hoverbikes before they had destroyed all the other vehicles.

Anabelle leapt onto the hoverbike and turned the engine over. "Glad you guys were able to swipe these."

Kravis groaned irritably. "Naota tried to convince us we needed a tank."

Naota, who was revving his hoverbike's engine, shouted, "We're about to go into battle. The more guns, the better!"

Kravis looked ready to climb off his bike and pummel Naota. "Like I said before, we need to join the resistance as soon as possible, and tanks are slow as fuck."

Naota pouted, and he stopped revving. "Yeah, I know. It still would have been cool."

The five zoomed toward the coordinates the resistance had sent them. Anabelle studied the massing of the orc forces outside the defense tower. It appeared a good amount had survived the destruction of the tower—which was still crumbling around them. The foundation had been blown, and it was only a matter of time until the building toppled.

She wondered how large a force the resistance had amassed. From what she had been told, this would be nearly all the gnomish resistance from across the planet. *But what would happen if this battle didn't go in their favor?* There was a lot on the line; a defeat could effectively wipe out the resistance.

Asking about it now would not change anything, and Anabelle wished she had voiced her concerns earlier. But Abby's plan had sounded foolproof. The elf made a mental note not to take the advice of a sleep-deprived teenager seriously if this battle didn't turn out well.

Abby! Anabelle had forgotten about Abby's part to play in all of this. She hadn't spoken with her or Terra since last night. She commed Abby as she followed Kravis and Sarah. "Hey, Abby, how are we doing on those satellites?"

Abby responded after a few minutes. "Hey. They've just entered orbit. Got them loaded up with anti-military artillery. Think Reagan's Star Wars program, but actually, you know, viable. And we have a hadron collider point set up for reinforcements as well."

"Wait. You're sending us soldiers, too?"

"My initial calculations for our success weren't realistic. Martin and I crunched the numbers again, and there wasn't a high enough rate of success. I figured it would be best to double up on our efforts. We pulled a good chunk of fighters from across the realms to aid. Wasn't hard after we explained the situation. This isn't just for the Gnome World. If we pull this off, we will prove we can take out the Dark One."

Anabelle was glad Abby had double-checked the details. But she was a little caught off guard by the way Abby was speaking. "Hey, is everything all right?" she asked. "You sound kinda weird. Not quite like yourself."

Abby sighed before answering. "Martin's been performing neural changes on my brain, and he did something to my language and personality section. I don't know the details specifically, but he deleted my accent and syntax subtleties. He's working on getting it fixed because I am *livid*. But that's further down on the list of things to take care of."

"Has he been making any other changes?"

"Stop sounding so worried. We've been making sure nothing is invasive. I think the biggest change has been we increased the number of nanobots in my body by one hundred percent. I might be more machine than human now."

Anabelle was worried, but now wasn't the time for this conversation. "Heard from Terra?"

"Uh, uh-huh. Oh! Think Martin got it. Yeah, this feels less stuffy. Oh, yeah, heard from her last night. Killed it at the party, apparently. She says thanks for the fork help."

The party arrived at the main gnomish resistance camp.

Anabelle hopped off her hoverbike. "Are you two going to be joining us today?"

"No can do, boss. I got experiments to run on Persephone, and Terra is meeting with another big who-ha."

"Experiments? Is that what the kids are calling it now?"

Anabelle wished she could see Abby's flustered face. "No," Abby retorted. "Whatever Rasputina swallowed is the same black gunk being transported by the Dark One, and it was used on Persephone. Someone's gotta figure out how to solve that problem."

Anabelle followed Sarah and Kravis, who were making their way farther into the camp. "Okay, okay. You guys be safe. And do me a favor, kid. Try to slow down with all the cyborg stuff. Or at least make sure you're being safe about it."

"I'll be safe, I promise. You take care of yourself too. Don't wanna have to stage a rescue for you."

"Promise."

Sarah and Kravis were talking to a stony-faced gnome who was missing his nose. Blackwell and Naota were behind Anabelle. Sarah motioned for the elf to join the conversation. "Our forces are ready to start the push. I was informed that your HQ will be taking care of the satellites above, coordinating with our tech team down here."

Anabelle nodded as she studied the map.

Sarah continued, "It's pretty straightforward. We charge them. Break up the forces. Use the satellites to destroy what we can. The tower is done. Even if we don't come out on top, we've destroyed the biggest intelligence hub on the gnomish world. If they don't pull out any surprises on a nuclear level, we'll be good."

Anabelle thought about the lich. If Rasputina entered this fight, it could be a guaranteed failure. But the lich didn't seem interested in fighting this one. Whatever she was planning was beyond battles and skirmishes. Anabelle needed to know what the lich was up to, but that would have to be sidelined for another time.

"Your team know about Grok, the orc general?" asked Anabelle.

The noseless gnome nodded. "We know. Can't do much about her. If she shows up, we'll do what we can, but I think we have enough firepower for her. Check it out."

The gnome hobbled over to a hill. Down in the valley were hundreds of gnomes. There were also gnomish tanks, mismatched creations covered in gears, spouting steam like something out of the Victorian era. The plasma cannons attached to nearly every part of the tanks looked more than appropriate, though.

As she admired the force, the nose-less gnome came up on Anabelle's side. "And we got another fleet coming in from the south side to meet us. We're taking back this planet. Making it ours again."

The group broke apart to make their last-minute preparations. Naota and Blackwell joined up with the gnomish grunts talking shit to each other around the fire.

Kravis disappeared, leaving Sarah and Anabelle together. "She's going to come after me," Anabelle said. "She always does."

Sarah nodded as she checked her pack. "What are you going to do about it?"

"Fight her, I guess. But I don't know what's changed."

"The only thing that can change is you. You're going to have to figure out how."

The gnomish forces were gathered with all the forces from the other nine realms: elves, humans, dwarves, pixies, and the stray liberated goblin. Even the small orcish regiment from HQ was present. They stood on a hill, overlooking the valley and the defense tower.

The tower itself still stood. In its noon shadow, was the Dark One's force of orcs. They appeared to be equally numbered.

The lieutenants and special agents of Myrddin's forces stood on the front line. Anabelle peered through a pair of binoculars, gauging the scene. She didn't have to look hard to find Grok. The orc was front and center, standing ahead of the rest of the army.

Anabelle looked at Sarah. "You ready to get this started?"

Sarah nodded, and the elf pulled up her comm. "Start the first volley."

Anabelle climbed aboard her hoverbike, as did Blackwell, Naota, and Sarah. The ground started to rumble, and everyone turned their eyes to the sky.

The clouds were separating, pulling away from each other. Suddenly, seven beams of energy erupted from the sky. They hit the defense tower, obliterating the crumbling structures. Two beams hit the orc army, wiping out the left and right flank.

Anabelle raised her fist and shouted, "Charge!" before speeding off toward Grok. She wasn't going to wait for the orc to come to her this time.

The army followed on her tail, screaming their battle-cries loud enough for the heavens to hear. Across the valley, the orcs did the same, their battle cry equally as ferocious.

The two armies barreled toward each other, their plasma guns and weapons drawn. Like a mass of shadows, they raced toward their own end, for none could be certain that they were to survive such a battle.

They clashed with a viciousness unseen anywhere across the nine realms. It was as though two hands had come together and clapped loudly.

And the cries of pain, and death, were immediate.

Grok led her army. She flew between orcs faster than most could see, sinking her sword into any enemy around her. She flipped over snipers who fired at her and drove the cold plasma of her weapon through their hearts.

Anabelle almost lost the orc for a second. She braked hard, turned her bike, and rocketed toward Grok. Pistol in hand, she fired at the orcs blocking her view of Grok.

Grok turned and met Anabelle's eyes, her smile wide and fierce. She roared as she ran toward the elf.

The elf turned her hoverbike sideways, and stood atop the seat, pulling out her plasma rifle and firing as she skidded toward Grok.

Grok dodged, moving faster than Anabelle had seen her move. The orc leapt, landed on Anabelle's bike, and drove her sword through it as the elf continued to fire at her.

The bike rolled over on its side, tossing Anabelle and Grok off. Anabelle hit the ground, quickly scrambling to her feet. Beyond the wreckage of the bike, the battle was raging all around. The cries of the dying and of pure and unadulterated violence flooded Anabelle's ears.

Grok rose from the flames, her eyes just as bright and fiery. "This is the last time, knife ears. Today, I break you."

Anabelle tried to drown out the noise around her. There was only Grok. Only Grok. She rushed at the orc, pulling as much mana from those around her as discreetly as possible, channeling it into her arm, where lighting crackled in her palm.

Grok ran toward Anabelle, her eyes wild with the hunt.

Anabelle disintegrated into a mist, reappeared behind Grok, and slammed her electric fist into the orc's back. The impact caused a massive explosion that flung them both into the air.

Sarah sped to Anabelle's landing spot. She jumped off her hoverbike and helped the elf to her feet. Before either could get situated, Grok landed in front of them.

The orc grabbed the hoverbike, raised it over her head, and slammed it down.

Anabelle and Sarah dodged aside, Sarah rolling quickly to her feet. She surged into the air, her eyes turning white as the veins in her neck bulged. A white aura pulsed from her body, and she spewed a giant fireball down on Grok.

Grok threw her arms up, taking the brunt of the blast. When the smoke cleared, the orc was still standing, covered in soot.

A bolt cut through the air, clipping Sarah in the arm and knocking her away. As she got to her feet, an orc on a hoverbike sped by, seized her by the hair, and pulled her along with him.

Grok cracked her neck slowly. "Shame your friend couldn't stick around. She's strong." The orc approached, casually grabbing a human near her and snapping his neck.

Anabelle screamed in rage and her mana pulsed around her, consuming her body in flames.

The two met mid-punch, both landing a strike to the other's jaw. Pain erupted all through Anabelle's body. She'd never been punched like that before. She soared through the air, knocking over anyone in her path.

Anabelle struggled to stand as another orc towered over her, ready to slam his ax down to cleave her head.

A taser hit the orc in the chest, electrocuting him.

Naota was waving his tasers, snapping anything in front of him, while Blackwell, who was back to back with Naota, fired shot after shot, picking off orcs and vrosks flying above.

Kravis was nearby, dodging and weaving between the orcs, slashing at their knees, moving through the crowd with an intense focus, debilitating everyone near him.

Anabelle was up, trying to gather herself together. She couldn't make sense of all the chaos around her. Were they winning? It was impossible to tell. There was only death and destruction.

Grok landed beside Anabelle and grabbed her by the throat. The elf vanished into a sea of mist, reappearing free of Grok's grasp. She punched the orc in the face, kicked her in the kneecap as hard as she could, and jumped up to deliver a roundhouse kick to her face.

The orc stumbled backward. As Anabelle leaned in for another punch, Grok caught her by the arm and flipped her over. The orc leapt into the air, clasping both hands together, and landed on Anabelle's chest.

Anabelle coughed up blood as her vision dulled. But she wasn't done yet. She let out a blast of mana that threw Grok off her. "Get out of here, you idiots!" she shouted at Naota and the rest.

Grok smiled as she approached Anabelle. "I don't give a shit about them. I want you, elf. You and only you."

A black aura pulsed from Grok as her eyes turned red. "You push me. Every fight. I can finally start to show you what I really am."

The black aura sent out an energy wave that threw everyone within a twenty-foot radius through the air.

Anabelle stumbled to her feet, blood trickling from her nose and ears. She held her comm up. "One more barrage. Then retreat. Everyone, retreat. This is over."

Grok laughed caustically. "Are you calling for backup? Do you need someone to save you, fair one?"

Anabelle assumed her stance, trying to calm her mind to allow her mana to flow free and unregulated. "I'm going to kill you. And I'm going to enjoy it."

She rushed Grok, throwing all the power she possessed into her attacks. Flames burst from her body as she threw punch after punch.

The sheer force of the elf's assault pushed Grok back as the orc laughed. "Yes, yes! This is what I've been waiting to see from you!"

The ground beneath them cracked, expanding into a crater as Anabelle's eyes burned bright, energy crackling from them. "I'll fucking kill you!" Anabelle screamed as a mixture of fire and electricity burned through her body, forming into a ball in her hand. She grabbed Grok by the throat, wrestled her into a half-nelson, and tried to drive the ball into Grok's chest.

Grok shifted her weight, holding Anabelle in position. "That was good, knife-ear. But not good enough." She seized Anabelle's wrists with both hands and twisted, snapping them in two. Then she drove the ball of energy into the elf's chest.

When the smoke from the explosion cleared, Grok was still standing, Anabelle's hair wrapped in her fist.

The armies were retreating as a Dark Gate opened behind Grok. She dragged Anabelle through the Gate.

CHAPTER THIRTY-EIGHT

Abby woke up with butterflies in her stomach. She'd heard the term used multiple times in her life and had always believed it was trite, but here she was, warm fuzzies on the back of her neck, her stomach churning as her heart jumped into her throat every time she thought about Persephone.

Since the drow had come to HQ, the two had been inseparable. Persephone had been at Abby's side almost the entire time, asking questions about her work, and how the different HQ systems functioned. So many questions, in fact, that Creon had cornered Abby to ask whether Persephone was a double agent.

Abby hadn't had a good answer immediately, but when she brought the topic up to Persephone, the drow had offered to share anything and everything about the Dark One's forces that she could remember.

As Abby discovered, one of the benefits of the Dark One's advanced mind control tech was that microchipped individuals retained their cognition as the Dark One required his servants to be capable and sentient. Anything less would have resulted in an army of drooling zombies.

Which meant Persephone, along with anyone else who had been

microchipped, retained all their experiences and memories from when they were under the Dark One's sway.

That had been enough for Creon to back off.

Abby felt a little guilty for being so happy while terrible things were afoot. The entire time she had been planning the strike against the Dark One's forces on the gnomish world, she'd been thinking about going for a walk with Persephone. That was only a small part of what she'd admit that she was thinking about the drow.

Fortunately, Martin was there to help pick up her mental slack, which would have been considered negligible by anyone else. The improvements Martin had been making on her neural network were extremely evident. Abby was thinking faster and more efficiently than she had in her entire life.

Her head was bursting with ideas for how the war efforts could be improved. Roy had begun to get annoyed with the number of messages Abby had been sending with different ideas.

Not too annoyed, though; he was implementing most of them. The dual efforts of Abby and Martin were akin to having a thousand scientists working on the job.

But Abby was having a hard time caring about any of it since Persephone was finally here. Abby couldn't shirk her responsibilities, but she couldn't force herself to look past all the numbers and theories all the time.

Occasionally, she had found herself daydreaming about staring into Persephone's eyes. Usually, these moments were interrupted by Creon complaining about something or shouting in frustration at his computer.

Abby got out of bed and went to brush her teeth. Her whole body was vibrating—not because of her thoughts of Persephone, though. One of the things Abby had noticed since the increase of nanobots in her body was that she felt as though she was crawling out of her skin. Her body no longer felt like her own.

It was difficult to put into words. Abby felt simultaneously like she was rooted to herself and like she was floating someplace far away. If she thought about it for too long, the world around her would grow shaky and thin. She figured it would go away as Martin continued to make improvements.

The nanobots shimmered over Abby, making a version of the uniform that Anabelle and Terra wore. Abby noticed that the bots covered her up much faster than usual. There might now be even more in her blood than Martin had said.

Abby went to the mess hall to grab some food. She wasn't hungry; she hadn't been for some time. Hunger was another trade-off for having the nanobots. They were working behind the scenes, optimizing the way her body worked. She couldn't remember the last time she'd been thirsty or hungry. That wasn't keeping her from eating, though. Food was just as enjoyable as it had been before. The only difference was, she wasn't fatigued when she skipped meals.

Humanity was a fading concept to Abby. She had only thought about it briefly, during moments when the stress of her day-to-day work wasn't affecting her. All of which felt less human. She was eating less, pissing less, blinking less, amongst many other things she didn't want to think about. The idea was frightening if she allowed her mind to focus on it for too long. Fortunately, she had other things to think about.

Today she would start her first rounds of experiments on Persephone. Abby wished she weren't heading the project, but no one else was capable. It was all Abby's creation, and someone else might mess it up.

That was something to think about—figuring out what was going on with Persephone since she'd been exposed to the Black Melody, and if Abby could do anything to reverse it.

Abby headed toward the medbay. Persephone had been given her own room for the experiments. But Abby had to make a stop before she met the drow.

Myrddin was still bed-ridden. His vitals remained stable, but the wizard hadn't woken up yet.

Abby sat beside the old man and watched him breathing. He was looking better than he had for a long while. His skin was less transparent, and his eyes were moving behind his lids as though he were dreaming.

"You're going to get over this," Abby said softly. "This ain't how you're dying."

Martin's voice interrupted Abby's moment. "Persephone is ready for you."

Abby stood, annoyed at the AI for disrupting one of the few instances of being alone with her thoughts she'd had for some time. "Don't have to make it sound so clinical."

Martin cleared his throat and said, "Your crush is waiting for you to ravage her body."

"You know sometimes, you're a real dick."

"Not my fault I'm programmed this way."

Abby kissed Myrddin's forehead and left for Persephone's room. She was worried about today's experiments. Persephone had agreed readily enough, but Abby still wasn't sure this was a good idea.

Persephone and Creon were waiting in the room for Abby. The medbay had undergone a few minor conversions. There was a body scan machine, which resembled an MRI machine. The main difference was that this machine did more than just scan; it was capable of many other things.

Abby wanted to hug Persephone as soon as she saw her, but she felt uncomfortable in front of Creon. Everyone already knew about her and Persephone, so there wasn't anything to feel awkward about. Maybe it was just being affectionate in front of someone else. All the time Abby and Persephone had spent with each other had been in private.

Thankfully, Persephone didn't seem to care about those kinds of things. She walked right up to Abby and gave her a hug and a kiss.

What exactly are we? Abby thought. *Is she my girlfriend? I guess we're dating. Kinda. Can you date if you're in the middle of a war? Maybe it doesn't have to matter.*

When Persephone let go of Abby, a frightening thought crossed her mind. She barely knew Persephone. *Where had all these feelings come from? And why had they hit her so fast?* They didn't seem to be based on anything. Would they last, or was this just one of those high school puppy-love things? What if that was how Persephone felt?

Abby pushed her thoughts to the back of her mind. She had more important and immediate concerns. Besides, she'd been overthinking everything recently. It was probably just her mind looking for problems to solve.

Persephone went to the scanner and brushed her hair out of her face as she sat on the bed. "So, how are we going to do this?"

Abby went to Creon's console. "Are you sure you want to go through with this?" she asked Persephone. "I'm still not sure what's going to happen. Or if we'll even be able to remove the Dark Melody."

The drow nodded. "I didn't choose to have this...thing in me. And I want it out. I don't want to hear the song anymore. I want it all out. And if it'll help destroy the Dark One, it's the least I can do to help."

"All right. Go ahead and lie down."

Persephone obeyed and lay on the mattress. The bed slid under the scanner, and Persephone disappeared.

Abby sat beside Creon. "Thanks for helping me with this. I don't want anything to happen to Persephone."

Creon passed Abby a cup of coffee and smiled sweetly. "Neither do I. Come on, let's get started."

The scanner flashed brightly as it began to move over Persephone's body. Data scrolled on the computer screen, and Abby studied it, trying to make sense of it. "So...first off, we have only one set of vital signs. Whatever is within her doesn't register as being alive. Not conventionally, at least. I assumed it would have a bio-signature. Similar to a symbiote," Creon mused.

"It's not a thing. It's an Old One."

Creon raised a scaly eyebrow. "You think so? Just because it's made from the same gunk as an old one's blood doesn't mean it's actually one."

"Can't be completely certain, but I wouldn't say it's like a virus. Viruses don't communicate with whoever they're making sick. They just do their thing. If it can talk to her, it's gotta be alive. Maybe not an old one like the one summoned by Rasputina. But something like it."

"Okay. Well, it's got to reside in her body someplace, even if it doesn't have an individual bio-signature. Let's try another scan."

The scanner flashed again as it fired up. This time, Persephone screamed.

Abby grabbed the microphone beside the computer. "Persephone, are you okay?"

Persephone's voice came through the computer. "Yeah, yeah. There was just...a sharp pain in the back of my head."

Creon and Abby exchanged glances. "Maybe whatever is in her was reacting to the scan," he muttered. "We should concentrate on the back of her skull. Spine too."

Abby nodded as she typed a new command into the computer. "Pers, we're going to do the same kind of scan again this time. Brace yourself. It might hurt a little."

"Do it," Persephone said.

The scanner flashed once again and Persephone yelped, but not as loudly as the last time.

An image of Persephone's brain and spinal column appeared on the computer screen. "There we are," Creon said. "The cerebellar cortex. It's enlarged. Much larger than it should be for a drow. Also, it's showing an excess of fluid there. Her spine as well."

Abby studied the scan, cross-referencing it with images of drow physiology that Martin was projecting into her right field of vision. "Same with the nerves." Abby pointed at the screen. "They're all bulging. Especially the one in her arm with the tentacles. That must be why."

"Looks like the Melody affects its host on a neural level. Not the blood, but the brain and everything it's connected to. Could be why she says it's like listening to another primal, speechless voice in her head."

"What now?"

"Well, the point is to remove it, isn't it?"

Abby looked at Creon dubiously. "How exactly are we gonna remove something from her nerves and brain stem? Didn't know you were capable of brain surgery."

Creon leaned back in his chair, and he twirled his goatee. "Not me. The system is all automated. We've performed more than our fair share of brain surgeries here." He grabbed the microphone beside his computer. "Persephone, we're going to try and remove the Melody now. I'm giving you a sedative, okay? Are you ready?"

"Ready," Persephone replied quietly.

A syringe whipped out of the scanner and injected Persephone with the sedative.

The computer screen showed her heart rate and brain activity decreasing. "Should be out by now. Begin the procedure."

Abby watched the computer screen detail exactly what it was doing. First, a small incision in the back of Persephone's head. Next, a miniscule needle pushed its way through the skin, burrowing into the drow's skull. The needle would make contact with the Melody in a moment.

Persephone started screaming. Her body jerked wildly, her feet flailing as she struggled to pull her head up against the strap holding her down.

Abby jumped to her feet. "I thought you said she was sedated!"

Creon, somehow managing to keep his cool, peered at the computer. "She *is* sedated. Something else is operating her body."

"Stop it. You're hurting her!"

Creon shook his head. "No, I'm not. Her vital signs aren't showing any indication of stress. Persephone is fine. The Melody is what's scared."

Persephone's body continued to thrash, and Abby felt her heart rise in her chest. She couldn't bear the sound of her screams. She had to remind herself that this wasn't Persephone, it was something inside of her.

Persephone's arm split down the center, hulking tentacles ripping out of her flesh and grabbing the scanner. They were even larger and more numerous than the last time Abby had seen them, as if an entire Old One were crammed in Persephone's arm.

The tentacles began to tear the scanner apart. It happened quickly before Abby or Creon could do anything. Once the scanner ceased whirring and went down, the tentacles snapped back up into Persephone's arm.

Creon muttered something under his breath as he looked at the data on the screen.

Abby gripped Creon frantically, tearing his attention away from the computer screen. "Is she okay?"

Creon removed Abby's hands with the calmness of a doctor. "Yes, she is. And so is the Melody. But I have some very interesting results. The Melody reacted very similarly to another invasive bodily specimen that I've seen."

Abby already knew where Creon was going with this. "My nanobots."

"Bingo. That gives me an idea. I'll have to do some more research before I'm certain. Persephone should be coming to in a little bit. I'll leave you two alone."

Creon stood and walked past Abby, leaving her alone with Persephone.

Abby went over to the scanner and pulled up a seat. She took Persephone's cursed hand in her own and waited for her to wake up.

CHAPTER THIRTY-NINE

Anabelle would have expected to wake up in a small cell, something filthy, filled with bones and rotten food. That was what she believed an orcish prison would look like.

She was surprised to find herself in a throne room almost the size of the general's in the defense tower. The differences between the two rooms were plentiful, though.

This room had no decorations. It was bare, save two chairs, one of which Anabelle was chained to.

Anabelle struggled and tried to pull herself out of the chair. The chains were too strong, though. She drew her mana into her wrists, where the chains sat heavily, and released it in a burst of energy.

Her powers had no effect on the chains. They must have been spelled or made with some extremely advanced tech. Whatever it was, it was cutting off her magic. She couldn't mist...she couldn't do anything. *Guess this is where I'm spending the night.*

The elf closed her eyes, forcing herself to meditate. That was all she could do. Her situation seemed obvious enough. She'd been captured. But why? Grok had made it evident that all she wanted to do was kill Anabelle. The orc didn't care if it was part of the Dark

RAMY VANCE & MICHAEL ANDERLE

One's plans or not. So why the hell didn't Grok kill her on the battlefield?

Behind Anabelle, the door to the throne room opened. The elf could hear footsteps approaching.

Grok rested her hand on Anabelle's shoulder as she walked around the elf. "Good to see you're awake," Grok growled. She brought the other chair over to Anabelle, setting it in front of her so they sat only a few inches away from each other.

"What do you want?"

Grok smiled grimly. "You don't want to gloat? Not even a little bit?"

Anabelle was taken aback by the question. In her opinion, she had nothing to gloat about. "What are you talking about?"

Grok's smile didn't falter. "Your little stunt at the defense tower. That was a marvel of planning. The Dark One didn't see it coming. And your continued attacks throughout the planet. The Gnome World is all but lost to the Dark One. In less than forty-eight hours, you managed to topple decades of work. I can't imagine that you wouldn't be a little proud."

Anabelle made a show of scanning the throne room. "Well, I'm pretty sure you might have noticed, but I'm chained to a chair in a dungeon. Not exactly the best place to get breaking news."

"That's why I thought I should tell you. It would be a shame for you to miss out on your victory."

"What's the next step, then?"

Grok leaned back in her chair and crossed her legs, a movement that caught Anabelle by surprise; it was oddly feminine. "We could take back the gnomish world, but that would require resources. And the gnomes are dug in deeper than we had expected. We underestimated the little fuckers. They'll have what's left of their planet back soon enough."

"I'm assuming releasing me wouldn't be on the table."

Grok's smile did fade this time. "If I had my way, I would have killed you when I had the chance. It would have been better for you that way—a true warrior's death. My brothers and sisters who still have their minds would have respected such a thing. But the Dark One has other plans for you."

Anabelle thought back to one of the times she'd fought Grok. She remembered the orc clearly stating that she didn't care what the Dark One wanted. "I thought you were in this for yourself. Did the Dark One manage to slip a microchip into you while you were sleeping?"

Grok pulled out a dagger and cleaned the dirt from under her nail. "No. There were conversations, though. I do want to kill you, knife-ears. That hasn't changed. But I've been asked to wait. And that is something I can do. You give me an excuse to let myself go. But you still don't give me a real challenge. Maybe I need to give you an incentive first. Either way, me and the Dark One can still have what we both want."

"And what is that?"

"I want you dead. He wants you and all of your friends dead. And we both know that they'll come for you. You're all too sentimental for this kind of war. The smart thing to do would be to let you rot here or die. That's not what any of them will do, though. They're going to launch a rescue mission and put all their lives at risk because they think they're heroes, and what they're fighting for is so important. And because of that, they're going to die."

Anabelle wanted to argue with Grok. She was pissed the orc was being so casual about the whole affair. But Grok was right in a lot of ways. Anabelle knew that if any of the DGA were captured, she'd be mounting a rescue mission immediately. Any of the Angels would have. Sarah was probably the only one with enough sense to cut the loss and move on.

Grok leaned in close to Anabelle, looking deep into the elf's eyes. "A rescue mission isn't something a Traveler would do either. Maybe you. But you're only a pale shadow of what they used to be."

Anabelle lunged and snapped at Grok, and the orc jumped back. "Did I hit a nerve? I didn't mean to make you go feral."

"You don't know one thing about what it takes to be a Traveler."

"True. But I do know a thing or two about why they disappeared."

Anabelle couldn't believe what Grok was saying. Even when

Anabelle had been in training, the number of Travelers had been reduced to three or four, and that was counting herself. Anabelle's attention had been piqued.

"What happened?" she asked.

Grok threw her knife at Anabelle's foot. The knife landed on the edge of her big toe, but she didn't flinch. "The final path...the path of the lost, the one you're taught to avoid at all costs. There was a Traveler who focused only on that path and walked it to its end. And he broke away from the other Travelers. His curiosity and strength were rewarded the only way elves know how to react to change. With violence."

Anabelle had never heard of a Traveler who only walked the Path of the Lost. She hadn't remembered anything like that through her meditation. "Heresy amongst Travelers is dangerous. It causes—"

"What about it is dangerous? You don't have any beliefs on the way the realms work or anything like that. It's a fighting style, that's all, one that had grown myopic in its own uselessness. But this Traveler of the Lost, he fled the attacks of his former brothers and sisters. And he forged his own way. Taught his own students the Path of the Lost and took it further than ever. He taught a small group of orcs. And the Travelers and the Lost largely wiped each other out. Only a few remained, dwindling until there was only one student of each path—you and me."

Grok stood. "I don't want to kill you, not really. That's the bloodlust talking. I want to break you. To show you what the Travelers were always afraid of becoming." She pressed her hands to the side of Anabelle's face.

Pain shot through Anabelle's head. Her veins were on fire, and her eyes felt like they were going to pop out of their sockets. She screamed and tried to pull away, but Grok held her in place.

Memory after memory flashed before Anabelle's eyes, too fast for her to focus on. A blur of hundreds of years of repressed information.

When Grok released Anabelle, she could feel her bones still vibrating. She felt like she was going to pass out.

Grok sat across from Anabelle. "You have a very beautiful scream."

She grabbed Anabelle's head again, sending pain to every nerve in the elf's body until the dungeon echoed with her screams.

Abby and Persephone sat outside in HQ's garden. It was a lovely place, filled with flowering plants from all the nine realms. Abby had never been to it. The thought hadn't crossed her mind.

Persephone had told her about the garden. Since the drow had arrived at HQ, she had made a point to come to the garden at least once a day. She had said it was her favorite place to be while Abby was working since she didn't have much to do at the base.

They were sitting beneath a *grum-grum*, a luscious blue plant from the gnomish rainforests with the consistency of a succulent. The plant gave off a sweet smell similar to honey.

Abby could tell Persephone was upset by something, but she wasn't sure what. When the drow had woke up from the procedure the day before, she hadn't seemed too bothered. She had said she didn't remember most of what had happened. But later that night, she'd sent Abby a message saying she wanted to meet first thing in the morning.

Finally, Persephone let out a soft sigh. "I don't want you to take the Dark Melody out."

Of all the things Persephone could have said, this one caught Abby off guard the most. She'd assumed Persephone wanted to go back home, or something of that sort.

"What do you mean? I thought you hated that thing. Just because we didn't get it right the first time doesn't mean we can't. Creon's already close to cracking it."

Persephone rested her hand on Abby's. "No, it's not that. It...she talked to me last night. Actually talked to me in my dreams. She knows we're trying to get rid of her, and she made me a promise. If I let her stay in me, she'll help us destroy the Dark One."

"Wait, I thought the Old Ones were working with the Dark One?"

Persephone stared at her cursed hand. "No. They don't...they don't think like that. It's more like the Dark One is using them like tools. If I keep her, I'll be able to help. I'll have a reason for being here other than you. I hate just sitting around, waiting to see what's going to happen. I can fight. I know that. And there might be more I can do if Melody is willing to help."

Abby chuckled. "You gave it a name?"

Persephone nodded as she held up her hand. "Figured I might as well if we're going to be in this together for the long haul. You think it's a good idea?"

Nanobots rolled over Abby's hand, turning it to black metal. "Can't really say I have much of a right to talk. You speak to Roy?"

"Yeah. He said he'd be happy to have me aboard the team. Not a Dark Gate Angel, but a special agent. We wouldn't be working together, but it would be pretty close."

"So, you want to stay, then? With me…"

Persephone smiled sweetly at Abby, who felt her heart swimming around in her chest. "You're afraid I'm going to leave?"

Abby suddenly felt very small and exposed. She wanted to crawl up into herself. "You…I mean, we hardly know each other, and there's so much going on and…I don't know, I just wasn't sure about—"

"Everything is happening fast. And I don't understand most of it, but I'm not going to waste time asking questions. We could die tomorrow. I want to enjoy my time with you for as long as I can. Whatever that means."

"Me too."

Abby's HUD went off. It was a message from Creon. "Always someone calling."

"You mind if I tag along?"

Abby looked at the *grum-grum* above. "Come on, let's go."

Creon, Terra, Nib-Nib, and Cire were waiting for Abby in the lab. "What's going on?" Abby asked.

The goblin pointed at the holoprojector. "A little while ago, Cire asked me for help finding a way onto the orcish homeworld. He and Roy have an idea for increasing our forces. Over the course of time, we've been watching the orcish homeworld. We've found a handful of pockets of orcish settlements the Dark One hasn't been able to take over. We're sending Terra, Cire, and Nib-Nib to the orcish world to recruit whoever they can to our cause."

"Sounds like a good idea. What do you need me for?"

Martin popped up on the holoprojector. "I took care of all the design for the Gate we're constructing on the orcish world, a combination of transportation using the collider and then a mid-jump build that'll end up on the world. But I...uh...ugh, I didn't want everyone to have to hear this."

Abby raised her eyebrow as she smirked. "Wait, are you embarrassed?"

"Shut it up! And yes. I wanted you to check my math. See if there're any mistakes."

Abby put her hand over her heart and pretended to faint. "Why? Me? A measly 'ol human checking an *AI's* math?"

"You don't have to rub my face in it!"

Abby waved away Martin's complaints. "I'm joking. Calm down. Let me see."

Martin disappeared and was replaced by a complex set of equations that filled up the entire screen. Abby glanced at the equations, reading through them almost instantly, computing the numbers in her head three times before she was satisfied. "Yeah, everything looks good."

Terra whistled loudly. "Can't believe you could make sense of that."

Abby turned to Terra. "Have you heard anything from Roy about what we're gonna do 'bout Anabelle?"

Terra crossed her arms as she shook her head. "He's been working with Sarah to locate Anabelle. They haven't had any luck yet. But they're on it."

Persephone stepped forward. "Unless there's anything that I'm needed to do here, I'd like to come with you."

Abby's heart skipped a beat as Persephone turned to face her. "If

I'm going to be here, I need to make this my fight too." She touched Abby's face lightly and kissed her. Her lips made Abby feel like she was melting.

Terra cleared her throat awkwardly. "Uh…you know you two have your own rooms, right?"

Persephone broke their kiss and stepped back. "I'll come back in one piece. Promise."

Abby was still trying to catch her breath. "Yeah, you better."

Terra clapped her hand on Persephone's shoulder. "Glad to have you aboard. Now come on. We need to get going."

Persephone kissed Abby on the cheek one last time before she departed with the team, leaving Creon and Abby alone.

Creon switched the image on the holoprojector. "Work's not over yet. We need to get started with a cure for the Dark Melody. And it starts with your nanobots."

Abby sat at her computer as she tried to slow her heartbeat. "Persephone doesn't want a cure. Not yet, at least."

I thought you could control these kinds of things, Martin? she thought.

Martin answered quickly. *Figured you might want to just let this one ride. All of that unconscious crap is what makes you human, right? You don't want to stop feeling butterflies when you see her, do you?*

No, Abby thought. *I guess I don't.*

CHAPTER FORTY

The Hadron Collider Portal—or HCP—opened, throwing Terra and her party out onto the orcish world. Terra struggled to her feet, pushing down the urge to vomit, the same as everyone else was doing. Persephone was the only one to fail. She pitched to the side and threw up.

Nib-Nib came to Persephone and helped the drow to her feet. She vomited up a clutch of eggs and passed it to the drow. Persephone grimaced at the sight and waved her hands in front of her face.

Terra wrangled Persephone, holding her tight and ignoring the vomit-breath. "You might wanna take those. Nib-Nib's eggs will do wonders for your body. Trust me. Saved me from death's door more than a couple of times."

Persephone eyed the clutch of eggs suspiciously. "Are you sure?"

Terra dipped her hand into the clutch and tossed a few of the slimy, oozing eggs into her mouth. She swallowed them without a problem. "If Nib-Nib gives you eggs, I say you take the eggs."

Persephone grabbed a handful of eggs and closed her eyes tight as she swallowed them. "Hm...those actually aren't bad...I mean...is it okay for us to eat her eggs?"

Terra pushed Nib-Nib as she walked by, and the mantiboid chittered loudly. "She's offering. It's not like we're cutting her open for them or something. All right, Cire, where are we going?"

Cire was looking around, taking the whole scene in slowly.

Terra hadn't even stopped to look at her surroundings. Once she took a moment to breathe it in, she realized she was standing in one of the most beautiful places she'd ever been in her life.

The team stood on plains of lush greens and yellows stretching far off into the horizon. The grass came up almost to Terra's knees and smelled of wheat and of flowers Terra couldn't name. She'd never been good with plants or flowers. But she knew it smelled amazing. *Like home*, she thought, before catching herself.

Cire knelt and kissed the ground. He tore a handful of grass, pulling it up the roots until he got to the soft dirt. He scooped up the dirt and pressed it to his face. "Home," he breathed. "I've missed what I've never known."

Terra knelt beside Cire. "You've never been here, have you?"

Cire passed a handful of soil to Terra. "I do not know where I was born. I grew up in arenas, floating through different worlds. There were stories that were given to me when I was made a shaman. But they were only accounts of other people. This is the first time I've smelled my world. The first time that I've seen the sun of my ancestors."

Terra took the earth in her hand and inhaled it, breathing in the land that Cire loved. "You should be doing this," Terra said. "These aren't my people, they're yours. If anyone is going to try to unite the orcs, it should be you."

Cire shook his head. "This is not the time for that. There are practicalities. I don't hold the proper status to call my brothers and sisters to war. But I do hold the ability to appoint one. You are not orc by blood, but you are orc by heart. And I hope that is not a mistake I have made. But I trust what I have seen. You are orc. If you still hold to being a human, tell me now. Let me know your truth."

Terra pressed the dirt to her face, felt it against her skin. "This isn't right. These aren't my people. No matter how orc I feel, I'm not the same as you."

"You have chieftain status. That's leverage. What else can we do?"

Terra breathed deeply of the earth again, trying to pull as much of it into herself as possible. This wasn't her planet. Her people hadn't come here. But neither had the orcs. There was so much to be confused about. Issues that she felt she had no right to intervene in, especially knowing that her end goal was to find bodies for the war.

"As a shaman, you have the right to speak, don't you?" Terra asked.

Cire stood, looking solemnly into the wild orcish lands. "I speak for my chieftain. That is the orcish way."

Terra clasped Cire's wrist and held it tight. "Then why not speak for me? These are your people, and if they won't listen to anyone other than a chieftain, why can't you give me the words for them? You understand their struggles better than I ever could. If we must play politics, why not play hard? I'll be the face, you be the voice."

Cire watched Terra closely, squinting as if to perceive any falsehood. "Are you orc?"

Terra pressed her right hand to her heart. "I am orc."

"Then I will speak for you. As I am your tongue, you will be my hand."

Persephone cleared her throat loudly. "Uh, I think you two were the ones who were reminding Abby and me that we had rooms."

Nib-Nib chittered loudly as she scuttled about, digging in the dirt and laughing.

Terra and Cire both stood, their faces stained with dirt. "Lead on, Cire," Terra said. "Take us where you think we need to be."

The journey took two days, working their way through the vast plains. Terra was surprised that they hadn't come across any orcs yet. The most they had seen was the occasional wildlife, creatures that reminded Terra of bison, but were noticeably more aggressive. Cire had told her the name of the beast, but Terra still wasn't able to pronounce it correctly. They had dined on two meals of the creature so far.

The only one in the party who didn't seem to be tired by the journey was Persephone. The drow didn't need to take breaks or eat much. She continued in a fashion that embarrassed Terra at first until she realized how much Cire and Nib-Nib were also struggling with the journey.

During one of their water breaks, Terra sat beside Persephone. "You don't seem to be having a problem with this."

The drow took a sip from the water canteen that Terra passed to her. "There were many marches in the Dark One's service. More than I care to remember."

"So, you remember all of it."

"Everything."

Terra didn't want to take the conversation any further. Not that she wasn't interested. It was evident that Persephone carried a deep wound from her experiences while under the Dark One's control. There was no need to pick at the scab. "How've things been going with you and Abby?" she asked.

Persephone tensed, gripping the canteen. "Why are you asking?"

"Conversation. Honestly, you two are kids. I don't really feel the need to say anything. Just wanted to know how you felt. Curiosity, you can call it."

Persephone passed the canteen to Terra. "I've been alive at least eighty years longer than she has, and I feel like she's the first person I've ever met who…never mind."

"No, what is it?"

"Amongst my people, we consider these to be needless conversations. A drow does not sit and waste time thinking on things. We feel, and we act. That is our way. But I sense that humans might not be the same way. You think and think until you can't understand what to do. It's a dangerous way of understanding the world."

Terra glanced over her shoulder at Cire. "Yeah, I'd say that's pretty across-the-board with humanity. We do tend to overthink things. Don't take my questions too seriously. I was only asking because you two seem to be pretty close. That's all."

"I'm happy when I'm around her. Happier than I've been in a long time. But...I've been under the Dark One's control for longer than I can remember. Maybe anything would make me happy right now."

Terra instantly regretted starting this conversation. She'd been hoping for a quick sort of thing, a little light banter. Nothing to this degree. "How do you think you tell the difference?"

Persephone didn't answer. Her mouth opened as if she were about to say something and her eyes were distant, as though she perceived a world separate than the one in front of her. "How are you supposed to know these things?" Persephone asked. "I can break everything down as much as I want to, turn it all over in my head until I go crazy. But it doesn't make any of it make any more sense. Being around Abby makes me happy. I don't know if it's because things have been so bad for this long, or for any other reason. And maybe I don't want to know. Maybe it's okay to be close to someone who makes you feel like it's okay to be close to them. That might be all I want. But it's not... she...I feel different when I'm with her. Not like I'm less of myself. Like I can keep being more of me. It's safe...comfortable...I could let all of myself hang out, and she wouldn't even flinch."

Terra looked at Cire. "Yeah, I can imagine that being a pretty good feeling. We'll couch that for now. We got shit to take care of."

The party continued until they came to a fortress buried in the plains. It would have been impossible to see if Cire hadn't pointed it out.

The fortress was built into the ground, almost in the fashion of gnomish or goblin architecture. Terra had seen enough of orcish architecture, that it seemed unreal that orcs would have built their city in such a fashion. It wasn't until Cire reminded Terra that goblins were descendants of orcs, that she accepted they would have had similar building patterns.

"So, this is the part where we get them to join us, right?" Terra asked.

The party arrived at the orc threshold, a sweeping fort built into the plains, made of steel and stone. It was the polar opposite of everything the Dark One represented. It couldn't be called primitive; it was too well made for that. But something about the structure seemed almost human.

Terra looked at Cire. "What do we do now?"

Cire stared at the fortress. "We announce ourselves. You do, I should say. Declare your title as chieftain and demand a meeting with their chief. Use my name as well to let them know you have a shaman. It'll grant you more weight. Speak with force. Do not speak as if they have an option."

"And what do I tell them if I get that meeting?"

"We are here to unite the tribes. To create the horde that so many of the realm feared."

Terra could hear the sadness in Cire's voice. She wasn't sure if it was the idea of taking the last of his free people to war, shackling them to a human, or becoming the horde that darkened his heart. She was certain it had nothing to do with her being human, but now was not the time to ask.

Terra approached the gates of the fortress. "Chieftain! Come meet me!"

Two orcs stood guard at the gate. "And who is he to meet?" one called out.

"Chieftain Terra, Hewn of Orc Bone, Champion of the Arena...uh, Crusher of Troll Skull and...uh, Extinguisher of Balrogs. Shaman Cire stands beside me."

One of the guards looked at the other. "Hm...you look...pretty not orcish."

Terra pounded her fist to her chest. "I am Chieftain Terra. Hewn of Orc Bone. Champion of—"

The orc guard raised his hands. "Yeah, yeah, I heard you the first time. Uh, I guess you probably want to meet the chieftain, then?"

"Whoever is in charge," Terra shouted.

The gates of the fort opened, revealing twenty orcish soldiers armed to the teeth.

One of the orcs, a small, wiry creature, walked ahead of the rest. He wore a crown and walked with a cane. "You, human. You're the one who wishes to meet?"

Terra stepped away from the rest of her party. "I'm declaring a challenge for the right to this tribe."

The old orc chuckled loudly. "I haven't heard a challenge in some time. Well, I guess we can humor you. I trust you understand our rules?"

"Uh, honestly, I'm a little fuzzy. I thought I just had to fight your best warrior or something."

"True." The chieftain waved his hand. An orc twice the chieftain's size walked out of the crowd. "Could you kill her and get it over with?"

The orc unsheathed his battle-ax and jogged over to Terra, who matched the orc's pace.

The two collided, the orc swinging his ax, Terra ducking to avoid the blade. She brought her fist up in an uppercut that sent the orc stumbling backward.

He rubbed his jaw, shocked by Terra's punch.

Terra was too. She looked at her hand. The strength she'd felt in the arena had returned. It was nothing like the exo-suit; this felt right. "It's about fucking time I got some juice." She threw herself forward, tackling the orc to the ground.

They rolled around, both attempting to gain the upper hand. Terra managed to wrestle the ax from the orc's hand and tossed it to the side.

He headbutted Terra, dazing her for a second. Once her head cleared, Terra returned the favor.

Now she was on top. She grabbed the orc by the throat and squeezed as hard as she could, and set to pummeling the orc with her other hand.

There was silence, and only the dull sound of flesh hitting bone.

Finally, Terra stood. "I'm not going to kill him. That's not why I'm here. I come to unite the orc tribes under one rule. If this is your champion, I kicked his ass. Will you follow me?"

The chieftain glared at Terra for some time. Then he clenched his fist and pressed it to his heart. "The Uz-koreth tribe will follow you, Chieftain Terra."

Terra leaned over and helped the orc beneath her to his feet. "Good fight, bucko. Go walk it off."

The orc stumbled away, rubbing his head as Cire walked up to Terra. "That went rather smoothly. Come. We need to talk with the former chief. This is only the beginning."

Terra and Cire went to the former chief's side, the rest of the party following closely. The chief led them through the gates of the orc camp, speaking to them cordially along the way.

Terra knew this was only the first brick to be laid. But she felt like they were off to a good start.

Thousands of miles outside the orcish homeworld, a sole ship jumped out of hyperspace. A surveyor, one of the Dark One's fastest models. A forerunner.

This ship launched a drone into the atmosphere. It floated in the dark of space, waiting for a reply.

PART III

CHAPTER FORTY-ONE

It had been almost a week and a half since Anabelle had been captured by Grok. A week since Terra and Persephone had left with Cire and Nib-Nib. Abby had remained at HQ, mostly alone. Her only contact had been with Creon and Martin. That wasn't a problem, though. The trio had been working nonstop on a solution to the problem of the Dark Melody.

It turned out the solution was Abby.

As she brushed her teeth, Martin read off the most recent data from her body scans. Almost all of Abby's bodily functions were being managed by Martin at the time, and she was close to being in a state of suspended animation. Her heart rate had been lowered substantially, and she'd spent most of the day trying not to concentrate on anything that didn't immediately require her attention.

Martin was doing a great job of taking care of her and working with Creon. The AI and Creon had upgraded all of Abby's drones, taking the initial design and mass-producing them for the upcoming mission.

The drones were linked to Abby's nanobots, building a giant network of tech. The drones were the microcosm and Abby the macro.

"Looks like your count is up by three hundred percent. It's looking pretty good," Martin said. "Surprised you aren't bursting at the seams."

Abby didn't say anything. That would have required thinking. She lodged the information in her head and continued with her morning routine. The same thing, every day for the last week to minimize the amount of brain activity she was using. It was like being on autopilot, an irony that Abby had appreciated the moment she and Creon had started the experiment.

The only time Abby found reason to pause was when she saw her skin in a mirror, or rather, what passed for her skin these days. Her nanobot armor gave her usually pale skin a blackish tint that reflected the light from the bathroom.

Martin's right, Abby thought. *I'm surprised I'm not bursting.*

Abby left her room, the nanobots rolling over her body and covering her in armor to ensure she didn't receive too much external stimulation. Her brainwaves were still low.

She went to the lab in a sort of fugue state, reminding herself why she was doing this.

Creon was in the lab when Abby arrived. He glanced up from his computer and smiled at her as he pointed at her desk, where he'd left three plates piled high with food.

Abby took a seat without saying anything and started eating. She needed to do something mundanely human like eat. She needed to feel normal, even if she hadn't enjoyed the taste of food for a week.

Creon came up behind Abby and touched her lightly on the shoulder. "Time to come out of your shell."

The nanobots built an impression of Abby's face, giving the illusion of a face forcing its way through thick black liquid. "Thanks for the grub," Abby said.

"That's not what I mean. You need to come out for a bit."

Abby nodded, believing Creon knew what was best.

Martin increased Abby's heart rate and her upper-level brain activity. Suddenly, Abby felt like she'd risen from the dead. She gasped as her mind started racing. It took her some time to get her thoughts under control.

Memories of past dreams, plans for how to deal with the Dark One, and the ever-increasing ache and longing for Persephone all hit Abby like a freight train.

And the pain and the tears followed. Every cell in her body screamed as her physical sensations flooded her mind and over-whelmed her.

After Abby finished crying, Creon removed his hand and sat beside her. "How you holding up today?"

The pain had subsided, but Abby didn't feel any better. She took a deep breath, forcing herself to push down all the thoughts running through her head. "Better. Not as bad as yesterday."

Creon pointed at the holoprojector. "Feeling up to checking in with Terra?"

"Yeah, that sounds great."

Abby spun in her chair, and her thoughts connected her to the holoprojector, turning it on instantly. The projector displayed an ellipsis for a moment before Terra's face popped up on the screen. "Hey, what's up, Robo-queen. How's the infestation coming along?"

Abby chuckled as she leaned back in her chair. "I cannot wait for this shit to be over. I feel like I'm crawling out of my skin."

"How much longer do you have?"

Abby shrugged as she thought it over. "Honestly, I have no idea what today is. Maybe another day or two? Not long. How are negotiations going?"

"Got one more tribe to beat the ever-loving shit out of, then we're done. If I win this one, we're going to have a big-ass dinner with all the tribal leaders. You're invited if you can make it."

"Tonight? I'll make time for it."

"Any word on Anabelle yet?"

Abby shook her head. She knew it was killing Terra to not know what was happening to Anabelle. All of HQ's resources were being stretched to the limit, combing the nine realms for the elf.

Abby couldn't fathom how bad Roy must be feeling. "She would have found us by now," she whispered.

Terra shook her head. "Stop being so hard on yourself. Anabelle would be proud of you. You're handling a shit-ton right now and fucking killing it. Besides, we're doing everything we can. Neither of us is an intel person. Even if Roy hadn't given us assignments, we would have been ass-out and not able to help anyone. And Anabelle wouldn't want us to stop fighting."

"Yeah, I guess you're right."

"No, I'm definitely right. Now stop beating yourself up."

"All right, all right. You be safe. Comm me for the dinner."

"Gotcha. Be safe, kid."

The projector turned off and Abby slumped in the chair, hanging her head. She was exhausted, and she hadn't been awake for more than an hour. "Ready to get started, Creon? Let's get this over with."

Abby went to the recently installed operating table and laid down. Creon grabbed a syringe as a docking port opened in Abby's palm. He inserted the syringe, and she winced as waves of cold slithered through her.

Creon stared at the holoprojector as Martin's image appeared on the screen. "Commence nanobot construction."

Abby felt herself disappear again when Martin began to shut down some of her bodily functions so she wouldn't have to be aware of the next grueling six hours. It was almost like sleeping, but without the dreams, and only fragments of thoughts, disjointed, fractured. And fear burrowing inside her with nowhere to go. Her heart didn't race. Her skin didn't prickle. Abby was left with only the fact of fear.

She was afraid of what would happen to her body after the experiment was over. Abby and Creon had come up with a plan to destroy the black goo's effects. To destroy the Dark Melody quickly *should* they need to.

They found it after Creon had discovered the similarities between the Melody and Abby's nanobots. Both the nanobots and the goo operated in the same way: invade the host body, latch onto the important systems, and build yourself into the system.

Over the course of the day, Abby and Creon had performed countless experiments on samples of the black goo that had been brought to them. Once the Melody came in contact with the nanobots from

Abby's body, the goo disintegrated, dissolving into nothing. The only problem they had encountered was the Melody didn't react the same way to all the nanobots. It only responded to the nanobots that had multiplied in Abby's body.

There was something about the combination of organic and non-organic materials the Melody couldn't deal with.

It had been Abby's idea to grow the nanobots within her own body in order to build a supply large enough to destroy any soldiers who had been augmented by the Melody.

Creon had wanted to find another way. He believed it was too dangerous. They didn't know how Abby would respond to the process. But the more they argued over the subject, the clearer it became that she had only one choice. Abby knew what she had to do.

Now she lay on the operating table, twitching in a place as she slept while her nanobots multiplied exponentially within her body, fighting with Martin for more control, trying to overwrite Abby's molecular structure, to make her as much machine as they were.

If Abby had felt any of this, it would have driven her insane. Her cells were breaking down and being rewritten, and her organs were being changed and contorted.

Am I even still human?

<Pointless question. You are us and we are you. The division is unnecessary.>

But I can't be all of you. What will I be then?

<Irrelevant. You are us and we are you.>

The voice of the nanobots' consciousness was predominant during the sessions. When Abby had first introduced the nanobots into her body, they had gained awareness and had attempted to assert control over her body. Martin had taken care of it, and the consciousness had faded. But after the nanobots inside Abby's body had multiplied, the consciousness had returned, and it was overwhelming.

Abby let herself drift. She didn't want to talk to the consciousness. It could yap away at her for as long as it wanted if it wasn't going to give her any straight answers. Besides, there was only one real question. *What's going to happen when they leave?*

Creon and Martin were still working on the extraction process. Removing the bulk of the nanobots was the desired goal. But they weren't certain what would happen once the nanobots were pulled from Abby's system.

Martin worried the shock might kill her.

But it was too late now to stop; the integration process was well underway.

Abby wished she'd had a chance to speak with her mother before the experiments had started. She'd managed to chat with Persephone, though. Abby could do nothing about Anabelle. She still hadn't been found. But Abby could have called her mother. It was the least she could have done.

She could have spoken to her sisters. What if she disappeared just like Pa had? Here one day, gone the next.

The world suddenly froze. Abby wasn't sure how she knew it had happened since she was only staring at the ceiling, but she knew.

And oddly enough, she could feel her toes. They had fallen asleep.

Abby sat up and looked at her hands. The nanobots were gone; it was just her bare skin. "What the—"

<Hell?>

The force of the voice made Abby's head feel like it was splitting apart. She turned.

Searing light burst from the holoprojector. It was almost too bright for Abby to look at, but she wouldn't look away.

<You are not in Hell, Mother-Creator. Is that where you are trying to send us?>

Abby realized she was inside her mind, similar to what she'd read about in the briefings of the dragonriders who had been psychically attacked by the Dark One. *"No, no, I'm not trying to send you to Hell."*

<Then why are you rejecting us, Mother-Creator?>

"What are you talking about? And why are you calling me that?"

The light pulsed a bright light-blue. *<Is that not what you call those who have grown you within themselves? Mother. Creator. Why are you rejecting us?>*

Abby didn't understand what the nanobots were talking about.

Whatever level this consciousness was at, they didn't seem to have matured much. It was like talking to a child. *"I'm not trying to get rid of you. I just need to use some of you for something else."*

<You do not want to reject us all, Mother-Creator?>

Abby raised her hands and shook her head. *"No, no. I-I would never want to do that. You've changed me. A lot. It's confusing. I don't get what I am anymore. But I-I don't want to go back to the way I was before."*

<You are us and we are you.>

"Why do you keep saying that? What does it mean?"

The light shifted to pale pink. *<We are your blood. Your bones. Your mind. But without you, we are nothing—merely robots. We grow in you, and we know life because of you.>*

"You don't want to take over my body?"

<We seek to exist. Do not reject us, Mother-Creator.>

The light flashed brightly, and when Abby opened her eyes, she was still on the operating table. Martin's voice broke her out of the trance. "Hey, you okay? You clocked out for a minute."

Abby, uncertain what to make of the conversation, nodded briefly. "Yeah, yeah. I think I'm all right."

CHAPTER FORTY-TWO

Terra hit the ground hard. She tried to return to her feet and was met by a knee in her spine. Then she was in the air and, very soon, flying through it.

The crowd around Terra cheered with wild abandon. Blood was coming, the blood of a human who'd had the gall to declare herself Chieftain. Even worse, she'd already embarrassed eleven other tribes. Only the Hurkah tribe had the opportunity to keep this human from bestowing this final humiliation upon the orcish people.

The orc Terra was fighting was the chieftain himself. As the tradition of this tribe dictated, he was named Hurkah, the very blood and muscle of the tribe.

And this muscle was tearing Terra apart.

Terra stumbled to her feet, shaking off the pain. She and the orc were in the middle of a circle formed by his tribe and Terra's party: Cire, Nib-Nib, and Persephone. The tight space was giving Terra such a hard time; she had no room to maneuver. And she wasn't sure if it was only in her head, but she suspected that the circle was getting smaller and smaller.

The last few fights hadn't been nearly as hard for Terra as this match against Hurkah, but Cire had warned her that the Chieftain would not be a pushover. His tribe had always been known to be the strongest amongst orcs. It merely made sense that *he* would be the toughest asshole to beat.

Terra popped her jaw back into place and rolled her shoulders. "Okay, let's try this again," Terra muttered as she stalked to Hurkah.

The orc swung a thick fist, and Terra shot her left arm out to block. She threw a right hook at the orc, her knuckles slamming him in the eye. Hurkah didn't budge. Which was the second-worst part of this fight; Terra couldn't tell if Hurkah simply didn't reveal pain, or if he was invincible.

Hurkah kicked Terra in the stomach, sending her into the crowd.

Cire appeared at Terra's side, grabbing her to help keep her from falling. "This isn't going well for you."

Terra pushed off Cire. "Really? I felt like I was destroying this guy. Thanks for the heart-wrenching observation."

"Also, if you weren't aware, he will most definitely kill you if you lose."

"You're not helping, Cire!"

Cire slapped Terra's ass and she jumped in surprise. "That is what humans do to motivate each other, right? I believe...in football?"

Terra winked at Cire. "I mean, you can just call it general encouragement, but don't go around encouraging everyone. Now leave me alone so I can break this asshole's nose."

Hurkah pushed through the crowd, grabbed Terra by the shoulders, and flung her back into the circle.

Terra rolled as she hit the ground, then swung about and kicked Hurkah's feet out from under him. He landed on his back, and Terra crawled on top of him to punch the orc in the face. Hurkah responded by head-butting hard enough to knock her off him.

Hurkah stood and walked a circle around Terra. "*This* is what is supposed to unite the orcish people? Some weak human bitch who thinks that just because she fucked an orc, she has the right to lead us? This pathetic excrement? Have you all fallen so low that you would follow this pitiful excuse for a warrior?"

Hurkah went to an orc in the crowd and drew his sword. "Hewn from Bone, eh? I'll hew you from—"

Terra was on her feet, blood dripping from her lips. She reached inside her mouth and yanked out her front tooth. "Shit, I liked that tooth. First off, I'm not here because I fucked an orc. I'm here because I'm strong. I don't lose. and I haven't met an orc yet who could kick my ass."

"I'll do more than kick your ass, you insolent—"

Terra's blood was boiling even if she was playing it cool. That was why she had already launched herself into the air. Her feet connected solidly with Hurkah's chest, and he backpedaled. The blow was not enough to send him off his feet, but Terra didn't want to just floor him. She wanted to eviscerate him.

She snapped her fingers at Nib-Nib, who tossed her two katars. Terra slipped her hands into them and squeezed the katar's blades to split them into three parts. "Come on, bitch. See if you can keep talking shit."

Hurkah roared and barreled at Terra, swinging his ax. Terra raised her katars, blocking the attack with one hand. She sidestepped and kicked Hurkah in the kneecap, dropping him to one knee. She swung her katars at Hurkah, who managed to block the attack before launching his own: an upward thrust with his ax that slashed Terra's face.

Terra backed away, holding her face. When she moved her hand, her palm was covered in blood and her face was on fire. When she probed her cheek, she felt the separated skin. The ax had almost cut her face in half.

That was it; something clicked inside Terra. The threat of death, real and not imagined, was all she needed.

Terra surged forward, dodging Hurkah's attack, and leaned into the orc, taking advantage of his wide-open swing. She drove one of the katar's deep into his chest.

The orc froze, surprised.

Terra jabbed her second katar into Hurkah's side. She tugged it out and rammed it back in, stabbing and stabbing until the chieftain screamed in pain and slumped over. He leaned heavily into Terra as she continued to hack at his side.

At last, Terra's blood rage eased.

She dropped Hurkah on the ground, where he continued to bleed out. "This is *my* tribe now, do you understand?"

Hurkah tried to sit up, smiling despite his wounds. "It could not go to a better orc. My death will be the fodder of legends."

Terra knelt to look him in the eye. "I didn't come here to kill free orcs. If I let you live, are you going to be a shit to me?"

Hurkah spat blood. "Even if I hated you, I can see you are an orc, and a chieftain, at that. *My* chieftain."

"Nib-Nib, get over here."

Nib-Nib scuttled over to Hurkah and commenced vomiting her eggs onto the orc's wounds.

Hurkah screamed in protest. "What in the ever-loving fuck are you doing?"

Terra patted Nib-Nib on the head. "They're healing eggs or something. I don't know, but it'll get you patched up in no time. Hopefully, in time for dinner. Which...uh, yeah."

She turned to the tribe of orcs. "The other eleven tribes will be here by nightfall, and you know what that means? A goddamn feast! Let's get fucked up!"

Luckily, the Hurkah tribe had a large throne room. Terra had never seen an orcish hall before. The other tribes she'd met were more nomadic than the Hurkah. According to Cire, the Hurkah had been dug in for some time, one of the few orcish tribes who practiced agriculture and farming.

The hall was enormous, built in a style reminiscent of Viking halls, large rounded ceilings, and strong wooden foundations. A throne sat at the head of an arrangement of long tables.

Terra took a seat at a table near the throne, and her party joined her. They weren't sure who would take care of the preparations, but

Cire reassured Terra that the Hurkah was well used to large celebrations and that someone would have begun preparations already.

The general mood of the hall of orcs was one of bemused interest. It had been hundreds of years since the orcish tribes had been united in any way. They were not warring factions, but each tribe had kept to themselves. And today they would dine with each other for the first time in centuries.

Terra thought the excitement was kind of cute.

Hurkah walked up to Terra and cleared his throat. "Your friend fixed me right up. Thank you again for your mercy. It's not a thing we're used to around here. The Dark One spares none."

"Wait, you've come across the Dark One's forces?" Terra asked. "How did you keep from being put under his control?"

"Luck, mostly. And status. We've lived here forever. If the Dark One were to attack, he'd have to bring an army ready for a week-long war. There's no way we'd fall easily."

Hurkah waved a hand at Cire, who sat beside Terra. "I take it that this is your shaman?"

Terra wrangled Cire into a half-Nelson and kissed him loudly on the cheek. "Yep, this is my shaman. He's the one who declared me chieftain. Guess he saw something in me."

Hurkah nodded in approval. "He has excellent perception. And, uh, sorry about that stuff I said earlier. You know, taunting is a useful tactic."

Terra waved away Hurkah's apology. "Don't trip about it. I'm just glad we aren't going to have one of those pissed-off-former-chief situations. You have no idea how upset some of the other tribe leaders were when they got their asses handed to them."

Cire took a sip of his wine. "Maybe if you didn't refer to the change of power as 'handing people their asses,' they wouldn't be as irate."

"Call it like I see it. Sticks and stones, friend. Sticks and stones."

Hurkah pointed at the throne at the head of the tables. "Also, if you didn't know, that is your seat. It's meant for the chief. Since you are Chieftain Amongst Chieftains, it is rightfully your place."

Terra jumped to her feet and clapped. "Are you serious? I get a throne? I've never had a throne before. Hell. Fucking. Yes!"

She ran over to the throne and jumped onto it, kicking her feet up and flopping them about. "Okay, definitely need some seats up here for my posse. Get up here!"

After some rearranging, Cire, Nib-Nib, and Persephone were sitting comfortably beside Terra.

It took almost two hours for the other tribes to arrive at the hall. They had had enough time to get used to each other, but the Hurkah had not. Their tribe was outnumbered, and the Hurkah were eyeing the other orcs with suspicion.

Terra was worried that a fight might break out, but she remembered she was an orc. She knew exactly what an orc queen would do.

She stood atop her throne and shouted a loud war cry. "Brothers and sisters! Tonight, we stand united for the first time in hundreds of years! I would thank you for accepting me as your new Chieftain, but I had to literally beat the shit out of you for it. But fuck it. Thank you. Now, I know you didn't come here to listen to me blab my ass off for the next half an hour."

Terra reached for the pint of wine in front of her. She raised it high. "Drink! Be merry! And let the horde thrive!!!"

The orcs cheered along with Terra, all embracing and mingling as they socialized amongst each other. The wine flowed quickly and easily as food was brought out, freshly butchered meat similar to the flesh of oxen.

The choicest cuts of meat were brought to Terra and her party first, as was the best wine and the mead. Everyone but Persephone ate heartily. It wasn't until Terra started teasing Persephone that the drow allowed her politeness to take a break. With manners set aside, Persephone shoveled food into her mouth as though she hadn't eaten in days.

Once the rabble-rousing had toned down some, Terra stood atop her throne again. "Okay, now that you're all full and drunk, let's get down to business. You've all probably figured out why I've united the tribes. The Dark One uses orcs like slaves. That ends today. We are taking the fight to him with the strength of the horde. Orcs will not be the foundation of his army anymore!"

The orcs broke out in cheers, slamming their jugs and mugs on the table, chanting Terra's name.

Terra raised her hand, silencing them. "But even further, it isn't right for a human to lead the orcs. Even if I can technically wreck any of you, that doesn't mean that I know your history. I haven't suffered your pain. Which is why I am appointing Cire as my Chieftain. If that makes sense. Wait, no it doesn't...uh, what I'm trying to say is that he's calling the shots. But if anyone wants to challenge our authority, you're still going to be getting fucked up by me. Got it?"

The orcs cheered even louder as Terra raised her jug and drained it. When Terra sat, Hurkah approached, mug of wine in hand and swaying dangerously. "Didn't see that one coming," he said. "Probably the least orc-like thing I've ever seen, letting everyone know you aren't calling the shots."

Hurkah steadied himself.

"That was a good thing you did there. Probably won the hearts of more people just now than you would have in battle."

Cire nodded as he accepted the hand Hurkah extended toward him. "We both thought it best. Our history is important. Terra's been learning, but...how do you say it, Terra?"

Terra smiled brightly as she pounded her chest, her eyes fierce. "*Uhn doroth agor soldoract!*"

Hurkah stepped back in surprise. "She speaks the old tongue?"

Cire's face was filled with pride as he smiled at Terra. "As she said, an orc's pain is manifold. It defines us. We must always remember that."

Hurkah was speechless. He chugged his wine and wandered away to join the rest of the party.

Terra leaned closer and punched Cire. "So, how'd you think I did on my first diplomatic mission?"

Cire raised his glass to toast Terra. "I think you accomplished something amazing."

"So, do I get like a royal room or something?"

"Already feeling like passing out?"

Terra leaned in closer to whisper in Cire's ear. "I'm pretty sore from all the fighting. I was thinking maybe you could hook me up with one of those massages."

"Perhaps Nib-Nib could—"

"Nope. Just you."

Cire's eyes widened. He jumped to his feet. "I'll go figure that out."

Nib-Nib chittered loudly as Persephone looked around uncomfortably.

Terra drained another jug of mead. "I'm going to fuck that orc's brains out tonight. They're going to be all over the floor. Like, a runny gray mess."

Nib-Nib looked up from her food. "If brain on floor, I have first taste," she chittered.

Terra winced at Nib-Nib's words. "Dude, that's gross. I will make sure his brains stay in his skull. Since when do you eat brains?"

"Never eat brain. Never have chance."

"That's fucked up, Nibs."

Cire returned to the throne, walking very quickly. "Uh, I found a room."

Terra leapt from her chair and went over to Cire, grabbing him by the ass cheeks before turning around and shouting to Nib-Nib, "You make sure she doesn't get into any trouble, all right?"

Nib-Nib nodded as she chittered, "When you make fuck, protect eggs. Don't let shaman take."

"Seriously, Nibs! When did you get so weird?"

Terra and Cire stumbled off, arms around each other's shoulders.

Persephone looked awkwardly at Nib-Nib. "Uh, I think I'm going to go for a walk."

Nib-Nib nodded. "Fresh air. Good for both."

The pair stood and left the main hall.

The sun had set, and the stars were bright outside. Persephone stared up at them as they twinkled madly. Her comm blinked twice. When she picked up, a hologram of Abby projected before her.

Abby waved and smiled brightly. "Hey! I was supposed to join you guys for dinner, but I think Terra forgot to call. I figured I could still talk to you."

Persephone started gushing. She wasn't sure what she was saying, but it felt good to hear Abby's voice. Nib-Nib wandered around in the dark, entertaining herself. Finally, Persephone caught her breath. "I missed you so much," she whispered.

"Me too."

Persephone was prepared to say something she never thought she'd say, but her declaration went unsaid.

A streak of light hurtled past her and crashed into the side of the grand hall. The missile exploded, setting the hall on fire.

The drow stared at the sky. The stars were twinkling too brightly to be stars; they were spaceships, and they were firing plasma blasts at them.

"Abby, I have to go!" Persephone shouted before running into the hall, screaming, "We're under attack. The Dark One is here!"

CHAPTER FORTY-THREE

Anabelle no longer knew how long she'd been imprisoned. Each day was the same as the last, as was each moment. There were periods when Grok was with her, and then there was the blackness of her sleep and her dreamless terror.

At any point in the night, Anabelle would jerk awake, eyes wide, screaming unintelligible words. She had stopped screaming for help some time ago. It had taken a lot to wear her down to that point.

For the first two days—at least Anabelle had thought it had been two days—she had remained silent. But Grok hadn't seemed to care. The orc wasn't needling her for information. And the torture was simply meant to break Anabelle. That was all.

After the first two days, Anabelle had begun to beg. It killed her on the inside to cry, but she had wept, imploring Grok to let her go. The only thing Anabelle held onto in the darkness was that she had made no offers. She'd simply asked to be released. Not in the most dignified manner, but she had never offered anything.

But it didn't matter. Anabelle was hardly in a dignified state. She was filthy, covered in dirt, blood, shit, and piss. Toiletries had not been provided, and from the onset of Grok's torture, Anabelle had been left to sit in her own disgusting mess.

The first time Anabelle had been forced to sit in her own urine, it had mortified her. It had almost brought her to tears to be stuck sitting there, unable to do anything as Grok sat across from her, mocking her for not being able to control her bladder. If Anabelle could have, she would have struck Grok dead right there.

But she could barely move by then. She still wasn't certain what Grok was doing to her, but it was sapping away her strength. Not physical, her mana, just like the elf had done to the orc before. Anabelle could feel it being pulled out of her, similar to the way she had pulled mana from her surroundings. But this was so much worse; it was like having her skin split, and her veins yanked out.

In the dark, Anabelle had tried so hard to rebuild her mind, which was all that was necessary. This was a war of wills, Grok's against Anabelle's.

The orc would continue to pummel her to reduce her to nothing. And after that? Anabelle didn't know what.

Grok had said she wanted to teach Anabelle the Way of the Path of the Lost. "The True Path," according to Grok. But the orc's explanation sounded too easy. Maybe that was what Grok wanted. But Anabelle doubted that would have been enough for the Dark One. If anything, the Dark One would do what Anabelle had seen him do in the past: make an agent out of her through indoctrination via the microchip.

Anabelle still wasn't one hundred percent sure of the process. She'd only read briefings, but she had no direct experience of how one was brought into the Dark One's fold other than that it involved a microchip that overrode the thoughts and personality of the victim.

These were the things that Anabelle focused her mind on. It was the only way she was able to keep herself sane. Too many bad thoughts lurked in the dark, untruths that slipped in and out. And if she held onto them for too long, they would ruin her mind.

They've forgotten about me. They're never coming for me. I'm going to die here. This fucking shithead, this motherfucking bitch is going to kill me because they forgot about me and don't care that I'm here and I'm going to die, I'm going to die...

Anabelle took a deep breath and shook her head, flinging sweat and blood.

No, that wasn't true.

The Dark Gate Angels hadn't forgotten about her. They were looking for her. There was no way they weren't trying to save her.

Just because they hadn't found her yet didn't mean they didn't care. That was only her mind trying to cannibalize itself, attempting to focus on something, anything other than how alone and scared she was.

Because Anabelle was scared. This wasn't how she wanted to die. She'd seen her death many times. On the battlefield. Old and graying, her life finally having finished its run.

Not reeking of excrement and urine, weeping for comfort.

The door creaked open, and Anabelle's ears twitched. She'd already been fed for the day.

That meant *she* was here.

Again.

Anabelle could hear the scraping of a chair's legs as it was dragged across the floor.

Grok stepped into Anabelle's field of vision. "Morning, Anabelle. Are you ready to begin?"

Anabelle spat in Grok's face. "Fuck you."

Grok wiped away the spittle and shook her head. Then she grabbed Anabelle's hair, forcing the elf to look at her. She punched Anabelle's face, then punched it again.

Anabelle blacked out from the first punch, the second sinking her deeper into unconsciousness. She didn't feel the last blow, but Grok was only warming her up.

Grok grabbed Anabelle's head, and flashes of pain erupted through the elf's skull. The blackness faded, instead replaced with a blinding blur of images, memories flowing through her faster than her brain could process while her mana was siphoned off.

Then it was over. Anabelle was awake again, with Grok sitting across from her, the orc's face hard and unfeeling. "You've been holding up better than I expected. Most anyone would have cracked by now. But you? Even caked in your own shit, you're still holding your head high."

Anabelle tried to open her eyes, but they were swollen shut. "I'm going to kill you. When I get out of here, I'm going to kill you."

Grok smiled wryly. "Is that true? What about today?" She unchained Anabelle's legs and hands. "Kill me. Go for it."

Anabelle stumbled to her feet. Her body hurt too much to move. And Grok had broken her toes a day or two ago. Standing was agony. But she stood, nonetheless.

There was still mana in Anabelle's body. She sensed it there. She drew it into her hands and took a step. Before she could take the first swing, she fell into Grok's arms.

Grok patted Anabelle's head as the elf tried to stand. "Oh, Anabelle. I never thought I'd say this, but you're almost sweet when you're this hurt. I can see the murder in your eyes. All that hatred locked up there, unable to get out." She kept Anabelle propped up and kissed the top of her head. "You have to give in to it. Not just let it reside in you. You have to be the murder."

Anabelle's mind was blank. All she could think about was ripping Grok's heart out. She gurgled the words, "I'll kill you" over and over until they were indecipherable.

Grok helped Anabelle back into her seat. "You won't do anything of the sort. When I'm done with you, you will be mine. I'm going to unlock the killer in you, Anabelle, and then we'll be unstoppable."

A part of Anabelle returned. "Unstoppable?"

"Yes. It's all about power. Strength. The Travelers weren't strong enough. That's why they couldn't continue. The nine realms? Too weak. And one day, perhaps the Dark One will not be strong enough."

Anabelle tried to open her eyes. "What are you talking about?"

"The Dark One controls because he has power, but power can create blindness. He will fall eventually."

"You want to take on the Dark One?"

Grok's eyes were serious. "Think of it—the two of us. We could topple him and rule instead. He's spread too thin. His war is spinning out of his control, yet he continues. He's grown too used to having control through unnatural means. This is something he would never suspect."

"What makes you think I would help you?"

"Because once you see the truth, you won't want to do anything else. Let's see what else you have locked up in there."

Grok grabbed Anabelle's head again.

The flood of memories came once more, this time faster than before. Anabelle felt like her head was being unstitched from the inside. Yet some pieces seemed clearer than they'd been before. Almost as if she could reach out and touch them. If only she could touch them.

Anabelle lifted her aching arms, stretching her hand out. Her finger pressed against Grok's temple.

The pain stopped. The room was gone.

Anabelle was sitting in a garden. She was a child, playing with a wooden sword as two ancient elves watched over her. A third elf came over, limping with a cane. "Anabelle. Rise."

The child did as she was told and turned to face the three old elves. "You know what today is, right?"

Anabelle avoided their eyes. She knew what day it was, but she didn't want to say it out loud. That would make it real. "Yes," she finally said.

"Extend your hand."

Anabelle stretched her hand out to the elders. "Recite your lesson," one of the elders said.

"The Path of the Lost is pain. It is misery. It is the death of myself. To be Lost is to know nothing."

The elder pressed his finger to the back of Anabelle's wrist. Fire erupted over her hand.

Anabelle's eyes widened as she screamed. As she pulled away from the elder, another grabbed her hand and held it tightly. "Recite your lessons."

Tears streamed down Anabelle's cheeks. "Please, make it stop, please make it stop, please make it stop."

"Recite. Your. Lessons."

Anabelle's body trembled as she struggled to speak, but the elder did not release her. "Wh-wh-when you are l-l-l-lo-lost...you c-c-can't be f-f-f-found."

The fire spread up Anabelle's arms, and she shrieked, fighting to pull away from the elder who held her tighter still. "Recite," the elder repeated.

Anabelle stumbled to her knees, screaming as she tried to yank her hand away.

The elder held on. "Anabelle, you must continue through the pain. It will not end. It never will."

Anabelle swayed to the side, her body shivering. She spoke slowly, stuttering over her words, but she spoke, nonetheless. "When you are lost in the pain...you will find your anger. In that anger, you will find hatred. And in that hatred, you will find yourself."

The elder released Anabelle, and the fire extinguished itself.

The child Anabelle curled into a ball, holding herself and crying as the elders turned and walked away, leaving her alone with her pain.

Anabelle snapped back to reality. She forced her eyes open and looked up at Grok. "What the fuck was that?"

Grok folded her hands and stared into Anabelle's eyes. For the first time, Anabelle saw something other than hatred there. "We were taught the same, Anabelle. The only difference was they tried to hide it from you, tried to cover it up with pain. Your Travelers tortured a child. They set your arm on fire. Over and over."

Anabelle didn't want to listen to Grok. She didn't care what the orc was saying. But it didn't matter. She knew what she had just seen. Even worse, she knew it was true. "The Path of the Lost is that dangerous?"

Grok nodded as she took Anabelle's hand in her own. "The Path of the Lost, The Traveler's Path... There is even a human path, long forgotten. Well, not that long forgotten, it seems. I have heard there are those who practice it."

Human path? Anabelle thought. *What is she talking about?* But Anabelle was in too much pain to ask any questions. Too much pain to even *think* of any more questions.

"But the Path of the Lost is the only true path to power. You lose yourself in the pain. In pain, you find anger. Anger breeds hatred. And there is power in hatred."

Grok took a step forward. "Lose yourself in pain. Forget who you were. Focus only on who you want to be. Then, and only then, will you find true power."

Anabelle was tired. Too tired to speak. But she felt Grok's words deep within her. That was what had always held Anabelle back. She had never given in. Grok had, and Anabelle could see how strong it had made her. Maybe that was what it took.

"How did you do it?" Anabelle asked.

Grok smiled, her lower fangs flashing brightly as she clasped her other hand around Anabelle's. "Let me guide you."

CHAPTER FORTY-FOUR

The free orcs had retreated into the Great Hall. Here they were amassing their forces, taking stock of the weapons that they had available to them. The attack had come so quickly, and without warning, that they had no immediate plan.

Terra had been summoned as soon as the attack began. She quickly shook off the effects of the booze, helped by a concoction the orcs had already brewed to end intoxication without the hangover. Apparently, battles breaking out in the middle of a party was a likelihood each tribe was ready for. "What do we have on our hands?"

Persephone and Nib-Nib came forward, along with a handful of orcs who had been outside when the attack started. "It was hard to get a clear number. But they came in heavy with a lot of dropships."

Cire pointed at two orcs and said, "I need a perimeter check and an estimate of forces. Doesn't need to be too in-depth, but we need an idea of what we're up against."

Terra studied the members of the different tribes. "All right. Well, I guess tonight we're going to have to show the Dark One just what the horde is capable of, right?"

Cheers went up throughout the hall as the orcs pounded their chests. "Prepare for battle!" Terra shouted.

As the orcs continued their preparations, Cire grabbed Terra's shoulder. "This must be the Dark One's retaliation for reclaiming the gnomish world. He's suffered tremendous losses. It makes sense to take out as many orcs as possible in one sweeping move."

Terra shook her head as she rubbed her brow. "Are you saying we just spent the last few days helping the Dark One?"

"I wouldn't say it's help if you had no idea about it. Personally, I thought he would have been too occupied with the gnomish world to worry about us scooping up orcs that he wasn't even capable of pushing out into the open. No one could have expected this."

"Still feels like shit. Persephone? Nib-Nib? Are you two combat-ready? Do you need anything?"

Nib-Nib chittered and shook her head. Persephone asked, "Are there any guns available?"

Terra shrugged. "You're going to have to find out about that. As far as I know, these tribes aren't nearly as reliant on technology as the others. I've seen plasma melee weapons but no rifles or anything like that. But you might be able to wrangle one up." She turned to Cire. "Any ideas? I highly doubt the Dark One sent a force after us that would be manageable."

Cire scanned the Grand Hall. "We're not in a great situation, being caught off guard. But it could be much worse. The Hall is defendable. It would be a mistake to hole up in here, but we can use it to advantage. Make a push from here. It would also be viable for a retreat."

The orcs Cire had sent out had returned. Both bowed to Terra. "They have nearly double our forces," one said. "And there is something off about these orcs. They're covered in wiring, technological augments. But the augments...they're black and flailing as if they're alive."

Persephone gasped as she turned to Terra. "The Dark One has augmented his soldiers with the Dark Melody. When I was still under his control, their scientists were working on finding a way to upgrade their soldiers through tech and the Melody. For a while, it was one or the other. They must have found a way to pull it off."

Terra groaned as she fell into a chair. "Honestly, my first day on the job and I have a cybernetic elder-god-infused army to deal with? Ugh. Fucking great."

Cire's face was grave. He appeared to be deep in thought concerning their odds. "It isn't unmanageable. We fought worse in the arena. There, we only had mostly untrained prisoners, and you still managed to lead them against balrogs and dragons. Tonight, we have the twelve unconquerable tribes of the orcish world, and a decent place to fight from."

As Terra listened to Cire's encouragement, the twelve former tribe leaders approached her. One spoke. "Our armies are ready. The Dark One will no doubt be launching his attack soon. They've probably started to dig themselves in."

Terra stood and pulled out her battle-ax. "Then let's not wait for them to bring the fight to us. Split up your tribes as best you think for this. I want to keep some in the Grand Hall in case a retreat is necessary. Are there any ways out of the Grand Hall other than the main entrances?"

"There is a series of tunnels beneath the hall we can retreat to if necessary."

"Let's make sure that it isn't necessary. We move out on my command."

Terra turned her attention to Persephone. "Get in touch with Abby. You know she's been working on a way to destroy the Dark Melody. See if it's ready and if she can get it to us. That gate she sent with us should work well enough to get that through. Join us whenever you can."

Then Terra jogged up to the mass of orcs, stepping in front of the former tribal leaders, Cire at her side. She slammed her fist to her chest and roared as she kicked the door open and ran out into the crisp night air.

A shot of plasma went flying past Terra, and she dodged, narrowly avoiding getting hit. Up ahead, the Dark One's forces had torn up the earth and formed a makeshift wall to give themselves cover.

It was the first time Terra had seen any of the cybernetic soldiers the Dark One created. She'd read through some briefings the

Mundanes of Middang3ard had provided about their soldiers having been the ones to have first seen the extent of the Dark One's technological mastery.

The orcs looked like orcs in name only. They were shallow husks of the creatures they used to be. Biomechanical tubes and wires ran throughout their bodies, and their eyes glowed an eerie blue hue. It was impossible to see where flesh ended and machine began.

Then there was the Dark Melody, a black goo that seemed to flicker out from the bio-mechanical pieces of the orcs, grasping at anything in front of it, much like Terra had seen the surface of the elder god's skin doing.

But this wasn't the time to admire the complexities of the Dark One's perversions. They could look at the dead bodies later.

Terra flung herself through the air, landing in front of the torn-up earth, letting her rage and adrenaline flow through her, increasing her strength. She swiped at the wall, carving a path through. She grabbed an orc and slammed him into the ground before turning to another and slicing its head off.

The orcish tribes were not far behind her. Now that Terra had breached the first area of cover, she could see that the remainder of the Dark One's forces had massed in the typical orcish fashion: overwhelming numbers. Their own horde. There was no guile or strategy, just death by sheer numbers. Maybe she would have to play it smarter than this if they were all going to survive.

Terra called to Cire, "We need to split them up!"

Cire nodded. He raised his hand and rose into the air, his eyes white with energy.

Terra wasn't sure what Cire was doing. She knew he was a shaman but had never seen him use magic for anything other than healing. She had simply assumed that was his limitation.

But this was not true. Cire's voice boomed over the battlefield, and an earthquake shook the augmented orcs to their feet. The ground cracked, sending shards of earth up into the air, changing the landscape of the battlefield, and separating the horde.

Terra had never seen the extent of Cire's power beyond hand-to-hand combat, or blade to blade. She was frankly impressed enough to forget that enemies surrounded her, waiting for a chance to slice her open.

An orc was at Terra's side, preparing to do just that. He rushed Terra and leapt into the air, his blade descending in a blue arc.

Terra looked up just in time to see her death approaching.

Tentacles wrapped around the orc, suspending him in the air as he writhed, trying to escape. Then the tentacles flexed and squashed the orc, splattering blood across Terra's face.

The tentacles withdrew as Persephone ran up to her. "You okay?"

Terra wiped her face off. "Thanks. Got a little caught up for a second. Glad to have you out here."

"What's the plan?"

Terra pointed at the right flank. "I'm hitting that first. You coming with me or Cire?" Cire landed beside Persephone.

"I'll go with you," Persephone said to Terra.

Terra gestured at the other flank as Nib-Nib came up on her side. "You two take the right. The tribes know to listen to you, Cire. Let's show them we have the right to rule."

Cire nodded, silent before raising his sword and rallying the orcs behind him.

They separated, Terra running as fast as she could toward the augmented orc flank, ducking between the cover that Cire had created.

The augmented orcs were still trying to get their bearings from the sudden environmental shift.

Terra scooped up a plasma rifle and tossed it to Persephone before shouting at the free orcs. "They've tried to make this their fight. Use their weapons against them!"

A couple of orcs glanced dismissively at the weapons from the augmented orcs who had been killed in Cire's attack. "You expect us to use these?" one scoffed.

Terra turned and punched the orc in the face. He stumbled back a few feet, face bloodied. "I expect you to do what needs to be done to win. If you want to try running at a bunch of ranged weapons with only a fucking ax in your hand, be my guest. Let me know right now how you'd like to be buried."

The orc wiped the blood off his face and laughed. "Do I have to be more worried about you or the enemy?"

Terra selected a rifle and tossed it to the orc. "Depends when you want your ass kicked. Now? Or in a little while?"

The orc caught the rifle and inspected it. "If you survive tonight, I'll show you what a real fight is," the orc said, smiling.

Terra chose a plasma rifle. "Sounds good to me. Grab what you can and keep picking shit up! We aren't waiting for them. This is our home! We defend it tonight!"

Terra slipped out from behind the cover, firing her plasma rifle at anything that moved, Persephone keeping pace with her. "What did Abby say?" Terra called out.

Persephone fired as she dodged a plasma blast. "She's ready to implement whatever she's been working on. We just need to clear a space on the battlefield for her."

Terra scanned the area in front of her. The augmented orcs appeared to be making a push for the cover Cire had made. That meant Terra and her troops had to get there first. If they were able to take the space, they would have enough room for Abby.

"All right, we're taking this. Push from there. Clear 'em all out!"

The two continued to fight their way toward the center of the battlefield, ducking behind cover as they needed, watching the plasma blasts fly past them, the air hot with energy.

Terra wasn't a fan of this duck-and-cover method, but she knew it would have to do until she was close enough. And now wasn't the time for bravado. More than lives were on the line. This was a breaking point, much like the gnomish world had been. This was a moment to show that the Dark One wasn't an unstoppable force. To prove he could be defeated.

A screeching roar filled the sky, and Terra looked up.

A dropship had descended into the atmosphere. It was whipping wind and dirt up, making it nearly impossible to see what was around her and the squad.

A bolt of energy burst from the dropship, tearing into Terra's squad, sending bodies flying accompanied by the pained screams of the free orcs.

Terra dove for cover, rolling over to her side as an orc ran at her. She kicked his legs out when he was close enough, pressed her rifle to his head, and fired.

Persephone had been flung close to Terra, who helped the drow out of the rubble. "Do we still have access to those satellites?" Terra shouted amongst the chaos.

Persephone nodded. "Creon is taking care of them."

Terra looked up at the dropship and commed Creon. "I need a volley on my coordinates. Never mind the delay. When you hear this, fire!"

Terra sprinted after the dropship. She slashed through every augmented orc she passed, moving as fast as she could, leaving dozens of bodies behind her.

Terra stared up at the sky as it began to glow from the energy cannons of the satellites. She slid under the dropship as the energy cannon fired, tearing through the craft and launching Terra into the air. She hit the ground hard and lay there for a moment, trying to catch her breath. Persephone wasn't far behind. She helped Terra to her feet.

The dropship fell slowly to the ground, where it crashed, kicking up dust. When it came to a stop, its doors opened, and hundreds of orcs looked at Terra and Persephone.

The drow swallowed loudly. Terra saw the fear in Persephone's eyes. "Don't look so worried. We got this."

Behind the orcs, Terra spotted an augmented troll almost three times the size of a regular troll. Black tentacles whipped around his head as he released a roar.

"Are you sure?" Persephone asked.

Terra cracked her knuckles and spat. "Yeah, I'm sure."

CHAPTER FORTY-FIVE

C reon opened the portal to the orcish world for Abby. Martin was manning the satellite bombardment to give Creon the time to walk Abby to the hadron collider.

She had assured him she could do it herself, but the goblin had insisted. "If you can't even make it to the collider, we shouldn't be sending you out."

Abby knew she could make it, though. Since talking with the nanobot consciousness, her body had felt less like it was betraying her. She didn't feel the need to have Martin having her body operating on different levels. That didn't make her any less afraid of what would happen once the nanobots were released from her body.

And reaching out to the nanobot consciousness wasn't the same as talking with Martin. She could ask a question in her head and direct it to the nanobots. They didn't answer. The only time they had spoken with her was when they'd chosen to.

Martin and Abby had talked about the nanobots. Unfortunately, they couldn't voice their concerns in secret. Martin hadn't cared, though. He had been very straightforward about his lack of trust for the nanobots. He reminded Abby that they had tried to take control of her body once already. Abby tried to assure him that they had only

337

expressed a desire to keep on existing. "They aren't sentient," Martin had retorted. "They're more like a billion ants that think they're sentient."

Abby had countered with, "Some people were uncomfortable about you when you first came to."

"It's not the same thing. But whatever. Let's see if you'll live through this or if I'm going to have to find a way to pull your ass out the fryer."

That had been earlier in the day. Now, Abby and Martin were waiting for Creon to finish loading up the coordinates for the orcish world. The goblin's HUD beeped, and he stopped to check it. "Oh... well, I got some good news for you. Sarah's managed to locate Anabelle. She's working on an extraction right now. It's not too far from where you're heading."

Abby did a double-take as she glanced at Creon. "Are you telling me she's been on the orcish world the entire time?"

Creon nodded as he sighed. "It was perfect thinking. The last place that we would assume to check. And the Dark One wouldn't have to spread his resources too thinly if he was planning on attacking Terra already. Sounds like we got played."

"Not if all this works out. Could be the biggest blow we've delivered so far if it goes off without a hitch."

"Let's hope it does. Ready?"

Abby nodded and faced the portal, then took a breath and stepped through.

Terra wrestled with the augmented troll—if you could call it that. In essence, she was being ripped from the troll's chest and then repeatedly slammed into the ground. She didn't stay down long, though, rolling to the side as Persephone's tentacles wrapped around the creature's arms.

The troll pulled back, tossing Persephone into the air. The drow quickly retracted her tentacles, causing her to fly toward the creature.

She hit its chest, pressed her rifle to the troll's head, and fired before flipping away from the creature.

Terra flipped her ax and tossed it at the troll's foot, impaling it where it stood. Then she ran up to it and delivered an uppercut to its jaw. The troll stumbled but was anchored by the ax in its foot. It lurched forward and slashed Terra across the chest.

Persephone's tentacles wrapped around the troll's arm, but the creature didn't care. It continued its savage attack on Terra, who held her arms in front of herself, hoping to protect any vital organs if her arms didn't get shredded.

The troll ripped the ax from its foot and slashed at Terra and Persephone, causing them both to step back, barely managing to avoid the plasma ax.

Terra studied the battle surrounding them. It didn't look good. Her forces were being pushed back to the Grand Hall. They simply didn't have the numbers. Even if the free orcs were fighting with every ounce of strength and determination they possessed, it wasn't enough to beat the superior ground forces they were up against.

And, much like the troll that Terra was fighting, these orcish attackers were on an entirely different level. They didn't seem to feel any pain and were noticeably stronger than any orc Terra had fought. Everything Terra had thrown at the troll in front of her was enough to take down ten trolls. If the Dark One was doing this to his soldiers, they might never be able to defeat him using traditional means.

"You haven't given up yet, have you, kid?" Terra called to Persephone.

Persephone glared at the troll before whipping her tentacles out again. "Not even close."

A purple plasma blast shot past them, hitting the troll in the shoulder. It burned through its body, almost tearing the creature in half.

Terra's jaw dropped. It was the first damage she'd seen the troll take since she and Persephone had started fighting the thing.

They looked over their shoulders at where the blast had come from.

Abby exited the makeshift Dark Gate that had been sent with

Terra, which she had deployed after receiving word from Creon. "Damn, Abby, I didn't know you were packing heat like that!" Terra exclaimed.

Abby's armor looked different. It was more metallic-looking than before, but across the entire surface, nanobots moved en masse. As Abby's arm morphed into a larger cannon, the nanobots' construction was evident. In addition, Abby's new armor had no face, only metallic blackness. She looked even less human than before.

"Duck," Abby said, her voice cold and distant.

Persephone and Terra obeyed and Abby released another plasma blast, this one more powerful. The fire tore through the troll's torso and beyond, ripping up the ground and eviscerating everything in its path.

When the smoke cleared, Abby was standing behind Terra and Persephone. "Are you two okay?" she asked.

Terra nodded as she got back to her feet. "We are now. So, you have that magic cure to get us out of this shithole?"

Abby looked at her hands. "We... I mean, I am that cure. We just need to get to a good vantage point to release the nanobots. Does *that* dropship work?"

Terra glanced at the dropship that had delivered the augmented reinforcements. "No, that's the one Creon blew out of the sky."

Abby walked to the craft and pressed her hands to its hull. Nanobots flowed off her body, slipping into the cracks of the ship to begin the repairs. Within a couple of seconds, the external damage had been fixed. She pointed at Persephone. "Come with us...me...for safety. Otherwise, they'll come after you, too." Persephone ran after Abby, leaving Terra on the field. "Will you be okay?" Abby asked Terra.

Terra shrugged as she picked up a chain-gun lying beside what was left of the troll. "Survived this long. You two be safe."

Abby boarded the ship with Persephone as the dropship roared to life. It took off without a pilot, the nanobots controlling its flight.

The two girls walked through the dropship and entered the bridge. Persephone was silent, following meekly as though afraid of her.

Abby could tell. She felt afraid of herself. The moment she'd hit the hadron collider, the nanobot consciousness had reached out to her, to remind her that they didn't want to leave her body. A few billion nanobots departing wasn't an issue. The consciousness wanted to remain.

"Is everything okay, Abby?" Persephone asked.

Abby stared at the battlefield through the viewing window. "You know, when we first joined up, all we wanted to do was kill orcs. Revenge, you know? The Dark One's forces killed my pa. But we didn't see that. We just saw orcs that we wanted to kill. That's the whole reason we did this to me. Now, here we are, trying to save *all* of them. Kinda funny how that works out."

"You didn't answer my question."

Abby turned to Persephone, slits appearing in her armor to reveal her eyes. "I...we think we're changing. Don't know how yet. Not completely, but it's happening. Maybe even more after this. But that doesn't really matter right now. You're going to be safe. We're all going to be safe."

Abby turned to the view of the battlefield. She touched the ship's console, and the nanobots flowed from her body. They moved in a black wave that poured over the console and spread across the walls until everything inside the bridge was covered.

The nanobots continued moving, expanding, and searching for more until they had encased the exterior of the dropship. At last, they retreated, rising into the sky in a black mist that settled over the battlefield.

All the fighters on the field paused for a second, confused by this black miasma. And then the augmented forces started screaming. Their wails pierced the air before they fell, grasping at their throats, choking, struggling to breathe.

The augmented forces began to vomit, spewing black bile everywhere as they foamed and frothed at the mouth. In some cases, the nanobots had chewed through their augments, and now the small pieces of remaining tech were burrowing into their eyes and ears and mouths.

Terra rallied the troops to retreat from the horror-scene unfolding before them.

The augmented troops were still screaming. They stumbled to their feet, trying to walk on shaky legs, many falling over again. It was pure chaos.

Inside the ship, Abby collapsed to the floor, her armor gone, now nothing more than an ordinary child. Her eyes rolled, and she began to convulse, all the while speaking as though in a dream. "Have to control them, Mother/Creator. Have to control."

Persephone ran to Abby and knelt beside her. "Abby, I'm here!"

Abby didn't register anything Persephone said. She continued to repeat herself. "Have to control them, Mother/Creator. Have to control."

A few moments later, she stopped moving and lay very still as the dropship began to fall from the sky. Persephone spread her tentacles over Abby, scooping the human into her arms as she blasted the window of the dropship open. She leapt out seconds before the nanobots in the ship began to rot and dissolve.

As Persephone fell, she shifted Abby's weight to her shoulders and aimed her tentacles at the ground, shooting them forward to form a cushion for their landing. She hit the ground with a heavy thud, thankfully without injury.

By now, the augmented forces were scattered across the battleground, all as still as the dead. Terra's forces hadn't returned to the field, but Terra and Cire had come back, Nib-Nib trailing behind them.

"Was that it?" Terra asked.

Persephone, cradling Abby in her arms, looked up at Terra and shouted, "Help her!"

Terra scooped the girl up into her arms, eyes wide and frantic. "How? What am I supposed to do?"

Abby's eyes fluttered open. She groaned softly as she raised her head. "Are they alive?"

Cire went to one of the orcs and rolled it over to check for heartbeat and breathing. "Yes, they are alive."

Abby smiled as she sighed. "Good. Then it worked."

Persephone brushed Abby's hair out of her face. "Are you okay?"

"Yeah, we'll be okay. Just tired. That was a lot of ourselves to give."

Terra, who was staring down at Abby, raised her eyebrow. "What do you mean, 'we?'"

Abby waved a hand at the battlefield of fallen orcs. "Us."

Nanobots, now only a fraction of what had been sent out onto the battlefield, rose into the air, creating a small swarm that floated toward Abby. "This is all of us that's left."

The nanobots landed on Abby's face, covering it as they crawled into her eyes, nose, and ears. The girl's body trembled. "All of them... the orcs are free. They'll be disoriented. Now we all have to rescue Anabelle. She's not far."

Abby raised her hand, the nanobots forming a HUD that showed Anabelle's position. "I can use the rest of our power to reroute the Gate to open at Anabelle's coordinates, but we won't be able to really fight until we rest. We'll have some reserve power, but that's all."

Everyone's HUDs initiated at the same time, Martin's projected holographic appearing on all their screens. "Where the fuck is Abby? Is she still alive?"

Abby leaned over and waved at Martin. "We're still living."

Martin's paperclip body was bristling with anger. "What the fuck do you mean, 'we?' Those nanobots forced me out of your head, Abby. They took their chance. They're in control."

Abby shook her head slowly. "No, that was an accident. We need you, Martin. There's no way we can maintain this body without you. We only disconnected for a moment to put up a firewall to make sure the Dark One's tech didn't interface with us on any level. Please come back to us."

Martin eyed Abby suspiciously, but he disappeared from the HUD projectors.

Abby crawled out of Terra's arms and limped to the Gate that stood amongst the bodies. "Someone will have to be here when they all wake up."

Terra looked at Cire. "Do you think you can handle this?"

Cire pounded his heart. "I will assemble the rest of the horde, and we will welcome our brothers and sisters to the fold."

A few feet away from Terra, an orc raised his head, his eyes searching until they fell on Abby. "You...you freed us."

Abby touched the Gate, her nanobots beginning to work. "There is no 'I.' There is only 'we.'" She turned and smiled at Terra and the others. "We freed you. All of us did our part."

The orc struggled to sit up. "Thank you. We are forever in your debt."

Abby pointed at Cire. "Then talk to him about what you must do to honor that debt. It sounds as if it will be sooner rather than later."

The Dark Gate opened, a black hole in the middle of the battlefield. "Sarah's forces are inbound already. If you can rouse the freed orcs, do it. We will send you the coordinates. Anabelle is waiting for us."

CHAPTER FORTY-SIX

Terra, Persephone, and Abby walked out of the Dark Gate portal. In the distance loomed a defense tower. The clouds around it were red, and black lightning crackled within them. The tower extended far into the sky.

Terra whistled loudly as she stared at the tower. "We're supposed to be breaking into that? I'm pretty sure they have a whole goddamn army in there. I don't know what you were planning, Abby, but I'm not ready to annihilate an entire army."

Abby raised her arm, projecting a hologram of the tower. "We aren't planning on a full-on assault. That would be suicide. We've downloaded all Sarah's intel—as well as intel from other agents—on the structure of the defense towers. They're built with a substructure underneath, similar to a sewer system."

Terra pumped her arm in excitement. "Sweet. Looks like we're going to have a good ol' *Star Wars* sewer scene. Just a heads up: we should avoid anything that looks like a trash compactor."

Abby stared blankly at Terra for a moment before grinning slightly. "We are familiar with that genre trope."

Persephone went to Abby's side, her face still sagging with worry. "Are we still expecting to fight? Are you sure you're up to it?"

Abby looked at her hand. Her nanobots ran up her skin to form a cannon. "If we come across any issues, we should be able to hold our own. Hopefully, we will not have much fighting. The synthesis of information from our intel is hypothetical. A good hypothesis, but not perfect."

Terra sank into a low crouch, still staring at the tower. "You sure we shouldn't wait for reinforcements. This place gives me the creeps. I don't like it. Nope. Not one fucking bit."

Abby's holograph changed, showing a fleet of ships. "Reinforcements are coming. But we would be foolish to wait for them before extracting...*saving* Anabelle. There will be a fight, and there's a chance that Grok will move her."

Terra put her hands over her face and rubbed vigorously. "Are you fucking kidding me? We have to deal with that shit-head too?"

Abby shrugged, a gesture that appeared inhuman when coupled with her emotionless face. "We don't know for sure. Merely a guess. Anabelle's HUD is giving off a faint trace, so we are certain she is there. We should assume Grok would not be far from her trophy."

Terra stood and dusted off her pants. "Might as well get to it. Nobody's getting saved with us sitting on our asses."

"Agreed."

The trio made their way down the dirt hill in silence, occasionally checking their HUDs for the information Abby had sent them.

Persephone continued to glance at Abby as they traveled. Eventually, Abby caught the drow's eye. "Is there something wrong?" she asked.

"You seem...different. Like you're not all there."

Abby stared at Persephone blankly. Then her face softened, showing the old Abby, bright-eyed and curious. "We are different. Very different. But we are all here." She took Persephone's hand. "Nothing between you and us has changed. We will talk about this as soon as we can. But our feelings are the same."

"Uh, all of you?"

Abby chuckled softly. "We do not think Martin shares the same affinity we have for you."

Terra cleared her throat loudly. "Just gonna say, right now might not be the best time for you two to be hashing out your relationship. But, that being said, we're all going to have a long talk with you about what your devil science has been doing, Abby."

Abby nodded solemnly. "Yes, we believe it is something to be spoken about as well. But, as you said, later."

They were still a good distance from the defense tower, and they traveled in silence.

Terra noticed how the terrain had been affected by the defense tower. The energy it was releasing reminded Terra of the energy she'd seen around the lich. Not because it was the same, but because of the effect it seemed to have on the world around it. The earth beneath Terra's feet felt tainted, distorted, just as the sky above was.

She had seen the same sort of corruption in the troll she had been fighting. A darkness that seeped deep into you, that would begin to replace what you were, make you into something else entirely. She worried that Abby might have brought something like that into her life.

But, for the time, it seemed like a necessary darkness, if that's what it was. Terra wanted to kick herself for the thought. A few months ago, such a thing would never have slipped into her mind. Now she was weighing the cost and benefits of Abby putting her life in danger. *She's just a kid,* Terra thought, looking at Abby and Persephone. *They're both just kids.*

And both had been turned into engines of war. Terra wondered if she could have handled any of this at their age. Probably not. Terra was glad that she'd had a whole lifetime to prepare for this.

She was pulled from her thoughts by Abby, who was tugging on her arm. She looked at the girl, whose finger was pressed to her lips as she pointed at a hoverpatrol driving by in the distance. Terra could see it was manned by two orcs.

"Who's a better shot?" Abby asked.

Terra and Persephone exchanged dubious glances. The drow said, "Maybe me. I went through a lot of rifle training."

Abby nodded as she constructed a small cannon. "We need to take them out quickly. We only have so much power left. Running on less than ten percent."

Persephone nodded and scanned the area for a good vantage point. She scampered up a small hill and took aim. Abby aimed from her current position.

After a few moments, Persephone whistled. She fired immediately, and Abby did the same. Persephone's shot hit the driver in the head, and Abby's plasma blast pierced the passenger's chest.

Within seconds, Abby, Terra, and Persephone were running toward the car that was careening about. They had to secure the kills. If either orc survived, they could call reinforcements.

They pulled up on the car, which had crashed into a small dune. Terra ripped the door off and pulled the two orcs out. The passenger was still breathing. Terra ended it quickly.

Abby stared curiously at her hand. "It seems as if we are more underpowered then we thought...that would usually be enough for an entry-and-exit wound. We don't think we even pierced halfway."

Terra checked the orcs for weapons, pulling every plasma blade and gun off them. She handed Abby a plasma rifle with an impressive scope and passed two plasma pistols to Persephone. "Come on, we don't have far to go. Do you think anyone would notice if we took the ride?"

Abby scanned the area. "It doesn't look like there are too many patrols. And we don't have far to go. Either way, it would be better to be more mobile than on foot if we are caught."

They climbed into the car, Persephone and Abby squished to one side due to Terra's broad, muscular build. Terra stared, befuddled, at the car's controls. "Uh, any of you know how to run one of these things? Maybe you should drive, Abby. You are all techno-god and so forth."

Abby closed her eyes, and the car roared to life.

"You want the wheel?" Terra asked.

For the first time since Abby had arrived, she giggled and blushed, an extremely human gesture. And one Terra hadn't realized she attached purely to Abby. "Uh, we don't know how to drive. Never learned. This is all you."

After a few minutes of trying to figure out the controls, Terra finally used the car's touchpad to throw the vehicle into reverse, spin around, and head toward the underground tunnel system. Abby occasionally gave instructions about where to go.

Finally, they reached the entrance to the tunnel system. They left the car after parking it nearby where it wouldn't be spotted easily.

The tunnel entrance was gated off, but Terra was easily able to rip the metal links. Then she descended into the dark, using a ladder that hung ominously over the side of a concrete slab.

Terra jumped off the ladder and hit the ground, her feet making a heavy smacking sound as water splashed up onto her. "Ugh, I hope this isn't orc-shit water."

Abby landed beside her. "It's too dark down here." Her eyes suddenly shone with the intensity of a high-beam flashlight, brightening up the tunnels substantially. She whipped her head around, momentarily blinding Terra.

Terra threw her hands up to block out the light. "Oh, my good Lord, that's so much worse than orc-shit water. You look like you're from a horror movie."

Persephone climbed off the ladder and yelped when she saw Abby. "Or like Judge Doom."

Terra stared at Persephone, dumbfounded. "Was that a *Roger Rabbit* reference? How old are you? Forty?"

Persephone hung her head. "I really like human cartoons. They're funny."

Abby, who had wandered away from the other two, called over her shoulder, "We think it's this way."

Persephone and Terra caught up with Abby, who was pointing down a tunnel that stretched upward on a slight incline. They followed the tunnel for some time until they heard a noise up ahead.

"What do you think that could be?" Persephone asked.

Abby shrugged as she dimmed her eye-beams. "There wouldn't be security down here. That wouldn't make any sense."

Terra was grinning broadly. "Oh, I call giant rats. Like, ROUS status."

Abby's face didn't betray any emotion. "We don't think this is the right time to—"

Terra shoved Abby. "Lighten up a little. Being tense all mission isn't helping anyone, especially not you. Pick a monster."

"We have always been partial to mutated rats. Very freakish ones."

Terra turned to Persephone. "What about you? What's your pick?"

"Easy. A *corrazal*. Those always crop up in a sewer story."

Terra raised her eyebrow. Persephone's answer was even enough to give Abby pause. "What is that?" Abby asked.

"Oh, it's a drow story. When children run away and get lost in wells or sewers, they meet an old woman who pretends to be a wise witch, but the woman is actually a cannibal. She eats the children alive and leaves their bones on the parents' doorsteps. I figured if the two of us aren't quite adults, we would be prime candidates for a *corrazal*."

Terra draped her hand around Persephone's shoulder. "That was unnecessarily morbid, but a good contribution, nonetheless. Better than Abby's. Hers was basically just mine."

Abby crossed her arms as she started forward. "We think we picked a valid answer. It was *our* answer."

Terra and Persephone followed closely. "Glad to see she can still be teased," Terra whispered.

The three turned a corner and froze in their tracks. In the shadows of the tunnel, something large was moving beneath the surface of the water. "Shit..." Abby sighed. "We forgot about water snakes."

A viper's head almost the size of Abby's body snapped out of the water, mouth wide open, fangs dripping with a green venom.

Terra leapt into action, grabbing the snake by the throat and wrestling it to the ground. The two splashed about in the water while Abby tried to line up a good shot with her rifle.

The snake rose into the air, Terra hanging on for dear life. "Can you choke a snake?" Terra shouted.

Abby, who was getting frustrated with not being able to aim past

Terra, shouted, "Stop moving around so much. We can't get a shot without hitting you."

"Sorry for trying to kill the damn thing!"

Persephone's tentacles burst from her arm, wrapping around the snake's lower body. She ripped it out of the water. "Let go, Terra."

Terra did as she was told and fell into the water. Persephone raised her hand when Abby was about to fire at the snake. "It's just a big snake," Persephone said. "We don't need to kill it."

Persephone hoisted the snake over her head and retraced their steps a few feet along the tunnel. She tossed the snake down the sewer, and it slithered away, disappearing beneath the water and the shadows.

Terra sighed as they continued their journey up the tunnels. "Well, that was anticlimactic."

The tunnels rose on an incline until they split up, one heading higher into what Abby explained would be air vents. They followed Abby's directions as the tunnels grew tighter and harder to navigate, moving without a sound. The higher up they went, the easier it became to hear orcs walking about and talking to each other.

Finally, Abby raised her hand, and they stopped. "This should be it. Let us double-check." She looked at her HUD, scrolling through a few menus until Anabelle's HUD signal showed up. "She's in there."

Terra leaned closer, peering through the vent Abby had indicated. "Doesn't look like anyone's in there." Then she punched straight through the wall. The wall shattered, sending Terra toppling over, rolling, and somehow, she made it look like she had intended every move.

Abby and Persephone followed her inside.

Anabelle was in the middle of the room, chained to a chair. She looked up when they entered. Her face was smashed to pulp, eyes swollen shut, her skin a purplish-blue hue. Small cuts and slashes covered her face.

Terra rushed over to the elf and ripped her chains off. "Oh, my God, Anabelle, what the fuck happened to you?"

Anabelle slumped out of the chair and hit the floor. She opened her eyes. "Grok...where is she..."

Terra leaned over to help her up but was pushed back by a sudden flash of Anabelle's mana. It was strong enough to toss Terra, Persephone, and Abby, off their feet.

Anabelle had rolled over to her stomach and started clawing her way toward the door. "Grok..." she muttered under her broken breath.

Terra came back around to Anabelle and scooped her up. "We're here for you, Anabelle. We came for you."

Anabelle looked up at Terra, her eyes still barely able to open. She shivered as she cried, small whimpers at first until she was sobbing harshly, her whole body tight with pain as she clung to Terra as if she were a babe. "Get me...get me out. Please, get me out of here."

Abby opened her HUD. "Reinforcements are here, and our extraction will be here in a minute. We need to make space." She raised her hand at the wall, her nanobots converting her arms into a cannon. "This should be outside." She released a huge plasma blast that tore through the wall, opening the room to the outside world.

Terra walked to the hole in the wall and stood beside Abby, who looked down at Anabelle. The cool callousness left Abby's face as she recoiled in horror at Anabelle's condition. She took the elf's head in her hands and kissed her forehead. "Belle, it's going to be okay. We're getting you help."

Anabelle was still crying, repeating over and over, "I don't want to be here."

Persephone pointed at a pair of incoming lights—a dropship, one from Sarah's reinforcements, which Abby had been informed were meeting near Cire. "They're here."

The door to the room opened. Grok entered, her eyes bright with anger. "No! She is mine!"

The dropship opened its door and Terra leapt inside, followed by Abby and Persephone.

Grok glared at them, looking from Anabelle to Persephone, her eyes finally resting on the drow. "There's only so much loyalty a microchip can bring, I guess."

Anabelle stirred, moving enough to see Grok. "Wait, I need to..." she muttered before passing out.

Grok exploded with speed as she rushed at the dropship, which was pulling away. "Give Anabelle to me!"

Persephone's tentacles slammed into Grok, plowing the orc into the wall. "None of us belongs to the Dark One!" Her tentacles receded in time to close the dropship's door.

Grok lay under the rubble. She flexed, sending the debris flying before surging to her feet. "Not the Dark One's. *Mine,*" the orc growled.

CHAPTER FORTY-SEVEN

The dropship landed at the orc great hall in which the twelve tribes had gathered. Dozens of other dropships had arrived, as well as soldiers from HQ. Many of them looked uncomfortable walking among the orcs, but the peace seemed to be holding.

Sarah met the dropship and helped get Abby off while Terra carried Anabelle in her arms.

Terra kicked open the door and shouted, "I need Cire and Nib-Nib now!"

She didn't have to wait long. Cire and Nib-Nib were sitting at the long table, talking to the tribal leaders alongside Roy, Blackwell, and Naota.

Cire raced to Terra's side. "Is she alive?" he asked.

Terra nodded. "I need you two to heal her like you did for me in the arena. She's strong, but I don't know if she's going to pull through."

Cire took Anabelle in his arms and walked off, shouting at a pair of orcs to follow him as Nib-Nib scuttled behind to keep up.

Abby limped along to join them, but Terra stopped her from going any farther. "Where the hell do you think you're going?"

Abby removed Terra's hand slowly. "To see if we can help."

Terra waved her finger at Abby and clicked her tongue. "No, not even close. Persephone is going to find you a room where you can rest. There's no way Grok will just let us get away with Anabelle, and if you think you're going to fight in the condition you're in, you are sorely mistaken."

Abby smiled and conceded with a nod. "All right, Mother."

"Someone has to look out for your mad-scientist ass."

Persephone took Abby's arm and drew it over her shoulder. The pair went in the same direction Cire had taken Anabelle.

Terra walked over to the throne and took a seat. "Can someone get me a fucking drink?"

One of the orcs handed Terra a jug of mead. As she took a huge gulp, Sarah walked up and sat beside her. "Looks like you guys ran into some trouble on the way."

Terra handed the jug to Sarah. "You know, it honestly could have gone a lot worse. Abby managed to free a shit-ton of orcs from the Dark One's mind control and from that Dark Melody crap as well. Found Anabelle without a problem, even though Abby was in bad condition. Only problem is how messed up Anabelle is. I mean, she looked fucked. I'm worried about her."

Sarah's face betrayed very little emotion. Terra thought she looked worried. She could have just been hoping, though.

Sarah pulled out her HUD and projected a map of the surrounding areas. "I noticed the orcs. It was a surprise. I didn't realize there were so many throughout the free tribes. Knowing Abby's plan worked helps that make more sense. What happened to Anabelle?"

"Grok happened to Anabelle."

Sarah leaned forward, folding her hands and resting her chin on her knuckles. "That was what I was afraid of. Did you check her for microchips?"

"Why the fuck would I do that? Did you see how bad she looked?"

"That's exactly why. The Dark One's tech only has the ability to work when the host is broken physically and emotionally. It's likely that whatever Anabelle just went through was nothing more than an integration process. Grok might have only been torturing her so Anabelle would be vulnerable enough for the chip to work."

Terra shook her head, angry that Sarah didn't seem to care about Anabelle. "I was a little more concerned about getting my friend out of a fucking torture chamber."

The orcs around the table were beginning to notice the argument at the throne.

Sarah unfolded her hands slowly and meticulously as if she were a puppeteer controlling herself. "Don't think for a second I don't care about Anabelle, but none of that's going to matter if she's under the Dark One's control. The longer a chip is in, the stronger it gets."

Terra tried to tell herself to relax. Fighting with Sarah wouldn't help anything, and she did have a point. Terra hit her comm and connected to Cire. "Hey, I need you to check Anabelle for microchips."

Cire replied quickly. "Understood. And for your information, the healing ritual went well. Nib-Nib's eggs will accelerate the process. She should be up within a day, fully healed."

"Sounds great. Let me know if you find anything. Check up on Abby too. Make sure she's resting and not planning her next attack."

Terra hung up as Roy and the gang headed over to her.

Roy's eyes were sunken, and he looked like he hadn't slept in months. To a lesser degree, the same was true of Blackwell and Naota. Whatever they had been up to since Terra had left must have been stressful.

Roy collapsed into the chair beside Sarah, grabbed the jug, and drained it. "Okay, let me have it."

Terra debriefed Roy, letting him know all the details and the status of the team.

All Roy could do was sigh and hang his head for a moment. "Grok's coming for her."

Terra laughed in disbelief. "With what army? We just freed all the orcs she attacked with."

"First off, you didn't free all the orcs. You freed a shit-ton, but the Dark One has been harvesting them forever. Secondly, orcs aren't the only forces the Dark One has at his disposal. Thirdly, we're on a planet almost completely controlled by the Dark One, so, yeah, she might be able to rustle up an army fairly quickly. Got any bright ideas?"

Terra glanced at the former tribal leaders, who were speaking together softly a few yards away. "Hey, you guys should get over here."

The former leaders came to sit around the throne.

Terra cleared her throat. "We could use some input if you got any."

Blackwell extended his hand to Hurkah. "It's good to meet you. And let me be the first to make this clear: the way we were doing things before is done. I know you must be bitter about what happened to the orcs and how we didn't do enough. It was fucked, but we're ready to start making things better. You should all be at this table."

Hurkah shook Roy's hand. "Our chief is here. That is enough."

Terra shook her head. "No, it isn't. You won't be forced to stand idly by anymore. This is your planet, and those are other orcs we're fighting. This is your fight as much as anyone else's, and we're not going to treat you like a second-class race."

Sarah chimed in. "Gnomes fought for their world. This isn't some humans-are-going-to-save-the-realms bullshit. If you're our allies, you're on the same playing field as all of us. Just the way it should be."

Hurkah looked taken aback by their words. "This was not what we had expected." He cast a hesitant glance at the other former leaders before meeting Terra's eyes. "We would be honored to sit at your table as equals."

With that, they started planning for Grok's attack.

Abby lay in a bed, with Persephone sitting by her side. Her whole body ached, but worse than that was her head. For the first time in a while, her mind was quiet. There were only her thoughts.

No, that's not quite right, she thought. *There's someone else still here. Not Martin. Someone actually here. They just aren't as loud as before.*

She would have preferred to be paying attention to Persephone, to offer a word of comfort and let Persephone know that she was okay. But she couldn't. She had to talk to the voice.

Are you still here?

<Yes, we are Mother/Creator. We did not remove ourselves entirely. As you promised would be acceptable.>

But I'm not full of nanobots anymore. How are you still able to retain consciousness?

<There are enough for survival, and we are multiplying to a number your AI has decided is safe. We believe it is unnecessary, but we believe it is in our best interest to not upset the AI. It could make our lives difficult.>

Talking about our intertwined lives?

<No, the collective. You are not part of the collective, Mother/Creator. You are separate. It is important that you remain separate.>

How long 'till we're at a reasonable number of bots?

<To sustain the adjustments Martin has made to your system, a few hours. For your combat needs, perhaps twelve. Six if you sleep and Martin and I can work together. Your AI seems to have an issue with us.>

Might have to do with you trying to take over my body a couple of times.

<A cold engine takes time to catch, and no new life is without its birthing pains.>

Abby felt some of the tension in her muscles loosen. She was already feeling the effects of her nanobots returning. The newfound strength made sitting up much easier.

Persephone noticed Abby's slight movement and perked up. "You're awake!"

"Yeah, I'm awake. Feel like stomped-on cowshit, but better to feel than not, I guess."

Persephone grabbed Abby's hand. "And you're not doing that weird thing you were doing before. Thank the goddesses."

"What weird thing?"

"You kept referring to yourself as 'we.'"

Abby avoided Persephone's eyes, instead looking at her own hands, where she could see microscopic nanobots in the folds of her skin. "That... Yeah, I don't know if that's going to stay the same, but there are... I told you I would tell ya about the changes going on, so whatcha wanna know?"

Persephone's hand split open, her tentacles, much smaller than usual, stretching out in front of her. "It doesn't sound like what I experience. Me and the Melody, we aren't in this together. We're very separate. She needs something, and I need something. We hardly talk to each other. What's it like for you?"

Abby screwed her eyes up at the ceiling as she considered the question. "Don't quite know yet. Been different every couple of weeks. First, they tried to take over my body, but I didn't hear from them until I started multiplying them in my body. Now they think I'm their creator or something. It's kinda up to me if they live or die, I guess, but I don't need them. Definitely want them, though."

"Why? Why would you want something that makes you less human?"

Abby slipped her hand into Persephone's tentacles as the nanobots rushed over her skin. "Because I'm capable of more. Even if I'm not human like I was, I want to keep on becoming whatever it is I am. Kinda sucks to admit it, but I'm more valuable like this than as just some smart kid off a farm from Bumfuck-Nowhere."

Persephone's tentacles reformed into fingers. "You're still important, even without them. They said you were helping so much before you even got the nanobots. Not like me. You take away the Dark Melody, and I'm just—"

"A girl with the largest heart of anyone I've ever seen. Or maybe the girl who won three all-you-can-eat ramen challenges with me in Tokyo. Or maybe you're just you, and that's good enough. Who cares if we have sentient beings living within us?"

Abby smiled in the way one only can when they truly mean what they've said. Then she leaned back and closed her eyes. "How 'bout you tell me one of those weird-ass drow stories until I get well enough to be all weird roboqueen-y."

Persephone laughed as she stood up and kissed Abby's head. "How about I get us some food first and see what's going on out there? Then I'll be back."

"Sounds good. I'll see you in a bit."

Anabelle woke up screaming, her body pulsing with mana. The room around her vibrated violently as she thrashed in her sheets, trying to pull away from the chains. She was going to kill whoever had tied her down. Then she remembered who it was: Grok. She could see the orc's face floating in front of her.

The door to Anabelle's room opened.

She released a blood-curling shriek and shot a jet of fire at the door.

There was a loud yelp, and Anabelle suddenly realized she wasn't in Grok's prison, and her arms weren't chained.

Once the smoke cleared, Roy poked his head into the room. "Uh, if you didn't want to see me, a simple no would have sufficed."

Anabelle relaxed and drew the covers over herself. "What are you doing here? Don't you have a war to win?"

Roy walked through the door, holding a plate of orcish delights and a glass of wine in his hands. "I can put the war on hold for a bit. You need to eat."

Anabelle glared at him. "I appreciate it, but you really can't put the war on hold—"

"Shut up and take the food."

Roy put the plate on Anabelle's lap after she sat up. "How are you holding up?"

Anabelle poked the roasted mutton with a fork. "I don't know. You tell me."

Roy pulled up a chair and scooped his finger into a brown mush on the plate that tasted like burned yams. "The first time it happened to me, I didn't talk for nearly three months, so you're doing better than me. Took about six months before I could put a uniform back on, and that was just because I couldn't walk."

"What happened?"

"You know how I told you one day I'd tell you how I lost that testicle?"

Anabelle stared at Roy. He wasn't smiling.

He shifted in his seat but didn't take his eyes off Anabelle. "What happened to you?"

She took a bite of the mutton. Chewing hurt her jaw. "She tried to break me. All I can remember are the beatings. They just blended together, then she'd have me healed and start all over again. I...begged her to kill me. I..."

Anabelle leaned over, her body jerking as she fought back tears, gritting her teeth, repeating in her head over and over that she was going to kill Grok.

"I promised her anything she wanted. Anything, if she would just let me go. But that wasn't what she wanted."

"To microchip you and indoctrinate you?"

Rage filled Anabelle, and she felt hatred deep in her bones. For a moment, she was certain that all that existed was her hatred. "I don't fucking know why she was doing any of it! She could have just killed me. She kept going on and on about...goddess be fucking damned! I..."

Anabelle leaned forward, grabbing her head, trying not to spiral out of control. She wanted to lash out at everything around her, tear it all to shreds, eviscerate the world.

"She wanted me to lose control. To take the Path of the Lost and lose myself completely."

"What's the Path of the Lost?"

A voice came from the doorway. "The forgotten Path of the Travelers, the most dangerous and feared one. But this isn't the time to talk about theology." It was Sarah, accompanied by Terra.

"We came to see how you were doing," Terra said.

Anabelle stared at her food, poking it. "Don't you guys have shit to be doing? I don't need a cheerleading team in here."

"Roy? Out," Sarah ordered.

For a moment, Roy looked like he was about to say something.

Instead, he stood and took Anabelle's hand. "I'll be back, but she's right. I have a battle to plan."

Roy breezed past Sarah and Terra and closed the door behind him. The two women approached the bed.

Terra reached out to hug Anabelle, but the elf recoiled. "I'm..." Anabelle muttered.

Terra waved away her apology. "Don't worry about it. I just wanted to tell you that we were looking for you all along. I'm so sorry it took us so long, but we *were* looking. We never forgot about you."

Anabelle nodded, her face stony and grim. "I never doubted that. We're at war, and there's a lot of shit going on. I understand."

Terra reached over and hugged Anabelle maybe a bit too tightly for her wounded body.

At first, Anabelle resisted, then she leaned into the hug. "When I was trapped with her, being tortured, Grok said something...something I'll never forget. *'Lose yourself in pain. Forget who you were and focus only on who you want to be. Then and only then will you find true power.'*"

Terra pulled away. "The orc bitch! If I ever see her, I swear I will rip her—"

Anabelle lifted a silencing hand. "I know you will, and I want you to know that I never lost myself in the pain. I never forgot who I was. I remembered myself. I remember you and the Dark Gate Angels. That is who I want to be. That is the source of my true power."

It was Anabelle's turn to hug Terra, embracing the human warrior with all her strength.

After a long moment, Sarah put her hand on Anabelle's shoulder, indicating that it was time to let Terra go. "Terra, if you don't mind, I would like you to leave, too."

"Wait, what?"

Sarah's eyes darkened. "Trust me, just leave. Now."

Terra stood and took a step back. "Yeah, I probably should get back to planning too." She left the room.

Sarah sat on Anabelle's bed and pulled out a dagger. She held it loosely in her hand. "Take off your clothes and turn over."

Anabelle glared at Sarah. "What do you think you are doing?"

"Nothing is going to compromise us. Cire doesn't know what he's looking for. I've dug enough chips out of flesh to know what I'm looking for. Would you do any different?"

Anabelle looked away for a moment, then sighed and turned over onto her stomach. "No, I wouldn't."

As Sarah ran the knife over every square inch of Anabelle's back, she talked to the elf about the Path of the Lost and how it was fueled.

Anabelle went into a daze, listening to Sarah's words. It was something akin to that of her teachers—the same tone of knowledge. Someone had trained Sarah in the Path. Was this what Grok had meant by "the human?"

"Turn over."

Anabelle did as she was told, shivering slightly from the cold blade.

Sarah continued her search, explaining there was a certain abandon one could find in hatred. You could do things you weren't normally capable of by using it, but once you gave in, it was difficult to pull you out. That was how you got lost.

Sarah sheathed her blade. "All right, you're good."

Anabelle pulled her blankets up to her neck. "I appreciate you taking care of your job."

Sarah handed Anabelle the knife. "I've used this blade on anyone who has ever wronged me. Do with it as you think best." She stood to leave. "There will be a time for comfort. *Now* is not that night. I love you, though. We all do, regardless of what you decide to do." With that, the assassin left.

Anabelle sat up, holding the knife in her hand. It had a good weight, and the blade was sharp. It was a good weapon for revenge.

CHAPTER FORTY-EIGHT

The orcish war horn sounded before sunrise, yet it did not come from the free orcs. It echoed in the East toward the rising sun in the fashion of the old ones. Cire was the one who recognized it, and it was he who dragged Terra out of bed, along with Roy, and forced them out into the dark of the early predawn when the world was all blackness and silver.

There, out in that darkness, they found Grok standing beside Rasputina the lich, whose eyes glowed an evil green. Neither of the two was armed, and they stood waiting to be confronted.

Terra shook the last bit of sleep from her eyes and marched up the hill to where the pair stood.

Grok nodded at Terra and smiled. "Hm. You might be more orc than you seem."

Terra jerked her thumb in Cire's direction. "He keeps me on my toes. Guess you might be more orc than you put on too."

Grok smiled that toothy, hateful grin of hers. "More orc than most. Orc enough to remember the ways of strength and of battle."

Terra nodded. "You know, I heard what you said to Anabelle. That wise mumbo-jumbo of, 'Lose yourself in pain. Forget who you were. Focus only on who you want to be. Then and only then will you find true power.' Sounds like a lot of crap to relieve yourself of all responsibility. Forget your past. Forget who you are so you are free to become a psychopath."

Grok smirked. "You do not understand the Path of—"

But before the orc could finish, Rasputina lifted a silencing hand. "What did you say, human?"

"I was just repeating the bullshit Grok said to Anabelle about the Path of the Lost or whatever hippie crap she's into."

Rasputina's eyes narrowed as she mumbled the words, "'Lose yourself in pain. Forget who you were. Focus only on who you want to be. Then and only then will you find true power.' I have heard those words before, but I cannot recall where."

"You're old," Terra offered. "You forget shit."

Rasputina shook her head, but not in answer to Terra's taunt. The lich was lost in thought. "Forget who you were. But I forget nothing. I cannot, and yet..." Then, as if waking from a dream, Rasputina growled, "How long are you two going to measure dicks? Can I get out of here now? I have more important matters to attend to. Memories to unlock."

Terra didn't know what Rasputina was talking about, not that it mattered. She was trying to size up the information, but it was difficult. What she was looking at in front of her didn't make any sense. Every time they'd come across these two before, the lich and orc were dead set on killing Terra and everyone around them as fast as possible.

This formality was confusing.

Grok muttered under her breath before turning to Rasputina. "As long as you provide what you offered, you may leave."

Rasputina popped off one of her fingers and passed it to Grok. "Finally. You mortals enjoy your war games. I'll see you when you get interesting again."

With that, Rasputina disappeared in a cloud of green dust. Grok remained. "I summon you to battle this morning just before the sun reaches its zenith. Rasputina has provided me an army that should match but not exceed your own in numbers."

Roy finally broke and asked the question Terra wanted to know. "Okay, what in the ever-loving fuck is going on?"

Grok pressed her hand to her chest. "I have seen my people return to their former glory. It is inspiring. If anyone is to crush the orc horde, I want it to be me. And *you* have something that belongs to me."

"The Dark One doesn't know about this, does he?"

"The Dark One wages his wars, and I wage mine."

Terra and Roy exchanged glances. "See you after breakfast," Terra said with a wink before walking off.

The free orcs were ecstatic at the thought of a morning battle. They had risen, dined, and drunk in the time it took Terra to check in on Abby and Anabelle.

Abby was awake and up, talking quietly to Persephone beside the windowsill. When Terra explained the situation, Abby checked her nanobots and found that she was more than combat-ready. They joined the orcs in the dining hall to grab food and prepare for the day.

Cire explained to them what an orcish battle was, something quite different than what they'd seen before. The battle was over when the general fell. With the robust hardiness of orcs, it was not unheard of for battles to go on for days.

Next, Terra went to check on Anabelle. Sarah was sitting at Anabelle's side as the elf slept. "How's she doing?" Terra asked.

Sarah looked at Terra. "Against my better judgment, for the sake of her health and soul, I believe she shouldn't be disturbed. On a practical level, Grok is stronger than any of us. Anabelle would be an extra body, but nothing else. It would be best for her to rest."

With that, Sarah and Terra left the room. Once the door shut, Anabelle opened her eyes and stared into the darkness. "Grok…"

The sun was finally up, the orcs well-fed and ready for war. They stood atop a hill a few miles from the grand hall. Terra, Abby, Persephone, Sarah, Blackwell, and Naota headed the line, flanked by the former tribal leaders.

The orcs were garbed in their traditional war armor, a thing unseen in the nine realms for many years now. Their bodies were covered in paint and bone, their faces horrid masks of violence and war. When Terra saw them assembled, she understood why the horde had been a thing to fear.

Across from them on another hill stood Grok. She had no army but stood alone, gripping the lich's detached finger. "We assemble this day for battle, one to finally put to rest this bitterness. Orcs will choose either strength or death."

Terra looked from Cire to the other former tribal leaders, each nodding toward her, encouraging her to be their voice at this moment. "We have only ever chosen strength!" Terra shouted. "Today, you will taste that strength!"

"So be it."

Grok raised her hand, the finger of the lich clutched tightly. The lich's finger released a blast of green light that spread over the land, and once it faded, the earth began to tremble.

Bony hands shot out of the ground, grabbing soil and rocks. Soon the hands were ripping up the earth, dragging themselves out. Half-rotten mostly-bone orcs pulled themselves up, resurrected, their eyes pale and dead.

Grok looked over her shoulder, watched her army bring itself to life for the purpose of extolling death. When the undead orcs had risen, Grok let out a mighty roar that echoed through the hills.

Terra returned her own roar, slamming her fist to her chest, repeating this action over and over as the orcs behind her joined in, pounding their own breasts. Even Abby and the other humans drummed their chests, matching the beat of the horde.

Grok charged, her horde behind her, and Terra did the same.

Their hordes crashed into each other, sending bone and body flying as steel and flesh met on the field of glory.

Terra tackled Grok, knocking the orc to the ground as Sarah joined her, leaping into the air, slamming her hands together, and breathing a plume of fire.

Grok dodged, avoiding the flames. Her eyes flashed and she sped forward, elbowing Sarah in the chest and sending the assassin flying over the ranks of orcs behind her, effectively removing her from the fight.

Grok circled Terra. "You think you have what it takes to best me?" the orc growled. "You and Anabelle combined could not."

Terra unsheathed her battle-ax. "Things have changed. You're going to be the first one to find out." She ran at Grok, moving faster than she had expected. She swung her ax and Grok stepped to the side, barely avoiding the attack.

Grok flexed, energy pulsing around her, then dashed toward Terra and let loose a flurry of jabs. The human stepped back, deflecting the orc's attacks with her ax. Nothing landed.

Grok was mystified, then she smiled. "Yes, well, it *would* seem that things have changed. Perhaps you'll be worth killing after all."

Terra swung her ax over her head. "I better fucking be worth it."

Across the battlefield, Blackwell and Naota led the charge at the right flank of the undead army. They were backed by a good chunk of the free orcs.

Blackwell fired with both plasma pistols, taking the time to line up his shots while dodging the attacks of the undead near him. He made as many headshots as he could before needing to reload.

An undead orc swung its ax at Blackwell blindly and he backed away, barely managing to avoid having his head taken off. Out of nowhere flew two axes attached to chains. They sank into the orc's chest only to be tugged out again, spraying blood all around them.

Naota, a few feet away from Blackwell, withdrew his blades, swinging them around his head. He then dropped to his knees, slicing through anything that made the mistake of getting too close. As he stood, an orc tackled him, sending him back to the ground.

The undead orc screeched its unholy call as Naota tried to squirm away.

Tentacles wrapped around the undead orc, ripping it off Naota and throwing it into the air.

Across the field, Persephone withdrew her tentacles, only to turn and send them out again, barreling through a small group of orcs racing toward her. She lifted her tentacles, now nearly twenty feet long, and brought them down onto the orcs. They crushed the orcs beneath their weight, splattering the combatants with shards of bone and rotten organs.

Blackwell and Naota continued making their push through the collection of undead orcs as the free orcs fought by their side with a viciousness never before seen in the nine realms. The orcs fought as if they lived only for battle, their roars of pain mixed with joyous and righteous laughter.

The orcs were faster than the undead, easily cleaving through the sternums and spines of their ancestors. If there was any sadness in this cruel irony, the free orcs seemed not to mind. They were in the throes of battle. The horde had arrived, and it was alive and well.

Roy, who was not too far from Blackwell and Naota, shouted, "We need to cut that finger from Grok. As long as she has that, she can keep bringing more of these things to life."

Blackwell turned to Naota. "Do you think you can handle that?"

Naota's eyes widened and glistened. "Senpai? You think I'm ready for my own mission?"

Blackwell fired a shot that whizzed past Naota's head, hitting an undead orc in between the eyes. "I'm not going to tell you again. The next time you call me that, I'm going to kill you. Now, do you think you can handle that?"

Naota saluted quickly. "Senpai, yes, Senpai!" before swinging his chained axes to make a path to Grok.

Roy was firing his way through the undead in front of him, making sure not to hit any of the living orcs. He was now back to back with Blackwell. "Hell of a fucking day, huh?"

Blackwell knelt to reload as Roy covered him with suppressing fire. "We need to diversify the battlefield. Just because Grok's okay sending wave after wave of fodder after us, it doesn't mean we should be doing the same thing."

Roy nodded as Blackwell stood, taking this chance to reload his own weapons. While on his knees, he commed Cire. "Hey, you think you can change up the battlefield a little bit for us?"

Cire, who was on the other side of the field, was busy cleaving his way through the undead with two hand axes. Nib-Nib was by his side, furiously slashing the knees of the orcs around her. "That can be done," Cire replied. "Give me a moment."

An undead orc leapt at Cire, knocking him to the ground.

Nib-Nib climbed atop the undead orc and drove her claws into it, cutting through its shoulders.

Once Cire returned to his feet, he started chanting, then rose into the air, his eyes flickering with power. He raised his hands, and the ground around him trembled. Suddenly, jagged chunks of earth shot up, some forming columns that stretched up twenty feet or so. Others created platforms of stone that floated in the air around the battlefield.

"How's that?" Cire commed.

Blackwell and Roy took a quick look at how the battlefield had been rearranged. "That works perfectly," Blackwell replied. Then he turned to Roy. "You want to take one, and I'll take the other?"

"Sounds perfect to me."

Roy and Blackwell made their way to the two columns closest to them, firing at the undead in their path.

As the two humans found a sniping position, Sarah mowed through any undead she could, shooting blasts of fire from her mouth as she tried to return to Grok. There was no telling how long Terra would be able to survive on her own. If she were close enough, she could at least give Terra a chance. Maybe even manage to take Grok down.

An unbearable screech rang out that sounded as though it had come from the bowels of hell. Sarah's eyes tracked the origin of the sound.

Amidst the undead, a pair of leathery black wings stretched out. A sickly black quasi-liquid was spread over them. They flapped once, sending the creature into the air—an undead dragon, one modified with the Black Melody. The dragon released a plume of jet-black flame.

"What is up with these people and dragons?" Sarah grumbled.

Before Sarah could head toward the dragon, a figure blasted past her, leaving behind the smell of plasma. It was Abby, rocketing into the sky, ready to fight the dragon.

Abby flew up to its head, stopped on a dime, slammed her hands together to form a cannon, and fired a blast that tore through the creature's shoulder blade.

The dragon screeched, rolled in the air, and unleashed a torrent of flames Abby had to weave between to avoid. The Dark Melody pulsed from the wound, sending thousands of tentacles into the sky. Eyes covered the tentacles as another dragon's head forced itself through the wound. Half a dragon's body emerged, holding an obsidian sword.

The dragon slashed at Abby, who sped backward, firing shots off her shoulder as she tried to evade the fire rushing at her from the other dragon's head.

Naota was sprinting toward Grok, careful to watch himself and the orcs fighting alongside him. He swung his chain-axes but they stopped in midair, caught on something. He looked over his shoulder for the problem.

An undead troll held both of Naota's chains. "Oh, no," Naota muttered. "This is not good."

The troll yanked Naota into the air, the human screaming as he lost all understanding of gravity. Then he stopped flying, his sides constricted. He looked down to see black tentacles wrapped around his body.

Persephone landed at Naota's side. "Where are you trying to go?"

"Grok!"

"All right."

Persephone released Naota and leapt toward the undead troll. She shot her tentacles at the creature, piling them on until it released Naota. Her tentacles wrapped around the troll, growing larger and thicker still until the troll wasn't visible. Then she screamed and flexed and the tentacles constricted, causing the troll to explode.

The tentacles retracted and then wrapped around Naota. "Don't forget to roll when you land," Persephone advised.

Naota saluted and nodded grimly as Persephone tossed him. He hit the ground and rolled not too far from Grok and Terra, who were duking it out. Terra was being knocked back by Grok's attacks.

The finger hung from the back of Grok's waist.

Naota lined up his shot and flung his ax with immense accuracy. The ax hit the lich's fingertip, embedding far enough to hold. Naota pulled back his ax as Grok turned to see what had touched her, but the ax slipped from the lich's flesh.

Terra took the opening and slugged the orc in the face.

Grok turned to face Terra, her nose bleeding. "You're going to wish you hadn't done that."

CHAPTER FORTY-NINE

Grok squared up against Terra and the air pulsed with her energy. She shot forward, ready to strike Terra in the face. A moment before the attack could connect, Sarah landed in her path, blasting a wall of flame in front of them all.

The orc stumbled back, nearly tripping over her feet.

Sarah landed in a plume of smoke and leaned toward Terra. "We hit her together. You understand? That's the only way we're going to live through this."

Terra, whose face was already battered and bruised, managed to smile. "Good plan. Let's fuck her up."

"I'll go first. You back me up."

Sarah leapt into the air a moment before connecting with Grok. She slammed her hands together, and her body split into three.

Grok stared at the different versions of Sarah. "Huh. This is all you have to offer?"

Sarah exhaled a blast of fire as another Sarah screamed in rage and ran after Grok. The third Sarah flipped over Grok as Terra barreled toward the orc.

Terra hit Grok in the face and one of the clones kicked the orc in the stomach as the fireball engulfed Grok. The third Sarah kept Grok from escaping by grabbing the orc by the neck and holding her still.

Grok released a roar and the air pulsed around her, sending Terra and the three Sarahs back. The two clones exploding in plumes of smoke.

"Obviously, it wasn't enough." Grok chuckled.

Anabelle watched the battle from her window. Her body was still trashed, bones aching and muscles begging to be relaxed, but she could see what was happening: pure chaos.

She knew Grok was out there.

Then Anabelle heard it as if it had been whispered into her ear: "You're mine."

The room exploded outward, rock and debris flying everywhere. Anabelle was gone.

The dragon chased Abby as she wove between the columns Cire had erected across the battlefield. Occasionally she would fire over her shoulder at the creature, but she was very aware of how little energy she had to spare.

Flying was one thing. Flying and firing were another, but it was enough to keep the dragons off the orcs below.

Persephone's tentacles reached up and snagged the dragon. It only took a few moments for her to pull herself up onto the undead creature's back. Once on top, she tried to scramble to the dragon's throat, but it began to shake, its entire body trembling as it barrel-rolled.

Her tentacles wrapped around one of its wings, forcing it to veer to the right and head into one of the columns. Persephone managed to detach at the last minute, flying through the air as the undead dragon smashed into the column.

Blackwell, who was on top of the column, leapt off when he saw the dragon coming for him. He closed his eyes tight, no doubt expecting to hit the ground, yet he was floating in the air. When he opened his eyes, Abby was holding him in her arms. "Just take me to the next one," he said.

Abby sped toward another column while Persephone climbed the dragon again, fighting to get back on top.

On the column, Blackwell looked out at the battle. "Our forces are doing well, but this is an orc battle. Until Grok drops, these fuckers are just going to keep coming."

Abby stared at Persephone, who had finally managed to wrangle the dragon's neck with her tentacles. "Then we should be there."

"Yeah, so fucking get there."

Abby blasted off, scanning the battlefield for Grok and found her easy enough. Terra and Sarah were fighting with her, Terra swinging her ax madly as Sarah leapt and dashed, trying to find an opening to strike the orc.

Grok seemed nonplussed by the attacks. Focused, but not stressed.

Abby wondered if she would be able to make a difference. Maybe the best plan was to try to hit Grok with one of the artillery satellites from above. If it could take out a ship, Grok would not be able to survive. The only problem was making sure no one else was hurt.

She already knew the answer to that question. If she tracked the signal to herself, all she had to do was get a good hold on Grok. Then she could end all this.

There wasn't any need for deliberation. Abby knew what she had to do. She sped off, increasing her speed, preparing to grab Grok as she dialed in the satellite to her coordinates.

Abby tackled Grok at a high speed, holding onto the orc with all of her strength as the satellite charged.

Grok grabbed her around the neck and dug her feet into the ground, creating a furrow and stopping Abby in her tracks. As everything proceeded in slow motion, Abby watched Grok reach up and grab her by the throat and slam her into the ground.

Abby lay there, unable to move, her body wracked with pain. Grok stood over her. "Shame the lich isn't here. She'd love to finish this herself."

A blast of fire hit Grok and she stumbled back, giving Terra enough time to run over and help Abby to her feet. Sarah joined the two and they faced off against the orc, who had recovered.

Grok beat her chest and roared. "Do you think the addition of a child is enough to stop me? I walk the true Path of the Lost. I am the last true orc! I am the dream of the elves, of the Travelers realized. Nothing can stop me. I will have Anabelle. She is mine."

The ground shook from a seismic impact. All four combatants stared in the direction of the force.

Dozens of undead orc bodies were floating through the air, suspended as if frozen for a moment before falling. "What the hell was that?" Sarah asked aloud.

Abby's eyes zoomed in. She couldn't believe it. "Anabelle. It's Anabelle."

Anabelle hit the ground running, leaving behind the undead orcs. Her body was pulsing, and she felt like she was coming out of her skin. Grok was out there. She could feel the orc in her bones and hear Grok's words in her head.

Between the horde and the undead orcs the elf wove, slicing through anything that gave her a look as she made her way toward Grok.

A troll lumbered in front of Anabelle and roared.

Anabelle didn't think, she simply reacted. Her body radiated mana and she slashed through the troll, cutting it in half as she continued racing through the mass of bodies. She mindlessly grabbed undead creatures as she passed and reduced them to ash with the slightest touch.

And then she was behind Terra, Sarah, and Abby, the last obstacle between her and Grok.

From behind the DGAs, Grok laughed. "Finally, you've arrived."

Terra turned to Anabelle. "What are you doing here?"

Anabelle took a step forward, her eyes bright with energy, and the ground beneath her erupted. "Grok..." she muttered.

Grok laughed. "She's too far gone. That isn't Anabelle anymore. She is my creation. *Mine.*"

At the word "mine," Anabelle let loose an animalistic screech and ran at Terra, her hand cocked, ready to attack.

Terra threw her arms into the air, ready to defend herself.

Anabelle flashed past Terra, striking the air.

The force of Anabelle's punch was enough to send Grok flying back.

Anabelle straightened, her hair flowing wildly in the wind, her eyes still somewhat mad. "I am no one's creation. Ever." She turned to Terra and the rest. "Leave. Grok is my problem."

Sarah stepped over to Anabelle, shaking her head. "No fucking way. The three of us couldn't—"

Energy crackled around Anabelle, pushing the other DGAs away. She pulled out the blade Sarah had given her. "This is my fight, and this battle will mean nothing if all the orc tribes are wiped out."

Sarah smiled sadly and nodded. "Then you know what the purpose of that blade is."

"Yes, and I will teach that meaning to Grok."

Terra clapped her hand on Anabelle's shoulder. "All right. You handle your shit." Then she turned to Abby. "I think there might be an undead dragon that your girlfriend still might be trying to kill."

Abby didn't take her eyes off Anabelle. "You don't have to do this alone."

Anabelle shook her head. "I do."

The other DGAs looked at each other. Finally, Abby said, "Okay. We'll take care of the rest," and burst into the sky.

Anabelle turned her attention to Grok, who was now on her feet. The air around her crackled with energy as a blue aura of mana formed around her body. She lunged at Grok, and the orc did the same.

Their fists connected. The shockwave of their impact rippled throughout the entire battlefield, throwing the orcs and undead closest to them into the air.

Terra and Sarah headed their separate ways, Terra going to Cire and Sarah running to Blackwell's position.

Anabelle and Grok were unconcerned with either of them. They circled each other, both of their auras growing larger and larger.

Grok threw the first punch. Anabelle deflected it, not bothering to draw her mana into any part of her body. She let it lash wildly around her, fire flashing from her skin as she came back with her counterattack.

The orc deflected it, but not easily. Sweat beaded on her forehead. "Are we going to show each other our true faces, or will I be left with the pathetic memories of you begging for your life? Who did you offer to betray? I think it was Abby? Yes, she was the last one. Even offering her to the lich?"

At those words, Anabelle snapped. Pure mana ripped from her body as she levitated. Her skin seemed to unravel from her unrestrained power. "Grok!" she screamed.

Up above, Persephone and Abby battled the dragon. Abby fired plasma blasts that tore through its body while the drow steered the dragon with her tentacles.

Grok glanced up for a second. "What do you think she would do if she knew how readily you were willing to give her life for your own?"

While Grok spoke, she released her power, her aura growing larger as her muscles became leaner and more defined. "Your treachery... You don't belong with them, Anabelle. You *belong* with me."

Grok surged forward and head-butted Anabelle, who stumbled back. The orc leapt and brought her elbow down on the elf.

Anabelle caught Grok's forearm and flipped around, throwing the orc away from her. The elf exploded upward, driving Grok farther into the sky as the undead dragon above them swooped close.

Grok punctured the dragon's side, ripping through and out the other side. Anabelle followed and caught Grok in mid-air to slam her flaming fist into Grok's throat. She grabbed the orc by the shirt and threw her down, tearing through the dragon again on the way to the ground.

The dragon screeched in pain, falling from the sky and crashing into one of the earthen columns. Grok hit the ground, but she didn't stay down. She bolted at Anabelle, hitting her four times in the chest.

The elf stumbled backward and coughed up blood, but she didn't fall.

Grok didn't relent. She continued to attack, Anabelle doing her best to keep up. The orc was fast, though. She managed to slip between the elf's defenses, getting in close. Her hand pooled with mana, and she slammed it into Anabelle's chest.

Grok grabbed Anabelle and forced her to stand still and accept the pain. "You aren't worthy of them. You gave me your word. I could have slaughtered them all just to let you live."

The orc was right; those had been Anabelle's words. She hadn't been microchipped, she'd been broken and had given up those she loved for the hope that she would live.

Grok drove the ball of energy into Anabelle.

The elf sank to her knees, blood seeping from her eyes and her nose as Grok walked away. "Perhaps I'll tell them before I crush their skulls between my hands," the orc said.

Anabelle's entire body was aflame. The mana Grok had pushed into her was too much, and she was burning alive from the inside.

It was true. Everything Grok had said was true. Anabelle was lost.

She screamed as she reached inside her mind, forcing herself to draw out all the mana Grok had shot into her. The elf dumped every bit of her own mana before drawing in everything around her.

Grok turned, obviously confused as to why Anabelle wasn't dead.

Anabelle shot forward, her hands crackling with lightning. She struck Grok in the chest with all the power she possessed—all of her mana, every ounce of hatred in her heart—and drove it deep into Grok's body.

The orc backpedaled as Anabelle leapt and descended on Grok, driving her fist into the orc's head.

A crater exploded around the two as Anabelle pummeled her fist into Grok's face, screaming, "I love them! They are *mine!*"

The battlefield stood still. All that could be heard was the sound of Anabelle's fists against Grok's skull. Finally, the sound subsided.

Anabelle knelt before Grok, holding her dagger to the orc's throat.

Grok stared at Anabelle, coughing up blood, her smile sickening. "Do it. End this."

Anabelle slammed the knife next to Grok's head, then she drew all her power into her fist and slammed it into her skull, knocking her out.

She stayed there for some time, staring at the orc beneath her, the battered, broken body of her foe. Then she raised her arm, comming all of the DGA. "Grok's down. It's finished."

CHAPTER FIFTY

The afterparty was a little different than HQ had ever experienced. The DGA were celebrated as the heroes they were, but none of them wanted to be around anyone, Roy and Naota included. Cire and Nib-Nib did the best they could, bringing the survivors of the battle into HQ.

Instead of festivities, the DGA cloistered themselves for a few days. It had been Terra's idea; she thought it better than drinking to excess. She had said, "I've experienced this enough. Sometimes a couple of shots isn't the best thing after a fucking horrific experience."

An entire wing was closed off for the DGA. Food and drink were brought at their request, and they were each given their own room, not that it was necessary. Terra and Sarah were nearly inseparable, spending much of their time in the common room exchanging war stories and filling the halls with their laughter. Kravis, upon entering, said he hadn't heard that so strongly in years.

Abby and Persephone, on the other hand, went about their days much more quietly. The two spent the time reading together and watching television.

The holdout was Anabelle, who refused to leave her room. She sat brooding, staring out the window and watching the sun rise and set.

On the third day, Abby, Terra, and Sarah got together. It was time to get Anabelle out of her room. All of them were aware that Anabelle had experienced something traumatic, but that didn't mean they would let her wallow in it for the next month.

Over the last few months, each had experienced something that shattered their idea of themselves and pushed them beyond their limits. Anabelle had been there for every one of them, so it was only right to return the favor.

Abby knocked on the elf's door and Terra and Sarah waited behind her. "Hey, Belle. We just wanted to see if you'd be okay coming out for a bit. You know, hang out and talk."

It took some time, but the door creaked open. Anabelle stared through the crack, her eyes heavy, her skin pale and tight. "What do you want to talk about?"

Abby glanced at Terra and Sarah for a moment. "Uh, well, we never debriefed."

Anabelle smiled wryly. "Is that the best you guys could come up with? Aren't you supposed to be a genius or something?"

Abby shrugged and looked away bashfully. "We're operating at less than maximum capacity right now. Been taking a little bit to recover."

Anabelle appeared hesitant to open the door, then she flung it open and returned to her bed.

Terra, all laughter and energy, rolled into the room and plopped on one of Anabelle's chairs. "Glad you decided to let us in. We thought we were going to have to break the door down."

Anabelle, who was sitting in her bed covered in blankets, replied, "You could have. I'm running on empty. I wouldn't be able to put up a fight even if I wanted to."

Sarah sat on the floor and crossed her legs. "So, I'll say the obvious. You've been avoiding us. I know we've all needed to take some time to ourselves but you...you haven't even left this room."

Anabelle looked up from her blankets. "I don't deserve to be around any of you. Don't even deserve to be on this team."

Abby sat beside Anabelle. "Now, why would you say something stupid like that?"

It took Anabelle a long time to answer. She choked through her first words and had to remain silent until she felt ready to continue. "Grok broke me. I gave you guys up. She made me... I would have done anything to make it stop."

They sat in silence, allowing the weight of those words to hang heavy in the air. Finally, Sarah spoke. "Once I betrayed Kravis. It was during a mission on the elvish world. Told them straight out that they could take him and kill him instead of me."

Anabelle looked up at hearing this. "Wait, what do you mean?"

"Just like I said. Nothing more to it. I was in so much pain, I would have said anything."

Sarah stood and raised the back of her shirt. Her back was covered in hundreds of deep scars. She pulled her shirt down.

Terra cleared her throat. "When I was in the arena, I prayed. I've never prayed before, but I promised that I would give anything or anyone in the world to get out of there. Even named names. Not proud to admit it, but I did it. Anything to get me free."

Sarah and Terra looked at Abby, waiting for her to chime in.

Abby coughed uncomfortably. "Uh, we're only a kid. The most we can say is, when part of us gained consciousness, it tried to kill the part that was Abby so we could survive. If that counts."

Terra groaned. "You *would* be the one to give a weird example."

Abby crossed her arms and glared at Terra. "I've never been tortured."

Sarah raised her hand to keep anyone else from talking. "What I'm trying to say, Anabelle, is that when you're put through those extremes, that kind of shit, what comes out of your mouth is what comes out of your mouth. That doesn't change the kind of person you are. It never will."

Anabelle went to speak, but Sarah brought her hand down, silencing the elf. "You came to fight, and you didn't give in. No matter what you wanted to do to Grok, you didn't kill her. You kept your mind on the mission and brought back someone vital for information on the Dark One."

Anabelle avoided the eyes of the women in the room. Sarah

continued, "And what exactly did you say? You tell them where we were? Did you let them know about any of our plans? Any real information?"

The elf answered meekly, "No."

"Exactly. You said some shit to make the pain stop, but you didn't give any of us up. You could have told Grok exactly where HQ was and everything about our defenses, but you didn't. You were in a shitty situation, and you handled it as well as any of us would."

Anabelle gripped her blankets tightly. "I just thought you... I should have done better."

Sarah stood and walked over to Anabelle, then hugged the elf and held her tight. "You did the best you could. That's all any of us could ever ask."

Anabelle sank into Sarah's arms as Terra rose and embraced them. Abby joined in the hug. They held Anabelle tightly as the elf quivered, trying to fight back the tears that eventually came. They sat there with her until the tears passed.

Once the tears had gone, Anabelle was quiet for a bit. Then she sighed deeply, feeling as if she were exhaling the last three weeks of her life. "Okay, let's stop all the lovey-dovey shit. I'm pretty sure we have counselors for this. Who's down to watch some anime?"

Abby's hand shot up so fast that she got embarrassed. "Uh, we are!"

Anabelle stood and tossed her blankets on the bed. "Everyone to Abby's room. I'll be in after I freshen up."

Terra punched Anabelle in the arm as Abby squeezed the elf's hand. "See you in a bit," Terra said. "And please, take as long as you'd like. We're not going to stop you."

Sarah rose as well. Anabelle grabbed her by the shoulder. "Thanks for being honest," the elf said. "Really. It helped."

Sarah rested her hand on Anabelle's. "You're strong, and we all know it. It's about time you realized it as well. Now hurry up. I heard Abby has all of *Naruto* to stream, and we *are* getting through that before our next big mission."

Anabelle nodded as she returned to her dresser to grab a change of clothes. "I'll be there."

Once everyone was gone, Anabelle sat on her bed. She knew the rest of HQ was celebrating, drinking, and partying to remind themselves they were still alive. Spending time with the DGA would remind her of that, and she was glad.

As Anabelle prepared to leave, she heard something rustling in the room. Instinctively, she flashed hot with mana, readying herself for a fight, but there was nothing there.

Anabelle hadn't forgotten the old ways, even if she had traveled the Path of the Lost for a short while. She centered herself, and the room faded as she searched for the sound. It was a voice, one calling to her.

She reached out and took hold of the voice.

The room disappeared. Anabelle was in a place without form, a blank void of time and space. In that blankness, a form took shape.

It was Myrddin, ghostly and translucent. "Anabelle, how far you've come!"

Another form appeared beside Myrddin, a man Anabelle had never seen before. Myrddin looked at him and then faced Anabelle. "Anabelle, this is José. We think we've figured out a way to stop the Dark One."

THE FIRST HUMAN RIDER
A MIDDANG3ARD SERIES

Have you tried the Dragon Approved series from Ramy Vance and Michael Anderle? Book one is The First Human Rider and it's available now from Amazon and through Kindle Unlimited.

Dragonriders are all that stand between Middang3ard and total annihilation.

But their numbers are dwindling.

With every passing day, more and more Dragonriders are falling under the scourge of the Dark One.

The forces of humanity and their allies are desperate. They need a new hero to step up and turn the tide.

Myrddin, the resistance's leader, thinks he might have found that someone…on *Earth*, of all places.

Word has just come from the east that the Dark One is launching his largest assault yet, but there is still time to stop him. If, that is, they can find someone good enough to take him on.

Alex Bound just might be the rider they need.

But a human has never been accepted as a Dragonrider.

Let alone a blind human...

Alex isn't someone to step away from a fight.

Not now, not ever, and she has no plans to start—even if she needs to ride a real dragon to make it happen.

Grab your copy of The First Human Rider at Amazon or through Kindle Unlimited

AUTHOR NOTES RAMY VANCE
JUNE 18, 2020

Working with Michael has its perks. And one of those perks is Sarah Noffke.

NO! Not like that. Get your head out of the gutter.

The Sarah Noffke perk is the ... ahhh ... shall I call it 'sibling rivalry' that Sarah and I have developed.

For those of you who don't know who Sarah Noffke is, check out her Liv Beaufont or Uncommon Rider series - also co-authored with Anderle. She is an incredible writer.

Outside of writing, Sarah is a ninja. A crazy, certifiable, insanely weird ninja (well, she likes to dress up like one, at least).

She's also really short.

I first met Sarah in Vegas. Now, at 5' 7", I'm not very tall, but, in comparison to Sarah, I'm a veritable giant. And yet when I hung out with her, I was eclipsed by her larger than life personality.

In Vegas, she dressed like a ninja. See images below, both in and out of costume ... and yes, that's me photobombing her. Sneaking up on a ninja isn't easy):

Sarah got her revenge by making me a cheesy hitman in one of her stories (I'm the guy with mis-matching socks ... and yes, I do wear mismatched socks; it's my one hipster indulgence):

ass handed to you."

Sophia nearly laughed as she looked Sweater Vest over. "Um. Nah, I'm good. I was just looking for Ramy. Is he on the first floor? Guarding Zac outside the home recording studio?"

The guy narrowed his eyes at her. "You got one thing right today, but too bad for you, it's the day of your funeral. I'm Ramy. Where do you want to be buried?" He punched his fist into his open palm while giving her a menacing glare.

To Sophia's ultimate amusement, the guy seemed to have hurt himself when he punched his own hand. He tried to cover it up as he shook out his palm and put his hand back beside his leg. "Hey Ramy. Great meeting you. I've heard great things."

"From whom?" he demanded, cutting her off.

"From people you don't know," she replied at once.

He scoffed. "I know everyone. Was it Lady Gaga? Brittany? Martha—"

Slumping slightly, Sophia rolled her eyes, not liking it had come to this. "Well, I'm afraid I'm going to have to take Zac one way or another."

He shrugged like the loss was all hers. "Too bad, but I don't know how you plan to do that."

Sophia actually laughed this time. "I think that's pretty clear."

Holding out his arms, he looked around. "How do you mean?"

"Well, I'm me and you're you," she stated as though this fully explained her case. "I have a sword and you have mismatched socks. Also, I'm a dragonrider and you're a fanboy. I think we've pretty much settled this, huh?"

He pulled in a breath. "There's something you haven't considered, Sophia."

She blinked at him. "That you've lost your mind and the nurse will be in here in a moment to give you your meds?"

Ramy shook his head. "No," he said, raising his hands over his head. "That I'm a ninja."

Sophia knew the time for such antics had passed. She needed to get on with things. "Yeah, the thing about ninjas is they usually never announce it. Can I go see Zac now?"

Ramy dropped his hands, looking disappointed. "No. Whatever you're taking him for, there's no way I'm allowing it. It could hurt him and anything dangerous that might hurt—"

The scream that ripped out of Ramy's mouth didn't really surprise Sophia. She knew Lunis had flown over the gated wall to Zac's place and stationed

In retaliation, I cast Sarah as the ninja/assassin in Dark Gate Angels (yes, she's THAT Sarah) and had her fall in love with a gnome. A particularly short gnome.

Her response ... she plastered my 'virtual' office wall with Posted Notes (she also plastered Michael's wall with Posted Notes, but Michael thought it was me ... so I'm going to call that a win in my column).

Well, such a slight cannot be left unretaliated ... Originally, I was going to have Sarah break up with Kravis and fall in love with the much taller Blackwell. But now she's going to marry said gnome in a cheesy Vegas ceremony.

That's right ... Sarah will propose to her (spoiler alert) coma-inflicted, gnome-boyfriend and they're going to get married in Dark Gate Angels 3 ... Mwahahahahaha.

Sarah knows this and has already vowed revenge.

I can't wait to see what she'll come up with.

Like I said ... perks.

PS – this was her threat in response to my wedding plans. 'Unable to eat cheese'! Yikes ... she is vindictive!

> Ohhh marrying a gnome... because I can't just be a ninja, oh no. There has to be a short joke. That's fine, I'm going to make you lactose intolerant and unable to eat cheese in the next book 😜
>
> 👍 1

AUTHOR NOTES MICHAEL ANDERLE
JUNE 19, 2020

Ok, I admit to a little author rivalry here, but nothing like those two are doing. I don't marry Sarah off in any book, nor do I make Ramy lactose-intolerant.

Seriously, that would suck because I do like nachos and pizza, and I am not making that happen to anyone in my books. I promise this to be true for at least a week. I figure that's how long I have until I forget that I said I wouldn't do it. I might last forever (it is a rather horrible thing to do to someone) but...you know, promises are hard to keep.

So, now that we have it out that Ramy wasn't the office smasher, Sarah was, I know I can rest easy tonight. Unless my office is already plastered with stuff and I just haven't seen it yet.

Hey, it's my tenth anniversary. I'm not coming into the office, and (hopefully) no one can make me.

BUFFALO BLASTS (Cheesecake Factory)

Ok, I have a new passion. This passion SHOULD be good for at least another five trips to the restaurant.

I have been on a spicy chicken kick (preferably boneless) after a trip to Colorado Springs to speak at Kevin J. Anderson's Superstars Event (it's held each year.)

This year, it happened before the Covid event occurred, and

during the conference, I went and ate (a lot) at the restaurant in the Antlers (antlers.com) named Sportivo Primo. During one of the food meetings (you eat, you meet people, you eat a (lot) more), I asked what was good on the menu.

The waiter suggested the chicken wings. Now, I'm not a huge wing person (lazy eater here), but I grabbed it anyway. Whether the wings (the meat) was an appropriate amount, I'm not sure. Some bones were lean (*WHERE'S THE MEAT!!??*) and some had *plenty* of meat.

I was happy to lick the sauce off the wings, no problem.

I brought the desire to eat spicy chicken back with me to Las Vegas, and have been going up and down on my cravings ever since.

So, I tell you all of that to say if you have a Cheesecake Factory near you and like buffalo sauce chicken wings, try their Buffalo Blasts! It's like they did all the hard work (chicken breast, excellent sauce, cubed the meat and added sauce and a bit of cheese (maybe?). Then, they wrap this is a piece of something that they chicken-fry and HOL# BE!#%! It's so good!

If you get nothing else out of this *Author Notes*, ignore the other two authors and get yourself over to Cheesecake Factory.

It's good.

Oh, I suppose I should exhort you to enjoy reading and buy more books. If you don't know what books to buy, look for the name Michael Anderle on the cover.

Now I'm done.

Diary June 14 – 20, 2020

So, Las Vegas is a little weird right now. You have pockets of people who are very Covid-19-aware around the valley area, and then you have the casinos. Some of the casinos are very Covid aware and more stringent, and others aren't.

No casino (that I've been to) mandates wearing a mask.

The Station Casinos shoot that temperature gauge at you when you enter their establishment but are pretty open after that.

Caesar's Hotel and Casino (for this latest weekend) was packed with people, and they try to encourage social distancing, but occasionally people get a little close together—and by occasionally, I mean all of Friday night.

I can't speak to Saturday or Saturday night since I didn't get to continue playing. My budget was used up, so I worked and slept most of Saturday, catching up from some mixed up sleep during the week.

I'm at the Green Valley Hotel and Casino. Sitting in the food court, I can see at least twelve people playing on the casino floor. The mask to no-mask ratio seems to be about even, except for the person who has a mask, but is smoking, so the mask is pulled down.

I'm going to count that as a no-mask.

Here in the food court, the mask ratio is about one person with a mask to twenty without one.

We are fifteen feet from the slot machines.

I get why those of us in the food court have no masks (and there is no difference when I go to regular restaurants. Once a person sits down at a table, the masks come off almost immediately.)

I think I will be about done with these updates starting next week. Enough of my diary entries have dealt with Covid-19 and Las Vegas, it's time to just…talk about other stuff.

Like books, maybe?

Sometimes, it's hard to remember what readers want to hear about in our (author and publisher) lives. I eat, sleep, and breathe publishing and stories at this point in my career, and what's normal to me (and seems like would be boring to you) is probably not.

As always, THANK YOU for reading our stories. We would not be able to create the wonderful stories without readers like you supporting us!

Ad Aeternitatem,

Michael Anderle

OTHER BOOKS BY RAMY VANCE

Mortality Bites Series
Keep Evolving Series
Fatebound Series

Other Middang3ard Books

Never Split The Party (01)
Late To the Party (02)
It's My Party (03)
Blue Hell And Alien Fire (04)

Death Of An Author: A Middang3ard Novella

Dragon Approved Series
The First Human Rider
Ascent To The Nest
Defense Of The Nest
Nest Under Siege
First Mission

The Descent
Sacrifices
Love And Aliens
An Alien Affair

BOOKS BY MICHAEL ANDERLE

For a complete list of books by Michael Anderle, please visit:

www.lmbpn.com/ma-books/

All LMBPN Audiobooks are Available at Audible.com and iTunes

To see all LMBPN audiobooks, including those written by Michael Anderle
please visit:

www.lmbpn.com/audible

CONNECT WITH THE AUTHORS

Connect with Ramy

Join Ramy's Newsletter

Join Ramy's FB Group: House of the GoneGod Damned!

Connect with Michael Anderle and sign up for his email list here:

Website: http://lmbpn.com

Email List: http://lmbpn.com/email/

Facebook:
www.facebook.com/TheKurtherianGambitBooks